Sergeant Pilot

by

Ken Fowler

Printed by CreateSpace, an Amazon.com Company
Available from Amazon.com and other retail outlets
Available on Kindle and other devices

Copyright © 2015 Ken Fowler

All rights reserved

To my Father
Sergeant George Fowler
RAF 1939 – 1945

Contents

Chapter One - Retrospective

Chapter Two – The Flying Club

Chapter Three - RAF Volunteer Reserve

Chapter Four – War Clouds

Chapter Five – The Tomcats

Chapter Six – Dunkirk

Chapter Seven – Battle of Britain

Chapter Eight – Rhubarbs and Circus

Chapter Nine - On the Run

Chapter Ten – Epilogue.

Chapter One - Retrospective

The shrill ring of the Smiths alarm clock rudely penetrated Harry Steed's deep and dreamless sleep. He reached out into the darkness, rapped the alarm-off button and peered drowsily at the offending timepiece. The luminous dial indicated that it was three-thirty in the morning. The clock ticked sulkily on. On the other side of the bed its twin also ticked monotonously towards its alarm detonation five minutes later, for it was imperative that he did not oversleep on this particular morning.

Steed crawled out of bed and clawed the sleep from his eyes, regretting that last beer in the sergeants' mess. It was his own fault; he should have gone to bed earlier instead of joining the party around the piano. He switched on the table-lamp, the low-wattage bulb casting a dim amber glow around the small room. A jug of cold water, a bowl and a black leather toiletry bag stood on a small mahogany table. Steed washed, shaved and put on his uniform. He surveyed the end result in the long wardrobe mirror, his eyes lingering with a sense of pride on the silver wings that adorned his tunic. Smart enough for the big day. Those lucky sods in the officers' mess had some batman servant to wake them with a nice cup of tea; RAF sergeants had to find their own!

Steed stepped outside into the cool pre-dawn and looked up at the sky with a pilot's eyes; broken cloud and a light wind, good flying weather. He filled his lungs with the fresh spring air and came alive. Already the sky was lightening to the east, an indigo dawn illuminating blood-red fingers of high cirrus cloud.

The throaty roar of a Merlin engine bursting into life broke the silence, the staccato popping of the twelve-cylinder Rolls-Royce brainchild suggesting that the mechanics were preparing one of the aircraft for the day's business. Steed peered around the side of the building. The purposeful shape of a Hawker Hurricane fighter was visible in the half-light outside the hangar, being run-up by the mechanics, with dancing blue flames emanating from her exhaust pipes. There would be more mechanics and more Hurricanes on the other side of the airfield, at the dispersal area. Perhaps there are people that get out of bed even earlier than sergeant pilots, Steed reflected.

It was cold outside before dawn, even though it was already late May. How quickly the last eight months seemed to have passed since war had been declared. Steed returned to the warmth of the sergeants' mess, one of the few brick-built buildings amongst the Nissen huts scattered around the wartime airfield. It was too early for breakfast of course, that would come later, after the operation and after debriefing by the Spy. It was tea that he wanted, hot tea and maybe some toast.

The mess dining area was almost deserted, but welcoming nonetheless. Two sergeant pilots, who were also scheduled to fly that morning, were seated at one of the wooden tables with their tea. Both, he knew, had started their careers in the RAF as fitters, but had jumped at the opportunity to retrain as pilots. The two pilots were very different. Johnny Walker was proud of his east end of London heritage, and was an extrovert cockney; he was well over six foot in height, fair-haired and with dancing grey-blue eyes. It never ceased to amaze Steed how he could possibly fit into the cockpit of his Hurricane fighter. Johnny was also the mess piano player, in great demand at every party. Toby Adams was almost the opposite, much shorter, slightly overweight and with an unruly mop of dark brown hair. Since joining the squadron a fortnight ago Steed had become firm friends with both men, and he now joined them at their table.

'Morning boys. Looking forward to an exciting day-trip to France?' he enquired breezily as he sat down.

'You'll think it exciting if you get a bloody great Messerschmitt up your khyber,' rejoined Adams. 'Not that there's much chance of that. We've been patrolling Calais-Dunkirk all week and still haven't had a sniff at the sods.' He gave a wink to Walker and added, 'Now that you've consented to join us, maybe our luck will change.'

'Yeah, glad that the Boss has given you the thumbs-up to join the party my son,' added the effervescent Walker as he slurped his hot tea. 'Not that you've missed much so far.'

'I was beginning to think that I had a personal hygiene problem,' quipped Steed. 'Everyone else has had a look at Frog-land except me. Guess that's the cross the new boy has to bear.'

Tea and toast consumed, the three sergeants piled into Adams's 1932 Hillman for the ride over to the aircraft dispersal area. They arrived before the officer pilots, who messed just outside the airfield perimeter. The three sergeants went over to their respective Hurricane fighters to speak to their ground crews. Each pilot was assigned two airmen who were responsible for his aircraft; the fitter looked after the engine and the rigger took care of the airframe. Steed's ground crew had guessed that the pilots would be going across the Channel once more, and they knew that this was to be Steed's first operation. Steed had developed a deep respect for his ground crew, and he greeted his fitter warmly.

'All tanked up and ready to go Denis?'

'She's in tip-top condition Sarge,' replied the fitter, looking up at the Hurricane with evident pride. He lowered his voice and added in a conspiratorial tone, 'Bob synchronised the guns at 250 yards on the range yesterday.'

Steed had been told that some pilots in France had changed the aiming of their eight Browning machine-guns from the approved wide Dowding spread, to instead converge at a point 250 yards in front of the fighter. This was guaranteed to give a devastating cone of fire at the aiming point, but relied on the pilot being a good shot and getting the aiming point right in the first place. Steed was of the opinion that he was a good shot and had asked the armourer to align his guns accordingly. The problem was that he suspected the C/O paid strict adherence to RAF recommended practice and would not sanction anything other than the Dowding spread if asked. Steed hadn't asked!

Steed's rigger joined them. 'Morning Colin,' said Steed. 'A bit chilly this morning.'

'Morning Sarge.' The rigger jerked a calloused thumb in the direction of the fighter. 'She's not brand new of course, but the old girl's in the best of health. Everything's tight and shipshape. She'll not let you down.'

'I'm sure that she won't Colin. I'll try to look after her for you and bring her back in one piece.'

'Just bring yourself back in one piece Sarge,' said the rigger with genuine concern. 'We can patch up any holes in her, but we're not sure if we can do the same for you!'

The three men continued with their discussion on the Hurricane, and with general small talk, for a minute or so until the officer pilots arrived in an assorted collection of motorcars. The officers' chatter reflected their public school backgrounds, and was peppered with RAF slang. It had surprised Steed, on joining the squadron, to find that he was older than most of them.

The pilots congregated inside the dispersal hut, some flopping into the battered armchairs others, like Steed, leaning against the walls. The pilots spent much of their time in this hut when at readiness, as testified by its lived-in appearance and well-used furniture permeated with cigarette smoke. The C/O, Squadron Leader Tomlinson, held up his hand for silence and then addressed his pilots in his distinctive, clipped and measured tone.

'I spoke to Group last night chaps; the situation on the ground over in France is starting to look rather serious. Things have happened pretty damn fast, and it's only now becoming clear just how bad things are. As you all know, the Germans invaded Holland and Belgium a couple of weeks ago. The British and French moved up into Belgium to check the German advance, so far so good, but then the enemy made a second breakthrough into France through the Ardennes, just beyond where the Maginot Line stops.'

There was a murmur amongst the pilots as Tomlinson indicated the position of the Ardennes forest on the map of Northern France hanging on the hut wall. 'Somewhere around here I think. It seems that the Huns have moved like lightning through France on a narrow front. They reached the coast near the Somme a couple of days ago, but now they have pushed on up the Channel towards Boulogne. Calais and Boulogne are both now coming under attack from the sods. The situation is fluid to say the least, and confusion reigns, but the latest reports suggest that the Germans have cut off our troops positioned around the Dunkirk-Calais region from the main French forces further west.' Again Tomlinson gestured vaguely at the map. 'Both the BEF and the French are putting in counterattacks to relieve the situation.'

Steed glanced around at the surprised and shocked faces of the young pilots as the squadron leader's words sunk in. They all knew that the German offensive had been devastatingly successful, but nobody had realised, until now, that the enemy was within twenty miles of England.

Tomlinson continued, 'The Germans are apparently very good at using their air force in support of their army. They use their Stuka dive-bombers like artillery and their bombers are causing absolute havoc along the allied supply lines. The sods are also strafing civilian refugee columns throughout France.'

Tomlinson surveyed his pilots through the fog of cigarette smoke engulfing the dispersal hut. 'The Luftwaffe has apparently achieved air superiority over most of France. Don't ask me what's happened to the Armée de l'Air. According to Group, the only area where the Huns do not have it all their own way is along the North Sea coast, where they are in range of people like us. The Hurricanes stationed in France have done an absolutely sterling job, but there were too few of them and they were overwhelmed eventually. Yes Pip?'

Pip Courtauld, one of the junior pilot officers, asked the obvious question. 'Sir, the Luftwaffe is obviously causing a lot of trouble, but we have been flying over France every day now for the past ten days. Why haven't we seen them?'

'Good question Pip. I suspect that things have moved too fast even for the Luftwaffe, so the Hun aircraft haven't been too active yet over the Channel ports. However, Group reported to me yesterday that the Luftwaffe has now occupied some of the French airfields. That puts most of their aircraft well within range of the Calais-Dunkirk sector. We seem to have been the only squadron that didn't see any of the blighters yesterday, but I think that is bound to change today.'

Once again Tomlinson pointed to the map. 'Our job today, as it has been for the past week, is to patrol ten miles inland along the line Calais-Dunkirk. We must prevent the Luftwaffe from getting through to our troops. By now you are all aware of our flight plan. Take off in sections of three, joining up on me at 2,000 feet. We will fly 'Aircraft Close Vic, Sections Close Astern' as far as France. I want to see a nice tight formation all the way as usual please. We will keep the speed down to conserve fuel. Everybody clear on all of that? Good, takeoff in fifteen minutes, navigation lights on until we have formed up.'

The pilots started out towards their Hurricanes. Squadron Leader Tomlinson came across to Steed as they left the dispersal hut. 'It's good to have you with us today Sergeant Steed. Your flight commander tells me that you have made excellent progress since joining us. So far I have only used my experienced pilots on these forays across the Channel, but now it's your turn. I am sure that you will do well. Keep a tight formation and if we get into a fight stay close to your section leader. Keep off the radio unless you have something really important to say, and then use the proper procedure, call signs and so on. You are better trained and have better equipment than the Huns. I know that you will do your duty.'

'Thank you sir, I won't let you down.' And with that, the C/O went bounding off after the B-Flight leader.

Steed walked towards his Hurricane and the waiting ground crew, his parachute carried over his shoulder, his helmet and cumbersome flapping oxygen mask draped over one arm. As he reached the Hurricane, his fitter helped him to clip on the parachute. He climbed into the cockpit, which was tight for his large frame; he consoled himself with the thought that a Spitfire's cockpit was even cosier. His fitter helped to strap him into the fighter while his rigger gave the canopy a final polish. It was important to have a spotless canopy; a speck of dust could look like a distant aeroplane. He adjusted his mask and plugged in the leads.

'Good luck Sarge,' said his fitter.

'Give Adolf one from me,' added the rigger. And with that both airmen jumped down from the Hurricane, leaving Steed to carry on with the pre-flight checks and engine starting procedures.

Now he was alone. This was what all the training had been leading up to; he was off to war. His father had fought in the trenches in the Great War, the war to end all wars they had said. And now, just twenty-one years later, the son was following in the father's footsteps against the same enemy. But Steed junior would fight in the clouds, not in the mud and misery of the Flanders trenches. Steed junior would emulate the Great War flying aces, especially James McCudden VC, the working class lad who had risen to captain and patrol leader in a Royal Flying Corps steeped in class prejudice.

Squadron Leader Tomlinson, the 'Boss', had given him that little pep talk as they had walked towards their aircraft a few moments ago. Jesus, it was the most the man had said to him since he had joined the squadron, what was it, a little over two weeks ago? Steed's section would be the last three aircraft to take off. He sat in the cockpit waiting for the Hurricanes to begin their taxi away from dispersal. His would be the last aircraft in the line-astern formation. Each section would then form up at the end of the airfield into the classic three-aircraft vic for take off.

As he waited, Steed allowed his mind to wander back in time, reflecting on how, at the tender age of twenty-two, he had come to be in this position, sitting in the cockpit of a RAF Hurricane fighter in May 1940, waiting to go to war. When had it all started? Was it his schoolboy passion for aeroplanes and the stories of the Great War pilots that had shaped his future? Maybe, but the crucial turning point was the day he went for interview at that small flying club northeast of London. He was just a boy then, so young, so naive. Was that really only six years ago?

Chapter Two – The Flying Club

Steed arrived for interview at Epping Flying Club on his Ariel motorcycle bright and early one Monday morning in April 1934. There wasn't much to see, a grass field, a clubhouse, a few parked aeroplanes and an aircraft hangar-come-workshop. A cheery man in his mid fifties, hearing the Ariel's throaty roar, greeted him at the workshop entrance. 'Morning young man, and what can I do for you?'

'My name is Harry Steed sir. I have come for interview as an apprentice aircraft mechanic.'

'Ah yes, you're a little bit early but never mind. I'm Bill Wheeler and I'm the chief fitter, foreman-mechanic if you like, of this little outfit. Come through into the office. The kettle's on so we can have a cuppa and you can run through your experience for me.'

The office was simply a wooden partition off the main workshop; it smelt of tobacco and engine oil. There was a large desk at one end with two chairs. Wheeler motioned to Steed to sit down. The desk was littered with buff folders and papers. Steed noted an aircraft maintenance schedule in front of the other chair, presumably work in hand. A bookcase stood at the far end of the office, on which perched a number of aircraft manuals and other assorted technical books. He was surprised to see that the bookcase also contained a few back numbers of his favourite magazine, *Aeroplane*. Steed invariably read every issue of the monthly periodical from cover to cover.

'How do you take your tea son?'

'No sugar, just a little milk please.'

Wheeler rapped on the office window that looked out over the workshop. 'Two teas please Sam,' he yelled. 'The lad takes it strong with no sugar.' For the first time Steed noticed the only other occupant of the workshop, a tall thin man who, like Wheeler, was in his mid fifties.

'Let's see,' said Wheeler as he rummaged for Steed's letter in the desk drawer. 'So Harry, you are sixteen, and for the last couple of years you have been apprenticed as a garage mechanic, that right?'

Not quite sir. I have been working at the garage for three years, since I was thirteen, but I only worked weekends and in the evenings until I left school at fifteen, just a year ago. So I have only been apprenticed for one year.'

'There's no need to call me sir, Mr Wheeler is fine for the time being. You're not at school now, nor in the army. What sort of things have you been doing in your garage?'

'Well, all the routine servicing stuff on cars and motorbikes they let me do more or less on my own now, you know, oil and plugs, replacing hoses, brake relining, tyres, that sort of thing. Recently I have also been getting more involved on the electrical side of things, repairing or replacing starter motors and dynamos. Oh, I don't touch bodywork, panel beating or anything like that. Only engines.'

'What about engine strip-downs?'

'For the big jobs like that, or the more complicated jobs, I help one of the qualified mechanics. Things like cylinder head removals, valve grinding, piston replacement, almost everything except gearboxes.'

'What about engine fault diagnosis? Do you get involved with that?'

'Yes, the simple stuff anyway, such as checking through for fuel and spark.'

'What sort of supervision do you get?'

'As I say, the routine servicing they let me do without too much supervision. I tell them when I've finished and they check to see it's okay. I work with one of the trained mechanics on the major jobs. The garage is pretty strict on that.'

The interview went on for half an hour, with Wheeler asking detailed questions about the range of jobs that Steed had undertaken, seeking the limit of his knowledge and experience. At last Wheeler stood up.

'Okay, that's enough about what you can do. Now follow me and let's have a look at what we do here. Basically the flying club has five Gipsy Moths available to club members to hire, which we also use for flying lessons. Sam and me are fitters and look after the engines and instruments. Another couple of guys, the riggers, look after the aeroplanes' structures. As well as the five Moths, we sometimes also take on jobs on the members' private aeroplanes. We even have a look at their motorcars now and again. Know anything about the Moth?'

'Only what I've read in the *Aeroplane*. The original de Havilland DH.60 Moth has a Cirrus engine; the Gypsy Moth is more modern and has an uprated Gypsy engine. That's why it's called the Gypsy Moth. Oh, and Amy Johnston flew one solo to Australia a couple of years ago.'

'Very good Harry, you've certainly been doing a lot of reading. Ever seen one up close?' They were now approaching a gleaming biplane parked just outside the workshop. The wings and tailplane were painted silver and the fuselage yellow. Steed thought that it looked magnificent. The cowling had been removed revealing the engine in all its glory.

'Not yet,' Steed replied.

'Well the engine is just brilliant. It's very reliable and easy to maintain. And it's not only used in the Moth; you see it in plenty of other aeroplanes.' They were now standing alongside the aircraft. Wheeler looked at the engine admiringly.

'You can see it's an air-cooled four-cylinder in-line. Not a lot different to a car engine really, in fact there are a few car parts inside it. But this beauty is designed for an aeroplane, so is both powerful and lightweight. About the only problem is the way the engine sticks up in front of the pilot. Look at this!' Wheeler gestured at the engine and then at the propeller. 'The engine is tall see, and the crankshaft at the bottom of the engine has to be connected at the same level as the propeller shaft. The propeller can't be mounted any lower or it will hit the ground. The end result is that engine has to be mounted high, and the top of the engine sticks out in front of the pilot. It obscures his visibility a bit, but that isn't too serious.'

Wheeler continued the tour around the small grass airfield. Steed warmed to the man. It was so obvious that Wheeler was a hands-on engineer and completely in love with his job. Finally they returned to the workshop office.

'Now then young Harry, why would you want to leave that nice cosy London garage, just around the corner from where you live, to come out to the wilds of Essex? A couple of years and you would finish your apprenticeship and be sitting pretty. Why leave the cars and motorbikes, and a secure job, for aeroplanes?'

Steed was half expecting this question. 'Well, I've thought about it long and hard,' he said slowly. 'Since I was a child I've been passionate about aeroplanes. My parents thought that I would grow out of it, but I guess that I'm stuck with it. I read Biggles novels, aeroplane magazines, RAF stuff, the lot! My bedroom is covered with pictures and models of aeroplanes. I just want to be around planes. I doubt that aeroplane engines are very much different from the engines that I'm used to, so I think that I could do a good job here. I would be learning about aeroplanes and their engines too. One more thing, and this is really important to me. I wouldn't expect much of a salary, but I do really want to learn to fly. Would it be possible, if you employ me that is, to offset some of my wage against a couple of hours flying instruction per week?'

Wheeler eyed him thoughtfully. At last he spoke. 'Flying lessons are very expensive my lad, well beyond apprentice pay. We charge nearly £100 for the course. Although I have the authority to hire and fire here in the workshop, I don't own the business; Mr Golding does. So I can't answer your question right now. It is true that there are occasions during the week when an instructor and an aeroplane are free, so that sort of arrangement might be possible.' Wheeler paused. 'I tell you what, I will offer you a month's trial as an apprentice aeroplane fitter. I will also have a word with Mr Golding to see what we can do about the flying lessons and how that might impact on your wage. I can't promise you anything now though. How about that we write to you later this week and let you know what's what?'

'That's wonderful Mr Wheeler. Thank you very much.'

Wheeler gestured to the motorcycle parked outside the workshop. 'I see you have an Ariel-Four, lovely motorbike that. What sort of journey did you have from your home this morning? North London isn't it? Will you do that every day if you join us, or will you look for digs around here?'

'The bike's my pride and joy. It was crash damaged by the previous owner. I think he damaged himself at the same time and his wife insisted that he give up motorcycling. It had also overheated at some stage so was difficult to start. That's the trouble with the Square-Four, you have to watch that the back cylinders are cooled properly in summer. Anyway, I got her as a non-runner at a very good price and fixed her up. Couldn't have afforded her otherwise. She runs beautifully now. The journey from home is fine, something to wake me up in the mornings!'

Wheeler smiled. 'Winter might be different.'

'Oh, I'm used to it. No problem if you wrap up warm. By the way Mr Wheeler, I'm free for the rest of the day. I worked half a day at the garage on Good Friday, so today is in lieu of that. If you have anything for me to do, I would be very happy to get my hands dirty.'

Wheeler beamed. 'You will find a pair of overalls over there. You can help me service the Moth outside.'

A few days later a letter arrived from the Epping Flying Club offering Steed a three year Aero Engine Fitter Apprenticeship, subject to a one month trial. The letter stated that two hours flying tuition would be given weekly following a successful trial, with an appropriate deduction in salary. Steed noted that, although the club was giving a substantial discount on the flying lessons, it would still be tough for him to make ends meet on what was left over. He discussed the offer with his parents; his mother said that he could reduce his contribution to the family to what he could afford. Overjoyed, Steed handed in his notice at the garage, and was very surprised to find that the owner offered him an immediate increase in salary if he would stay!

So it was that one sunny Monday morning in late April 1934 found Harry Steed happily riding up to the Epping Flying Club workshop on his motorcycle. He was early, and the workshop was locked, but he didn't care. He was happy to breathe in the fresh country air, a delight after the sooty atmosphere of Inner London. Bill Wheeler arrived half and hour later to open up the workshop, followed soon after by Sam, the other fitter, and the two riggers.

Wheeler got straight to the point. 'Right then Harry, for the time being you will work with me so that I can see the quality of your work, what you can and cannot do. We will fit in your flying training as and when an instructor and aeroplane are free. I have convinced Mr Golding that it would be a good thing if at least one of the fitters could fly. It would make it much easier for us to verify fault clearance and generally sign out the aeroplanes, because at the moment we have to ask one of the instructors to undertake the flight tests. That, and the fact that you were so keen to learn that you wanted your salary docked, convinced His Nibs to let you have a go.' Wheeler paused, and then said ominously, 'I have to warn you that not everybody takes to flying. Many students fall by the wayside. If the instructor gets the idea that you are not safe, or if you are not making good progress, that will be it. Okay?'

'Yes Mr Wheeler. Thank you very much.' Steed had no intention of not making good progress!

'One last thing. The members pay through the nose to learn to fly. They won't take it kindly if they see a boy fitter getting freebies. So keep a very low profile when you are in your flying kit. Don't go near the clubhouse and for heaven's sake don't talk to any of the members about flying.'

Steed settled into the new routine at the flying club and he passed his probationary period. Bill Wheeler was quietly impressed by the youngster's ability and willingness to learn and, for his part, Steed enjoyed the friendly atmosphere of the workshop and now called his colleagues by their Christian names. Then, at last, came the time for his first flying lesson.

Steed waited for his instructor alongside one of the Gypsy Moths. The dual-control Moth seated instructor and pupil in a tandem open cockpit; the pupil usually sat in front. He knew all the instructors by sight, but had not yet been introduced to any of them; they were all ex-RAF pilots. Presently his instructor, an athletic looking character with curly brown hair, strode up and amicably introduced himself.

'Hi Harry, I've seen you around. My name is Tom Clancy and I'm the chief instructor here. I will take you up. Ever flown before?'

'No sir, I'm really looking forward to it.'

'Good show. Now I know that you are an aeroplane fitter here and probably know what all the bits are called, and what they do, but I want to start from the beginning, okay?'

'Yes sir.'

They walked around the Moth as Clancy described the control surfaces and the rudimentary aspects of flying. Power, lift, drag, rudder, elevators, ailerons; Steed knew the theory already from many hours poring over aeroplane books, but he listened attentively to Clancy's explanations. Clancy smiled. 'Now then Harry, just to show me that you have understood, please repeat to me as much as you can remember about what I have been saying.'

Steed drew breath and then delivered an almost perfect explanation of all that he had just been told. He was careful not to overdo it and to avoid straying into areas that Clancy had not covered.

'Well done my lad, very good indeed. Right-ho, jump up into the front seat and strap yourself in, good and tight.' Steed needed no second bidding. Clancy checked the harness and then climbed into the seat immediately behind and leaned over. 'Now then, tell me what you know of the controls and instruments in front of you.'

Steed had read so much over the years about aeroplanes that he already knew the purpose of the basic controls and instruments by heart, long before he had arrived at the flying club. Not that there was very much to see because there were only half a dozen instruments in front of him. Speaking in a steady voice, despite his excitement about his first flight,

Steed pointed at each control and each instrument in turn and gave a few words of explanation.

'Wonderful, so you have at least some idea of the theory,' chortled Clancy cheerily. 'That's a good start. A darn sight better than most of the first timers. But you are one of our fitters, so that's what we should expect. Now then, shall we go for a spin?'

'You bet!'

'First thing is to carry out the pre-flight checks. We have already had a walk around the old girl, kicked the tyres and generally seen that her hat's on straight. We know that the aeroplane is cleared for flight and that we have fuel. Before we fly we also need to find out what we can about the weather. Take a look at the cloud base; what is the wind direction and strength? Is a storm brewing? Last thing to do before we start up is to check the controls, like so.' Clancy moved the stick and rudder bars. 'Now you do it. No, not like that. Take a good look behind you when you move the rudder and elevators. Make sure the bloody things are following the stick and bar movements properly. That's it! Good.'

Clancy signalled to Sam to come over to start the Moth.

'Listen carefully Harry. I will give a running commentary on what I am doing over the voice tube. If you need to say anything you must shout down the tube, otherwise I will never hear you above the din made by the engine and wind. Keep your hands clear of the stick and your feet clear of the rudder bars. We will take off, climb to about 3,000 feet and then stooge about a bit to give you an idea of what it's like. If you feel sick use the bag. If all goes well, I will invite you to have a go. If at any time I say 'I have control' you make sure you bloody well let go. Ready to go?'

'Absolutely sir!'

'Contact,' yelled Clancy throwing the magneto switches. Sam swung the propeller. At the second attempt the engine roared into life.

'Important thing to do is to keep a good lookout,' yelled Clancy into the voice pipe as they taxied out onto the grass airfield. 'Make sure that the engine is warm, we don't want that cutting out on us as we lift off, now do we? Remember, we take off into the wind, although it is pretty light today as you can see by the windsock. Final checks. Oil pressure good, everything seems to be working. Okay, now we point the nose up the runway, put the brakes on and gun the engine. See, no hesitation; the engine is nice and responsive. Last look around to make sure that no other aircraft are in sight or landing. Now, we release the brakes, give her full throttle and off we jolly well go!'

The Moth sped across the grass airfield, thudding and bumping, and then they were airborne. 'She would lift off and climb gently all on her own once she has the airspeed, even if you held the stick steady. But once you feel her lifting off, pull back the stick a little and you climb away faster. Much safer that way.'

Clancy climbed out to the east of the field, to around 3,000 feet, and then levelled off. It was a beautiful early summer's day with hardly a cloud in the sky. Steed was exhilarated, his head turning from side to side, up and down, as he tried to take it all in. Essex was spread out below like a patchwork quilt, the diverse crops and field demarcations creating those particular patterns in the countryside that Steed was later to recognise as being quintessentially English. The Thames estuary was to their front right, and the sea opened out on the horizon in front of them. Steed let out a joyful cry as he recognised Southend-on-Sea in the distance, a place of happy childhood memories.

Clancy shouted observations and instructions down the voice pipe at intervals. He made a few gentle turns and other manoeuvres, all the time encouraging Steed to watch the instruments such as the compass bearing, the altimeter, the airspeed indicator, the inclinometer and the turn and slip indicator. Presently he shouted, 'Okay Harry, I want you to hold this course and height. She is nicely trimmed so GENTLE hands and feet please on the controls. Put your feet on the rudder bar and take the stick. Are you ready to take control?'

'Yes sir.'

'Right, you have control.'

Not a lot happened. The Moth continued on her merry way. The instruments did not move. After a short while Steed became aware that the nose was dropping slightly, confirmed by the inclinometer. He eased back on the stick, but over corrected. The nose went up and the right wing started to drop. The aircraft was making a very gentle turn to starboard. Steed corrected by pushing the stick to the left, but again over corrected and found himself in a shallow left hand dive. Gradually he got the Moth back on an even keel, at the right height and going in the right direction.

After a couple of minutes on a steady course and height, Clancy shouted, 'Very good. Remember, gentle hands. Feel the aeroplane. Now take a good look around the sky and in your own time execute a 180-degree turn to starboard, that's a turn to the right remember. Don't just use the rudder and yaw around, use the stick and bank a little as you go around. And keep the nose up. Try not to lose height. Gently now, nice wide turn.'

Steed had a good look around. The sky seemed to be empty apart from the little Moth, although the biplane's wings and fuselage obscured a full panoramic view. Steed concentrated on the turn. He knew the theory even before Clancy's recent demonstrations, he had been through this manoeuvre a hundred times in his mind's eye, but now this was for real. Stick over to the right, now centre, and now back a bit, a little rudder. The sun was dazzling as they passed through south but Steed squinted determinedly at the horizon as he turned the little aeroplane onto a westerly heading and then levelled out. Blimey! He had actually turned the aeroplane around without spinning out of control!

'Not at all bad young Harry. You only lost two hundred feet in height during the turn. Let's try that again. A 180 degree turn to starboard in your own time please.'

And so it went on. Gentle turns, climbs and dives. Always looking around the sky, checking the instruments, the altimeter, the inclinometer, the turn and slip indicator and the compass. With the modest climbs and dives, Steed was instructed how to vary the throttle settings to maintain the airspeed dictated by Clancy. Steed was perspiring with the effort. A 90-degree turn to port, a 180-degree turn to starboard, descend to 2,000 feet, climb to 2,500 feet. It went on and on. Steed no longer had time to gaze at the landscape below, so it came as a great surprise to him that he suddenly found himself at 1000 feet with his airfield immediately ahead.

'Well done Harry. That really was very good. That's our field below, so I will now land the aeroplane. I have control.'

Clancy took control, but continued to shout down the voice pipe. 'I am joining the circuit on the down-wind leg. Look at the windsock, it's not exactly blowing a gale but you can still see the wind direction. Notice how I am losing height. Now we execute a 180-degree turn and line up on the field into the wind. The nicest way to land is a three pointer. Over the fence, throttle right back as we lift the nose so that the tail wheel can touch down a fraction after the main undercarriage. Hey presto, perfect landing, not a bounce in sight.' Clancy taxied back to the workshop and switched off. They jumped out of the aircraft.

'Let's have a cup of tea,' suggested Clancy. 'And you don't have to call me sir, Tom is fine.'

'Right Oh Tom! I called you sir because you are an ex RAF officer, and my instructor. I thought that it was more polite. I can put the workshop kettle on for you if you don't mind you tea in a mug.'

'Workshop tea would be lovely. So, what did you think of it?'

Steed was still exhilarated. 'Bloody fantastic! Every bit as good as I hoped. Absolutely wonderful! I can't get over it. I've read all the books and magazines on how to fly an aeroplane, and I've rehearsed those turns a thousand times in my head. I'm amazed that I managed to carry them off without the old girl falling out of the sky. And the view from up there was marvellous. The sun was so bright, especially when we turned into it. I feel like Biggles!'

'You did very well. You were able to keep her straight and level after only a few minutes of trying. You got the hang of those turns pretty quickly too. Most students lose bags of height or even spin when they first try. On a clear day like today, when we are not stooging about under the cloud base, it is worth wearing smoked goggles. Cuts down the glare.

'There seems to be so much to do at the same time,' Steed ventured, 'I was in a real two and eight. I lost all sense of where we were. I was really surprised when the field came up in front of us.'

Clancy sat back and smiled, 'Okay, so where do we go from here?' The question was rhetorical. 'First up, you haven't scared the pants off me, you weren't scared either – don't laugh – I've had a couple of students that were so put off by their first flight that they decided against the idea. A few more gave up when we started pulling out of spins. You showed a good aptitude for flying so, all in all, I am satisfied that your tuition can continue.'

'Oh fantastic! Thank you very much.'

'The club are prepared to subsidise your flying up to the level of the Class-A pilot's licence, provided that you continue to make good progress. That means they will give you a substantial discount on the normal fees; they will not pay for everything. The fees will be deducted from your wages. I assume that you have discussed all of this with Mr Golding.'

'Well not directly with Mr Golding, but Bill has told me what the deductions will be, and I guess that they will be taken from my salary now that I have started flying lessons.'

'Very well. With the Class-A you will be able to take aircraft up for tests, if Bill Wheeler decides that's what he wants you to do. Now this is very important,' Clancy looked sternly at Steed, 'If Bill asks you to jump in and start the engine or to fiddle with the controls as a part of your job then that's okay. What you are not allowed to do yet, under any circumstances, is to taxi the thing around when you are not being supervised by an instructor. Is that clear?'

'Absolutely.'

'I will continue to be your instructor for the time being to give you some continuity. Mid-week, about this time, things are quiet, so I will try to fit you in for an hour or so every Wednesday and Thursday. We will fit in the flying when we both have some free time. Work comes first okay? I will also get some books for you and I will be setting you some homework. The theory is very important, not just the skill of flying the aeroplane. You have to study rules of the air, lights and signals, navigation, all sorts of stuff. How's your maths? Do you have a School Certificate?'

'No, I'm afraid that I had to leave school at fifteen. My parents couldn't afford for me to stay on for another year. My maths isn't too bad though.' Steed omitted to say that he had been top of his class in maths.

'Well, we will have to see how you progress. I am sorry, but you cannot join the theory classes with the other students. That puts you at a big disadvantage I know, so you just have to spend plenty of time studying the books that I give to you. I will try to answer any questions when we meet for your flying lessons. As you know, the students here are mostly high society types. They are here as much for socialising as they are for flying and they pay dearly for it. You must keep out of their way.'

Clancy was as good as his word. As the summer of 1934 wore on, Steed made good progress in both the practical and theoretical aspects of flying. He learnt to exit from a spin, to take off and to land. He also learnt quickly about Moth engines and instruments and so became a valuable member of the engineering team.

Steed's only problem was an acute shortage of cash. Even though the flying club charged only a fraction of the usual fee for his tuition, and in spite of the long hours and weekends that he worked to improve his wage, his apprentice pay left him bordering on poverty. His powerful motorcycle was a necessity for the journey between home and flying club, but it was heavy on petrol. His parents subsidised him as best they could, but Steed still felt obliged to give his mother something for his keep.

All of this meant that his social life was virtually non-existent. His life revolved around the workshop, flying, and studying for his pilot's licence, all of which he loved, but he missed the company of people his own age. He spent such long hours working and travelling that he started to lose contact with his old school friends, and with those he had met at the garage. When he did have the time to go out, he could rarely afford it.

Then came the day when Clancy, with a twinkle in his eye, leaned forward from the back seat of the Moth and said, 'I want you to repeat the circuit that we have just completed, but this time solo. Think carefully about what you are doing. Remember your height and your turning points. If you are in any doubt whatsoever, or if you bounce badly on landing, open the throttle and go around again. Keep a careful lookout. Keep calm. Do everything that you have been taught and everything will be fine. After you have landed, taxi around for a second circuit unless I stop you. Clear?'

'Yes, clear.'

'As soon as I get out you can go. Remember, take a good look around first.' With that Clancy jumped out and gave a cheery wave.

In spite of his excitement, Steed forced himself to stay calm and methodically go through the procedures. Line up the aeroplane on the runway, check the oil pressure, gun the engine, release the brakes and off we go. The little aircraft gathered speed and then they were up. Check the height; a 90-degree turn away from the field and then another to bring them onto the downwind leg, parallel to the field. Now, for the first time, Steed was able to fully take in that he was flying solo. He could see Clancy below, looking up over his shoulder as he walked back to the taxi line. Now the next turning point was approaching. Check the speed, check the height and check around for other aeroplanes. A 90-degree turn, then another and they were on the landing approach. Settle into the final glide and choose the spot to land. And now for the tricky part. Check the speed, judge the height, a slight cross wind today so straighten up, throttle right back, stick back a bit to bring the nose up, a bump and she was down. Not quite a three-pointer, but no bouncing. Apply the brakes, keep her straight, look around as we prepare to turn and taxi back to the downwind end of the field.

Steed looked across to Clancy as the Moth taxied by; Clancy simply gave a nonchalant thumbs-up. Steed repeated the solo circuit a second time and then taxied back to the workshop. Clancy greeted him. 'Well done, I'm sure that you will enter that one in your log. We'll do a few more solo circuits next time. Cheerio.' And with that he was gone.

The flying club gained many new members during that summer of '34 and business was brisk. The terrible years of the depression seemed to be slipping behind and a new dawn beginning. The fitters hardly had time to draw breath, and the instructors were similarly busy. Steed still managed to fly a couple of hours each week as the summer wore on, and by November he was ready to take his Class-A private pilot's licence exam. The exam consisted of a medical, a practical flying test and a technical examination in London. The medical was no problem; he was a fit youth with excellent eyesight. The flying examination, although stringent, was similarly straightforward. Steed had been well prepared by his instructors and was an above average pupil. The theoretical examination in London included subjects such as lights and signals, rules of the air including those around aerodromes and international air legislation. He passed!

Steed was now able to take aircraft on test flights as a part of his work, and in that way maintain flying experience in his logbook, essential for retaining his pilot's licence. Deductions from his salary for flying tuition also ceased, which was very welcome. As winter deepened and the days shortened, flying club business slackened and the fitters were less busy. There was flying at weekends, but midweek was quiet. From November through to the following March, Steed worked a five-day week without overtime, with a day off midweek in lieu of Saturday working. It was just as well that he no longer needed to fund his flying lessons. Life for the young Harry Steed settled into a routine. He enjoyed his work as an apprentice mechanic, especially the flying. He joined a cross-country running club and made new friends of his own age. He was also a frequent visitor to the swimming pool and to the library where his choice was invariably historical non-fiction.

In the spring of 1935, Bill Wheeler introduced Steed to clay pigeon shooting. Using Wheeler's shotgun, for his apprentice wage did not stretch to purchasing a weapon of his own, Steed developed into quite a useful shot. Bill also taught him some of the ways of the country, including a little illicit poaching. Occasionally, Steed would spend the night with Wheeler and his genial wife Emily. Then, he and Wheeler would go out into the fields and woodlands of rural Essex to snare rabbits. The idea was to locate a rabbit run and then to carefully place a snare, concealing it not only from the rabbit but also from inquisitive people such as farmers or gamekeepers. Generally speaking, the farmers didn't object to a little rabbit poaching, since the rabbits ate corn, but when Wheeler and Steed went after pheasants it was a different story.

One had to be very careful when going about poaching pheasants because the gamekeeper and the local bobby were always on the lookout. Wheeler's method was simple. At night, for that was when the poacher worked, the pheasants would fly up to sleep in the lower branches of the trees, or into the hedgerows, where they were safe from the foxes.

Pheasants were stupid birds, Wheeler said, and he would creep up on them and shine a torch into their eyes. Steed would then grab their legs while they were still stupefied by the bright light. Wheeler and Steed never sold their booty; their ill-gotten gains went into the pot.

Steed was well aware that what he was doing was illegal. In law, the wildlife belonged to the landowner whose property it happened to be on at the time. There was money to be made by the landowner from pheasant shoots, so sporting estates hired gamekeepers to protect the birds. The local magistrates, who probably classed the local landowners as personal friends, took a dim view of poaching.

But Steed enjoyed the closeness to nature that he felt when moving quietly through the countryside at night, always vigilant, his senses razor sharp, learning the skills of the countryman. He knew that in the eyes of the law he was trespassing and stealing the game, but he felt no sympathy for rich landowners and farmers who paid their labourers and farmhands a pittance. He was becoming more and more politically aware and was influenced by the leftwards-leaning politics of Wheeler, whom he admired. Steed's father's views were now also left of centre, hardened by the less than humanitarian treatment of soldiers returning from the Great War trenches. Steed was beginning to appreciate the class system that permeated English society in the pre-war thirties, as he saw it to the detriment of most of the population.

Fuelled by the many books that he was reading on history, politics and religion, Steed's mind began to expand. He started to question the established British political system of a King and House of Lords who derived their power through birthright. Steed's parents had a relaxed attitude towards religion; it was simply not an important aspect of their lives. Steed had neither attended traditional Church of England services nor Sunday school as a boy and, as he grew into adolescence, he considered himself at first an agnostic and then an atheist. With this new outlook on religion, he also found himself at odds with the privileged position of the Church of England in British society.

By that summer Steed had grown into a tall, good looking and athletic seventeen year-old. The outdoor life and the summer sun had bleached his hair blond and the cross-county running, on which he was so keen, had toned his body.

Generally, the mechanics were under management orders to keep their distance from the flying club's wealthy clientele. However, when things were slack, they were sometimes tasked with general maintenance and repair jobs on the clients' vehicles. One warm and pleasant morning during the Indian summer of 1935, one of the members, a vivacious brunette of about thirty called Sophie Richards, brought her Humber 12 across to the workshop. Steed greeted her politely, 'Can I help you madam?'

She looked at Steed through her expensive sunglasses and smiled. 'I do hope so,' she murmured. 'Mr Golding suggested you might be able to do something about my car. It's overheating and there seems to be steam coming from under the bonnet.'

'I'll take a look for you.' Steed opened the bonnet. The cause of the problem was immediately apparent. 'You have a split hose madam, so you're losing water. We don't stock that type in the workshop, so I'll have to go to the local garage. I can have your car ready for you in about an hour and a half, say two hours to be on the safe side.'

'You are an angel. What's your name?'

'Harry Steed madam.'

'You don't have to call me madam. My name is Mrs Richards. I've seen you around. You fly don't you?'

'Yes Mrs Richards. I'm one of the mechanics here, but I also have a pilot's licence so that I can flight test the aircraft.'

'Yes, I've watched you do that. I have also seen you running around the airfield in your shorts. You look very fit. Are you in training for something?'

Steed blushed, 'Oh, I try to keep fit. I like cross-country running. I sometimes run around the airfield during my lunch break.'

'Do you take part in competitions?'

'Sometimes Mrs Richards, but I work here most weekends, so I don't get much chance to compete these days.'

'Well it's nice to meet you Harry. I'll come back in a couple of hours.'

Steed crossed the workshop to tell Bill Wheeler where he was going and then took the workshop van into town for the hose. He was back and had the repair completed in just over an hour.

'It's all ready for you Mrs Richards. I've changed the hose, filled the radiator including anti-freeze, and checked it over. She doesn't overheat now. The bill will be added to your account.'

'That's very kind of you Harry, but will you come for a short drive with me please. I want to be sure that it doesn't overheat again and leave me stranded in the middle of nowhere.'

'Sure thing Mrs Richards.'

Steed sat back in the comfortable passenger seat as Mrs Richards drove briskly along the country roads. It was a warm summer's day, and both windows of the large saloon were down, letting in a welcome breeze. Mrs Richards was wearing a light chiffon dress, and both this and her long auburn hair fluttered in the wind. She turned to Steed and smiled. 'It's a warm day Harry, just the day for a ride on that motorbike of yours. I bet the girls melt in your arms after a fast ride on the back of that.'

Steed was at a loss for words. Mrs Richards seemed to have noticed an awful lot of things about him, his flying, his running and now his motorcycle. Flustered, he answered, 'The motorbike's lovely in this weather, but it's not quite so much fun in the winter.'

'Hmm,' she whispered, 'It must be lovely having so much power between your legs.' It took Steed a moment to grasp the innuendo. Had she meant to say that, or was it an innocent comment about the power of his motorcycle? He did not reply, but stared fixedly ahead.

'I would adore having that power between my legs,' she continued, 'But my husband doesn't understand a woman's needs. He's away most of the time on his business. He leaves poor little me all alone. He's away on business right now.'

Steed gulped and started to tremble a little. This woman was trying to seduce him! She was certainly very pretty, but she was married and much older than him. She was sophisticated and obviously rich. Why would she take any notice of an apprentice mechanic?

Mrs Richards slowed the car and turned onto a farm track. The track entered a wood; a hundred yards into the wood she stopped the car under some trees and turned off the motor. Steed did not know where to look or what to say. She was speaking once again.

'How old are you Harry?'

'Seventeen, Mrs Richards.'

'Oh, I think that you can call me Sophie when we are alone like this, don't you Harry?' She was leaning towards him now. He was keenly aware of her presence, her sensuous perfume, and the closeness of her body. Her chiffon dress had ridden up her leg, or had she helped it on its way? Her hand moved towards his leg and her lips were now very close to his cheek. He was trembling and his heart was pounding. His eyes were bulging from their sockets as he looked down, in spite of himself, at that perfect leg now visible from her ankle almost to her thigh.

She didn't say a word, but started to kiss and nibble his ear. Her left hand was around his shoulder and stroking his hair. Her right hand was stroking his leg, at first in the region of his knee, but then moving inextricably up towards his groin. He was very aware of her breasts under her chiffon dress, rising and falling with her breathing. He had an uncontrollable desire to put his hand on her breast, over that thin chiffon dress. Jesus, he had never even kissed a girl properly before, let alone touched her breasts!

He stammered, 'But you are married. Your husband, what if...'

She cut him short, 'Don't worry Harry. My husband is far away. Nobody knows that we are here. I want you to make love to me right now. This will be the one and only time, and afterwards, neither of us will speak about it ever again. I just want to experience you this once. You understand? No strings attached, no regrets and no worries about tomorrow. Here and now, just for fun. Now kiss me.'

For the first time in his life, Steed placed his hand on a girl's breast and squeezed gently. For the first time in his life he kissed a girl with feeling. She responded, and then said, 'Open your mouth slightly when you kiss me darling……mmm….that's right.' His hand traced a path down her cleavage, beneath her dress, beneath her brassier. For a moment Steed thought that she was going to push his hand away, but she simply undid the buttons at the front of her dress before returning her hand to his groin area.

Her skin was soft and he stared in wonder as her right nipple appeared from underneath her brassier, coaxed out by his trembling hand. Her nipple, which had been soft, was now hard. He moved his lips from her mouth to that wonderful pert pink nipple. Her hand was rubbing his groin, and his manhood was now rock hard. She pulled away, now slightly breathless, 'Outside darling, on the grass,' she said urgently.

They both got out of the car. She pulled the car blanket from the rear seat and spread it on the grass; then she lay down. Her lips were large, red and inviting and her right breast still peaked out from her unbuttoned dress. Steed kissed her hungrily, his hand now probing her underclothes for their hidden secrets. With wonder he touched pubic hair and something moist and warm.

With surprising strength she pushed him over onto his back and unbuttoned his fly. Steed gasped with surprise as she produced a condom and pulled in onto him. She held his penis firmly as she lowered herself onto it. At some stage she must have removed her knickers, but things were by now a blur to Steed. And then he was no longer a virgin. She moved up and down, moaning softly. All too quickly the feeling came over him and he could not stop himself.

She rolled away from him and kissed him gently. 'You seemed very ready for that my darling. Now it's my turn.' Naively, Steed did not have a clue what she meant, but she guided his hand once again to that moist area of her groin. 'Just here my darling, gently here with your finger…ohhh, that's nice, that's very nice.'

She lay back on the grass and closed her eyes. Somewhere above, Steed heard an aeroplane, probably from the club, but the two lovers were hidden from view under the foliage of the trees. While he did her bidding with his right hand, his left hand explored her bosom. She said nothing, but lay back with closed eyes as he undid more buttons on her dress and then pulled up her brassier to reveal both magnificent breasts. He kissed her breasts gently, paying special attention to those exquisite nipples, all the time doing her bidding down there, in that mysterious area of her groin. She murmured her approval. Her breathing became heavier, and then suddenly her whole body quivered and she let out a muffled squeal of pleasure. She arrested the movement of his hand on her groin and rolled into his arms, kissing him softly on the lips and cheek.

'That was your first time, wasn't it my darling?'

'Why do you say that?' he said defensively.

'Ah well, a woman knows these things, especially a married woman like me.' She put a finger over his lips as he tried to speak. 'Don't think too badly of me my pet. I admit that I've watched you and connived to get you to make love to me. You shouldn't blame me; you really are a dish you know. Some day soon you will find a girl of your own age, and when the time comes to…well you know…you will have a pretty good idea of how to give her pleasure. Maybe that's my gift to you in return for the pleasure that you have given me. Now listen my darling. I am married and you have your job at the club. This is both the first and last time that we can be like this. In a moment we will get in the car and drive back. I will tell Mr Golding that I insisted on a full road test after the repair, and I will expect to be billed accordingly. If we meet again, I must once again be the remote Mrs Richards, the flying club member who once gave you her car to repair.'

'I will always remember you Sophie, and this afternoon,' was all that Steed could say.

'I bet you will Harry, I bet you will!' she said standing up and re-arranging her clothes. 'Come on. Time to get back.'

Steed could never be sure just how much Sophie Richards had planned his seduction, and how much it had been by chance. Had she really had a problem with her car, or had she engineered the split hose with a knife? By the time he had thought about it, the hose was long gone and past all examination. That farm track leading to the woods, where her car could not be seen from any club aircraft that might happen to fly overhead, surely that did not happen by chance. She must have reconnoitred that in advance. Whatever, Sophie was right. He would always remember her and that hot afternoon when he lost his virginity to an older married woman.

The final two years of Steed's apprenticeship passed uneventfully, although the happenings in Europe were far from uneventful. Mr Hitler and his Nazi party chums were busy building a nationalistic and militaristic Germany, while in Spain civil war broke out between the republican government and a conservative rebellious army led by General Franco. In England, the abdication of King Edward VIII reinforced Steed's republican instincts.

Steed completed his apprenticeship in April 1937 and at last moved on to something like a reasonable wage for the job that he was doing. As the season got into full swing, the flying club was busier than ever. But the political situation in Europe was deteriorating and war clouds were gathering. In August 1934, following Hindenburg's death, Adolf Hitler had become the undisputed leader of Germany. Two years later his forces had marched unopposed into the Rhineland. Few people in Great Britain had the stomach for a round-two clash with Germany after the catastrophe of the Great War. Peace and disarmament were seen as laudable objectives and had received strong support in both parliament and in the country generally. But now, sadly, in the summer of 1937 it had become apparent that Britain must rearm, and rearm quickly, or nakedly face an increasingly belligerent Germany.

Steed too, began to consider how he should respond to the growing likelihood of war.

Chapter Three - RAF Volunteer Reserve

As war clouds gathered, the government decided upon an expansion programme for the RAF. The traditional method of service entry for officer cadet pilots remained Cranwell, the RAF equivalent of the British Army's Sandhurst. Virtually all the RAF officers passing through Cranwell came from the public schools, because the establishment believed that only public schoolboys would preserve the best traditions of the officer class.

The Auxiliary Air Force, which was established in 1924 for reservist pilots, was also being expanded. However, the AAF required the candidate to be of a 'certain background' and invariably wealthy; it soon became a social club for the upper echelons of the British class system. The third method of entry was the RAF Volunteer Reserve.

The RAFVR was formed in 1936, with the objective of providing an immediate reserve of trained pilots in the event of war. It was a part-time air force, similar in concept to Britain's Territorial Army. Its members trained in the evenings and at weekends but otherwise retained their civilian jobs and lifestyle. Although it was not publicly admitted, the VR was brought into being to provide a reserve of pilots who could fill the places of those permanent RAF pilots who might expect to be killed or wounded in the first phase of an air war. All entrants had to be between eighteen and twenty-five, and were required to sign on for five years.

This 'citizen air force reserve' was far less elitist than the AAF, or the RAF proper, and was aimed at middle and even working class young men; it was not necessary to have been to a public school. VR pilots were neither seen as gentlemen nor air leaders, so consequently successful candidates became sergeants. There was no cost penalty for the part-time aviators; in fact there was a £25 per year bounty. The VR was naturally very popular and consequently oversubscribed.

Initially the RAF had relied on its own elementary flying schools to train the new influx of pilots, but it was soon discovered that these could not cope with the increased demand. The RAF therefore decided to pay civilian flying schools to train its fledgling pilots. Consequently, Epping flying club took delivery of three shiny new Tiger Moth aeroplanes in May 1937 and started to provide basic flying training for RAFVR pilots at weekends, with plans being made for summer camps.

Steed made his decision. War with Germany was looking more and more likely, although he hoped that it might still be avoided. Yet if war came, he would much rather fight in the air than in the trenches. Joining the RAF as an officer pilot was impossible for a working class boy without a School Certificate, but the VR offered a way in as an NCO. Steed might not have a School Certificate, but he did have a pilot's licence and he felt that must count for something. He resolved to apply to join the RAFVR as a weekend flyer. If war came it would be a fast route into the RAF proper and a squadron.

He informed Mr Golding of his decision, but it was met with hostility. 'We need you here more than ever, as a full-time fitter on the ground, not as a weekend RAF flyboy. We have trained you as a fitter; we have even helped you to get your pilot's licence. Weekends are our busy time, especially so now that we have the RAF here. No. It's out of the question.'

'I am very sorry Mr Golding, but my mind's made up. I believe that we might have to go to war with Germany. Look what's happening in Spain right now. I really hope that I am wrong, but if we do go to war we will need all the trained pilots that we can get. I want to do my bit. The VR is only part-time, at weekends and some evenings. It's designed for people like me that have full-time jobs. We train when we are not at work. Anyway, if they send me here to train I will always be on hand in case of emergencies, even if I am off duty as a fitter I can always help out.'

'That's another problem. Knowing those silly buggers in the Air Ministry, they are just as likely to send you to some other training school and then where will we be?' And then came the threat. 'If you cannot guarantee to work here at weekends and in the evenings, I cannot guarantee your job. We may have to find a replacement for you.'

But they both knew that was an empty threat. Steed had become an essential part of the workforce. Not only was he a first-class aircraft fitter, with aircraft fitters in short supply, but he was also the only fitter capable of flight-testing the aeroplanes. Instructors were now too busy to take on that task.

'We may be worrying unnecessarily,' commented Steed wryly. 'From what I've read, the VR is heavily oversubscribed. My chances of getting in are pretty low, but I thought it only fair to tell you that I was applying.'

'Hmm. Well if you do get in, I will see if our instructors can pull a few strings to get your training done here.'

'Thank you Mr Golding.' And with that Steed took his leave and returned to the workshop. The new apprentice was waiting for him when he arrived. 'Right then Brian, let's have a look at how your valve seating is going.'

Steed submitted his application in May 1937, and was duly invited to attend for interview and a medical examination at Store Street, the London headquarters of the VR. Steed found himself in company with a dozen other young hopefuls. The medical examination was surprisingly thorough, but Steed was fit with excellent eyesight and so passed A1.

Steed waited in a long room as, one after another, all of the other candidates disappeared off for interview. None of them returned. Eventually it was Steed's turn and he was ushered into the interview room. A wing commander in his mid forties, seated behind a desk, greeted him. Steed noted the wings and the DFC. The wing commander introduced a squadron leader sitting nonchalantly alongside whom, he said, would be taking notes. The squadron leader smiled. Steed was invited to sit facing the two of them.

The wing commander looked at the papers in front of him; it was he who spoke first. 'Mr Harold Steed aged nineteen I see. Working as an aircraft fitter and with a Class-A private pilot's licence.' He looked up, 'How did you manage that?'

'The flying club gave me discounted flying lessons during my apprenticeship. I managed to fly a couple of hours each week. I had to work weekends and in the evenings to make ends meet, but now it means that I not only work on the engines but I can also flight-test the aeroplanes.'

The wing commander studied the papers some more. 'I see here that you have a fair amount of flying experience on training aircraft. But service flying is very different you know. What you learn first, take offs, circuits and landings, simple turns, that's the easy bit. What comes later sorts out the men from the boys. Tried any aerobatics?'

'Loops in training sir, and of course recovering from a spin. But these days I'm only allowed to check out engines and instruments on flight tests. No aerobatics or fun flying. My flying tuition ceased as soon as I got my pilot's licence.'

'Pity. Ride do you?'

Steed was caught off guard for a moment. Ride? He means horses not a motorbike you fool. 'No sir, I have never ridden a horse.'

'Pity, you need sensitive hands for aeroplanes. Riding's good for developing sensitive hands. Hunting's good too. Follow a pack do you?' This man was from a different world!

'No sir, but I do play the piano, you need sensitive hands for that as well,' Steed said brightly.

'Humph, what about sports. Say's here that you do cross-country running. Done any team sports? Played cricket? Rugger?'

'I used to play football at school, and I still swim a bit, but my main sport is cross-country running. I came third in the East London trials when I was sixteen, running over on Hackney Marshes. These days I spend so much time working and travelling to and from the flying club in Epping that I haven't the time to play team sports like football. I would miss too many of the matches, not to mention the training sessions. But I still keep fit by running.'

'Team sports are important. They build team spirit; that's very important in a squadron. Become team captain and you demonstrate leadership. All officers and NCOs in the RAF must show leadership. How can you show me that you can fit into a team and can lead?'

Steed groped for inspiration. After a moment he said, 'Well sir. I am a part of a team at work. We all pull together to keep the aeroplanes flying.' God, what else was there to say? 'Oh, and we now have a new apprentice. The chief fitter has put him under my wing.'

There followed some general questions on Steed's hobbies and home life, and then the wing commander moved onto his academic studies. 'I see that you went to a grammar school but that you left school at fifteen. Why didn't you stay on for your School Certificate?'

'I wanted to, but I am afraid that my parents simply could not afford it. I had to start to earn a living and contribute something towards my keep.'

'Was you father not working?'

'Oh yes sir, but with the depression and all, his wages were very poor. We were lucky, some of my friends had to leave school even earlier because their fathers had lost their jobs.'

Steed went on defensively 'My mum and dad were very good to me later, when I said that I wanted to learn to fly. The flying club gave me lessons at a much reduced price, much less than for club members, but after paying for the lessons and the petrol for the motorbike that I needed to go back and forth between Islington and Epping, there wasn't much left over. I gave my mum some money for my food and rent, but it really wasn't enough.'

'Indeed,' said the wing commander thoughtfully. 'But you need a decent standard of mathematics for flying you know. For navigation especially.'

'Yes sir, I know. I have tried to brush up on maths since leaving school. The chief flying instructor at the school lent me some books on navigation, and of course I needed some maths to pass the Class-A.'

The wing commander nodded and went back to the papers in front of him. He looked up, straight into Steed's eyes. 'Why do you want to join the RAF Volunteer Reserve?'

At last, the expected question. Steed drew breath.

'I've been passionate about aeroplanes since I was a boy. I read aeroplane magazines, Biggles novels, everything there is to read about the RAF. I left school at fifteen and started an apprenticeship at a motor garage. I was doing well, but I just wanted to be around aeroplanes.' Steed had a sense of déjà vu going back to his first meeting with Bill Wheeler, when Bill had asked him why he wanted to work at the flying club. He continued, 'I applied for a job at the flying club miles away from my home, just so that I would have the chance to work with aeroplanes and to fly them. Now I think that a war is likely, although I really hope that I'm wrong. My dad was an infantry sergeant in the Great War and it would be terrible to see all of that happen again. But if there is to be a war, then I understand aeroplanes. I am a pilot. I want to join the RAF Volunteer Reserve so that I can train to be a fighter pilot and be ready to defend our country, just in case the worst happens.'

The wing commander looked at Steed quizzically. 'Why a fighter pilot? Why not bombers? Don't you fancy the idea of dropping bombs?'

Steed gave himself a moment for thought. 'I think that I have the aptitude to be a fighter pilot. If enemy bombers dare to attack our country, I want to be the one who shoots them down. I like the idea of being a hunter, of out-thinking the other fellow whether he is an enemy fighter or a bomber. I just think that I would be good at it.'

The wing commander persisted, 'Say we asked you to become a bomber pilot. How would you feel about dropping bombs on enemy cities?'

Steed said quietly, 'I don't suppose that anybody likes the idea of killing women and children. I think that the RAF would probably ask me to bomb military targets in preference, but we can see the way that things are going in Spain. If Britain is strong, if she has a powerful bomber force, then I think that the enemy would think twice about bombing our cities. We could retaliate by bombing theirs; they would know that.' Steed paused, and then said simply, 'I would do my duty sir.'

The wing commander nodded. 'Do you think that the bomber will always get through?'

'I don't really know. That's what people say. It depends on how many fighters we can deploy and whether they can get up in time. I suspect that our fighters would be able to shoot quite a few of the enemy down, but I guess that some might get through.'

Steed warmed to his point. He had to demonstrate to this man that he knew what he was talking about. 'But things are changing all the time. The Hawker Hart bomber was faster than our fighters when it was first introduced a couple of years ago, so the fighters of the day would have had a tough time shooting that down. But then new fighters were introduced, like the Hawker Fury and Gloster Gladiator, to redress the balance.'

Steed continued, 'The Bristol Blenheim is our latest bomber. She is a streamlined monoplane with a retractable undercarriage, so she has low drag and is fast. Our biplane fighters are very manoeuvrable in a dogfight, but they are hampered by drag in out-and-out speed. I think that if a bomber like the Blenheim had height advantage it would probably get through.'

The wing commander nodded. 'Very well Mr Steed. That's about it for the moment. The corporal outside will take you for some tea. The group captain will see you later and let you know the result. Anything that you would like to ask me?'

'No sir. Thank you.'

Steed stood up to attention, feeling slightly conspicuous because he was a civilian and not in uniform. But he wanted to demonstrate by his manner that he would readily assimilate into the RAFVR. The wing commander nodded and the squadron leader, who had been scribbling throughout the interview but without speaking, smiled kindly as Steed left the room.

The corporal led Steed to a large room where his fellow candidates were assembled. 'Tea and buns over there,' said a stocky youth of about Steed's age. 'You're the last one aren't you? How did you get on?'

'Yes, I was last. I was feeling quite lonely towards the end in that waiting room.' Steed laughed, 'You all left one by one and nobody came back. I thought that you had all gone home. Difficult to say how I got on. I had a wingco asking the questions and a squadron leader who didn't say a thing, but kept scribbling away on a piece of paper.'

'Yep, same for the rest of us,' said the youth.

Wing Commander Beresford looked across to Squadron Leader Warren as Steed left the room. 'What did you make of him Bunny?'

Warren looked down at his notes. 'I was very impressed. The lad is from a poor family background, but he has the drive to carve out the life that he wants for himself. He wanted to fly and, in spite of his background, he has moved hell and high water to achieve his ambition. That shows real spirit. He has a pilot's licence and plenty of hours in his logbook. What's more, he has a mechanical bent and understands aircraft engines. He has a good knowledge of RAF aircraft with positive and imaginative thoughts on strategy. All in all, I think that he's easily the best candidate we have seen all week. Medical is A1 too.'

'I agree.' said the wing commander. 'He was very respectful towards my rank as well, unusual for a civilian of his age, almost as if he was in the service already. We will take him on as a pilot. I did rather wonder at first if he might not do better as an aircraft fitter, but he has his Class-A and he is dead set on becoming a fighter pilot, so we will give him a shot at getting his wings.'

The corporal retuned and asked Steed and one other of the candidates to follow him. The two of them were ushered into the interview room and were duly sworn in by a group captain as sergeant pilots under training in the RAF Volunteer Reserve. The other ten candidates were informed that there were no vacancies at that time; such was the competition for the VR in 1937.

That evening, Steed joined his mother and father for a celebratory drink in the local pub. Steed's father was bursting with pride that his son had become a sergeant, be it in a part-time capacity and with the RAF and not the army, but his mother was more circumspect. Later, when they were alone in their bedroom, his mother whispered quietly to her husband, 'The RAF needs aircraft fitters as well as pilots. Why oh why can't Harry settle for that? If war comes it would be so much safer for him. It was so horrible when you were at the front; so many of the other wives received those dreadful telegrams. You came back thank God, but must we go through it all again worrying about Harry?'

George Steed held his wife in his arms. She was sobbing quietly. 'Chin up old gooseberry. War won't come; and in any case the RAF's not like the army. No sitting in muddy trenches getting shelled and gassed for the boys in blue. A life of old Riley for them. Even if war comes, which it won't, Harry will be all right.' But, hidden from his wife's view as he held her in his arms, the old man's face betrayed his inner thoughts. The life expectancy of an RFC pilot in the Great War had been considerably inferior to that of a Tommy in the trenches. One month on average at the time of the Somme. Death was more common than being wounded for fighter pilots: and when death came it so often involved being burnt alive. Hitler had been a frontline soldier in the Great War. He must have shared in the terrible misery and suffering of all the soldiers, regardless of nationality. Shelling, gas, machine-guns, the bayonet! Surely Hitler wouldn't want to start another war? No sane man that went through that would.

The VR required its student pilots to pass a 15-day *ab initio* elementary flying training course to demonstrate their flying aptitude. Successful students would then progress to further flying training at weekends or during summer evenings. At the same time, students were required to attend lectures on flight theory, navigation, engines and generally all things aeronautical, at a local venue twice per week.

For Steed, evening lectures commenced at Store Street, in London, towards the end of June 1937. Steed knew already much of what was taught in those first months, but he found it useful revision. He did not volunteer the fact that he had a private pilot's licence to anybody, least of all to the instructors; he simply carried on quietly with the work he was given, obtaining top marks along the way.

Golding and Clancy had pulled strings such that Steed's three-week RAFVR flying training *ab initio* camp was located at Epping. Steed's course commenced in mid August 1937; by then he had seen a number of similar courses pass through Epping and had a fair idea of what to expect. Golding, despite his grumbling that Steed could not be spared at this busy time, reluctantly agreed to allow him to take his two weeks annual holiday, with a third week without pay, to attend the summer camp.

Epping had by now been virtually taken over by the VR for flying training purposes, and there were far fewer private flyers to be seen. A RAF flight lieutenant instructor had also appeared; his job was to routinely test all of the students for progress and general flying ability. There was fierce competition for VR placements, with new applicants eagerly waiting to fill the shoes of those VR trainee pilots that fell by the wayside. It was made clear at the inaugural meeting of the three-week camp that the standards were high; if trainee pilots were not 'up to scratch' they could expect to be 'washed up'.

Steed had hoped to fly with one of the Epping instructors that he knew so well, but as he approached the Tiger Moth, he saw the RAF flight lieutenant.

'Good afternoon Sergeant Steed, my name is Flight Lieutenant Harris. Mr Clancy tells me that you are an aircraft fitter here at Epping and that you have a Class-A licence. What's more you regularly take aircraft like this Moth up for flight tests. Is that correct?'

'Yes sir,' said Steed respectfully. He thought it better to wait for the questions rather than to volunteer further information.

'Do you have your Class-A with you?' Steed kept it with his logbook, and so handed over both documents. Harris studied the logbook in particular. 'Okay Steed, you have plenty of hours logged and a Class-A licence, so it would be a waste of our time and yours for you to sit through the basics with the other students. But in order for you to move on, you first have to prove to me that you have reached the required standard to pass the *ab initio* course. You can start by telling me all about the control surfaces and instruments of this aeroplane.'

They walked around the aircraft. Steed described the aeroplane controls and instruments as he was bid, with Harris asking occasional questions. Harris then asked, 'Apart from the flying that is necessary for the Class-A, what other flying have you done? Any cross-country or aerobatics for example?'

'No sir. The flying club agreed to give me discounted flying lessons just sufficient for me to get the Class-A licence. When I achieved that, the flying lessons stopped. I routinely take aircraft up for flight tests, but I am not allowed to do anything more than that. I don't stray too far from the airfield. No aerobatics. The club is very strict about that. No flying for fun either, just for my work, just for instrument and engine checks.'

'Right,' said Harris as they settled into their seats in the Tiger Moth, 'I want you to start up. Taxi to the downwind end of the field, take off, circuit and land. Do that three times. Pretend that I am not in the aeroplane with you. I want to see three landings. Clear?'

'Yes sir.' Steed did as he was bid, executing three near perfect three-pointed landings. Harris did not say a word.

After the third landing Harris shouted above the noise of the engine through the voice tube, 'Take off again, set a course due east and climb to 2,000 feet. I don't have to tell you to keep a lookout around North Weald do I?'

'I'll keep a sharp lookout sir.' Steed knew all about the RAF types from the North Weald aerodrome and their Gloster Gauntlet aeroplanes. Steed had often seen these handsome open-cockpit biplanes frolicking around the sky, playing with the clouds and showing off their power and agility. Sometimes several of these aircraft would practise their aerobatics in unison, performing an exquisite aerial ballet.

When they reached altitude, Harris told Steed to carry out a number of turns climbs and dives of varying intensity and in various combinations, finishing with a recovery from a spin. Satisfied, Harris simply told Steed to head for home and land. As they were taxiing after landing Harris shouted, 'Stop here and let me out. Do three more take off and landing circuits, this time solo, then come back here and we will call it a day. All right?'

At the end of the session, as they walked away from the aeroplane, Harris said, 'That was good, but no more than I expected from a pilot with your flying hours. You have satisfied the practical flying requirements for the basic course. Tomorrow you will progress to more advanced flying with one of the other instructors. I will come up with you again sometime during the next couple of weeks.'

The other students soon discovered that Steed not only worked as an aircraft fitter at Epping, but that he also had a private pilot's licence and had the job of flight testing their Tiger Moths. He was therefore in great demand during breaks and in the evenings for advice on all things aeronautical. One by one his fellow students went solo, usually after around 10 to 12 hours dual. Two of the students lagged the rest in ability, demonstrating numerous aborted and bumpy landings. It acted as a sharp reminder to the rest when both of these students were 'washed up' after a flying test with Flight Lieutenant Harris.

Steed was alone in moving onto instrument flying, simple aerobatics and cross-country navigation. He flew dual with one of the instructors from Epping that he knew well, but he was shown no favours. He suspected that Flight Lieutenant Harris had told his instructor to find the limit of his abilities and then stretch them further. This was certainly what it felt like. Steed was convinced that his instructor was putting him under pressure just to see how he reacted. He was fortunate in that he knew the Tiger Moth so well. He had made so many landings on the Epping field that he could put her down with pinpoint accuracy whatever the weather.

What was new to Steed was the reliance on instruments now insisted upon by his instructor. Sometimes an instrument-training hood was rigged around the rear cockpit, cutting out all visibility to the outside; on these occasions the instructor sat in front. Steed was then told to carry out various manoeuvres relying solely on instruments. Steed had climbed through cloud before on instruments, but he found that the complete lack of vision outside the confines of the cockpit played tricks on his senses. Now and then he became sure that the aircraft was banking when the instruments told him that she was flying straight and level. In these situations he learnt to rely on his instruments and not to give way to his instincts.

Flight Lieutenant Harris accompanied Steed twice more during the three-week course to check on his progress. The final flight with Harris was on the penultimate day of the course. Harris set Steed a particularly arduous set of tasks. After they landed, Harris gave Steed his debrief. 'How do you think that went Sergeant? Any issues, any problems?'

'I guess there is always something that one feels could be better. It is never perfect. Some of my barrel rolls were a bit off the mark I think, but generally I was happy.'

'Yes, not at all bad. You have a big advantage of course, not just that you had a pilot's licence before you started, but also you know the airfield and the aeroplane so well. Nevertheless, you have made good progress during the past three weeks.'

'Thank you sir.'

Harris continued, 'I really think that you have gone far enough with the Tiger Moth, you need to move on to an advanced trainer. Also, I want to move you away from this airfield. Send you somewhere where you are less familiar with the people and the geography. It will be good for you.'

'Yes sir. Would that be for weekend flying from now on? And would that be from another London aerodrome?' Steed sounded a trifle concerned.

Harris smiled, 'Yes Sergeant, if we can arrange it we will move you to another London aerodrome where they have advanced trainers.

Don't worry, we won't expect you to travel backwards and forwards to Scotland every weekend.'

Steed was instructed to report to Monks Hill Flying Club to the northwest of London for his weekend flying training, commencing in October 1937. As Steed expected, this was not popular with Golding. Monks Hill Flying Club, like Epping, had also been a private flying club, but by now had been completely taken over by the RAFVR. The airfield was slightly larger than Epping and operated Tiger Moths for the elementary courses and Hawker Harts for the more advanced courses. Steed was to fly the latter.

The Hawker Hart light bomber had caused quite a stir when it first entered RAF service in 1930, being faster than any of the contemporary RAF fighters. The Hart had been the mainstay RAF light bomber of the early to mid thirties and had seen service throughout the Empire, often operating in harsh climates; for example it had been used most successfully to drop bombs on the wayward tribesmen of the Northwest Frontier. Monks Hill was equipped with the trainer version of the Hart, and Steed marvelled when he had a close look at the engine, a huge 12-cylinder Rolls-Royce Kestrel.

Steed found the Hart a delight to fly, so much more powerful than the Tiger Moth and very manoeuvrable. He went solo in the Hart after just two dual lessons. The intensity of the training increased. The Hart, like the Tiger Moth, could be fitted with a hood to simulate night flying and this prevented the pupil from seeing anything outside the confines of the cockpit. At first, instrument-only lessons consisted solely of turns, climbs and dives on given headings; then came the day when, with plenty of height in hand, Steed was instructed to put the aircraft into a spin and then recover on instruments.

Steed had of course been taught how to recover from a spin; indeed it was mandatory knowledge prior to any pilot going solo. Steed knew the theory. A spin usually results when an aircraft is stalled; the aircraft is unstable at the moment of stall with the stick held back in a climb, and it usually develops into a roll or yaw. At this point the up-going wing is less stalled than the down-going wing so the aircraft rolls towards the down-going wing and keeps on going, losing height rapidly. Recovery from a spin relies on a combination of stick and rudder movements. First the power is reduced to idle and then the rudder is applied in the opposite direction to the spin. As the spin slows and then stops, the rudder is centred and the stick pushed forward to unstall the wings and the aircraft enters a steep dive. Finally one pulls back on the stick to exit the dive, reapplies the power and so gets back to level flight. So much for the theory! Steed had, by now, deliberately stalled, spun and recovered many times in the Tiger Moth, and also a few times in the Hawker Hart, but always in clear air and with a good view of the horizon.

Now his instructor asked him to do the same thing with the hood on. In the blackness, Steed concentrated on the glowing instruments as his instructor told him to induce a spin. Steed set a nose up attitude of 15 degrees and watched the airspeed drop. He forced himself to rely on his instruments and not on his instincts as the nose dropped on the onset of the stall. Haul back on the stick and then put the rudder over to the left to force the spin to the left. The gauges started to spin and disorientation set in. Power back to idle. There was no horizon outside to check the speed of rotation, although he could be fairly certain of the direction of the spin since he had induced it. Rudder over to the right, and the spin was slowing. Order was returning to the gauges although now the altitude was going down at an alarming rate. Ease the stick forward and Steed could see from the instruments that they were in a steep dive. Ease back on the stick and up she came back towards level flight. Now increase the power. The instruments had settled down, they were straight and level. Now come back onto course and regain height. Made it!

Chapter Four – War Clouds

Steed continued to make good progress in the VR as autumn turned to winter, and then winter to the spring of 1938. But in Europe, war clouds were gathering apace. In March of that year Germany annexed Austria in the Anschluss on the pretext of uniting the German speaking peoples. In September Hitler demanded that Czechoslovakia cede the Sudetenland to Germany for much the same reason. The British Prime Minister, Neville Chamberlain, met with Hitler during the Munich crisis and famously waved a piece of paper bearing Hitler's signature purporting to guarantee peace if Hitler's demands were met. Czechoslovakia was forced to surrender the Sudetenland.

In March 1939, not content with the Sudetenland, Hitler ordered the German army to march into the heart of Czechoslovakia. There were no ethnic Germans in central Czechoslovakia, unlike the Sudetenland, only financial and manufacturing prizes such as the large Skoda works, very useful if one was considering a war and wanted to make tanks and aeroplanes! It was now obvious to most people, including Steed, that war with Germany was almost inevitable. Poland was next on Hitler's wish list; he wanted the Poles to cede territory to provide a land corridor to East Prussia. The Poles were not going to allow this, and here Britain and France would make their stand. Steed applied to join the RAF, and the RAF accepted his offer.

It came as something of a surprise to Steed that, instead of giving him a Spitfire to play with, the RAF sent him to Herne Bay, a small seaside town in Kent, to learn how to march and drill. He was billeted with other new recruits in a seaside boarding house behind the seafront. They learnt how to form ranks - shortest on the left, tallest on the right -, march, slow-march, halt, turn, about turn and countless other parade ground movements. They also learn how to do peculiar things with Lee Enfield rifles of Great War vintage. They even had the opportunity to fire the .303 rifles on the range. Although he had never fired a rifle before, shooting clays appeared to have given Steed an edge because, much to his surprise, he made the highest score in the class by a fair margin.

Steed was very glad that he had kept fit through cross-country running because that now paid handsome dividends when under the cosh from the seemingly sadistic PT instructor. Steed lacked the speed and agility of some of his companions, especially the football and rugby players amongst them, but none could match his stamina. He actually enjoyed the daily marches in the fresh sea air, along the cliffs towards Reculver Towers, but he despaired of some of the 'bull' that the RAF authorities seemed so keen on.

'What is the point of all of this crap?' sighed one of his companions to one and all as he attempted, without much success, to shine his boots using the 'spit and polish' technique they had been taught. 'Are we supposed to dazzle the Germans with our shiny boots so they can't shoot straight? Will they be so impressed with our synchronised marching that they will take fright and go home? Seriously, can anyone tell me the point?'

An earnest young recruit, Arthur Stevenson, fresh from working as a clerk in a city bank, piped up, 'It's all about developing teamwork and team spirit. Drill helps us to act like a team.'

Steed answered with a cynical laugh. 'The idea, young Art, is that all of this bull, all of this drill, takes away your freedom of thought. You react instantly to the order without thinking. Just what's needed for the Tommy going over the top.'

'That's unfair,' said earnest Arthur. 'They want pilots to think for themselves, not to act like a herd of sheep.'

'Agreed,' retorted Steed. 'But drill was invented for the brown jobs. Say you're sitting in your nice warm, safe dugout when your officer comes along and tells you to jump up and run over open ground towards the enemy machine-guns. If you think about it, if you weigh up your chances of getting shot for the sake of twenty yards, you might decide against the idea. No, when you're ordered to do something you do as you're told without thinking. You're conditioned to do it. That's what drill is for.' There was general laughter and ribald comments all around.

At that moment Squadron Leader Madams was sitting in the barrack commander's office, which was attached to the students' barrack. The door was open so, although out of sight, the squadron leader could hear the banter perfectly well. Unbeknown to the student pilots, Madams had the power to recommend gifted students for officer training. Steed was the only student in the batch under consideration for this honour. Certainly Steed's flying merited a commission, but could he lead men? Perhaps his comments about drill, although said in jest, suggested an underlying cynicism with the system. Later, back in his office, Madams again consulted Steed's file. Under the heading 'Religion' was the word 'Atheist'. Madams was a devout man and he grimaced. Not C of E like most of the other students; not Roman Catholic or even Jew. This boy had rejected God altogether. Steed would probably make a fine pilot, but could he lead men and tend to their needs, including their spiritual needs? Could he be relied upon to support the status quo? No, thought Madams, he is a maverick, too much of a rebel. Not officer material. Steed's career path would continue as a sergeant pilot.

A second choice now had to be made on Steed's future career in the RAF; that choice was between fighters or bombers and was always made in the RAF based on the student's aptitude, the needs of the service and to some extent the student's personal wishes. To date, service priority had been to build the bomber fleet, given the belief that parity with the German bomber force would act as a deterrent, coupled with the conviction that 'the bomber would always get through'. Now it was obvious to both the Government and the RAF chiefs that the German bomber fleet had too much of a head start to be matched before war broke out, and the new Hurricane and Spitfire fighters, together with the secret radio detection of approaching enemy formations termed RDF, had given RAF fighters a good chance of mauling enemy bombers if they should attack Britain. The balance thus shifted towards building up RAF Fighter Command.

Steed had always wanted to be a fighter pilot, to follow in the footsteps of his Great War heroes, not to mention Biggles! He had expressed this wish already, as forcibly as he could, while still a part-time pilot flying Hawker Harts. The reports from Monks Hill had put him as an above-average pupil, good at aerobatics and formation flying with a softness of touch on the controls. Steed got his wish and was allocated training as a fighter pilot.

Steed was posted to Durnwaite Flying Training Station, near the city of Carlisle in northwest England, for advanced flying training. FTS Durnwaite was equipped with the new Miles Master advanced trainer, a low-wing monoplane with a retractable undercarriage. The engine was a Rolls-Royce Kestrel, similar to that in the Hart.

The Master had a reputation as an unforgiving aeroplane if abused, but Steed quite liked it. The aeroplane was so much more modern than the fixed undercarriage, open-cockpit biplanes that he had flown at Epping and Monks Hill. After a few hours dual with his instructor, Steed went solo. He lined up the aeroplane at the end of the runway, set the mixture control to normal rich and the propeller to fine pitch. He opened the throttle, released the brakes, pushed the stick forward slightly to raise the tail as the aircraft gathered speed and corrected the slight torque-induced tendency to swing to one side with a touch of rudder. As he lifted off he raised the undercarriage – a new experience – and checked that the green lights turned red as the wheels clunked home. He adjusted the trim controls and climbed to 1,000 feet. He made the necessary turns to bring the Master on a reciprocal course back alongside the runway and throttled back to around 150 miles per hour. He lowered the undercarriage and watched with satisfaction the appearance of the green lights indicating that the wheels were down and locked. He turned crosswind, reduced his speed to 130 miles per hour and lowered the flaps. He made the final turn to line up on the runway and started to lose height, making sure that the airspeed remained above 80 miles an hour; finally a neat landing without bounces - an uneventful first solo in a monoplane.

A few days after Steed's arrival at FTS Durnwaite, all the students and their instructors were summoned to the crew room to hear a special broadcast from the British Prime Minister, Neville Chamberlain. It was 11.00 am on the third of September 1939. Everybody knew what he was going to say. As this man of peace announced that Britain was at war with Germany, the student pilots clapped and cheered almost to a man. Steed did not join in the cheering, but he nodded quietly in agreement. His instructor, Flying Officer Stephenson, noted Steed's subdued reaction to the declaration of war amongst the general hullabaloo, and rather wondered if this was the response to be expected of a fighter pilot who should be keen to do battle with the aggressor. Later, when they were walking together towards the Master for a dual lesson, Stephenson gave the subject an airing.

'What do you think about war with Germany Steed, do you think that Chamberlain was right to declare war?'

'I don't think that he had any choice sir. War with Germany was inevitable from the moment Hitler invaded Poland, possibly from the moment their Fuhrer became Chancellor. I've read his book, *Mein Kampf*. Hitler has a chip on his shoulder left over from the last war. He thinks that the Germans are a superior race and deserve more living space. That means taking over other people's countries. He has to be stopped and this is the time to do it.'

'Ah, I see. It's just that when everybody else was cheering during Chamberlain's speech, I couldn't help noticing that you looked rather solemn.'

Steed looked a little embarrassed. 'Well sir, I agree very much with our declaration of war, and I want to fight. It's just that my dad told me about the jingoistic reaction in Britain when the first war with Germany was declared. The Great War caused so much suffering and so many good men were lost, I'm not sure that anyone won; Germany simply lost a lot more than we did if you know what I mean. Now we are at war again. As a pilot I will have to kill other men. I will do it because it is my duty and because I think it is right. There is no alternative now, but I still didn't feel like cheering this morning.'

Stephenson looked at Steed in a new light. True, the boy was a little older than the majority of the students on the course, but even so he was so much more thoughtful than the others. 'You have read *Mein Kampf*? You read German?' he said.

'Oh no, I read the English translation.' Steed warmed to his point, 'I wanted to try to understand why the Germans follow this man.'

'And do you know why?'

'I think so. The Germans are a very militaristic and proud race. They were devastated and shamed by losing the Great War. German speaking peoples and territories were annexed into other countries and the repatriations that they had to pay under the Versailles treaty bankrupted their country. It was bad here in Britain after the war, but it was much worse in Germany. Hitler restored their pride, restored their economy, regained their lost territories and generally made the people feel that their country was great again.'

Steed paused for a moment, and then continued, 'But they've been hoodwinked. Hitler wants more than to rule Germany and to restore its prosperity. He wants land, living space for Germans, from other countries like Czechoslovakia and Poland. Who is next to be annexed, Holland or Denmark maybe? Does he call these people Aryans and think that they should be a part of a Greater Germany like Austria? And then what? Sweden, Norway, Great Britain? He will divide and conquer if we let him. That's why we have to stop him now, before it's too late.'

'You certainly have a way with words Sergeant Steed,' Stephenson said, not without a little admiration. 'You should have been a politician.'

Steed laughed, the mood lightened, 'No thank you sir, I'd much rather be a fighter pilot!'

Many people expected the German bombers to attack British cities immediately, with horrific results reminiscent of the Spanish Civil War. The RAF fighter squadrons went onto full alert, but no attack on Britain came, at least not from the Luftwaffe. On the first day of hostilities, RAF Spitfires succeeded in shooting down a couple of Hurricanes in the 'Battle of Barking Creek' in the mistaken belief that they were the enemy. Such was the fog of war.

The Germans made short shrift of Poland, and it came as a nasty shock to many people in Britain to see the Russian army invading Poland from the east, ostensibly to prevent the Germans moving up to their border. To Steed, it looked like poor Poland had been carved up between Hitler and 'Uncle Joe' Stalin. Britain and France did little to save Poland, perhaps there was little that they could do, and both countries wisely refrained from declaring war on Russia!

The war on the Western Front in France then entered the 'phoney war' stage, as the Americans called it. The RAF sent a few Hurricane fighter squadrons to France to support the Fairy Battles and Bristol Blenheims of the somewhat outmoded RAF bomber force, but the Western Front remained very quiet. The Allies were content to sit behind their defences, including the much-vaunted French Maginot Line, awaiting the expected German attack. If, as in the Great War, the Germans attacked through neutral Belgium, the French and British planned to move forward into Belgium to take up defensive positions.

At least this respite gave the RAF more time to convert its front line fighter squadrons from obsolete biplanes to Spitfires and Hurricanes, and to complete the training of the many RAFVR and AAF pilots who been called up on the outbreak of hostilities.

That first winter of the war was very harsh. Steed's fighter training intensified, he was airborne whenever the atrocious weather allowed. He learnt how to apply the RAF's set piece attacks on bomber formations, with friendly Wellingtons, Whitleys and Hampdens pretending to be the enemy bombers. These flew beautifully straight and level as, one after one, Steed and his chums flew in and pretended to shoot them down. There was also some fun shooting at aerial drogues, towed behind some brave pilot and his aeroplane. Steed confirmed that his .303 rifle exploit in basic training was no fluke. His excellent eyesight, experience with clays and, most of all, his understanding of deflection shooting proved invaluable in hitting the towed drogue, and not the tow plane! Unfortunately, gunnery was not a skill that the RAF at that time thought worthy of too much attention, and so the pilots lacked practice.

Sometimes students would pair up, each in their own aeroplane, for cross-country navigational exercises. Away from the prying eyes of the instructors, this was always an excuse for mock dogfights. One of Steed's favourite techniques was a full-throttle climbing turn away from his opponent and then, following the practice of his Great War heroes, bounce his prey from out of the sun. He also learnt to creep up on the blind spot, behind and underneath his adversary. By the same token, he learnt not to fly straight and level for too long to thereby allow himself to be caught by the same technique.

He perfected the Immelmann turn, named after the Great War German ace Max Immelmann. The idea was to attack the enemy bomber head-on and then, after diving below the bomber at full throttle, pull up into a loop, straighten out at the top of the loop, and then roll from inverted into normal flight. Assuming that your enemy has continued to maintain his course – perhaps a big assumption – you should then find yourself behind and above your bomber. You were then in a position to use your height advantage to increase speed and dive down on the bomber in a stern attack. That was the theory!

Low flying, and especially aerobatics at low altitude, was expressly forbidden. Too many student pilots had been killed that way. Nevertheless Steed and his peers often disregarded the rules when they were out on their own. Steed was sometimes paired with one particular pilot, 'Pete' Peterson, a cheerful Liverpudlian who was especially skilful at low flying. The two of them would take it in turn to try to shake the other off their tail. They would roar around the border country at treetop level, twisting and turning and scaring the living daylights out of the sheep. They had glorious fun in the Lake District, skimming the waves over Ullswater, soaring and barrel rolling over the peaks and thundering along the valleys. Steed was later to be very grateful to Pete for this illicit, but invaluable, low-flying experience.

The talk in the sergeants' mess was often of the war and especially the RAF's part in it; little seemed to be happening in France, either in the air or on the ground. People in Britain were relieved that their cities had not been bombed, the only Luftwaffe activity over Britain being occasional reconnaissance sorties.

'Looks like this war is going nowhere,' said Peterson to Steed one night in the mess as they sipped their beer. 'What do you think Harry? You're the only one of us who has bothered to read Adolf's book. What's he up to?'

'Funny you should say that,' retorted Steed. 'Herr Hitler telephoned me only the other day. He's heard that ace pilot Pete Peterson is going to join in the war, so he's going to made peace with Mr Chamberlain before it's too late.'

'Too right,' laughed Peterson, 'I'll shoot up his arse in his Chancellery!' He added more seriously, 'With Poland taken care of, I'm surprised that we haven't seen the Luftwaffe trying it on over here, bombing our cities I mean, just like everyone expected at the beginning. I reckon it must be that they are scared that we would retaliate.'

'You bet we would!' exclaimed Steed. 'But I think that the Jerries would target French cities rather than ours. Think about it. If the Jerries want to bomb Britain they would have to cross neutral Holland or Belgium, or come through France. Crossing neutral countries risks bringing them into the war, and Hitler doesn't want that. Crossing France means a long flight being attacked by French fighters all the way to Britain, and back again. In any case, whichever way they come, their single engine fighters probably don't have the range to escort their bombers all the way to Britain. If their bombers come here without a fighter escort we will blow the sods apart.'

'Sounds good to me,' replied Peterson. 'And it would be pointless their coming at night; they would never find their targets in the blackout.'

'I think they will send us to France when we join our squadrons,' suggested Steed thoughtfully. 'The action will be at the front, just like the last war. I reckon that Adolf will start something in the spring, just in time for us.'

'*Zut Allors. Ahh weel dreenk to zat*' said Peterson in a mock French accent. '*Just zink of all zose French floozies just waiting for mah arhreeval en Paris.*'

'I'll give you that! France has got to be more exciting than England at the moment,' said Steed. 'I can't understand what the government is playing at. People need cheering up, but Chamberlain's lot seem hell bent on depressing everyone even more. All the theatres and cinemas are closed in case Jerry drops a bomb on one of them, and the BBC only broadcasts news and public service announcements, oh and that terrible organ music by Sandy whatever his name is. No wonder people listen to Lord Haw Haw. The BBC should play dance music or American jazz and swing to liven things up a bit.'

Flying accidents, sometimes fatal, were an accepted fact of life. Steed had seen the results of numerous misfortunes since joining the RAF. He liked the Miles Master, but it was much less forgiving than the Tiger Moth basic trainer or even the Hart. Sometimes, inexperienced pilots misjudged a landing approach and, instead of going around again for another try, persevered through pride or ignorance and consequently crashed. Several student pilots forgot to lower the Miles Master's undercarriage, despite the warning buzzer or the flare fired from the control tower, and inadvertently belly-landed. Most pilots walked away from a belly landing on grass, something that certainly did not happen if they flew into a hillside while descending through cloud, and there were plenty of hillsides around FTS Durnwaite. Recently, Steed had witnessed a student failing to recover a Master from a spin above the airfield. The aircraft had crashed just outside the perimeter, bursting into flames as it went in, incinerating the pilot.

Steed had been fortunate in not having too many mishaps during his time at Durnwaite, although he came close to disaster several times during his low flying escapades with Peterson. However, danger was always at hand, even seemingly straightforward navigational exercises had their risks.

The winter of 1939-40 in the border region was severe, with flying often impossible. Even when the airfield was cleared of snow, low cloud often prevented serious flying activities. On one occasion, when the weather forecast predicted a spell of clearer weather, Steed was instructed to undertake a round-trip navigational exercise from FTS Durnwaite. His objective was to plot a course eastwards across country to Newcastle, then to turn south to refuel near Catterick, before finally returning northwest to Durnwaite.

The journey started without problem. Steed picked up Hadrian's Wall and the old Roman military road running alongside it. He could see the Carlisle to Newcastle railway line a few miles to the south and followed it towards the industrial sprawl that was Newcastle upon Tyne. He turned south, keeping the hills on his right, and found the small grass airfield between Scotch Corner and Catterick. He landed, reported to the duty officer and refuelled.

The weather now started to close in. Steed had noted the dark clouds to the west as he flew south, but the latest weather forecast available at Catterick was still not too bad. If he stayed the night in this godforsaken place, there was no telling when the weather might clear enough for him to get home. Despite warnings from the duty officer, Steed decided to go for the return journey.

Once airborne, Steed realised that the weather was now significantly worse. The cloud base was lower and the wind had increased. He set course across the Pennines but the cloud base was now so low, merging with the hill peaks, that he was forced to climb up through the cloud. Up here at 4,000 feet, in the watery winter sunshine, he could see a curtain of unbroken cloud stretching away to the horizon before him. Worse, the high wind was making navigation difficult. He considered turning back to Catterick, but dismissed the idea because he was not certain that the weather had not closed in there as well. Looking behind, the blanket of white cotton wool disappeared into the distance. He pressed on.

Like all the aircraft that Steed had flown to date, the Miles Master was not equipped with a radio. He was on his own, at 4,000 feet with unbroken cloud and high peaks below. He could feel the wind, stronger now, gusting on the Master, making his dead reckoning navigation highly suspect.

At length, based on his flying time, airspeed, compass bearing, estimated wind speed and estimated wind direction – he was far from happy about the last two assumptions – he concluded that he was somewhere in the vicinity of FTS Durnwaite. But what was he to do now? There was still endless cloud below. To descend down through that murk, when there was a good chance that navigational error would put him above the hills, was courting disaster. He still had a decent reserve of fuel and a couple of hours of winter daylight left. He decided to head west towards the sea and then let down below the cloud. He studied the map on his knee. West should take him out over the Solway Firth, but if he went too far in that direction he would strike landfall in Scotland. On the other hand, if navigational error had put him further south than he thought, and he did not fly far enough west, he might still be over the cloud covered hills of England when he let down. He settled on a south-westerly course for a time period that he was quite certain should put him out over the Irish Sea.

At the appointed time, Steed started to let down through the cloud. As he did so, ice particles began to form on the windscreen, and then they began to form on the leading edges of the wings. He became very worried when, even at 500 feet, he was still in the all-enveloping, gloomy murk. Eventually, at 400 feet, peering down he saw the cold, grey sea, with the wind whipping up frothy white sea horses on the wave crests. He turned east, straining his eyes for landfall through the salt splattered canopy. Even below the cloud at 300 feet, it was still very dismal, and now it was sleeting. After what seemed an age he spotted the coastline ahead and turned left to follow it. Almost immediately he recognised the coastal town of Workington. Feeling much happier now, he stayed below the cloud flying a north-easterly course up the Solway Firth, finally turning inland to land at Durnwaite.

In retrospect, Steed was satisfied with the flight, and with the actions that he had taken. But he was also well aware that, had he taken different decisions, it could have resulted in his death, just as it had with so many other student pilots.

Danger was also present during the mandatory night flying test. The minimum requirement was to complete three solo landings. A strict blackout had been imposed throughout Britain on the outbreak of war and airfields used for night flying did not operate peacetime flare paths for fear of German bombing. Rather, they made use of low-intensity 'glim' lamps that were much more difficult to see once a pilot strayed too far from the airfield.

Night flying was dangerous for the trainee pilots. They had to rely entirely on instruments and could easily become disorientated. The instructors stressed the importance of cockpit drill before take-off. On the previous course, a pilot had failed to uncage his artificial horizon and directional compass before taking off. Confused by the incorrect readings, the pilot had allowed his aeroplane to climb too steeply, then to turn and bank to starboard; finally, out of control and beyond redemption, the Master plummeted into the ground. Those watching on the ground saw the navigation lights disappear, heard a dull thud and saw the sky lighten with a red glow beyond the airfield. The luckless pilot had of course been killed.

Steed sat in the front of the Master with his hands lightly on the controls, following the movements of his instructor who was flying the aeroplane. He listened carefully as his instructor demonstrated and talked through the correct procedure. 'Remember Steed, as soon as you leave the ground put your head down into your instruments. Do not look outside, you won't see anything and you risk losing control. Get up to 700 feet and then start a climbing rate-one 180-degree turn to port. When the compass shows that you are flying back on a parallel course to the runway, and when everything is steady, have a quick look for the glim lights. Don't be in too much of a hurry. Morse your identification to the control tower and wait for their green light. Remember, stay on instruments on the parallel leg; don't rely on the glim lights even if you can see them, they will play tricks on you. Turn in, and then the final approach is the same as in daylight. Finally, line up on the glims and in we go. The glide path indicator lights make the approach easy. Remember, you should see a green light like it is now, which means that your approach is just right. If you see an amber light you are too high, and a red means too low.'

It was then Steed's turn to pilot the Master for three further landings under the watchful eye of his instructor.

'Not bad Steed, tomorrow you can solo.'

The following night was icy cold and pitch black, with cloud obscuring the moon and stars. The trainee pilots huddled in the warmth of the crew room in a fog of cigarette smoke. Steed was grateful that he was the first to fly. He was confident of his instrument flying abilities, and his plan was to bash off the three compulsory landings and then get back to the cheerful sergeants' mess for a beer. Out on the runway his instructor, standing on the wing of the Master and leaning into the cockpit, shouted a last few words of encouragement above the noise of the engine. Steed taxied to the start of the flare path, carried out his final checks, received a green light from the control tower and then he was on his way.

As soon as the Master lifted off, Steed took his eyes away from the runway lights and concentrated on his instruments. Once he reached 700 feet he began the climbing 180-degree turn. At 1,000 feet he was heading back on a parallel course to the runway. Inside the cockpit the Master felt cosy, warm and friendly. The instruments glowed dimly, for Steed had turned the brilliance down to improve his night vision. The artificial horizon, altimeter and compass were all rock steady. No dramas.

Steed looked outside for the glim lamps. Nothing to be seen except the impenetrable blackness and his wingtip navigation lights, red on port and green on starboard. A minute went by, then another. He should have seen the runway lights by now, but still nothing, no even the bright Chance lights at each end of the runway. Steed felt a lump in his throat and the first pangs of anxiety. Until now, he had wondered why everybody made such a fuss about night flying; it seemed relatively straightforward to him. Now he knew the reason!

By this time in his flying career, Steed flew an aeroplane almost instinctively. He was an accomplished pilot before he had joined the RAFVR, more than two years ago now, and this had given him a tremendous advantage over his fellow trainee pilots and had enabled him to more easily assimilate the advanced flying training required by the RAF. While he was searching for the runway lights, Steed was also revisiting his actions to date, checking and rechecking his instrument readings. He was certain that had carried out the correct manoeuvres on take off. The climb to 700 feet, the climbing rate-one 180-degree turn to port and finally levelling out at 1,000 feet. He was on the correct course and at the correct height, flying straight and level, so why couldn't he see the runway lights? Maybe there had been a problem and they had been turned off. Was a German bomber force about to attack the airfield? His single machine-gun wasn't even loaded, so he hoped not!

Time to make a decision. His aircraft was not equipped with a radio so he had to think his way out of the situation alone. By now, assuming that he could believe his instruments, he should have over-flown the runway and it should now be somewhere behind him and to his left.

Steed checked the time and made a 180-degree turn to port to have another look. He peered ahead and to either side, still nothing. There was something slightly different about the navigation lights, a slight glow around them. And then it hit him, and he was annoyed that he hadn't thought of it before. Sodding hell, am I in cloud? The instructions had been to climb to 1,000 feet, but it was always possible that cloud base had dropped.

Steed started a descent, and at 600 feet the runway lights thankfully appeared. But he was almost on top of the runway and too high. Did he have the time and space to sideslip down, line up on the glims and land? Probably, but he hadn't followed the correct procedure and flashed his identification on the down-leg, got a green and so on. No, he had to go around again, but this time staying at 600 feet. This he did, getting the green from the tower and landing without further fuss.

As he taxied back he wondered if he was supposed to carry out another two landings as previously instructed, given that the cloud base had now dropped to 600 feet. It was also starting to look a bit misty on the ground as well. His instructor solved his conundrum for him by waving him in. All flying was cancelled for the rest of the night.

The next night was again cold, but this time clear with a three-quarter moon. Perfect for night flying. Steed completed one landing and was coming in for his final landing of the night when he received a red warning light to go around again. As he passed over the airfield he saw the navigation lights of another aircraft on the runway. The Chance light, that large floodlight positioned at the end of the runway to provide illumination, did not seem to be on either. Steed made his 180-degree turn and started back on a parallel course to the runway. He received a red light in answer to his next flashed identification; they wanted him to go around again. He could see the flashing navigation lights of the other aeroplane still on the runway. There was obviously a problem, some sort of crash landing maybe, and they had to clear the runway before he could be cleared to land. Ah well, he had plenty of petrol, the cockpit was cosy and warm bathed in the glow of the instruments, and he was enjoying flying around alone on this beautiful, clear, calm winter's night.

After four more passes, and still not cleared to land, Steed was getting a little bored flying straight and level up and down above the runway. He wanted to experiment a little more, climb and try a few loops, but he knew this was absolutely forbidden and the sound of the engine in a loop this close to the airfield would give him away. He decided on a gentle roll or two when he was clear of the runway at the end of a leg. He was up at 1,000 feet, so they shouldn't notice that down below. So, for ten minutes or so, Steed amused himself with some gentle rolls and a spot of inverted flying. At long last he received a green to land, the offending crashed aeroplane having been cleared from the runway; the pilot had misjudged his landing and smashed his undercarriage on the Chance light. He was lucky to walk away.

Upon landing Steed was immediately summoned to the flight commander's office. The man was furious and Steed stood rigidly to attention in front of him.

'What do you mean by performing crazy aerobatics while night flying? Your instructions were crystal clear, take off, circuit and land, nothing more. Don't you realise how many pilots have been killed while learning to fly at night? You need to be experienced at night flying before you start trying something like that. You can very easily tip the artificial horizon and the compass, and then where would you be? Spinning into the ground and dead. You would also wreck a very expensive aeroplane. Explain yourself!'

'I am very sorry sir. I have no excuse.'

'You thought that we couldn't see you flying inverted parallel to the runway didn't you? Well answer me boy!'

'Yes sir. That was deceitful. I am very sorry.'

'Everybody saw you, you stupid fool. Everybody was pointing at you. And do you know why?' The flight commander did not wait for an answer. 'I'll tell you why, you idiot. Your navigational lights Steed – your navigational lights showed us that you were upside down.'

'Yes sir,' gulped Steed. 'I'm very sorry.'

'Oh get out. You're very lucky that I don't wash you up. Get out man.' Steed saluted smartly, about-turned and left the office very red-faced. But back in the sergeants' mess, Steed found that he was something of a celebrity.

The wings test comprised both flying and written exams. Passing the wings test was of crucial importance because it meant that the pilot was entitled to wear the coveted RAF wings on his tunic. The flying test examiner was Chief Flying Instructor, Squadron Leader Hammond.

Steed was reasonably confident in his flying abilities, and his instructor had given him good advice on what the examiner would be looking for.

'Remember Steed it's not just your flying ability but your general awareness that is being tested. The instructor will ask you to do a series of manoeuvres, no problem for you there, but he will also expect you to know where you are and what is going on around you at all times. A favourite ploy is for the examiner to suddenly close your throttle and tell you that you have engine failure. Somewhere in the vicinity will probably be an airfield and you will have sufficient height to glide towards it. But, and this is crucial, you have to know where you are first in order to find your airfield.'

Steed was one of the first pilots on his course to take the flying test. True to form, CFI Hammond took Steed through the entire gamut of aeroplane manoeuvres. Steed was told to execute barrel rolls, loops, stall turns and spins; mid-way through all of this, and as expected, CFI Hammond shut down the throttle and held it closed, telling Steed that he should assume engine failure. Steed's preparation for the wings test had been thorough and he knew Haydon airfield to be close at hand.

Later, his flight commander, who seemed to have forgotten the inverted flying incident, told Steed that he had done well in the flying test. Steed then buried his head into the reference books in preparation for the theoretical examination. He was significantly more worried about this than the flying test, but at least he had more time to prepare for it as, one by one, his colleagues took their flying tests with CFI Hammond. The entire course sat the written exam together, sitting at separate desks inside a cold hanger.

Then came the day that the notice was put up in the training block. Steed had been awarded his wings! In spite of his excitement, he could not help but spare a fault for a couple of his course whose names were not on the list. Even at this late stage it was possible to be 'washed up'.

Steed was full of pride when he returned home on leave and took his mum and dad out for a celebratory meal in London, sporting the brevet sewn on his uniform that told the world that he was a recognised RAF pilot.

'I know it's what you've always wanted son,' said his father, 'so here's to you and God bless.' His parents raised their glasses in the toast.

'Thanks Dad, thanks Mum. I couldn't have done it without you. You supported me during those early days at Epping when I said that I wanted to learn to fly. I know that it wasn't easy.'

'When do you get posted to your squadron?' asked his father.

'It will be some time yet I think. Even though I have my wings I am still in training. After I finish at Durnwaite they will probably send me to an Operational Training Unit. That's where I learn to fly a front line aeroplane, rather than the Miles Master that I fly at the moment. My guess is that I will join my squadron around March.'

His mother asked, 'Your squadron son, do you know where it will be based?'

'I haven't a clue Mum. They don't tell us much in case Hitler gets to hear about it, but my guess is they will send more RAF squadrons to the front pretty soon, just like the last time. Could be that I will go there.' Steed saw the concern in his mother's eyes. 'Don't worry Mum. I am far too good a pilot to be shot down by some goose-stepping Jerry. It's the Huns that will have to watch out. Anyway, just in case they send me to France I am brushing up on my French. Got any tips on how to speak Froggie Dad?'

'They all spoke English when I was there son, at least they did when they wanted to sell you something. If they pretend not to understand, just speak in English slowly and loudly. Changing the subject, what are you going to do with that motorbike of yours Harry? It is still in the shed where you left it.'

'I know Dad, I didn't want to take it all the way up to Durnwaite in the winter, and I would have had precious little time to ride it up there anyway. Let's see where my squadron is based first.'

The next day, the last full day of his leave at home, Steed's parents threw a party in honour of their RAF pilot son. Aunts, uncles, cousins and neighbours came along, those that could anyway, for the war had placed many of the younger generation in uniform. Harry played the old songs on the family piano, and there was singing, dancing and general merriment. At one point, as his mother sang with her arm around his shoulders as he played, Harry noticed the tears in her eyes. He mistook them for tears of love and pride in her son; he was right about the love and pride, but the tears were of apprehension for her only child in this dreadful, second war with Germany.

In April 1940, prior to joining his squadron, Steed was posted to Number 103 Operational Training Unit in Lincolnshire for a conversion course to a front-line fighter. Like all potential RAF fighter pilots of his day, Steed had hoped for a posting to a Spitfire squadron, but instead he found that he was going to be taught to fly Hurricanes. The Hawker Hurricane and Supermarine Spitfire were similar aeroplanes in many respects. They were both streamlined single-seat monoplanes with retractable undercarriages and eight-gun armament, and they also shared the same Rolls-Royce Merlin engine, but the Spitfire was a more modern design and had a definite edge in performance.

Steed was presented with a manual for the Hurricane and told to study it, and to memorise the positions of all the cockpit controls and instruments. The following day he climbed into the cramped cockpit of a Hurricane for the first time and, with the manual for company, thoroughly familiarised himself with all the gadgets. There followed a lecture on the do's and don'ts of flying a Hurricane, and finally a short dual 'airfield familiarisation' flight in a Harvard advance trainer around the locality. Then Steed was invited to try a 'control familiarisation' practice flight in the single-seat Hurricane, followed by a few take-off and landing circuits.

An airman assisted Steed into the Hurricane, positioned the straps over his shoulders and clipped them home into the central 'quick-release'. Steed reached down for the straps between his legs and clipped these in too. He signalled to the airman with the starter trolley, and the Merlin roared into life. The Hurricane's nose, under which resided that large and powerful Merlin engine, restricted the view forwards to some extent when taxiing. Steed needed to swing the aircraft from side to side to make sure that he didn't hit anything. He remembered the do's and don'ts lecture. 'Don't forget to put the propeller into fine pitch before you take off, or you will end up in the potato field at the other end of the runway.'

He moved the throttle forward and released the brakes. A push forward on the stick and up came the tail as they gathered speed; now he had a clear view in front. What power! He corrected for the torque, something else that he had been warned about, and then they were airborne. He retracted the undercarriage and climbed away. He levelled out at 3,000 feet and tried a few turns, rolls and loops. What a beautiful aeroplane, a real thoroughbred, and such power. Steed returned to the airfield and joined other pilots on the circuit waiting their turn to land. The landing was uneventful, but again he remembered the advice from his instructor, 'Sometimes you can get an air lock in the hydraulics. Even after you see the green light, continue pumping the handle to make sure that the undercarriage is solidly locked down.' He even remembered to put the two-bladed wooden propeller back into fine pitch.

Chapter Five – The Tomcats

Steed was posted to 126-Squadron at Colne Martin, northeast of London, on the Essex-Suffolk border. He reported to the squadron adjutant, a man of about fifty with a handlebar moustache and wings on his tunic. Steed saluted and stood to attention.

'Good afternoon sir, my name is Harry Steed. I have been instructed to report to 126-Squadron.'

'Ah yes Sergeant Steed, we have been expecting you. Please sit down.' Steed did as he was bid. The adjutant searched his desk drawer for some papers. 'You have come straight from the OTU where you have flown Hurricanes, is that right?' He looked expectantly at Steed.

'Yes sir.'

'Excellent. Your arrival puts us up to fifteen pilots, not yet full strength but we are well on the way. The C/O's out at the moment, but I will fix you up with an interview with him this afternoon. His name is Squadron Leader Tomlinson by the way. Take your logbook along when you see him. You will almost certainly be in B-Flight, but I had better let the C/O confirm that. In the meantime, let's get the domestics sorted out.'

RAF Colne Martin was a new wartime grass airfield that supported just the one fighter squadron at that time; it was therefore bereft of many of the facilities and luxuries normally associated with the established RAF aerodromes. In addition to the hanger and workshops, a collection of Nissen and wooden huts were dotted around the airfield; everything looked to have been put together in a hurry. The sergeants' mess was housed in one of the few brick buildings on the airfield, but the officers messed in a large country house a mile or so outside the airfield perimeter.

Steed was shown into Squadron Leader Tomlinson's office later that afternoon. Tomlinson, a short stocky man of about twenty-five with a pencil moustache, and recognisable to Steed by the three rings on his tunic, was talking to a flight lieutenant. Steed saluted and stood to attention. Tomlinson turned and spoke. 'Sergeant Steed, good to have you aboard, settling in okay?'

'Yes sir'

'Sit down will you.' Steed sat in the offered chair. Tomlinson sat in the chair on the opposite side of the desk while the flight lieutenant leaned casually against the wall to one side. 'Let's see now.' Tomlinson briefly consulted the papers in front of him, 'Passed out above average, good. How many hours on Hurricanes?'

'Fourteen sir.'

'And how old are you?'

'Twenty-two sir.'

'I'm going to put you into B-Flight. Your flight commander will be Flight Lieutenant Dix.' He nodded towards the flight lieutenant, who smiled. Dix was taller than Tomlinson, almost as tall as Steed himself, clean-shaven and with a mop of black wavy hair. Tomlinson continued, '126 is a new squadron and we have only been operational for two months. With your arrival we now have fifteen pilots, twelve officers including myself, and three sergeants. We are training hard, and before you fly with us I want to be very sure that you can hold formation without wandering about, and also change formation smartly and accurately when ordered. Also, I want to make sure that you can follow us in all the Fighting Area Attacks. When you have proved to us that you can do these things, you can join us in full squadron exercises. Flight Lieutenant Dix will bring you up to speed in the way we do things here and generally look after you. Any questions?'

'I was told to bring my logbook to you sir, would you like to see it now?'

It was Dix who answered. 'Leave it with me Sergeant Steed and wait for me outside would you?' Steed stood up, saluted and left the office. A short time later Dix joined him and handed back the logbook. 'Good to see that you have plenty of flying experience Sergeant Steed, you already had a pilot's licence when you joined the Volunteer Reserve I see.'

'Yes sir. I was a mechanic at a flying club and one of my jobs was to flight test the aircraft.'

'Excellent, but it's how well you can handle a Hurricane that counts. Come with me and I will introduce you to one of the other sergeant pilots in B-Flight. He will show you the ropes, settle you into the sergeants' mess and so on. Tomorrow afternoon we will take a couple of Hurricanes up and you can show me how well you can fly.'

'Thank you sir.'

'In the meantime, I will give you some homework to do,' said Dix with a grin. 'Read up on squadron orders and study the maps of the area. I don't want you getting lost when we let you out with one of our aeroplanes. Also brush up on the Fighting Area Attacks. Do you have the '38 Training Manual?'

'Thank you sir. I have the manual. May I ask if the squadron seen any action as yet?'

'We get scrambled every now and again to intercept the occasional German reconnaissance plane, but so far without much luck. Since moving down south several of us have chased shadows in the clouds. I even got in a burst in the general direction of a Dornier somewhere over Ipswich once, but none of us has achieved anything conclusive. Even if we manage to catch sight of the blighters, the Huns disappear into the clouds as soon as they see us. In this weather it's like finding the proverbial needle in a haystack. The squadron's still looking for its first victory; the boss has put up a magnum of Champagne for the lucky blighter that gets it, so you're in with a chance Sergeant Steed.'

Dix continued, 'I should tell you how we do things in the squadron. The RAF isn't quite like the army. As you know, RAF NCOs and airman are far more skilled than soldiers, who are pretty good at firing their rifles but haven't a clue about maintaining or flying complex aeroplanes. Sergeant pilots do much the same job in the air as pilot officers. For these reasons, the relationship between junior officers and NCOs is much more relaxed than in the army. Nevertheless, the RAF is a command and control outfit and there are certain, and very necessary, distances between ranks. There is a very definite step-change between officers and NCOs, and the two are not encouraged to get over-friendly. You call me sir, Flight Lieutenant Dix or Mr Dix, whatever seems appropriate, and I always use your title of Sergeant. But you don't need to call me sir in every sentence. The first time that you see me each day we return salutes, but from then on we don't bother. With the junior officers, either in the crew room or off duty, things are more relaxed. If they use your Christian name, rather than call you Sergeant, you can do the same. In the air we all use call signs.'

Toby Adams was waiting for them outside the sergeants' mess. 'Sergeant Adams is also in B-Flight. He will show you around and introduce you to everybody. He will also take you up for a ride in the squadron Lysander, which we use for general communications duties, and point out all the local landmarks. Don't forget to have a good look at the map before you go up.' With that he was gone, leaving Steed with Adams.

'He's not a bad sort, that Mr Dix. He's certainly a very good pilot, but like all the officers here he has to keep his distance from the NCO pilots like us. They are told not to get too friendly; it is bad for discipline apparently.'

'Yes, he told me the form. Do you call most of the pilots by their Christian names in the crew room or when you are off duty?'

'By and large yes, or their nickname. You like to be called Harry? You haven't been saddled with a nickname as yet?'

'Harry is just fine. I like your sergeants' mess by the way, very cosy, just like a country pub.'

'Isn't it just? The mess committee do a great job. We live well in there, a lot better than they do in the officers' mess I think. That's one of the problems for the pilots, separate messes. There are only two of us sergeant pilots in the squadron, well three now that you have arrived, and we do feel a bit left out at times. I think that much of the discussion on things that should really concern us all goes on in the officers' mess. Still I wouldn't want to be a pilot officer – couldn't afford it. Unless Daddy is rich, or you have a second income, you are far better off financially as a sergeant.'

Steed spent the evening reading the squadron orders and studying the maps of the area, trying to commit to memory roads, railways and other geographical features of the surrounding countryside. The next afternoon, after B-Flight was released from readiness, he met up with Toby Adams who introduced him to the flight sergeant in charge of aircraft maintenance. 'We're cleared to take up the Lysander Flight, is she ready?'

'Yes Toby, all ready for you outside.' He turned to Steed, 'Mr Dix asked me to get your Hurricane ready for later this afternoon. That's the old girl over there. She's not new, one of the officers bagged the latest one in from the factory and you have his cast-off, but she's in tip-top condition.'

'I bet she is Flight,' said Steed, 'She looks magnificent. I'll try to take good care of her.'

'We are just finishing off the final checks now. Do you have a moment to meet your fitter and rigger?'

Steed looked at Toby who nodded and said, 'Sure Flight, plenty of time.'

The three men walked across to Steed's Hurricane. Two airmen were working on the aircraft, which was on a trellis. They jumped down as the flight sergeant called to them. The flight sergeant then addressed Steed as the two airmen approached.

'Sergeant Steed, this is your fitter Denis White, and your rigger Colin Stuart. You will always have the same two ground crew to look after you and your aircraft.'

'Pleased to meet you Sarge' said White, in an unmistakable London accent.

'Likewise Sarge' echoed Stuart. One met people from all over the country in the melting pot that was the RAF, and by now Steed was pretty adept at guessing where people were raised from their accents. He could not be sure, but he judged that Colin Stuart was probably from Yorkshire.

'Are you servicing her?' he asked the fitter, nodding towards the Hurricane.

'Flying Officer Edwards, he's the chap that was her pilot before his new aeroplane arrived, reported sticky undercarriage hydraulics. We've stripped it down and replaced a part and have just finished checking it out. Everything looks good, so it should be ready for you in an hour Sarge.'

'It's really a nice little aeroplane,' added the rigger. 'Never given us a serious problem. Don't know why Mr Edwards wanted to exchange it. It's been well maintained and is exactly the same spec as his new one, but more miles on the clock of course.' The four men spoke for a few more minutes about Steed's Hurricane before Adams led Steed across the grass airfield to the waiting Lysander.

The flight around the environs of the airfield in the Westland Lysander was fun. Adams pointed out the local geographical features, shouting above the din of the Lysander's engine. 'That's Colne Martin village. The church is very distinctive and it also makes a good marker for landing. That's the local pub, the Queen's Head, and over there, that large country house, that's the officers' mess.' They climbed higher. 'Down there is the main London railway line. London is to the southwest and Colchester to the northeast. You can see Colchester over there.' Adams pointed along the railway line towards the town. 'Keep following the railway line past Colchester and the next big town is Ipswich. Once you have the railway line in sight, it is easy to find the airfield. Look over there and you can still see Colne Martin church. The River Colne is also a good marker to get your bearings. There are no serious hills around here, so even with a low cloud base you can let down to get an indication of where you are. You go much faster in a Hurricane of course, and your visibility is worse than in the Lysander.'

The Essex countryside was very familiar to Steed from his days at Epping Flying Club so he felt confident of finding the Colne Martin field on even the murkiest of days.

After his flight in the Lysander with Adams, Steed met up with Dix in the dispersal crew room. In addition to Dix, there were three other pilots in the room, all lounging in easy chairs and reading. They looked up as he entered. Steed noted the ranks, a flying officer, a pilot officer and Sergeant 'Johnny' Walker who he had met the previous evening in the mess.

Dix introduced Steed to the assembled company. 'This, my merry men, is the latest addition to our ranks, Sergeant Harry Steed. He will be in B-Flight.' He turned to Harry, 'These boys are Yellow Section, A-Flight, and it is their pleasant duty to hang around here on stand-by, just in case Adolf sends over the odd reconnaissance aeroplane to visit us. Allow me to introduce Flying Officer 'Roger' Daily, a real hit with the ladies, hence his name.'

A square-jawed rugged character rose from his chair and spoke in an Aussie drawl, 'Glad to know you Harry.'

'Next we have Pilot Officer 'Bunny' Burroughs.' A callow looking youth rose from his chair to shake Steed's hand; he did not look old enough to shave. 'Nice to have you on board Harry.'

'And finally, Sergeant 'Johnny' Walker.' Johnny was a good-looking, quick-witted, outgoing character from East London. Steed thought that he too would be a hit with the ladies. Walker gave a wave from his chair and grinned. 'We met last night in the mess. How's it going Harry?'

Dix picked up his flying gear. 'Let's go for a spin, shall we Sergeant Steed?' As they walked to the two waiting Hurricanes, the ground crews sprang into action.

'I see that the Hurricanes here have the new three-bladed constant-speed variable pitch propellers. We had the two-bladers at OTU. Is there much difference?'

'You will get more power with the new screw. We are also using 100-octane petrol here; you probably had 87-octane at the OTU, and that makes a difference too. Now listen carefully, we will make sure the radios are working before we move off. We will take off together. As soon as the wheels are up you will take station just behind my right wingtip. The number two position in the vic we normally fly. Understand?'

'Yes sir.'

'I am Blue Leader, you are Blue-2. We will climb to 12,000 feet keeping in tight formation, which means oxygen of course; don't forget that because I won't remind you when we are in the air. I've known pilots fall out of the sky because they have forgotten to switch their oxygen on, so don't let it happen to you. Once I am satisfied that you can hold formation we will play at dog fighting. Your guns are loaded because we are at war, but for God's sake keep the safety on.'

They took off and started the climb. Steed took up the Blue-2 position about thirty feet away from Dix, and with his wingtip slightly behind Dix's Hurricane. Dix held his plane perfectly steady in the climb and Steed found it easy to maintain position. After a short while Dix came in over the radio, 'Blue-2, come in closer.'

'Roger Blue Leader, moving in.' Steed edged in to reduce the distance between the two Hurricanes to about twenty feet. They climbed up through a layer of cloud and came out into bright sunshine.

Dix came in again, 'Blue-2, come in still closer.'

'Roger Blue Leader, moving in.' Steed edged in to about ten feet of Dix's wingtip. At 12,000 feet they levelled out.

'Blue-2, I'm going to start a gentle turn to the left, hold position.'

Steed held position, as Dix executed one turn after another, each turn steeper than the last, so that Steed found himself almost on his side either above Dix in a steep left turn, or below Dix when they turned to the right. Eventually Dix levelled out. 'Blue-2, very good. Now come in still closer.'

'Roger Blue Leader.' Steed gently edged in until his wingtip was within five feet of his leader. This was getting dangerous; it wouldn't take much of a misjudgement, a freak downdraft perhaps or maybe if he was to stray too far into Dix's slipstream, and there would be a very nasty bang! Dix was either very brave or more likely very foolhardy to try out this clever stuff with a pilot fresh out of training. One thing was certain however, Dix was a very good pilot. He held his Hurricane rock-steady in level flight, and all of his manoeuvres, even those steep turns, were very smooth.

'Blue-2, I am going to make a gentle turn to port, hold your position.' Steed swallowed nervously; Jesus H Christ! I hope to God that he doesn't want us to stay this close during those tight banks! But after turning through 180-degrees Dix came back to straight and level flight.

'Blue-2, I am going to pull away from formation now. I will come back and try to get on your tail. Pretend that I am the enemy and try to shake me off. Try to get into position to shoot me down if you can, but guns on safety and do not press the button!'

'Roger Blue Leader,' and then Dix was gone.

He's not going to shoot me down thought Steed and he put his Hurricane in a climbing turn to the right. Height was everything in a dogfight. He will try to bounce me from the sun; but Dix was nowhere to be seen. Steed put the Hurricane into a full throttle turn to the left, still climbing. Is he below me in the blind spot? Steed banked then weaved, trying to cover the blind spot. Ah there is, coming down out of the sun. Steed broke right to meet the attack. Dix turned to try to get on his tail, and Steed turned to counter. They were circling each other. He isn't going to get the better of me hissed Steed, and tightened the turn. Both pilots were now circling ever tighter, as if they were riding on some mad carousel.

Steed had been through all of this before. Height was everything in a dogfight. Turn as tightly as you can, do not stall and do not lose height. The G-force was going to make him black out soon, he could feel it coming on, but Dix was turning tighter. Soon Dix would be on his tail. If he were a real enemy it would be all over. Steed could feel his Hurricane approaching the stall as he fought for height as well as tightening the turn. He was fighting blackout now, with the aircraft banked almost to the vertical; he had to look up and back over his shoulder to keep Dix in view. Dix was almost in a shooting position, but he was a little lower.

But suddenly Dix had lost it! To aim his guns, Dix had needed to point his aircraft up, which had brought on the stall. He was falling away and Steed was coming around the turn into an advantageous position above and behind his leader. Now for the Steed bounce. Steed put his aircraft into a dive to bring it behind and under his adversary, into the blind spot. Now up and hit him with a deflection shot. But Dix suddenly broke away to the left and Steed overshot. Steed used his speed from the dive to climb away, turning into the sun as he did so, intending to attack Dix from out of its blinding rays. The two pilots twisted and turned in their aerial ballet for several minutes, making machine-gun noises whenever they thought that they had the other in their sights. At length Dix called, 'Blue-2, formate on me and home for tea!'

'Roger Blue Leader.'

When they landed, Dix came over. 'How did you enjoy that Sergeant Steed?'

'It was really great fun, but tell me, how can I delay blackout in those steep turns?'

'Yes, I was very impressed with those turns. You held your height and that gave you an advantage. The word from France is that the Germans have nothing that can out turn a Hurricane. So if you can live with turns as tight as today the Huns shouldn't worry you, at least not in that kind of a situation. You just have to put up with the blackouts. It's because the blood drains from the brain under the G-Force of course. Taller people like us seem to have more trouble than the shorter types. Try tensing your muscles, that might help; you get used to it after a while.'

'I'll give it a try next time.'

'I thought that you did very well. I know that you have plenty of hours in your logbook, but you don't yet have many on the Hurricane, so well done. You are able to hold formation without problem, but I still need to make sure that you are bullet proof when it comes to following formation changes and the Fighting Area Attacks. Come back to the office now and we will run through it all. Tomorrow you can fly with me in a section and we will see how well you can put it into practice.'

Steed finally took his leave of Dix an hour later, with visions of Fighting Area Attacks dancing before his eyes. Dix had set yet more homework for the next day, but Steed needed to clear his head; he needed to go for a run. The problem was that he was now at an operational RAF station in wartime. Maybe they wouldn't take too kindly to a bloke in PT kit running around near the dispersed aeroplanes. He found Toby Adams in the mess. 'No problem,' advised Adams, 'Airfield defence is pretty rudimentary, just a few ancient Lewis guns dotted around the place. People go for walks around the airfield all the time without anyone batting an eyelid.' Confident that all would be well, Steed changed into shorts and vest and set out for a run around the airfield perimeter.

It was a beautiful spring evening. The world smelt fresh and clean and he was running well. Today had gone rather well he thought; he was going to enjoy life in 126-Squadron. Suddenly Steed was shaken out of his daydreaming as a large black dog came bounding up. He stopped running and stood still. 'Don't worry,' said a voice behind him, 'He only wants to play.' Steed turned to see a middle-aged flight lieutenant smoking a pipe approaching from the small wood bordering the airfield. The dog, which Steed now recognised as a Labrador, stopped alongside Steed wagging its tail and looking up expectantly.

'Good evening sir,' began Steed, 'My name is Sergeant Steed. I joined 126-Squadron as a pilot yesterday.'

'Pleased to meet you Sergeant Steed. My name is Bob Rose, the local intelligence officer, known to one and all as the Spy. I am fairly new here myself. This young chap,' he motioned to the dog, 'is called Dion, named after Dionysus, the Greek god of wine, merrymaking and the theatre.'

'He looks in fine shape,' said Steed, after surreptitiously checking that it was indeed a dog and not a bitch, 'And very friendly too.'

'He wants a run, but being somewhat out of condition, unlike you I might add young Sergeant, with me he only gets a walk.'

'I would be pleased to take him on a run for you sir, that is if he would stay with me and not go running off. I would hate to lose him or get him run over by one of the aeroplanes.'

'Would you my lad? That's very decent of you. He would appreciate that, and he's very obedient. And you don't have to call me sir. Just call me Spy like everyone else. I am not regular RAF, simply hostilities only. Not so long ago I was teaching classics at university. To me you are all pilots doing the same job. Please feel free to question me at any time on any intelligence matter, what the Luftwaffe is up to, their tactics, the performance of their aircraft, what Goring had for lunch, anything.'

'Thank you Spy. Dion can run with me now if you like, that is if he will follow me.'

'Dion would love to go with you now I'm sure. He will probably run just in front of you, looking back every so often to make sure that you are still there. He may charge off after a rabbit, if he sees one, but just whistle and he will come back immediately. When you get back, simply leave him outside the station office. You will see his water bowl there. Command him to stay and he will sit down and wait for me there.' Steed nodded, and started to run off. He slapped his thigh and shouted for the dog to follow. Dion looked up at his master, who signalled to the dog to follow the young pilot. The dog did not wait to be told twice, but happily bounded off in pursuit.

The following day Steed had the opportunity to put his homework on Fighting Area Attacks to the test. Dix led a section of three aircraft in a vic formation. Pilot Officer Courtauld flew Blue-2 and Steed flew Blue-3.

A single Hurricane, flown by Toby Adams pretended to be an enemy bomber, flying sedately along at 200 mph, straight and level.

Pilot Officer 'Pip' Courtauld had recently graduated from the RAF Officer Training School at Cranwell and had only been in the squadron a fortnight longer than Steed. He was also member of 'B-Flight' and Dix had brought him along today for some additional training. He seemed a nice lad and had chatted amiably to Steed as they prepared for the flight, but Steed was surprised how young the boy was, not yet nineteen and the baby of the squadron. Steed, at twenty-two, felt positively ancient in his company. Once in the air, Steed noted that Pip was having trouble maintaining close formation in the turns.

'Number One Fighting Area Attack, Number One Attack, GO,' said Dix curtly. FAA-1 was designed for attacks on lone bombers. The three Hurricanes moved into line astern, Dix first, followed by Courtauld with Steed bringing up the rear. Dix led the dive down coming up on the rear of Toby's 'bomber'. Dix went in first shouting 'rat tat tat tat tat!' Courtauld followed him, 'bang bang bang bang!' And then Steed, 'buda buda buda!'

'Reform Vic,' ordered Dix, and then, 'Number Two Attack, Number Two Attack, GO.' This was an attack from below. Each of the Hurricanes climbed in turn up to the rear of the luckless Toby Adams, pretended to expend their ammunition and then broke away to allow the next Hurricane to attack. FAA-3 was next. For this they held vic formation and 'fired' together as they came up behind Adams.

They continued by practising other FAAs and making formation changes. After they landed Dix took Steed aside. 'You did well today Sergeant Steed, tomorrow you will join the rest of B-Flight in training. You will fly in Green Section. Flying Officer Bishop will lead the section, with Sergeant Adams Green-2 and you Green-3.'

The following afternoon, Squadron Leader Tomlinson called all the pilots together for an important briefing. 'Gentlemen,' he began, 'It looks like things are happening across the Channel. This morning, German forces invaded neutral Belgium and Holland. Our forces are moving up to help to defend these countries. I do not know yet what impact this will have on 126-Squadron, but it may be that we will move to France. In the meantime, it is imperative that we stay on our toes and be ready for anything.' It was the 10th May 1940.

Afterwards, he spoke to Steed. 'How are you settling in Sergeant Steed? Flight Lieutenant Dix has told me that you are making good progress, you have good formation discipline and you have been practising Fighting Area Attacks I understand.'

'I'm settling in just fine sir. I flew with B-Flight this morning.'

'Capital,' enthused Tomlinson breezily, 'We fly good tight formations in squadron strength. It's very important that individual pilots know what they are doing and don't get in the way of everyone else when we change formation or go for the FAAs. It's even more important now as it seems that the balloon is going up in France.'

'I look forward to joining the rest of the squadron on air exercise sir.' Tomlinson nodded and walked away.

The news from the front over the next few days was confused, but did not seem too encouraging. The British Expeditionary Force had advanced into Belgium and their line was reported to be holding firm, but the Germans appeared to be advancing through Holland and had taken the key Belgian strongpoint of Eban Emael. On a positive note, the Maginot Line, the massive French defensive fortifications along the Franco-German border, remained unyielding.

Steed now flew with the full squadron as they practised formation flying and FAAs. Steed was impatient to try more dogfighting, for he had really enjoyed his lesson with Dix, but Tomlinson was only following Fighter Command directives with his preponderance for disciplined squadron formation flying and FAAs. At least Steed had a chance to fire his eight Browning machine-guns at ground targets on the gunnery range, and later at a towed drogue.

Steed noted that the two flight lieutenants, Dix and Chamberlain, were easily the best shots. They went in close to the targets before firing, which then virtually disintegrated. Steed tried the same thing; he hit the target but without such dramatic results.

Later he spoke with his armourer, 'Can you check that all the guns are correctly aligned please Bob?'

'The guns are aligned as they should be Sarge. I checked them just the other day on the range. But I can have another look. Is there a problem?'

'No, it's probably just me. The squadron had some shooting practice earlier today and my shooting seemed a bit off. The two flight lieutenants practically blew the targets apart. I went in close and hit the target, I am sure of that, but not with the same effect.'

The armourer smiled knowingly, 'You know that your guns are set up in a Dowding spread?'

'What's that?'

'Well it's named after the C in C of Fighter Command of course. The RAF thinks that pilots can't shoot straight in air fighting because of the high speeds and G-forces. With eight guns you can afford to point them in slightly different directions so that you get a spread of fire. You have a better chance of hitting the target with at least some of your bullets. That's how we are supposed to align your guns.'

'I didn't know that.'

'Now then,' said the armourer in a conspiratorial manner, 'There are two pilots in the squadron who have asked for their guns to be aligned to converge at 250 yards. Both of these gentlemen believe that they are first class shots, having massacred half the British populations of pheasants and grouse between them. With eight Brownings all converging you decimate anything in your sights at 250 yards. Apparently some of the pilots in France have done the same thing with pretty good results. It only works if you are a very good shot in the first place. If you are a bit off target with the Dowding spread at least some of your bullets strike home, a bit off target with your bullets converging at 250 yards and you miss completely. But if you tell me to set the guns like that, I will.'

Steed thought about it for a moment, 'Okay Bob, I'm officially asking you to align my guns to 250 yards please, but let's keep it to ourselves for the time being.'

Steed was not too sure of the reaction of the C/O to any changes in gun alignment, especially if requested by a lowly sergeant. He rather suspected that the C/O would follow the party line and prescribe the official Dowding spread for all squadron machines if asked. Dix and Chamberlain might not be too happy about having their gun alignment changes made public either. Steed felt sure that his shooting war was going to start soon, and when it did he would need every advantage that he could get. I may not have massacred pheasants, he thought, but I have shot clays. What's more, the one time I fired a 303 rifle during basic training I came top of the class, and I did pretty well on the air-firing course too. Yes, let's align the guns but keep quiet about it.

The news from the front was still sketchy, but definitely getting worse. On the 14th May Rotterdam was bombed and on the following day the Dutch surrendered. That evening, a sombre Squadron Leader Tomlinson once again called all his pilots together for a special briefing.

'Things are serious in Belgium boys. Group tell me that the British Army is making a strategic withdrawal, quite why and to where I just don't know. Squadrons from the South of England will provide fighter protection to cover the withdrawal, and that includes us. We will carry out standing patrols in the Calais Dunkirk region, twelve miles inland from the coast. The twelve most experienced pilots will be selected for our first sortie tomorrow at 10.00 hours. The plan is to stay over the patrol line for about 30 minutes before returning home. Then we refuel, rearm and go back for a second bash in the afternoon.' Tomlinson and the flight commanders then continued with the detailed briefing.

The next day at 10.00, twelve Hurricanes of 126-Squadron climbed away from Colne Martin in a perfect formation of four vics on their way to war. Steed was disappointed, but not surprised, to find that he was one of the three pilots to be left behind. The other two reserves were Sergeant Johnny Walker and Pilot Officer Courtauld. The twelve aircraft returned, again in an impeccable formation of four vics. They changed to line astern above the airfield and came in to land one by one. Their gun ports were still covered. They hadn't fired a shot.

Steed bounded over as Toby Adams's Hurricane came to a halt. 'Hi Toby, what was it like?'

'A non-event my boy. France was very pretty, but there were no Germans coming out to play. We went over the Channel at a snail's pace to conserve fuel, went 10 miles inland from Dunkirk and chugged up and down for half an hour, and then we came home. All we saw was half a dozen Spitfires going in the opposite direction as we came back. A big disappointment all around!' Two hours hour later, after refuelling, the same pilots took off again, only to return that evening still without seeing any Germans.

The next day the squadron sortied at 08.00 for the same patrol line. The same pilots were selected with the same result. In the afternoon the squadron remained at Colne Martin on readiness. Squadron Leader Tomlinson explained the reasoning to the pilots. 'The Germans have moved up into Belgium and Holland and their bombers now occupy airfields much nearer to us. Our orders are to wait by the Hurricanes on immediate readiness in case of an attack on Britain.' The war news that evening was bad. The Germans had entered Brussels, which had been declared an open city.

That evening, Steed sat with Toby Adams and Johnny Walker in the sergeants' mess. 'It's a bugger that you two aren't allowed to join in the party yet, but you're not missing anything,' said Adams.

'The only thing that seems to be missing is the Luftwaffe,' replied Walker. 'Never mind, our turn will come. The Boss has to rotate his pilots to spread the load. Otherwise, he might as well send those of us left behind off on leave.'

'God knows where the Luftwaffe kites are,' said Adams, 'They are supposed to be bombing and strafing all over the place, but we haven't seen a sausage. The Jerry army seems to be doing all right on the ground without them though. See Brussels fell to the sods today. Pity that Wellington's not around anymore, we could have done with him in charge of the Pongos.'

'Trouble is that the Jerries were on our side at Waterloo and the French were the enemy,' said Steed with a chuckle. 'Maybe that's the reason why Wellington won.'

For the third day in succession Squadron Leader Tomlinson selected the same twelve pilots for the morning sortie over Calais-Dunkirk, and again there was no contact with the enemy. In the afternoon, however, Steed, Walker and Courtauld replaced three of the morning's pilots for afternoon readiness. The pattern of patrols inland of Calais-Dunkirk interspersed with periods of readiness continued for the next six days. Steed was always nominated for the readiness shift, but both Courtauld and Walker were promoted to flying patrols as Tomlinson started to rotate his pilots.

Dix allowed Steed to fly 'instrument check' missions when the others were on patrol. 'For heaven's sake Sergeant Steed, keep out of trouble. Always head inland and on no account fly out over the Channel. I'm only doing this so that you can log some more hours on the Hurricane and keep your hand in. Don't let me down!'

The war news became much worse. Antwerp fell, and on the 20th May the German spearhead reached the coast at the mouth of the Somme. On the 23rd May RAF patrols from England skirmished with the Luftwaffe over the Channel ports; on the following day the air fighting was much more intense. During all of this time 126-Squadron remained out of luck, arriving on-station over Calais-Dunkirk either too early or too late to see action.

At last Steed's name appeared on the flying roster. He was selected to fly the dawn patrol on the 25th May.

Chapter Six – Dunkirk

At 04.40 on the 25th May 1940, Steed was sitting in his Hurricane, canopy open, engine running and pre-flight checks completed, waiting for the other aircraft to move off. The 'Boss' had ordered take-off in sections of three. Steed's Green Section would be the last to take off. The other aircraft, their engines warm by now, started to taxi in line astern towards the end of the airfield with Tomlinson at their head. Steed snapped out of his daydreaming and joined the end of the queue.

Steed's section assembled in their vic formation at the end of the field, ready for take-off. Steed looked across to Green-Leader, the Hurricane to his right and slightly in front. He could see Flying Officer 'Billy' Bishop in the cockpit. Bishop was a genial, fair-haired boy of roughly Steed's age who had joined the RAF on a short-service commission. Bishop had flown Gladiators prior to joining the newly formed 126-Squadron on promotion. Steed liked and respected Billy Bishop, who had taken the time to brief his novice sergeant pilot on what he might expect on his first offensive patrol over France, and to generally make him feel at ease. Bishop's Hurricane looked purposeful in the morning half-light, every inch a rugged fighter. As Steed looked towards his Section Leader, Bishop turned and gave a cheery wave followed by a thumbs-up. Steed's eyes strayed further to his right towards the third aircraft in his section, piloted by Sergeant Toby Adams. But Toby was looking up the field to where the pilots of Blue Section were already taking off.

Bishop looked behind and to either side to check that Adams and Steed were paying attention and then he too commenced his take-off run. The three Hurricanes retained their perfect vic formation as Bishop led them in a climbing turn, bringing his section in behind and slightly lower than the other nine Hurricanes already forming up.

The twelve aircraft were now arranged in four vics in line astern, each vic slightly lower than the one in front. Squadron Leader Tomlinson was at their head with Red Section, followed by Yellow and Blue Sections, with Steed's Green Section at the back. Steed and Adams, at the very back of the squadron, had a spectacular view of their ten closely packed companions stepped-up in front.

They headed out over the Thames estuary, climbing to 12,000 feet into bright sunlight, the first young men in England to witness the dawn of the new day. They held a tight formation out over the still murky English

Channel, where the morning sun had yet to reach. Behind and to his right Steed could see the white cliffs of Dover receding, and ahead the coast of France advancing ever closer. Steed thought the squadron looked a magnificent sight, purposeful and powerful, sunlight glinting on their canopies. They would make a nasty mess of any Hun bomber formations they came across.

As they approached the French coast, Tomlinson's voice crackled over the radio, 'Tomcat Aircraft Close Vic, Sections Close Echelon Starboard, GO.' The twelve Hurricanes changed formation, smartly and crisply, like guardsmen on parade. Tomlinson and Red Flight out in front continued on their way, but the other sections, each still in a vic formation, moved to their right such that they were now strung out in a diagonal line stretching back from the leader, with Steed's Green Section on the far right and to the rear.

Tomlinson retained the tight formation as he led his squadron inland and then turned parallel to the coast towards Belgium. Below, the fields and woodland of Northern France were speckled with irregular shrouds of ground mist. Steed could see what he assumed to be Boulogne behind his left wingtip, but smoke obscured much of the town so that he couldn't be sure. He did his best to scan the sky for enemy aircraft, but in such a tight formation he had to keep one eye on Bishop's Hurricane just a few feet away, otherwise there would be the danger of a mid-air collision. It occurred to him that this was his first time abroad.

Tomlinson's voice again came over the radio, calm and precise, 'Tomcat Squadron from Leader. Three bogeys nine o'clock, angels five.' Tomlinson turned left, with Steed's Green Section on the outside of the turn having to increase speed to hold position. Steed could see the unidentified aircraft now, three twin-engine aircraft scuttling along in line astern towards the smoke of one of the coastal towns. Tomlinson came in over the radio again, 'Tomcat Squadron from Leader, three Dornier bombers, at eleven o'clock angels five.'

Steed could see the enemy more clearly now. They had long, slim fuselages and he was sure they were indeed Dornier-17s. He switched on his reflector gun sight and armed his guns. The Hurricanes had the height advantage and the sun behind them. The perfect bounce; the three Dorniers didn't stand a chance unless they acted now and bolted for cloud cover. Steed almost felt sorry for them. Almost, but not quite. The Huns were killing British troops down there; it was time for some payback.

Tomlinson now put the squadron into a gentle dive towards the enemy in order to increase speed and close the gap. Tomlinson's voice once more crackled over the airwaves 'Tomcat Squadron Number 5 Attack, Number 5 Attack GO.'

As the squadron manoeuvred into the Fighting Area Attack formation, there came a sudden shout, 'Huns coming down six o'clock, Break, Break!' Steed later discovered that the shout came from Dix.

The twelve Hurricanes of Tomcat Squadron, hunters that a moment before had been stalking three German bombers, now found themselves the prey. Steed put his Hurricane into a vicious climbing turn to port, just in time to see a Messerschmitt-109 whistle past on the starboard side. The four single-engine German fighters had come down in a dive from out of the sun and attacked the Hurricanes from behind. They carried on through the broken formation of 126-Squadron, firing at targets of opportunity as they went, then climbed away using their speed from the dive to regain their height advantage.

Steed searched the sky, especially that area around the bright sun, for enemy aircraft while at the same time jinking his Hurricane to left and right in the hope of making himself a difficult target. Everybody was shouting at once over the radio. Steed saw the four Me-109s climbing away, seemingly without a scratch, and aircraft from his own squadron wheeling about in disorder. Tomlinson's urgent voice again cut in over the radio, 'Shut up! Radio discipline! Shut up!' and calm returned to the airwaves.

'Tomcat Squadron from Leader, reform over Calais, reform over Calais.' Steed saw Bishop and Adams below and, still exploring the sky and keeping a wary eye on the four climbing Messerschmitts, dropped down to rejoin Green Section. Steed watched as the Me-109s reached the zenith of their climb and then, having selected their next victims, rolled easily into another dive. Jesus thought Steed, they're coming for us! Green section, now back in vic formation, was making its way west towards Calais, where Tomlinson was attempting to reform the rest of the squadron. The Me-109s were again coming down out of the sun, straight towards them. Bishop had seen them and his voice came calmly over the radio, 'Green Section from Green Leader. Huns coming down out of the sun, prepare to break port,' a moment's pause and then, 'Green Section break port GO.'

The three Hurricanes of Green Section turned to meet the attack. Steed selected his target and returned fire as the German fighters pounced. The Me-109s swept by and Steed pulled his Hurricane around in pursuit. The Messerschmitts were now diving away and heading southeast, probably low on fuel he thought. Steed chased after them at full throttle, but they were too fast. He gave up the pursuit and looked around for friend or foe, weaving to cover the blind spots; but as far as he could tell he was alone in the sky. He had travelled another fifteen miles or so further inland during the chase, and he now set a course back towards the patrol line.

The sky over France, Steed decided, was a dangerous place for a lone Hurricane. And then he admonished himself. It would be a far more dangerous place for a Hun bomber, if he should come across one. He reached the patrol line and circled for some minutes. The sky seemed empty, and there was no response to his radio calls. With one eye on his fuel gauge, he decided to head for home. As he approached the coast he spotted a single engine monoplane below. Was it an enemy fighter, a French aircraft perhaps, or maybe it was one of his own squadron? If it was a Hun then the German was at a height disadvantage. No, it was a Hurricane, travelling slowly and alone towards the Channel.

Steed, for what seemed the millionth time checked the sky for a lurking enemy, but it was empty. He dropped down to join the friendly fighter. As he approached, he recognised the markings of Flight Lieutenant Chamberlain's aircraft. Chamberlain was the A-Flight commander, and today he had been leading Yellow Section. Steed called him on the radio, 'Yellow Leader, Green-3 joining you.'

Chamberlain's voice came over the wireless immediately, 'Good to see you Sergeant Steed. Take a look over my kite will you? She's a devil to fly straight and level and she won't turn right. She's shaking like mad.'

As Steed slowly drew alongside, he could see that Chamberlain's aircraft had suffered significant damage. 'Yellow Leader, you have a large hole in your rudder, and it looks like your tail-plane has taken some hits too.'

'I had a run in with some Messerschmitts. Do me a favour and ride shotgun would you Sergeant Steed? I should be able to make it back across the Channel if I don't have to turn any right-hand corners!'

'Will do Yellow Leader,' said Steed and he took up a position above and behind the A-Flight Leader. And then he spotted them. 'Yellow Leader, two Bogeys at 5 o'clock, same height as us.'

'Keep your eye on them Sergeant Steed, with luck they are friendly.'

The Bogeys were not acting in a friendly manner. They had dropped down a little lower than the two Hurricanes and were now almost directly behind. That is exactly what I used to do in training mused Steed.

Hide in the blind spot behind and below, and sneak up on the unwary. Well I'm not bloody unwary! He was weaving from side to side, keeping an eye on the Bogeys, which he was now sure were Me-109s.

'Yellow Leader, the bogeys are Me-109s, and they mean to attack from behind. I will turn to engage them, you press on for home.'

'Afraid that I am not going to be much use to you Sergeant Steed, unless they agree to go around in left-hand circles that is.'

'No worries Yellow Leader. Head for home. I promise that they won't get through me.' With that Steed wheeled his Hurricane around and flew straight towards the enemy.

Steed was scared, not of dying because he hadn't yet thought about that, but of failing. This was his first operation. The A-Flight commander was helpless and depending on him. If the Me-109s got past him and shot down Chamberlain, he would be thought at best incompetent and at worst a coward because he had failed to protect the flight lieutenant.

The two Me-109s were in line astern, approaching head-on and fast. The aerial dance of death was approaching its climax. Steed was calm, surprisingly calm, as he lined up his sights on the lead Messerschmitt. 'Hope these synchronised guns do the business,' he whispered to himself, 'This bastard is not going to get past me.' And then he opened fire, dead on target. He held the button down, aiming his Hurricane at the Messerschmitt as the two aircraft closed at something like 500 mph. The German fighter pilot was not going to yield; he held course straight for the Hurricane, flame spitting from his machine-gun and cannon armament. As the Messerschmitt filled the sky in front of him, Steed closed his eyes and, still with all guns firing, waited for oblivion.

'Fuck me!' screamed Hauptmann Hans-Otto Steinhilper as he heaved on the joystick to send his Me-109 into a steep climb, missing Steed's Hurricane by a hair's breadth. A 'Spaniard' as the Condor Legion veterans of the Spanish Civil War were called in the Luftwaffe, Hauptmann Steinhilper had chalked up nineteen victories to date, having fought in the Polish campaign last autumn and in the present Battle of France. He had spotted the two Hurricanes flying serenely along at low altitude, seemingly without a care in the world, and had decided that they were easy meat.

Although getting low on fuel, Steinhilper had led his wingman in a stern attack, creeping up in the blind spot behind and slightly beneath the two Hurricanes. And then, of all the luck, he had been spotted at the last moment. One of the Hurricanes turned sharply towards him in a head-on attack. It was too late for any other option but to meet the Englishman in a head-to-head dual. But this Englishman was bent on suicide. He did not yield. Steinhilper had opened fire as the Hurricane approached, but at the last moment he had been forced to pull back the stick in order to avoid certain death.

But, in the split second that Steinhilper had presented the Me-109s vulnerable underside to Steed's machine-gun fire, serious damage had been done. An oil pipeline had been severed, spaying oil over the hot engine. The oil pressure started to fall, ringing the death knell for the Daimler-Benz engine. Feldwebel Voss, Steinhilper's number two, faithfully followed his leader in the climb and away from Chamberlain's wounded Hurricane.

Steed opened his eyes to see his bullets flying harmlessly underneath the second Me-109, which cast a dark shadow over the Hurricane's canopy as Feldwebel Voss pulled up into his steep climb. Steed was panic stricken as he hauled his Hurricane up into an Immelmann turn. The two German fighters had managed to get past him and must even now be attacking his defenceless leader. He was still alive but he had failed to protect the flight commander.

As the Hurricane went up into the loop, Steed sought the enemy. Ah, there was one of the sods, and there was the other. They had both climbed away and had bottled out of the attack on Chamberlain. Steed reached the top of the loop inverted and then rolled right side up to complete the Immelmann, but he had lost all momentum and the Hurricane was now only just above her stalling speed. The two Me-109s were at much the same height as his Hurricane, but turning away from the coast. Thank God! Chamberlain would be making good his escape. He looked towards the Channel and then, with alarm, spotted the Hurricane circling anticlockwise. The damn fool, what was Chamberlain doing? Brave of him to hang around and try to help out, but the flight commander was not of much use with a duff aeroplane.

As he climbed, Hauptmann Hans-Otto Steinhilper considered his next move. There were two of the enemy, but at that moment he wasn't sure where either of them were. The important thing was to gain height; that gave him options. He levelled out at the top of the climb, and then banked his aircraft to look down for the Tommies. His number two Voss was still there, good, he didn't have to worry about his tail. He could concentrate on seeking out and destroying the enemy, earning yet more victories.

And then Steinhilper smelt the oil, worse he could see the smoke coming from somewhere down there by his feet. He looked at his oil pressure gauge. It read zero! Where were the Hurricanes? Then he saw Steed. The idiot Englishman that had nearly killed him had also climbed and was more or less at the same height as Voss and himself, but still some distance away and heading back towards the coast. The second Englishman he could not see yet, but yes, there he was below and circling. The smoke was much worse now inside Steinhilper's cockpit, the fire would be next; it was time to get out. He radioed his number two, 'Voss, I have lost all oil pressure and I am on fire, I need to get out now while I still have height.' Then he jettisoned the canopy.

Steed looked across to the two Me-109s, and saw with some amazement that the leader was trailing black smoke. As he watched the stricken aircraft turned onto its back and the pilot dropped out. Steed had his throttle wide open and the Hurricane was slowly picking up speed. Steed aimed to put himself between the second Me-109 and Chamberlain, still circling a mile or so distant.

Feldwebel Voss assessed the situation. He now faced two enemy fighters and he was low on fuel. He knew that his Me-109 was faster than a Hurricane, and he could choose whether to fight or retire. He needed to protect his leader, just in case the Tommies decided to use the Hauptmann for target practice as he hung defenceless in his parachute; but he could see that the Hurricanes were not about to do that. Feldwebel Voss turned for home.

Steed dropped down to join Chamberlain. 'Yellow Leader, are you okay, can you make it home?'

'Bloody good show Sergeant Steed. You certainly nailed that Hun bastard. I saw the pilot jump.'

Steed took station above and behind Chamberlain as they left France and headed out across the English Channel. Considering the damage to the rear of his aircraft, Chamberlain made a creditable landing back at Colne Martin.

Steed learned in his debrief by the intelligence officer, the Spy, that the squadron had two pilots missing, both from 'A Flight'. Pilot Officer 'Bunny' Burroughs had been shot down in the first pass by the four Me-109s that had attacked Tomcat Squadron just as they were forming up for their 'Fighting Area Attack Number 5' on the Dorniers. His plane was seen going down with half the back end missing. Nobody had seen a parachute. Bunny was only twenty years of age and one of the recent intake of pilots to the squadron. He was a Cranwell graduate and had seemed to Steed to be a very serious youth, quiet and reserved and a staunch member of the God Squad. Steed hoped that he had managed to parachute out of his doomed aircraft.

Steed was very pleased to see that Billy Bishop and Toby Adams had made it back. The four Messerschmitts had not done so well in their second attack, although they had managed to scatter Green Section. Bishop and Adams had eventually found each other and reformed, but by then they had lost sight of Steed and indeed the rest of Tomcat Squadron. After stooging around over France for a bit, and failing to raise the rest of the Tomcats on the radio, they had headed for home undamaged and without further incident.

The rest of Tomcat Squadron, minus Bunny Burroughs, had reformed over Calais but by then the Dorniers and the four Me-109s had disappeared. The Tomcats then saw some Stukas attacking Calais and formed up for a Fighting Area Attack to intervene, but before they could engage they were attacked, again out of the sun, by a gaggle of Me-109s. In the ensuing dogfight several Hurricanes were damaged, including Chamberlain's, and Flying Officer Dougie Smith went down. Dougie Smith was one of the senior pilots who had formed the nucleus of experience when 126-Squadron was created. His Hurricane had crashed into woodland behind Calais and exploded. It seemed probable that he had been killed. Several pilots claimed hits on the German fighters, but Steed's was the only confirmed victory, and the first for the squadron.

A number of the Hurricanes had sustained damage. Steed examined his own aircraft with his ground crew. Several machine-gun bullets had passed through the cowling and hit either the engine or the front bulkhead, but the damage was slight and the Hurricane could be speedily repaired and available for that afternoon if needed. Steed had been lucky. None of Hauptmann Hans-Otto Steinhilper's cannon shells had found their mark, neither had the vulnerable Glycol header tank at the front of the engine been hit.

The squadron was put on thirty minute's readiness for the afternoon. Tomlinson and the two flight commanders were absent from the crew room, but discussion amongst the rest of the pilots centred on the lessons to be learnt from the morning's adventure. There was almost universal condemnation of the Fighting Area Attacks. Flying Officer 'Roger' Daily, the straight talking Australian who always told it as it was, being the most vociferous.

'These bloody FAAs are all very well if all you have to worry about is a bunch of Jerry bombers flying along in a nice straight line. FAAs take no account of the bloody fighters waiting up there in the sun.' He jabbed a finger upwards. 'We sod about getting ourselves into a nice formation for the FAA, but while we are doing that we are wide open to being bounced by the bloody escorting fighters.'

Billy Bishop expressed similar sentiments. 'One thing that bothers me is that we all need to keep a sharp lookout for the Hun in the sun as the saying goes, but we are also blind behind and below. It is difficult for individual pilots to look around properly for the Huns when we are flying such a tight formation; we are too busy avoiding bumping into each other. You are right Roger. We have even less chance of spotting the Huns when we are manoeuvring into the FAAs. We need a tight formation when we climb through cloud of course, and tight formation flying certainly helps with pilot training, but maybe we need to speak to the Boss about the possibility of opening the formation out a bit when the Hun fighters are about.'

Steed listened to the other pilots but didn't say much. He strongly agreed with the outspoken Aussie Roger Daily and with the more circumspect Billy Bishop, but he was very much aware that, as the most junior pilot in both the squadron and in rank, it was best for him to keep his own counsel, at least for the moment.

Later in the early evening, immediately after the squadron had been stood down, Tomlinson and the two flight commanders, Chamberlain and Dix, joined the rest of the pilots in the dispersal crew room. Tomlinson addressed the pilots.

'Gentlemen, this morning the squadron had its first brush with the enemy. Congratulations to Sergeant Steed for achieving our first kill.' Whoops, cheers and whistles echoed around the crew room, much to Steed's embarrassment. 'As you all know, Douglas and Bunny are missing. I have been talking for most of the afternoon to Group and to the leaders of other fighter squadrons, trying to make sense of what is happening over in France, and trying to get some idea of how best to deal with the Hun fighters. We,' he indicated the flight commanders, 'have also been going over our operation this morning. I think that there are some changes that we need to make in the way we do things. Firstly, let's deal with the Fighting Area Attacks. For a number of years our training has assumed that we would be up against fast enemy bombers without fighter escort; that was why the FAAs were developed. Squadron leaders were told not to deviate from FAAs in training. I have now been given more freedom of action. FAAs take time to execute, time that we do not always have. While we are doing all of this, we are vulnerable to enemy fighter attack. In future, I may not always order FAAs when we spot the enemy, especially if I think that there are enemy fighters around.' There were nods and general murmurings of approval from the assembled pilots.

Tomlinson continued, 'We normally fly four vics into battle, but recent practical experience in France suggests there are some deficiencies in this formation. We need to spot the enemy before he sees us and, more especially, enemy fighters must not catch us out again as they did twice today. From tomorrow, I propose to adopt a slightly different formation, similar to that now being implemented by some of the other fighter squadrons. Red, Yellow and Blue sections will still fly vics, but from now on, we will have two or three 'weavers' at the back. These weavers will fly in an open line abreast formation behind the main squadron, well spread out, and slightly higher than the rest of us. Their job will be to spot enemy fighters sneaking up behind us. Each weaver aircraft will independently and constantly weave from side to side to ensure that they cover all the sky behind the squadron, including the blind spot behind and below.' Again there were murmurings of approval from the pilots.

'Our job tomorrow is to go after the enemy bombers, to thereby protect our troops fighting below. While most of us concentrate on that, our weavers will warn us of any impending attack by enemy fighters. This is a system that has been shown to work in other squadrons and I am confident that it will work for us.'

Before leaving the crew room for his office, Tomlinson made a point of speaking to Steed. 'That was a very good show on your part this morning Sergeant Steed. Flight Lieutenant Chamberlain has told me all about it. I looked over his Hurricane after he landed, it's amazing that he made it back at all; he was certainly in no position to fight off an attack by two Me-109s. He told me that you flew straight at the lead 109 and got in so close that you damn near rammed it. You sent it down in flames, damn good shooting that! It was nice to see that the pilot got out. Then you chased off the second 109. You also have the squadron's first victory Sergeant Steed. Capital!'

'Thank you sir,' stammered Steed. 'I was trying my best not to let the Jerries get past me. I didn't see flames, but I did see a fair bit of smoke, and then the 109 turned upside down and the pilot bailed out.'

'Damn good show,' said Tomlinson as he left. 'We must have a party tonight to celebrate the squadron's first victory. There is also a magnum of Champagne with your name on it Sergeant.'

Flight Lieutenant Dix called together Bishop, Adams and Steed. 'You three are Green Section tomorrow, which means that you will all be weavers. I want you to be absolutely clear what your duties are. Billy, as Green Leader you take station three hundred feet or so behind the last plane in the squadron, dead centre, and about three hundred feet higher than the squadron leader. You will weave from side to side and make sure that nothing sneaks up on us from behind. Keep a special lookout for the Hun in the sun when the sun is behind you. Sergeant Adams, as Green-2 you take station level with Billy, but on the extreme right of the squadron You also look behind, but you have the special job of keeping a sharp lookout to the right. Sergeant Steed, you will be Green-3 on the left, and of course you have the special job of keeping a lookout to the left, as well as behind. So to reiterate, you three must look out for the enemy fighters coming in on our tail or on the beam, and especially out of the sun when it is within your sector. The squadron leader is responsible for looking ahead and finding our targets. Clear as mud everybody?'

Steed replied, 'What if the Boss changes formation, say from sections astern to line abreast. Do I move out to always stay behind the Hurricane on the extreme left?'

'Absolutely,' said Dix. 'Always keep behind the squadron on their left hand edge. Similarly Sergeant Adams, you must mirror that on the right. Give yourselves plenty of room to weave around and look out for the Hun in your blind spots. You boys have a very important job.'

That evening all of the pilots went to a local pub for the party to celebrate the squadron's first victory. Toby Adams gave Steed and Johnny Walker a lift in his beloved Hillman, with the officers racing along behind in an assortment of vehicles. Adams was determined to win the race to the pub, which was only a few miles from the airfield, but Tomlinson saw his chance on a straight stretch of road and went hurtling past in his open-top Bentley, his passengers giving catcalls and making rude signs as he did so. Adams managed to keep the other pilots behind by weaving all over the road; he said later that he was getting into practice for his new job. As a motorcyclist, well aware of his vulnerability in a collision with almost any other vehicle on the road, Steed was more than a little concerned with the lack of road sense and consideration for the safety of other road users shown by the drivers. The closeness to death in the skies, that was now apparent to all, seemed already to have promoted a feeling of live now pay later, and to hell with the rules. Maybe this was a necessary release valve for them.

This was the first time that Steed had been in the company of the other pilots in an off-duty environment. The mood in the pub was relaxed and friendly, with most of the junior pilots calling Steed by his Christian name. The senior pilots were also significantly more informal than in the crew room. Even so, Steed still detected the barrier between the three sergeant pilots and their officer comrades, with one exception. The irrepressible Australian pilot Roger Daily treated everybody as a bosom pal.

Chamberlain made a point of buying Steed a beer and talking through their engagement with the two Me-109s that morning. He was particularly complementary about Steed's tenacity and good shooting in the head-on attack against the Messerschmitt. Steed was on the point of letting Chamberlain in on his discussions on gun synchronisation with the armourer and his consequent change from the spread, but he decided to hold his tongue for the time being. Steed knew that both Chamberlain and Dix had also quietly had their guns synchronised at 250 yards, and it was really up to the two flight commanders to broach the subject with the squadron leader and the rest of the pilots. Generally, everyone refrained from talking shop though, and the two downed pilots Burroughs and Smith were not mentioned. Steed had a few beers that night, but his mind was on the Dunkirk-Calais operation the next morning.

Spitfire squadrons covered the early shifts over France the next day, so the three sergeant pilots had time to breakfast in their mess before squadron take-off at 09.00. 'I thought it went well last night,' said Adams, 'It's really unusual for all the pilots to go out together. Usually the officers and NCOs do not mix.'

'Last time it happened was when the squadron was declared operational,' added Walker, 'The Boss stood a slap-up meal in London for all of us that night.'

'It's a pity about the them and us attitude,' said Steed. 'They seem a nice bunch of guys.'

'Terribly immature, some of them,' said Adams disdainfully.' You hear them talking in the crew room about the antics that they got up to in their mess the previous night. Pillow fights with the sofa cushions, spraying soda siphons at each other, trying to climb around their mess without touching the floor. A bunch of overgrown schoolboys if you ask me.'

'That's what comes of a public school education,' said Walker. 'They think they're still in their dormitories playing silly games after lights out. It wouldn't surprise me if half of them aren't a bit ginger.' In answer to Adams' quizzical look he added, 'You know, a bit ginger beer, homosexuals.'

'So how do you know what goes on after lights out in public school dormitories' asked Adams with a grin?

'Ah well you see, I've read the Magnet comics. I know all about Billy Bunter and his chums. Our lot even speak the same language. Have you heard them? Wizard prang old chap, absolutely spiffing! I'm surprised they don't resort to a few gadzooks, yaroos and huzzahs while they are about it.'

'I'm not sure about the homosexual bit,' contributed Steed. 'One or two of them seemed to be doing very well with the ladies last night. Anyway, I feel a bit sorry for them, those that got packed off to boarding school at age eight or whatever.'

'Well that's the British class system for you my son. But they have a different way of life from the proletariat, much better opportunities, and the system keeps it that way. The pilot officers do exactly the same job as us, but they live in their mess and we live in ours.'

Steed mused over their conversation as he followed the rest of the squadron out over the Channel. It was a pity that there was a division between the pilots, for one certainly existed; experience and information should be shared. But that was the way things had been done in the armed forces since time immemorial. There are the officers who lead and the men who follow. Sergeants were positioned somewhere between the two. His job was to follow those that led the squadron, the Boss and his flight and section leaders, and give them his full support. Today that job was to be the eyes of the squadron, a weaver. He concentrated on his new role.

The squadron was once again flying vics in sections astern, but Tomlinson had relaxed the formation slightly and they were not quite so close together as yesterday. Bishop had positioned the Green Section weavers well behind and above the rest of the squadron, and the weavers were well spread out in line abreast. Freed from the necessity to hold a tight formation, they were far better able to act as squadron lookouts.

Steed used his preferred method of searching the sky. Firstly he looked behind and above, weaving his Hurricane slightly to cover the blind spot behind his head. Then he weaved more robustly so that he could search the area behind and below. He then banked his aircraft first one way and then the other in order to look below, beneath his wings and fuselage. Finally he searched the vast sky to the squadron's left. The bright sun, which at this time in the morning was to the front left, over France, was on the edge of his responsibility, but he did his best to seek out the enemy within its dazzling ring. He constantly repeated this procedure, scanning the sky to protect the squadron from the Hun bounce that had claimed two victims yesterday; it was tiring but very necessary work.

Steed had renewed confidence in Tomlinson. He had started to believe that the Boss was inflexible, simply carrying out his orders regardless of their justification. But Tomlinson had acted quickly to rectify yesterday's errors. The squadron's formation was a little more relaxed, although Steed suspected that most of the pilots were still rather too preoccupied with keeping formation. Tomlinson had actively and quickly sought out opinion from other squadron leaders and consequently had introduced weavers as the eyes of the squadron.

They crossed the French coast in the vicinity of Gravelines, north of Calais, and headed inland. Steed spotted a small group of aircraft on the left beam and slightly higher. 'Tomcat Leader from Green-3, bogeys at nine o'clock, angels twelve.'

Tomlinson acknowledged Steed's sighting and ordered the squadron to climb at full throttle towards the unidentified aircraft, at the same time ordering a formation change to vics in echelon starboard. The weavers behind spread out to match the formation change and continued with their lookout duties. It was soon obvious that the approaching aircraft, now slightly lower than 126-Squadron, were six enemy bombers, twin engine Junkers Ju-88s. Their leader must have seen the Hurricanes coming towards him but he pressed on towards his target, allowing Tomlinson to put his twelve fighters in the most advantageous position, above and behind the enemy bombers.

The bombers now started their run on Calais, entering a shallow dive. Tomlinson did not waste time setting up a Fighting Area Attack. He led his men in a dive to break up the small German formation, each pilot selecting his own target. As they neared the enemy Steed was well to the rear of the Hurricane formation and on the left. He had held back, continuing with his weaver's duties until the last moment, but now he was fully occupied in selecting a target.

The six Ju-88s were grouped in two parallel sections of three aircraft in line astern. They held their formation admirably in the face of the onslaught by the Hurricanes and put up concentrated and well-aimed defensive fire. Steed selected the lead aircraft on the left column for special attention. The Ju-88 was the best bomber that the Germans possessed, an excellent machine, fast and modern; it could even be used as a heavy fighter or as a dive-bomber. Steed thought that it had a weakness because all of the crew sat together under a large glass canopy. Eight Browning machine-guns aimed at this vulnerable spot were bound to cause casualties amongst the crew. That was the theory that Steed put into practice that morning.

Things happened very quickly. Steed needed to aim well in front of his target at this steep angle of attack, and his view of the bomber was partially obscured by the nose of his own aircraft, but deflection shooting was his forté. Most of the squadron pilots were already through the Ju-88s as Steed aimed his guns, with the result that every available defensive weapon in the Ju-88 squadron swivelled to aim at Steed's plunging Hurricane. But he was a difficult target to hit, and most of the gunners switching their sights from the other attackers either did not have time to fire, or at least to aim properly. Steed did aim properly and was rewarded by seeing his tracers at first pass in front of the lead Ju-88 and then dance on the large glass canopy, showering pieces of wreckage in their wake. At the last moment he was aware of a blur in front as a German bullet smashed into the armoured section of his windscreen. He ceased firing as he rocketed only a few feet past the Ju-88s large tail. He threw the aircraft around for a few moments to put off any final efforts by the enemy gunners, and then pulled out of his dive to follow the rest of the squadron. It was only then that he became aware of the other damage that his Hurricane had suffered at the hands of the experienced German gunners. In addition to the bullet that had hit his windscreen there were holes in his left wing and a couple that he could see in the engine cowling in front of him.

Steed's Hurricane still answered to the controls as if she had not been hit, and as far as he could tell the engine was behaving itself as well; all the gauges were normal. Tomlinson's voice again came over the radio, 'Tomcat Squadron reform on me.' Steed was at full power as he manoeuvred to rejoin the rest of his squadron. Tomlinson was leading them in a steep turn in order to get after the Ju-88s once more, but they had lost time reforming and the Ju-88s had a head start. As he followed Tomlinson and the rest of the boys in their pursuit of the Ju-88s, Steed remembered his duties and began once more to scan the sky for enemy fighters.

The Ju-88s were well out of range and travelling very fast in their shallow dive towards Calais. But not all of them. One Ju-88 on the right was lagging behind his fellows with smoke gushing from one engine. Another on the left was in a steep dive away from the rest of the formation; it hit the ground with a tremendous explosion of a full bomb load.

Even at full throttle, the Hurricanes were not going to catch the main body of enemy aircraft before they reached Calais, but the damaged straggler was another story. He must have realised his plight because he turned sharp left away from Calais and jettisoned his bombs. Tomlinson's voice cut in over the radio. 'Yellow-One, take your section and put down that fellow with only one engine.'

Chamberlain, who was again leading Yellow Section responded, 'Roger Tomcat leader. Yellow Section, follow me.'

Suddenly there was a burst of well-aimed flak from below, scattering the Tomcats. 'Stupid bastards!' yelled somebody. 'Can't the bloody Pongos recognise Hurricanes?'

The German gun crew below had indeed recognised the RAF Hurricanes, and directed fire from their quadruple 20mm guns accordingly; 126-squadron was over enemy territory!

'I've been hit,' a worried voice announced.

Tomlinson cut in, 'Use the correct radio procedure, who's been hit and how badly?'

'Sorry sir. Tomcat Leader from Blue-3. I've been hit by ground fire, cannon shells I think, there's smoke in the cockpit,' responded a shaken Pip Courtauld.

'Climb to parachute height. Try to make it home, but if you can't, get out over Calais.'

'Will do Leader.'

'Green-1 from Tomcat Leader. Escort him home Billy. Good luck Pip. Go now.'

The surviving Ju-88s were now dropping their bombs on the unfortunate inhabitants of Calais, but the ground fire incident had allowed then to open up the gap between themselves and their pursuers. This time it was Toby Adams on the radio 'Green-2 to Tomcat Leader. Bogeys at three o'clock, same height as us.'

Tomlinson came in after a short pause, 'Green-2, keep your eye on them. We will stay after to Huns in front.' 126-Squadron was now positioned to the east of the fleeing Ju-88s, cutting off their retreat, but the enemy aircraft swept over the Calais foreshore and dropped down to wave top height as they hugged the French coastline heading southwest. Minus their bomb load, the Ju-88s were even faster. The Hurricanes were still in an approximate vic sections in echelon starboard formation, but they were now spread out in a tail chase, with the faster Hurricanes edging out in front. Steed's Hurricane was lagging behind in spite of being on full throttle emergency boost, and he was getting worried about the punishment the motor was taking, not to mention the punishment to the rest of his aircraft so recently dolled out by the German air gunners. Weaving was out of the question at this speed, although he did his best to look out for enemy fighters coming down from behind.

As they passed Boulogne, the leading Hurricanes opened fire at maximum range. The Ju-88s turned inland, hedgehopping at full speed, only marginally slower than the Hurricanes. The leading Hurricanes expended most of their ammunition without obvious result, and the squadron was being drawn further and further inland. The return fire from the Ju-88s was uncannily accurate; they were using a method of directed fire, where all the gunners tried to concentrate on just one of their attackers. At length, Tomlinson called off the chase. 'Tomcats from Leader, sorry boys, they're too fast for us today and they've dropped their bombs anyway. Throttle back and reform. Green-2, are your Bogeys still around?'

'No leader,' from Adams. 'The sky is clear.'

Tomlinson climbed to 10,000 feet and led the remaining seven members of his squadron back towards the English Channel and home. Presently, Steed spotted aircraft out over the Channel, coming towards them.

'Tomcat Leader from Green-3. Bogeys at eleven o'clock, angels twelve.'

Tomlinson answered almost immediately, 'I've seen them, probably friendly, but we'll keep an eye on them.' They were indeed friendly. The twelve Spitfires waggled their wings in salute as they passed by.

Steed's ground crew were examining the damage to his Hurricane even before his propeller had come to a standstill. Steed was also keen to see the damage, especially to his engine. He rather liked his synchronised gun settings and didn't want to revert to a replacement aircraft with a Dowding spread. 'Looks like you've got moths Sarge,' said his rigger.

'Too right Colin,' said Steed. 'But you should have seen the other fellow! Can you patch her up for this afternoon? I don't want to take one of the spares unless I have to.'

'We'll get onto it right now and give it our best shot Sarge. Did you get another one?' All the ground crews took a keen interest and pride in their particular pilot's exploits. Steed's ground crew were no exception, and they were developing a close bond with their man. Steed's victory the previous day had been a source of deep satisfaction for them.

'I knocked bits off of a Ju-88, that's when I copped this lot from his mates. One of the Ju-88s went down, we saw it crash, and another one was flying on one engine when last I saw it, with three Hurricanes up its arse.' Steed turned to his fitter 'Dennis, there are a couple of holes in the engine cowling. She seems to be running well, and all the indicators are okay, but you had better have a good look inside to see if anything vital got hit.'

'I'll do it right now Sarge.'

'I am sorry, but I had to give her a long dose of emergency boost in order to keep up with the others in a tail chase after the Ju-88s. I'll come back to see you after I've been debriefed by the Spy.'

'No worries Sarge. Glad you got back okay.'

The pilots were elated. Chamberlain's Yellow section had successfully downed the lame duck. The German dorsal gunner had bravely returned fire as the Ju-88 had vainly tried to make cloud cover, but Chamberlain had silenced him in his first pass. The other two Hurricanes of Yellow Section, attacking in line astern, had finished off the German bomber, which dropped into a shallow dive and exploded on impact as it crashed into a potato field; there were no survivors.

Chamberlain and the other two pilots in Yellow Section, Johnny Walker and Roger Daily, were each credited with 1/3 kill. Nobody was sure who had bagged the other Ju-88 to go down, and most of the pilots claimed to have hit something, so Tomlinson awarded 1/12 kill to everybody. Steed would never know it, but his devastating concentrated fire from eight Browning machine-guns on the glass canopy of the Ju-88 had killed or wounded most of the crew, and it was that aircraft that the Tomcats had seen crash.

Courtauld, escorted by Billy Bishop, had made it back to Colne Martin with two large cannon shell holes in the underside of his aeroplane.

Steed returned to his ground crew. Dennis White greeted him, 'I had a good look at the Merlin Sarge. One of the bullets that went through the cowling caught the glycol header tank a glancing blow and dented it. I am replacing that now, so it will be ready for your next op. Another bullet hit the bulkhead in front of the reserve petrol tank, but it didn't cause any damage.' The mechanic's calloused hand reached into his oil smeared overall and withdrew a deformed 7.92mm bullet, which he handed to Steed. 'Here you are Sarge, a souvenir.'

Steed's rigger appeared, 'Hi Sarge. You picked up a fair number of holes from the Jerries, but the Hurricane's a tough old bird and there's no lasting damage. There are a few holes in the fuselage, but I'll have those fixed in a jiffy. The holes in your wings will take a bit more time. The early Hurricanes used to have fabric-covered wings, but they changed them for the new stressed metal wings that you have. Tough as old boots, but they take a little longer to repair. I can make a temporary fix so that you can fly later today, and I can tidy up the paintwork when you come back, ready for tomorrow. The screen has to be replaced as well, but that isn't a problem. We can do that by the time you take off this evening.'

'That's great Colin, thanks a million. We have the last shift this evening, take-off at 19.00, but I guess you know that already.' Steed cast an expert eye over his Hurricane, but he knew better than to interfere with the work of his ground crew. He had told them that he had been a mechanic in Civvy Street, but he had so far avoided telling them that he had been an aircraft mechanic. Aside from Tomlinson and Dix, the only other two people on the squadron that knew about his work at Epping Flying Club were his fellow sergeant pilots Toby Adams and Johnny Walker, and that was because they had both started out as RAF ground crew fitters themselves.

126-Squadron took off for their second mission of the day at 7.00pm. They had two hours of daylight left, and as usual they were to patrol ten miles inland of Calais-Dunkirk. Reports were coming in from other squadrons of increased German air activity, with both Dunkirk and Calais bombed by small formations of Heinkel 111s, Ju-88s and Stukas. The operation was something of an anti-climax after the last two days, because the Luftwaffe did not put in an appearance. The Tomcats landed shortly before sunset.

Steed met up with Adams and Walker in the mess that night to celebrate Walker's 1/3 kill. There was grudging admiration for the German aircrew, and for the aeroplane that they flew.

'Damn fast aeroplane, the Junkers-88,' commented Steed. 'Once they had jettisoned their bombs they were the Devil's own job to catch.'

'Too right,' added Adams. 'And even when the lads in front caught up with them, they took a hell of a lot of punishment without going down.

From what I gather, a couple of our boys used up all their ammunition in the attempt.'

'I think maybe they should have got in closer before they opened fire,' suggested Steed.

'We had the same problem with our bugger,' chimed in Walker. 'Peter Chamberlain had a bash at it, then Roger and finally me. It took all three of us to put him down. The Hun gunners were firing back at us all of the time, pretty accurate stuff too; you can't fault their courage.'

So ended the 26th May, Steed's second day in the shooting war. Already he had nearly been killed twice! Steed put his magnum of Champagne behind the bar in the sergeants' mess, but he also made sure that his ground crew had the opportunity to sample the booty. He made his excuses after a couple of glasses and had an early night; he was scheduled to fly in the morning, and take-off was at 06.30.

Tomlinson's face was grim as he briefed his pilots the following morning. 'Gentlemen, I am afraid that the war news is bad. The BEF is cut off and an evacuation had been ordered from Dunkirk. Our job, as it has been for the past week, is to protect our troops from the German bombers. I say that, but there are also reports of Messerschmitt fighters, the 109s and the 110s, strafing the roads, railways, troops, ships and anything else that they see. So our task, as I see it, is to patrol just inland of Dunkirk and break up any enemy bomber formations that are attempting to get at our troops. But in reality, we will take on anything in the air that is German. We must cover the evacuation of our troops.'

Courtauld piped up, 'Are the troops coming home to Blighty sir, or is the navy taking them down the coast to land again in France?'

'Good question Pip. As far as I can gather, when the Germans invaded Holland and Belgium, the BEF and some French units moved up into Belgium to form a defensive line. That was all okay and the line held. But then the Germans made a second thrust through the Ardennes, through Luxembourg at the point where the French Maginot Line finishes. In no time at all the Germans broke through all the way to the Channel, cutting off our troops holding the line in Belgium from the main French armies down here in the south.' Tomlinson indicated the positions on the wall map in the crew room. 'Our boys are now surrounded by the Huns at Dunkirk, with their backs to the sea. In answer to your question Pip, it is my understanding that the evacuation is from Dunkirk back to England. Now it may be that in a day or two our troops can be ferried from England to somewhere down here,' Tomlinson gestured vaguely towards Normandy, 'and carry on the fight. To be honest Pip, I just do not know.'

Once again, Green Section was flying as weavers, and Steed was again positioned on the left side and behind the main squadron. Steed's ground crew had worked into the night to tidy their earlier repairs, repaint the damaged areas and to generally check over the aeroplane. Steed's Hurricane was almost as good as new, if a little slower than some of the fresher machines allocated to the more senior pilots.

As they approached Dunkirk, the pilots received a shock. There was a huge pall of coal black smoke above the town. The oil storage tanks were alight and Dunkirk was a mess. There was an assortment of boats offshore, but the harbour looked a shambles. Tomlinson circled the squadron above Dunkirk. Steed, on the outside of the turn, spotted the dive-bombers first. 'Tomcat leader from Green-3. Stukas at nine o'clock bombing the shipping.'

Tomlinson led his squadron straight into the attack. The weavers watched for any escorting fighters. It was Bishop who spotted them this time, 'Tomcat Squadron from Green-1, bandits at six o'clock high, coming down.' Steed saw them. Around a dozen twin engine Messerschmitt 110s. Bishop's voice again, 'Tomcat Squadron prepare to break port.' As the first person to spot the enemy, Bishop was in the best position to call the break, 'Break port GO.'

The twelve Hurricanes turned to meet the oncoming Me-110s. After the first pass the Hurricanes turned to follow the Me-110s and a dogfight developed. Although big and heavy, the Me-110s were if anything slightly faster than the Hurricanes in level flight, and each carried a formidable armament of four machine-guns and two cannon in the nose.

Steed found himself chasing a 110, which then climbed away using its superior speed generated by its dive. The 110 rolled over the top of the loop and looked for a target below, intending to dive down for another pass at the Hurricanes. Steed followed the 110 through the loop and again attempted to get on its tail. The 110 went into a tight turn and the rear gunner opened fire. Steed followed the turn, ignoring the fire from the gunner, and was soon in a position to open fire himself at close range with a deflection shot. Steed saw the results of his work as twinkling lights and smoke crept along the nose and long glass canopy of the Messerschmitt, killing its pilot and silencing its gunner. Steed broke away violently, just in case another enemy fighter was closing in on him, but there was only his Hurricane and the vanquished Me-110 in the immediate vicinity; the Messerschmitt was entering its terminal dive towards the cold and foreboding North Sea below. Steed circled, once again scanning the sky. He spotted a Hurricane coming towards him, and then recognised it by its markings as Roger Daily's machine. Steed slotted in behind Daily's aircraft as the twin engine German fighter hit the water below.

The airwaves were full of shouts, warnings and curses, some of them becoming quite faint. The squadron seemed to be spread out all over Northern France. During a short lull in the general hubbub, Steed transmitted, 'Yellow-2 from Green-3, I'll cover your tail.'

'Glad to have you there Harry, I'm making for those Stukas.'

Steed was still on the lookout for enemy fighters and weaving like mad as he followed Daily. This weaving was habit forming, the muscles in his neck ached. He saw a group of Me-110s away to his left; they had formed a defensive circle, each one covering the tail of its companion in front. What a pointless exercise for an escort fighter! They were supposed to be defending the Stukas. Hurricanes were milling around them like moths attracted to a light.

Around half a dozen Stukas were circling slowly at 13,000 feet, slightly higher than Daily and Steed. Others were either diving towards their targets or, having dropped their bombs, were heading for home at low level. One after another, Stukas were leaving the circle to make a straight bombing run towards the shipping, diving almost vertically down to around 3,000 feet where they would release their bombs.

Daily led the two Hurricanes into a position behind and below the last two Stukas remaining in the circle. It felt like murder, the two divebombers never stood a chance. Without a word to each other, Daily chose his target and Steed selected the other. Both Stukas literally fell apart in mid air under the onslaught of the Brownings at point blank range. Steed thought that Daily would go down after the remaining enemy divebombers, but Daily instead chose to return to the battle with the Messerschmitts.

As a defensive formation, the circling technique seemed to suit the Me-110s. An attack on one of them immediately drew fire from its companion behind. There was also the rear gunner to contend with. As Daily and Steed approached the melee, they could see that virtually every Hurricane in the squadron was making firing passes at the circling Me-110s. Suddenly the Germans lost their nerve and, as one, put their noses down in a steep dive, followed by several of the Hurricanes.

Although well behind the rest, Steed and Daily followed suit. The Me-110s pulled away from the Hurricanes in the dive and headed east for home. Tomcat squadron was by now dispersed over a wide area, and would be difficult to reform. Daily then spotted a lone Stuka below, hedge-hopping home. 'Steed from Daily, Stuka at ten o'clock, low-level. Going down.'

'Yellow-2, following you.'

Daily brought the two line-astern Hurricanes to a position directly behind the Stuka, which immediately started to jink, twist and turn at treetop level. The Stuka was a slow aeroplane, compared to the Hurricanes, so Daily's main problem was to avoid overshooting. The rear gunner started firing short bursts well before Daily was in range, perhaps to put the Hurricane pilot off his aim. The tactic did not work, for when Daily did open fire the rear gunner was the first casualty. As Daily overshot the dive-bomber and climbed away, Steed, who had dropped back, lined up his sights. But he had no need to open fire, because the Stuka dropped lower and then ploughed into a farmhouse. I hope to Christ that there was no one at home thought Steed as he once more closed up on his leader. As they began to climb, Steed spotted the aircraft above, 'Yellow-2 from Green-3, four Bogies at five o'clock high.'

'Can't see them Harry, are they coming down?'

'Yellow-2, don't think so. Four single engine aircraft, up there at five o'clock, maybe angels ten? Fighters I think, but can't tell what type.'

'No, I still can't see them,' said Daily slowly, and then after a pause, 'Got them. Strewth cobber, you must have eyes like a hawk. Keep them in sight if you can, I'm heading back towards Dunkirk.' As Daily climbed northeast in the general direction of Dunkirk, Steed continued in his search of the sky. The bogies, nearer and now almost directly above, were heading in the opposite direction. 'Yellow-2 from Green-3, I am pretty sure it's a *schwarm* of 109s. They are almost directly above us, heading southeast.'

'Let's hope they stay that way. I'm up for a fight with some Hun bombers, but I don't fancy a blue with a swarm of 109s with just the two of us, and I'm low on ammo as well. Err, I make it four of them up there, do you see any more?'

'Yellow-2, I see only four 109s.'

They left the Messerschmitt fighters behind. Ahead lay Dunkirk, now unmistakable with its resident plume of grimy black smoke. Daily circled at 5000 feet over the town. They had the sky to themselves, but below there was plenty of evidence of recent visits by the Luftwaffe. Daily climbed, still circling, with Steed 150 feet behind and slightly higher. Again it was Steed who saw them first.

'Yellow-2 from Green-3, bogeys at seven o'clock, angels twelve, over the coast. About half a dozen of them; single engine types I think.'

Daily immediately turned towards the sea and home, climbing steeply at full power. 'If they are 109s Harry, we are out of here. We will dive down to wave-top height at full boost.'

After a minute, Steed called his leader. 'Yellow-2, they look like Hurricanes to me.'

Tomlinson's voice came in, indistinct but still recognisable. 'Yellow-2 from Tomcat leader, Yellow-2, can you hear me?'

Daily throttled back and levelled out. He turned back towards the bogeys, now recognisable as Hurricanes, and responded, 'Yellow-2 and Green-3 rejoining Tomcat squadron. There were only seven aircraft in the squadron, two vics in echelon and a single weaver behind. Tomlinson came in again.

'Nice to have you back Roger, you too Green-3.'

The rest of the trip was uneventful. After a while, low on fuel, Tomlinson led the squadron back across the Channel to Colne Martin.

As soon as they landed, Daily bounded over to see Steed, who was examining his Hurricane. 'Hey, look at this,' laughed Steed. 'It's the first time that I've made it back without any bullet holes. I must be improving!'

'Good on you mate!' Daily clapped Steed on the back with a hefty whack, 'That worked well today. Bloody bonzer! With you guarding my tail it was easy for me to get into position for those attacks.'

'Yes it did work well didn't it? You put in some nice shooting too. Did you see that Stuka hit the farmhouse? I hope that there wasn't anyone inside.'

'Sure did, we can claim half each for that one. I also saw you get the Me-110 by the way, and we both got a Stuka each over Dunkirk of course.'

'I didn't shoot at the Hun that hit the farmhouse, he's all yours. What happened to you when the 110s dived on us?'

'I am pretty sure that I hit the one that came down on me. I turned after him but he wasn't interested in making a fight of it. He just kept going down and then he pulled away for home at top speed. The rear gunner took a few pot shots at me but he was well out of range. I couldn't catch the bugger so I turned around to get after the Stukas. That's when I saw you hit the 110 on the turn; that was damn good deflection shooting. I saw him go straight down into the drink. You had me worried when you said there was a swarm of 109s above us. I could only see four and I thought there must be more. A swarm obviously means more in Australian than in English.'

'It's not English Roger, it's German. It's *schwarm* not swarm.' Daily looked quizzically at Steed. 'I asked the Spy the other day what he knew about German fighter tactics. Apparently the Jerries used to fly vics in Spain, just like us, but they changed to handier formations. The Spy said that the German fighters never fly alone, their most basic formation is two aircraft, a leader and a wingman; they call it a *rotte*. Two *rotte* pairs make a *schwarm* of four fighters, which is one of the most common formations used by the Germans apparently.'

'You learn something every day,' chortled Daily. 'So today we were a rotten pair!' They both laughed as they walked off to debriefing by the Spy.

126-Squadron had enjoyed a very productive morning. Steed and three other pilots each claimed a 110 destroyed, Daily shot down two Stukas and Steed one. Billy Bishop had been shot up during the Me-110s' first pass and was obliged to head back across the Channel; Billy had been forced to crash land at RAF Marston, a coastal airfield near the Kent coast, but he was none the worse for wear apart from a few minor cuts and bruises. The squadron's tally over the last couple of days now stood at seven kills for the loss of Smith and Burroughs. Steed was the squadron's top scorer with three confirmed victories.

The Tomcats were airborne again at five o'clock in the afternoon for their second sortie of the day. They were without Billy Bishop, who was still on his way back from Marston by road, so Green Section, who again supplied the weavers, was led by Flying Officer 'Teddy' Edwards. So far in the battle, Tomlinson had been able to rest at least one of his pilots per sortie, but now, with two pilots lost out of the original fifteen and Billy Bishop still on his way back from Marston, Tomlinson had to put up his full complement of twelve pilots.

Edwards kept Green Section further behind the main squadron, and a little higher, than was Billy Bishop's practice. Steed thought of his attack on the Ju-88s; when being the last to attack he had become the subject of their concentrated gunfire. This far back, he might find himself in the same position again. On the other hand, as a weaver, he did not have to follow a vic leader. He had more freedom for manoeuvre. Another point suddenly occurred to him, this far back from the main squadron the weavers themselves made a tempting target for the Huns. With this uncomfortable thought in mind he doubled his efforts to find the elusive enemy fighters in this big, blue sky.

Dunkirk, signposted by its shroud of black, oily smoke, loomed ahead. Far below, a Royal Navy destroyer creamed through the grey sea. There were other destroyers lying offshore; several small boats were ferrying men to them from the beaches. Steed rebuked himself. Amazing though these scenes were, he should not be looking at them. His job as a weaver was to be on the lookout for the baddies. This time it was Dix's voice that came over the radio. 'Tomcat Leader from Blue 1, bogies at two o'clock, same height as us.'

Steed looked across to where a line of smudges indicated the unidentified aircraft, almost certainly enemy bombers. He looked above them. Were there enemy fighters lurking up there? Maybe, but his job was to search to the left, not to the right; best to leave that to Toby Adams. The sun was behind them, lower now and out over the sea, as the evening drew on. Tomlinson was climbing. Good, if the bogies were enemy bombers then Tomlinson could attack them head on out of the sun. What was that glinting high overhead and a bit to the right? He called over the radio, 'Tomcat Leader from Green-3, bogeys almost overhead and slightly to the right. Very high, maybe angels twenty.'

After a while Tomlinson came in, 'Green-3 from Leader. Can't see them, are you sure?'

'Yes Leader. I can see them glinting almost directly above us, but a bit to the right, at three o'clock. Maybe four of them.'

'Still can't see them,' said Tomlinson, with an unwarranted degree of suspicion in his voice thought Steed.

Dix cut in, 'Tomcat Leader from Blue-1. I can see them now, at least I can see the sun glinting on them.'

'Thank you Hugh, and well spotted Green-3,' said Tomlinson. 'They are not bothering us up there. The aircraft in front look like Heinkels.' Tomlinson was now manoeuvring the squadron for a frontal attack on the enemy bombers from out of the sun. Steed could now see that the aircraft were indeed Heinkel-111s; there were about twelve of them, flying in a tight formation towards Dunkirk.

Steed continued to scan the sky, keeping a special watch on the high-flying bogies. Apart from these companions high above, the sky seemed to be clear; it looked like the Jerries were going to give the Tomcats a clear run at the bombers. Was it his imagination, or were those bogies lower now? He could see them more clearly now. They were definitely coming down. 'Tomcat leader from Green-3. The bogies are coming down now. About four single engine fighters I think.'

Tomlinson responded, 'Green leader, take your section up to deal with those fighters. Everybody else attack the Hun bombers. Choose your own targets, Tallyho.'

Edwards went to full power and started to climb, followed by Steed and Adams. Below, the rest of the squadron headed for the bombers. Having gained height, Edwards, still climbing, turned towards the enemy. The four Me-109s, for Steed had been correct, were now above and in front of the three Hurricanes, but they were coming down out of the sun and the Hurricanes were still travelling relatively slowly after their climb. The Messerschmitts made their first pass at high speed and then split into two pairs as they climbed and turned behind the Hurricanes, ready to come in again. At least, thought Steed, we are preventing the sods from attacking the rest of the squadron; they can get on with their job of breaking up the bomber formation.

The Me-109s came back, trying to get on the tail of an unwary Hurricane. They work well together, these Jerries, thought Steed, using their extra man to good advantage. One of the Germans attempted to turn inside of him, but Steed turned tighter, tightening the muscles in his neck to try to prevent the G-forces from draining the blood from his head. He was turning tighter than the German, in a moment he would have the correct deflection and could open fire. The Hun fighter would be toast!

But suddenly the German dived away. Steed was on the point of following when he saw a second Me-109 getting into position behind him. Diving would be fatal; the Jerry behind would get him. Steed continued to turn tightly, and he found that the Messerschmitt could not stay with him. Steed had a sense of déjà vu. It was just like the first time that he had practised this manoeuvre with Dix, but this was easier. The Hurricane could easily turn inside a Me-109, at least he could against this particular pilot and at this altitude. The German pilot wisely bottled out and dived away. This time, his tail being clear, Steed followed. But the Me-109 was too fast; it easily pulled away and headed off towards the east.

Steed looked around first for danger, and then for another target. The Hun bombers were heading towards Dunkirk with Hurricanes dancing around them like hornets. Steed's first instinct was to join them, but then he saw a lone Heinkel heading east away from the fight. One of its engines was feathered and it had obviously sustained some damage, but it was still flying. Steed licked his lips and set off in pursuit. He approached the Heinkel from behind and underneath. The Heinkel was flying slowly on one engine, and was in no position to take evasive action. Steed was careful to throttle right back; he didn't want to overshoot the bomber and give its gunners a juicy target. Steed had developed a healthy respect for German air gunners by now. He weaved to check his tail. Good, no enemy fighters around, this should be easy.

The rear gunner in the gondola beneath the bomber started firing far too soon. Probably trying to put me off, thought Steed. Now, what was it that the Great War German ace von Richthofen had said? 'When attacking two-seaters, kill the gunner first.' Well, this wasn't a two-seater, but if one had the time it probably made sense with a bomber too. Steed carefully lined up his sights on the Heinkel's belly, ignoring the tracer from the gondola, and opened fire. He watched his bullets draw a line from just forward of the gondola, though the gondola, which virtually disintegrated, and then continue their destructive path back towards the tail. He ceased fire as the Hurricane approached stalling speed, then fell away turning through 360 degrees to return for a second attack, again from behind and below. The bomber was still flying straight and level but, unsurprisingly, the return fire from the gondola gunner had ceased.

This time Steed took careful aim at the starboard engine. The Heinkel did not take evasive action and there was no return fire. Steed could hardly miss. The engine burst into flames and the Heinkel, now with both engines stopped and full of holes dropped towards the ground in a shallow dive. Flames took a firm hold on the starboard engine and along the wing. The aircraft twisted in its death throes as the dive became steeper then finally hit the ground in a mass of flame and twisted metal. There were no parachutes, although the aircraft had been too low for them to be of much use anyway.

Steed headed back towards Dunkirk. He circled the town for a few minutes, but everybody seemed to have gone home. He was low on ammunition and this was no place for a lone Hurricane, so he decided to do the same.

After debriefing by the Spy, Tomlinson called all of the pilots together in the crew room. 'We had another successful day gentlemen. Flying Officer Edwards is missing, but he may yet turn up. Sergeants Steed and Adams, can you add anything to that?'

'No sir,' replied Adams, 'Mr Edwards led the section into action against four 109s. There was a dogfight. I was turning with a 109 when it suddenly dived away. I followed it down, but it was too fast and he got away. After that I was alone. I headed back towards Dunkirk; then I met up with the rest of you.'

'And you Sergeant Steed?' Tomlinson's stare was icy cold.

'Much the same sir, in fact it happened twice. I was circling a 109 and managing to turn inside. When I had almost reached the point of firing, it dived away. I didn't follow it because another one came up behind me. The same thing happened. We turned, I managed to turn inside it and then it dived way. This time I followed but it was too fast and it headed away east. I didn't see what happened to Mr Edwards. I didn't see anyone go down, neither did I see any parachutes.'

'What happened next Sergeant Steed?' Again Tomlinson's tone was harsh.

'I headed back towards the fight with the Heinkels. I saw one on its own and I shot it down. It crashed west of Dunkirk.'

'I saw what happened Sergeant Steed.' Tomlinson laid heavy emphasis on the word Sergeant. 'Our duty was to break up that formation of bombers before it hit our troops at Dunkirk. You were perfectly well aware of that. Instead you chose to attack a lone damaged aeroplane that had jettisoned his bombs and was heading home.' Tomlinson's face was red with anger, 'You attacked a defenceless lone aircraft in preference to the much more dangerous job of helping your fellow pilots to break up the bomber formation. Your only concern was to increase your personal score.'

The crew room went deathly quiet. Steed slowly stood up, thinking fast. Squadron leader or not, the man was out of order. Steed made up his mind and stood to attention.

'With the greatest respect sir, a damaged bomber can be repaired. The crew of a damaged bomber can return the next day and kill more of our troops. The bomber that I attacked today is beyond all repair. The crew of that bomber will not return tomorrow because they are dead. Together with my colleagues in Green Section, I engaged a superior force of enemy fighters and kept them from attacking the rest of the squadron. I obviously misunderstood your orders, but I am not a coward sir and I resent that accusation, if that is what you meant.'

Steed stood rigidly to attention, staring straight ahead, awaiting the coming onslaught. Tomlinson was of the old school; squadron leaders were one rung down from God and NCOs were to be seen and not heard.

'You insubordinate wretch! You dare to question my judgement? You are very lucky that we are short of pilots in this critical time for our men in France, otherwise I would ground you right now and have you kicked out of the squadron. Do I make myself clear?'

'Yes sir.'

'You will continue to fly with us for the time being Steed, but you will no longer be a weaver. Instead you will fly in a section and woe betides you if you do not follow your section leader instead of gallivanting around on your own. And you will obey my orders to the letter. Do you understand?'

'Yes sir.'

Tomlinson turned away to speak to Dix. Steed could feel his own face burning like fire, and he was shaking slightly from a mixture of anger and embarrassment. Should he have said what he did? Well it was done now. He would have to leave the squadron; there must not be any bad feeling amongst the pilots. He sat down slowly, lost in his own thoughts. Conversation in the crew room was muted and there was a sense of embarrassment amongst the pilots. Nobody spoke to Steed, and some of the pilots left the room.

Steed was shaken out of his reflections by Dix. 'A word with you outside please Sergeant Steed.' Once outside, Dix said, 'Shall we walk?' And as they walked he said, 'What are your thoughts about what went on back there?'

Steed thought for a moment and then said quietly, 'Well I meant what I said. It may have been better if I hadn't said it, but it's done now and it cannot be undone. I certainly didn't intend to be insubordinate. But I am not a coward. I attacked that lone Heinkel because I thought that it was the right thing to do, to shoot it down I mean, not because I was frightened of attacking a formation of the buggers.'

Dix nodded and said quietly, 'I know that Sergeant Steed.'

Steed continued, 'The Boss ordered Flight Lieutenant Chamberlain's section to attack a lone damaged Ju-88 yesterday, after it had ditched its bombs. I don't see much difference between that and my Heinkel. It has left a bitter taste in my mouth, and it saddens me that the squadron leader has obviously lost confidence in me and that he wants me kicked out of the squadron. You could have cut the atmosphere in the crew room with a knife after he bollocked me. God knows what the other pilots think of me now. I guess that I will be moved on after this Dunkirk thing is over. Until then I will do my best to follow the squadron leader's orders. I have been trying to do that since I arrived anyway.'

'Hmm, I think that you are overreacting a bit,' said Dix. 'The Boss is under a lot of pressure at the moment, and he isn't used to sergeants saying anything but yes sir and no sir to him. I think that he probably regrets his outburst, but it is difficult for someone in his position to retract. He would say it is bad for discipline. My advice is to keep your head down for a few days, and all of this will blow over.'

'I'll do my best. Do you know what section I will fly in tomorrow?'

Well, Billy Bishop hurt his wrist in his crash landing this morning and the Doc has put him off flying for tomorrow at least. If Teddy Edwards doesn't turn up, that means we have only eleven pilots. The Boss has decreed that we will have three vics and two weavers. You will probably fly in Blue section tomorrow with Pip Courtauld and me.'

That evening in the mess, when Adams and Walker made a joke of Tomlinson's outburst, Steed simply shrugged and said, 'Dix had a word with me afterwards. He told me to keep my head down and it would probably all blow over.'

Take-off on the 28th May was at 9.00 a.m. Tomlinson had decided to create two new weavers, Pilot Officer Stephen Cavendish and Pilot Officer James Hunniford, and to return Adams and Steed to the vics. The weather was overcast, with low cloud obscuring Dunkirk, although there was no mistaking the tower of oily residue marking its position. Tomlinson orbited above the tormented town at 6,000 feet, but couldn't find any targets. The two weavers took up station well behind the squadron, and slightly higher.

Nobody saw the two Messerschmitt 109s that crept up behind the weavers, taking advantage of cloud cover. Nobody saw the Me-109 that killed Hunniford with its first burst from point blank range, not even the other weaver Cavendish who happened to be looking the other way at the time. But a few seconds later everybody heard Cavendish's scream as a cannon shell from the second Me-109 exploded in the footwell of his Hurricane, neatly severing his left foot. Seconds later his Hurricane was going down with the port fuel tank on fire. The fire quickly spread along the wing and up into poor Cavendish's cockpit, burning him alive. The remaining nine Hurricane pilots heard him screaming in pain and terror until, mercifully, his aeroplane exploded half way on its journey to the Earth below. Of the assassins, the two Messerschmitt 109s, there was no sign.

Tomlinson radioed his pilots, 'Leader to Tomcats, if we can't see anything to bomb, neither can the Germans. The Huns will be below this muck. We are going down. Tight formation through the cloud please.'

Tomlinson headed out over the sea as the safest place to let down in cloud. Normally that would have been the case, but not today, off Dunkirk, with a harassed Royal Navy below. As the squadron broke cloud cover, a Destroyer sent up a stream of anti-aircraft fire. The sailors firmly believed that every aeroplane in the sky was German, and with good reason; they had been suffering heavy air bombardment for days and, from their vantage point, they had seen very little of the RAF.

'Jesus!' exclaimed somebody. 'Who taught these matelots aircraft recognition?'

There were soldiers on the beaches and in the dunes behind the beaches. As the Hurricanes flew above them, most of the soldiers dived for cover, although a few men recognised the friendly aircraft and waved. A twin-engine bomber suddenly appeared beyond the dunes, difficult to see amongst the smoke and dust, and then promptly disappeared into a patch of low cloud. As the bomber emerged from the cloud, Tomlinson swung the Tomcats into the attack. 'Ju-88, eleven o'clock, Tallyho.'

Steed looked at the enemy aircraft looming ahead and then did a second take. 'Tomcat leader don't shoot! It's a Blenheim.'

Tomlinson, in the lead Hurricane, was on the point of blowing the RAF light bomber out of the sky when Steed's hurried call stopped him. He saw the RAF roundel on the side and recognised the Blenheim's silhouette. 'Who said that?' he snapped.

'Blue-3, leader, it was definitely a Blenheim.'

'Well spotted Sergeant Steed,' replied Tomlinson after a pause. 'Although what the hell it was doing over the beach God alone knows.'

Tomlinson led the nine Hurricanes inland, a little to the west of Dunkirk. His idea was to catch any incoming bomber squadrons before they reached the town or the beaches. He was in luck. Away to the right he spotted three low-flying bombers. 'Leader to Tomcat Squadron, three Dorniers at three o'clock. Tallyho!'

The Hurricanes turned to attack the Dornier-17s from behind. The two weavers had already met their demise, and none of the remaining pilots spotted the two Me-109s popping in and out of the clouds above and behind the Dorniers, waiting for an opportunity to pounce on the unwary.

The Me-109s swooped down behind the Hurricanes, but at the last moment Chamberlain saw them coming and shouted a warning. Steed's eyes were on Dix. He was going to follow his leader come hell or high water. Dix broke hard to the right and Steed followed. He was aware of Courtauld on his right as his leader now climbed. Steed risked a quick look over each shoulder as he followed his leader, but he couldn't see any Messerschmitts lurking behind.

Steed could now make out Dix's target, a 109 heading for cloud cover. It was well out of range when Dix gave it a vain burst from his eight machine-guns. Dix followed the Me-109, into the cloud, a dangerous exercise Steed thought. Steed kept close to his leader as they ploughed upwards through the cloud, breaking out into bright sunshine above. Courtauld had disappeared, but miraculously there were two Me-109s in line astern formation directly in front of the two Hurricanes.

Without Courtauld in attendance, Steed adopted the position of the number two in a German *rotte*, much as had done with Daily, was it only yesterday? He was now behind Dix and to the right, but he climbed slightly higher in order to get a clear view of the sun, from where death might strike. His job was to guard his leader against attack from behind, while Dix concentrated on the enemy in front. As Dix approached the two German fighters from behind, the leader broke left while his wingman went right. Dix selected the German leader for attention.

As Dix and Steed closed in on the enemy leader, his number two reappeared some distance behind them. Well worked, the crafty buggers, thought Steed.

'Blue leader, 109 behind, but out of range.'

The lead Me-109 went into a sharp right hand turn, followed by Dix. Steed broke hard left. Following Dix would be suicide; the leader would get him for sure. Steed saw the German number two go past, aiming for Dix. Steed continued his turn to position himself on the Messerschmitt's tail. Just in time the Me-109 pilot realised his peril and put his nose down into a steep dive. Steed instinctively did the same. His Merlin engine coughed as the carburettor float was pushed upwards by the G-force and starved the Merlin of fuel; the Me-109, with its fuel injected

Daimler Benz engine had no such problems and rocketed down towards the protective clouds.

Steed did not follow, but pulled up to look for Dix. His leader was circling the first Me-109 and was just about in a shooting position. As Steed approached the duelling pair, he saw Dix fire a long burst. Although the tracers streaked behind the German fighter, the pilot panicked and applied opposite rudder. That was his downfall because it made him a perfect target. Dix did not miss a second time. Another long burst and the Me-109 climbed, stalled and span towards the clouds below, with Dix still shooting at it. It entered the clouds still spinning. Dix followed it into the clouds still firing, but reappeared almost immediately.

Steed took station behind his flight commander. Dix circled, calling the squadron on the radio, but his only reply was static. After a few minutes Dix said cheerily, 'Home for lunch Blue-3. I am out of ammunition anyway.'

The two Hurricanes set course for home. A few minutes later, through a break in the clouds, they spotted a lone Hurricane travelling slowly just above the sea. Dix and Steed dropped down and recognised the squadron leader's aircraft. Dix transmitted, 'Tomcat leader, Blue-1 and Blue-3 joining you.'

Tomlinson replied in a weak voice, 'Glad to see you Hugh. Afraid that I am a bit shot-up.' On closer inspection, Steed could see that Tomlinson's Hurricane had several holes in the fuselage.

'Are you hurt leader?' asked Dix with concern.

'Bloody right hand – been shot in the right hand,' responded Tomlinson. The squadron leader sounded feeble and in great pain. Dix, by now, was on the left hand side of Tomlinson's Hurricane and Steed was on the right. Tomlinson looked at each of them in turn and smiled thinly, 'I would be obliged if you would lead the way home Hugh, I'm not too sure where I am at the moment.'

Dix replied cheerily, 'Be glad to Tomcat leader,' and then added, 'Blue-3, take up station as a weaver behind.

Steed was already looking over his shoulder and he didn't like what he saw. 'Blue leader, there are four bogeys behind and slightly below us, Me-109s I think.'

'Shit!' exclaimed Dix. 'Blue-3, remain with the squadron leader. Get him home.'

'Blue leader,' pleaded Steed, 'you are out of ammunition. It has to be me.'

There was a moment's pause before Dix spoke again. 'Very well Sergeant Steed. Try to keep them busy for a minute or so, and then break for the clouds. Good luck.'

Steed opened the throttle and climbed steeply above Tomlinson and Dix before wheeling the Hurricane around to face the oncoming *schwarm* of 109s. The tactic worked. Their leader was reluctant to attack Tomlinson and Dix with the probability that Steed would be on his tail. The four Me-109s climbed and then split into two pairs. The leader's *rotte* dived towards Tomlinson and Dix, the other *rotte* came at Steed. Steed did not hesitate; he dived to cut off the leader and his wingman, allowing the other two Me-109s to come around onto his tail.

'The next bit is all about timing,' Steed said quietly to himself. He selected emergency boost and prepared for a deflection shot on the German leader. The leader saw him coming and turned towards him. Good, the Me-109s had been distracted from their prey and now all four were after him, two in front and two on his tail. He corkscrew dived below the two oncoming Me-109s, who both had a fleeting shot at him, and then climbed steeply in a tight left hand turn; as he did so tracer from the fighter on his tail flashed past on his right. The German number four suddenly appeared in front of him, time enough just for a quick deflection shot.

The Messerschmitts were getting in each other's way. The Me-109 was easily superior to a Hurricane at high level, but close to the sea the difference in performance was marginal and here the Hurricane was a far better dogfighter. In Steed, the Germans had met a natural pilot who could wring the maximum out of his aeroplane.

At first, the German pilots thought that they had a guaranteed victory, and their main concern was to prevent the lone Hurricane from climbing towards the safety of the clouds and eluding them. In pursuing this tactic they allowed Dix and Tomlinson to escape. In fairness, the Germans had not realised that one of the Hurricanes was damaged with a wounded pilot and that the other was out of ammunition; if they had, then the outcome may well have been very different.

After a minute, a very long minute for Steed, of twists and turns and brief bursts of fire from all of the combatants, Steed pulled off his masterstroke. He corkscrew dived for the sea, knowing that the Me-109 on his tail would follow. At the last moment he pulled out of the dive, just above the waves, and then turned hard to his right. The Me-109 pilot on his tail sensed victory. The corkscrew made the Hurricane a difficult target, but the Englishman had nowhere to go. The German pilot prepared to give the coup de grace. With his mind focused on the target in front of him, he realised just in time the closeness of the Channel. He heaved back on the stick, and by the slimmest of margins pulled out of the dive in time, his slipstream causing spray on the water surface. Steed looked back, disappointed that his trick had not worked. The German airman was badly shaken.

Steed, now down to within a few feet of the sea, continued with his ploy of tight turns, playing to the advantage of his Hurricane. It was easy to lose height in a tight turn, and to do so a few feet above the sea would be fatal. The Me-109 pilots were not so accomplished at this game and suddenly Steed found himself behind and beneath one of the Me-109s with a perfect opportunity to cause serious damage. Fortunately for the pilot, Steed only had time for a very brief burst before being forced to turn sharply away by another Messerschmitt on his tail. Even so, that brief burst had been enough to wound the German pilot in the leg. The unfortunate man, or rather unfortunate boy because he was only nineteen, radioed his comrades that he had to make for home. One of the other Me-109s broke off to escort him.

That left only two Messerschmitts for Steed to deal with. Things were much easier now, and Steed began to believe that he was not destined for a cold and watery grave, at least not this time. As long as he didn't make a mistake he would be all right; he might even bag a 109. He had plenty of fuel, but he needed to conserve his ammunition; he must only shoot when he was sure of hitting something, no longer simply to put off the opposition.

But the Me-109s were running low on fuel, and they didn't like the way this Englishman flew so low and turned so tightly. They couldn't use the climb and dive policy that had served them so well on their previous encounters with Hurricanes or they would plough straight into the sea. Down here this particular Englishman, in this particular aeroplane, held the initiative. It was time to make an exit, but pride made them stay to fight it out.

The end came during one of the tight turns. The leader's wingman had seen Steed coming up behind him; the wingman was in no real danger, his leader was about to force Steed to break away. But the wingman turned too tightly and stalled; the 109's wingtip hit the water first, followed by the rest of the fighter, cartwheeling in a shower of spray. The remaining Me-109, the pilot still shaken from the narrowness of his escape following

Steed's earlier corkscrew dive towards the sea, decided to call it a day and powered away in a steep climb for the clouds. Steed circled the flotsam from the crashed 109 as it slipped into the depths, and for the first time noticed a Royal Navy Minesweeper making for the wreckage. Steed was certain that the German pilot could not have survived such an impact, but at least the little ship was going to have a look. Steed set course for Colne Martin, extremely relieved.

Steed landed to learn that six aircraft from the squadron, including Pip Courtauld, had eventually reformed after the attack by the Me-109s. In the absence of their squadron leader, Chamberlain had led the six circling above the clouds, dust and smoke covering Dunkirk for twenty minutes or so without catching further sight of the enemy, and then turned for home low on fuel. Tomlinson and Dix had landed safely at Marston, but Tomlinson, barely conscious, had lost a lot of blood from his mauled right hand and was in hospital.

Once again there were a few holes in Steed's Hurricane, but the damage was superficial and the plane was ready for take-off at 5.00 pm for the second patrol of the day. Chamberlain called the pilots together for a briefing shortly before take-off. Chamberlain, looking serious, stood together with Dix and addressed the pilots.

'We were caught napping this morning. It shouldn't have happened. Our two weavers were too far back and the Huns picked them off. The Boss is in hospital and I'm afraid that they have amputated his hand; it was virtually hanging off when he landed apparently. It must have taken a superhuman effort for the squadron leader to get back at all in that condition; he must have been in great pain. He was lucky that Flight Lieutenant Dix and Sergeant Steed happened along.'

Chamberlain's face betrayed a thin smile as he looked across the crew room to where Steed was sitting. 'You're making a habit of riding to the rescue and jousting the 109s aren't you Harry?' A couple of the other pilots looked quizzically at Steed, who blushed. This was the first time that either of the flight lieutenants had used his Christian name.

Chamberlain continued, 'He hasn't told you the whole story about this morning's adventures. The Boss was in a bad way, almost delirious through loss of blood and his kite was shot up. He needed somebody to guide him back across the Channel or he was finished. Who do you think then spotted four 109s sneaking up on them? The same body who always seems to spot the buggers, Hawkeye Steed!' Everybody was now looking at Steed.

Flight Lieutenant Dix ordered Sergeant Steed to escort the Boss home. But Hawkeye here, knowing that Mr Dix was out of ammo, volunteered to keep the bad guys busy while Mr Dix got the Boss home. Not only did he drive off all four of the bastards, but he also downed one of the blighters in the process.' Steed's cheeks were by now deep crimson. The crew room erupted in a crescendo of cheering whistling and stamping of feet.

Chamberlain continued, his face once again serious. 'Okay, settle down. The Boss isn't going to be back with us for some time. Group will no doubt find us a replacement in the next day or so but in the meantime, as the senor flight commander, it falls to me to run the squadron, with Flight Lieutenant Dix's help and support of course. As you all know, 126-Squadron is well under strength. We had not worked up to our full quota of pilots when this Dunkirk thing started, and we have taken losses since then. I doubt that we will be able to get up to full strength in the near future, so each one of us is likely to be flying around the clock until the evacuation is completed. Our troops are counting on us. The country is counting on us. We will be dog-tired but we must not, we will not, let them down. The re-arranged sections are on the notice board. You have all seen them. Billy wanted to join us this afternoon since we are short-handed,' Chamberlain gestured towards Billy Bishop, 'but I have said no. Maybe tomorrow if the M/O gives the okay. We have only eight pilots available, so we will fly two sections and two weavers. I will lead Red Section, with Roger Daily and Sergeant Adams. Flight Lieutenant Dix will lead Blue Section with Pip Courtauld and Ian Graham, and finally the Green Section weavers are Sergeants Adams and Steed.'

In view of his earlier reprimand by Tomlinson, Steed was very surprised to be reinstated as a weaver. Chamberlain obviously had his own way of doing things.

The weather that greeted the eight Hurricanes over Dunkirk that evening was much worse than it had been in the morning. But the weather was a godsend for the troops and naval craft of all kinds that lay off the beaches, for low cloud and rain made life difficult for the dive-bombers. Steed and Toby Adams, weaving at the back of Chamberlain's squadron, imagined that they saw 109s lurking in every cloud, hiding in the dust and gloom, awaiting their chance to pounce. But the squadron saw neither friend nor foe during their sojourn over France, and they returned to England with the masking tape still over their gun ports.

Chamberlain reported in his morning briefing of the 29th May that Group had promised replacement pilots within the next couple of days, but there was no word yet on a replacement C/O; the pilots hoped that Chamberlain would get the job. Billy Bishop insisted that his wrist was much better and was passed fit to fly. He rejoined Steed and Adams to lead the Green Section of weavers, but otherwise the formation remained the same as the previous afternoon.

Group had allowed 126-Squadron a little respite because of their recent casualties and the loss of their C/O, and they were scheduled for only one stint over the beaches that day, with take-off at 13.45. The morning had been overcast with low cloud and pouring rain, but by the time 126-Squadron arrived over Dunkirk the weather was clearing. Looking down through breaks in the cloud, Steed saw ships lying off the beaches. Further towards Dunkirk town he could see the mole, stretching out like a bony finger into the sea, with a ship of some sort at its end. But these were only fleeting glimpses, his job was to keep a sharp lookout and prevent the bounce.

Chamberlain's voice rang out over the airwaves, 'Tomcat Squadron Tallyho, Stukas at eleven o'clock.' Chamberlain turned towards the enemy dive-bombers and began to climb. Steed looked briefly in front and slightly above to where some of the Stukas were circling while others were straightening into level flight for their bombing run, and then peeling off towards their targets below. Steed knew enough by now about the Luftwaffe's way of doing things to expect a fighter escort somewhere up above, perhaps in the sun. He could not see anything there or to the left, he checked behind, still nothing. Were the Tomcats to get a clear run at the Stukas?

It was Toby Adams who saw them first, 'Green-2 to Tomcat Leader. Bandits at three o'clock high, coming down.'

Chamberlain responded immediately, 'I see them Green-2. Blue and Green Sections, engage the fighters. Red Section, follow me into the Stukas. Good luck everybody.'

Dix's voice cut in, 'Blue and Green Sections, prepare to break left into them.' A pause and then, 'Break left GO.'

Steed followed Billy Bishop into the turn and towards the 109s. Another hard turn and Bishop was on the tail of a Me-109, but the German's wingman was coming up behind Steed.

'Green leader, 109 behind us, I'm taking him on!' Steed hauled his aircraft into a tight turn in an attempt to get on to the Me-109's tail, but the German pilot countered by turning in behind the Hurricane. Steed had a glimpse of Billy Bishop's fighter still behind the first Me-109.

'Green leader, your tail is clear now Billy.' Steed hoped that his message had got through because the airwaves were now full of shouts, oaths and warnings. I wish radio discipline was better, reflected Steed as the blood drained from his head through the G-force in the tight turn.

As Steed expected, his Hurricane was turning inside the Me-109 and soon he would be able to fire his guns for the first time that day. But the Me-109 sensed the danger and, again as Steed expected, the German pushed his nose down into a dive. Steed followed, but this time he rolled the Hurricane inverted before pulling the stick back into his stomach to pursue the 109 down. The manoeuvre at least prevented fuel starvation in the Merlin engine, caused by the negative G-force, but the Me-109 nevertheless had a good start and he was out of firing range. The German fighter pulled away into the safety of a cloud below and Steed gave up the chase, breaking sharply in case one of the pilot's friends was on his tail.

Initially the sky in the immediate vicinity appeared empty, but then Steed saw a Stuka in its dive towards the shipping below. He pushed forward the throttle and set of in pursuit. Very quickly he realised his mistake. The Stuka had dive brakes and could hold a steady speed in a dive. Steed did not have that luxury and he overshot his target without having the chance to fire, although he sensed that the Stuka's rear gunner did not miss the opportunity for a quick burst. Steed pulled back hard on the stick but, with the sea coming up fast, he only just managed to pull out of the dive in time. That was absolutely stupid, he thought to himself. You only just about got away with that Harry, my old son.

He turned above the shipping and was about to climb back to the fight above when he spotted a Stuka, probably not the one that he had stupidly tried to match in a dive but a Stuka nevertheless. The dive-bomber was just releasing its bombs in the direction of a stationary paddle steamer below. The Stuka was a perfect target, Steed couldn't miss and he didn't. Steed opened fire from behind and underneath the gull-winged brute. The effect was impressive and instantaneous; the Stuka fell apart in front of his eyes.

Steed began to wonder if he might find better opportunities down here immediately above the beaches, rather than above the clouds and inland. The aim of breaking up the bomber formations before they could reach Dunkirk was laudable, but Stukas seemed very vulnerable once they had pulled out of their dive, and the escorting Me-109 fighters lost many of their advantages over the Hurricanes at this low-level.

He was shaken from his ponderings by an almighty bang and the Hurricane being thrown upwards. His immediate thought was that an enemy fighter was attacking him, and he threw the Hurricane into a tight diving turn, but he then realised that the fire was coming from a Royal Navy destroyer below. The Hurricane was hit again and the engine stopped. The destroyer ceased firing, the gunners at last realising their mistake. The cockpit filled with smoke and dust, and there was a strong smell of cordite.

Steed was far too low to bail out, his only chance was to ditch in the sea. The paddle steamer, which mercifully had not been hit by the Stukas bombs, was close by on his left. He turned his ill-fated, gliding Hurricane towards the elderly pleasure boat and into the wind, just a few feet above the waves and close to stalling speed. He transmitted, 'Green-3 ditching near beach, Green-3 ditching near beach.' And then he hit the water.

Steed was thrown forwards, despite the straps, and hit his head on the reflector gun-sight. He pulled back the canopy, which fortunately didn't stick, undid the straps, oxygen mask and other paraphernalia and hauled himself out of the cockpit. He jumped onto the wing, but the wing was already sliding beneath the waves, so he simply settled gently into the water, supported by his May West life jacket. The nose of the Hurricane slid beneath the surface and the tail rose above his head, but fortunately followed the rest of his doomed fighter to Davy Jones' locker without hitting him.

'Hell's bells!' Steed said under his breath. 'Shot down by the bloody navy!' He looked around. The paddle steamer was motionless in the water about 300 yards away, and so he decided to swim towards it. He soon found that swimming on his back was a darn sight easier than on his front when supported by the Mae West life jacket. As he swam he saw a fast motor launch approaching. It was a Royal Navy motor torpedo boat, and it was crammed to the gunwales with soldiers. 'I'm a RAF pilot,' he yelled as the MTB slowed and stopped alongside him.

'Climb aboard at the stern, through the torpedo hatch mate,' a rating shouted. Helping hands dragged Steed out of the water and dumped him unceremoniously in the boat. The soldiers made room as he sat up. The boat started moving once again towards the paddle steamer.

'We saw you blow that Stuka out of the sky.' A naval sub-lieutenant had appeared from nowhere. 'Did he get you with his return fire?'

'No,' said Steed. 'That destroyer over there got me with his anti-aircraft fire, but it was my fault for getting too close to him. I'm very grateful that you stopped to pick me up. I can see how busy you are.' And Steed looked around at the exhausted troops.

'Oh I see,' said the sub. 'But, you know, we haven't seen too much of the RAF fighters around here, and we have seen rather too much of the Luftwaffe. The gunners tend to assume that anything flying too close is the enemy.'

'You are quite right,' replied Steed ruefully. 'It was my own stupid fault. I was looking for another target and just got too close to the destroyer. By the way, there are plenty of RAF fighters upstairs, above the clouds and inland. Our job is to break up the enemy bomber formations before they reach the beaches. We've shot quite few down before they could get here, but there are an awful lot of the blighters up there, and Hun fighters always escort them.' The sub did not seem convinced. 'We have taken casualties too,' Steed added evenly.

The MTB by this time was drawing alongside the paddle steamer. As it approached, Steed could see a small fishing boat pulling away, heading back to the beach to pick up more soldiers. There was a door leading into the steamer's hull positioned just above a running board. The exhausted soldiers were helped onto this narrow walkway and then through the hatch. Steed was recognised as a pilot. 'Are you the chap who got that Stuka?' a seaman queried.

'That's right,' replied Steed.

'The captain would like a word with you on the bridge. If you would follow me please.'

The captain shook Steed's hand warmly. After the introductions he said, 'We saw what happened. You blew that Stuka apart, absolutely beautiful that, and then HMS Fullsome got you. Great pity, but that's one of the reasons I've asked you up here.' He pointed to a group of soldiers by the handrail with two Bren-guns. 'These boys are our anti-aircraft defence. We fire at anything that comes within range, but we are not too good at aircraft recognition. Most of the stuff around here is Jerry, but now and again we do see RAF roundels. Can you help us to identify who's on our side?'

'Of course sir,' said Steed. 'I would be glad to. By the way, is there any chance that you can radio your people back home and ask them to tell the RAF that I am on my way back? Just tell them Sergeant Steed, 126-Squadron.'

'I'll ask the radio operator to send it. You have a nasty cut on your forehead. The Medical Orderlies are busy at the moment, but when one becomes free I'll send him over.'

'It's not important,' said Steed. 'I caught it on the gun sight when I ditched. The wounded soldiers need the MO's help much more than I do.'

'I'll try to find a blanket or something for you, but most of the soldiers are wet though as well, so blankets are in short supply. Keep your life jacket on – you never know when you may need it!'

'I'll survive sir, and thank you.' Steed went over to the group of soldiers, headed by a corporal. 'Hi guys,' he began, 'I'm the pilot of the shot down Hurricane that the Navy has just fished out of the drink. The captain asked me to help out with aircraft recognition.'

'Glad to have you help us sir,' said the corporal. 'We have the two Brens, and the boys also take pot shots with their rifles. The Stukas are the real bastards. They always seem to come down on the seaward side of the ships with that bloody screaming noise of theirs. We have a go at them when they pull out of their dive, although they are still pretty high. That's why we have set up the Brens here. Their rear gunners fire back.'

Steed considered the corporal's reply. 'Looks like they are bombing into the wind. Have you had many attacks from them?'

'Only two Stukas have had a go at this old tub so far sir, one of which you shot down. Both of them missed, but bomb splinters from the first one killed a few people back there at the blunt end. But we've seen the Stukas hit other ships around here, and those bastards gave us a rough time in Belgium. The Germans also machine-gun and bomb with all sorts of other planes, mostly twin-engine stuff.'

'I see,' said Steed thoughtfully. 'By the way, don't call me sir, I'm only a sergeant.' Steed looked across the water. In the distance, two aircraft were attacking a destroyer. 'Those two over there are Junkers Ju-88s,' he said to the soldiers. As he spoke two waterspouts grew towards the stern of the ship, which was turning sharply in an effort to spoil the bombers' aim. An orange flash and smoke appeared on the stern. 'Poor sods,' said one of the soldiers.

Steed turned to the corporal, 'Where have you blokes been fighting?'

'Well Sarge, we started off in France, but not very much happened for months. When the German's invaded Belgium, we moved up to meet them. We were holding them when we received the order to pull back. We have been pulling back ever since, until we arrived here. We lost our officer and some of our soldiers during a run-in with the Jerries on the way.' Steed noted the determination on the man's face as he added firmly, 'We saved the Brens and some ammo though. It's the same ammo that we use for the rifles, which makes things easy, but each magazine only holds thirty rounds so we can only fire short bursts. We had a whip round among the boys on board for some extra bullets, but we're running low now.'

Steed was fairly sure that Stukas had armour plating underneath as protection against small arms ground fire. Armour piercing ammo would be better he thought, but the soldiers had what they had, and nobody could do anything about it now. 'How long were you on the beach?'

'We arrived the night before last. We tried the jetty in Dunkirk town, the mole they call it, yesterday, and again last night. The ships can load troops from the end, but there were long queues. This morning we thought that we would give the beach a go. We pushed some abandoned vehicles into the water to make a kind of jetty, because the small boats can't come right in or they get stuck on the sand.' He gestured to the paddle steamer, 'This thing arrived about eleven o'clock, and a fishing boat picked us up from our makeshift jetty and brought us out here. All sorts of little boats have been ferrying people out here all afternoon. I don't think that she can take many more, she looks overloaded to me now, I hope the Captain gets going soon.'

Steed couldn't help but agree. Men were packed onto the decks. Heaven alone knows how crowded it must be below. What chance would those trapped below have if the old paddle steamer were to be struck by a bomb and went down?

Steed had been studying the sky through habit. Two twin-engine aircraft appeared in line-astern formation some way behind the ship. Steed pointed at them and said to the soldiers, 'Me-110s, German heavy fighters.' The fighters were following the beach line, staffing the soldiers and small boats in the surf. Suddenly they veered towards the paddle steamer. The soldiers hoisted the two Bren guns.

The two Me-110s thundered past overhead, their murderous cannon fire raking the old paddle steamer's wooden deck and mowing down the soldiers like skittles. The two Brens each delivered their 30 round burst of fire in the general direction of the attackers, and some of the soldiers fired their rifles, but Steed doubted that any of it had been effective and the 110s appeared undamaged. Steed thought that the two enemy aircraft would turn back for a second pass, but they continued on towards the damaged destroyer some distance away.

Another two-engine aircraft appeared and the soldiers rammed a second magazine into each of their Bren guns and lined up on the intruder. 'Don't shoot!' yelled Steed. 'It's RAF, an Avro Anson.' The Anson lumbered past them at low altitude, now clearly displaying its RAF markings, heading for the now departed Me-110s. Steed glimpsed a machine-gun protruding from the side and was filled with admiration for the brave crew. 'That's a Costal Command Anson, nice aeroplane as a transport or maritime recognisance, but not designed to take on German fighters.'

'At least he's here,' murmured one of the soldiers, and Steed couldn't help but agree.

The Captain had seen enough. With his decks covered with the wounded, dead and dying, and awash with their blood, he ordered his ship to get underway. The large paddle wheels started slowly to rotate and the brave little Thames pleasure steamer turned for home. Steed looked back at the beaches; there were still so many men to bring away. The whole beach was littered with wreckage from a shattered army. Most of the soldiers on board had brought their rifles with them, but the heavy equipment, the guns and transport; these things would not be coming home. As they chugged along the narrow channel, about a mile or so out from the beach, another raid was building. The Anson came back, circling the paddle steamer protectively.

Abruptly, a Stuka appeared streaking down towards the steamer. The soldiers with the Bren guns didn't need any advice from Steed on aircraft recognition. They raised their weapons. The Anson did just enough; he closed on the Stuka just before the German released his bomb load. The machine-guns twinkled from the side of the Coastal Command reconnaissance aircraft and the Stuka was sufficiently distracted. His bombs missed. As the Stuka pulled up from its dive, Steed was certain that he saw smoke coming from its engine. The Anson chased after it.

Elsewhere, the raid simply added to the general carnage and Steed saw one of the smaller Royal Navy ships bracketed by bombs. Where were the Spitfires and Hurricanes? They should be down here. No wonder that the brown jobs were annoyed. Above the clouds he could hear the unmistakeable sound of a Merlin engine and the rattle of machine-gun fire, but neither he nor the long-suffering soldiers saw the RAF fighter.

The hours passed as they headed out to sea. In front of them was the destroyer, damaged earlier by the Ju-88's bomb. It was soon apparent to Steed that many of the soldiers bore ill will towards the RAF, who they believed had let them down. Steed could hardly blame them. They did not know that RAF pilots were fighting and dying inland and above the clouds, trying to break up the bomber formations. He tried to explain a few times, but the soldiers were convinced that the RAF had deserted them, and they were too tired to understand his explanation.

Steed was cold, outside in the open, his sheepskin flying jacket was sodden. The rest of his clothes were not much drier, and his head throbbed from its earlier contact with the Hurricane's gun-sight; one of the medical orderlies had bandaged it for him an hour ago. The soldiers were quiet; virtually all of them were asleep. It was becoming darker and getting foggy. Steed still could not see land. The sea was empty, save for the paddle steamer and its wounded destroyer escort up ahead. Surely the journey from Dunkirk to Ramsgate, for that was where they were going he had been told, should not take this long. He didn't like to bother anyone, but as one of the seamen stopped nearby to peer over the side, he asked the question.

'Ah well mate, we couldn't go straight across the Channel because of the sandbanks see, both on the Frog side and the Goodwin Sands off our coast. The best thing for us would have been to go down the Frog coast towards Calais and then cross straight over to Dover, but the Jerries have taken Gravelines and have installed some bloody great big guns there. We would be blown out of the bloody water. So we have to go the long way around.' The seaman warmed to his explanation, 'But we're nearly home now. Can you see that light over there? That's the North Goodwin Lightship. Given our slow speed, the best thing for us is to go around that and then drop down into Ramsgate. Not long now, as long as we don't run into a mine that is,' he added darkly. The seaman moved on.

As they rounded the Lightship, Steed saw the most amazing sight. Lights dimmed, and following an old destroyer, some twenty or so small craft were heading out to sea. The seaman had reappeared at his shoulder. 'Going over to Dunkirk to collect their Tommies,' he said quietly. 'They have been assembling at all the ports along the coast. Let's hope the fog holds for them. That's the only thing that will keep the Luftwaffe off their backs.'

The aging paddle steamer pulled into Ramsgate harbour at dusk. The small pleasure boat had spent her mediocre working life ferrying day-trippers from London to Southend-on-Sea, plying her trade across the Thames estuary to Margate, or working her way around the Essex coast to Clacton with her compliment of holidaymakers. Now, in the twilight of her years, she had found true glory. Machine-gun bullets and cannon shells scarred her decks, her hull was peppered with bomb splinters and blood everywhere testified to her suffering and that of her cargo of exhausted soldiers. Here in Ramsgate was sanctuary at last from German bombs and mines. But Steed knew that, after disembarking her soldiers, she would be going back to the beaches of Dunkirk. He wished her Godspeed.

Almost all of the soldiers had snatched some sleep during the crossing, many had slept for the whole voyage, but now they came to life as the paddle steamer drew alongside the quay. The medical teams were the first on board to attend to the badly wounded. The walking wounded and the other soldiers then started to disembark. Steed was impressed at their discipline. Nearly every soldier carried a rifle, even though their uniforms were mostly filthy and many were missing other parts of their kit. One group of Royal Engineers actually formed up and marched off as though on the parade ground. For the most part though, the soldiers were simply glad to be home in one piece.

Steed disembarked and looked for an RAF officer. The organisation at Ramsgate seemed first class. Steed gratefully accepted the tea and corned beef sandwiches on offer from the ladies of the WVS. The soldiers from the paddle steamer, together with more troops disembarked from all kinds of little ships in the harbour, naval and civilian, were being herded onto buses. Failing to find an RAF officer, Steed spoke to a naval sub-lieutenant. 'My name's Sergeant Steed. I am an RAF fighter pilot shot down over Dunkirk earlier today. I must get back to my squadron near Colchester as soon as possible. Is there any transport going in that direction?'

The naval officer looked tired, but he tried to be helpful. 'These soldiers are going by bus to a train siding outside Dover. From there they will take troop trains to various reception areas all over the country. It is imperative to get everybody away from the ports as quickly as possible, before still more people arrive from Dunkirk and, God forbid, before the Luftwaffe arrives. If you don't want to go down that route, you could try the railway station. You may be able to get a train to London. If you can't, come back here and you can join the army. You've been wounded I see, go over to the casualty clearing station first, they will dress your wound.'

Steed thanked the man. He didn't want to miss the London train, if indeed there was one. The bandage that the medical orderly on the paddle steamer had applied was still in good order, and so he set off for the railway station immediately. Steed was in luck. The last London train for the day was just about to leave. Steed did not have the money to purchase a ticket, so he simply boarded the train, found a quiet compartment, took off his damp flying jacket and tunic top, and closed his eyes.

Somebody shaking his shoulder awakened him. For just a moment he was in his Hurricane. He had ditched in the Channel and the Hurricane was sinking, but he could not open the canopy. His eyes focussed on the ticket inspector. 'Can I see your ticket please?' said the man.

The railwayman was eyeing Steed's dishevelled clothing in distaste. Steed was suddenly aware that he no longer looked much like an RAF pilot. He reached for his tunic above his head and showed the ticket inspector his Sergeant's stripes and wings. 'I am sorry. I don't have a ticket. I am an RAF pilot. I came down into the sea this morning. I must get to London tonight.'

The ticket inspector was not going to give up so easily, 'I am sorry Sergeant, but to travel on this train you must have a ticket. You will have to leave the train at the next station.'

Steed controlled his anger and said evenly, 'Well, I refuse to leave the train until we get to London. You are at liberty to call the police or the military police, if that is what you must do, when we get there. I couldn't buy a ticket at Ramsgate because I don't carry money when I fly. I must get back to my squadron as soon as possible.'

The ticket inspector thought for a moment, 'You were at Dunkirk Sergeant?' Steed nodded. 'And now you are trying to get back to your squadron?'

'That's right.'

'Well, you have our thanks and admiration. You are a brave man and I am sorry to have bothered you.' And with that the ticket inspector left the compartment.

Steed felt somewhat humbled, and for the first time became aware of the other two occupants of the compartment, a middle-aged man and woman. 'We have only just heard that soldiers are coming home from Dunkirk,' said the man. 'It was on the news this evening.' He pulled out a packet of cigarettes from his jacket pocket, 'Would you like a cigarette?'

'That's very kind of you, but I don't smoke.'

'Were you hurt when you came down?' asked the woman, looking at Steed's bandaged head.

'Not really,' said Steed. 'I banged my head on the side of the aeroplane when I ditched in the sea, but it's only a scratch.'

'Please don't be offended, but we would like to offer you some money to help you to get back to your squadron,' said the man. 'We heard you say that you don't carry money when you fly.' The man took five pounds from his wallet. The woman added, 'Our son has been called up. He is in the army, training. He's not in France, thank goodness.'

Steed was touched. 'That's very kind of you, but I'm okay, really I am. My mum and dad live in London, so I will stay overnight with them. Dad will pay for the taxi, so I don't need any money. But it's very kind of you. Thank you so much for offering.'

Steed telephoned the squadron, reverse charges, when he arrived at London Bridge station. He spoke to the adjutant and was pleased to learn that the squadron already knew that he had been picked up by the paddle steamer. The adjutant agreed that he should stay overnight with his parents and return to Colne Martin the next day. Steed found a taxi outside the station and gave the taxi driver his home address. The cabby looked carefully at him as he got in. 'Are you all right mate? You look as though you have been in the wars.'

'I'm fine. I've just had a very tiring day.'

Even late at night, London cabbies always want to talk. 'Heard the news about Dunkirk? Looks like they are bringing our boys home.'

'No,' said Steed truthfully, 'I haven't listened to the radio today, nor seen a paper. What are they saying?' The cabby was driving across London Bridge. It was strange, like most North Londoners, Steed always felt so much happier on the north bank of the river.

'Hitler has come straight across France like a dose of salts. So much for the Maginot Line! Belgium has surrendered and our boys fighting in Belgium have made a fighting retreat to Dunkirk. Now an evacuation's been ordered and the Navy are bringing them home. A right rum do if you ask me.'

The driver turned round for a quick look at Steed, who had his eyes closed in the back of the cab. Steed's Flying jacket was open and the driver caught a glimpse of the wings on his tunic. The cabby's brain whirred as he drove through the night. The dishevelled pilot's uniform and flying jacket, the bandage around the head, the train just in from the coast. 'Are you an RAF pilot mate?'

'Yes,' said Steed.

'And you've just arrived from Dunkirk, haven't you?'

'Yes,' said Steed again.

'Stone the flaming crows! I am sorry mate, I should have realised. I'll have you home in a jiffy. Just settle back and go to sleep if you like.'

When they arrived at his parent's house, Steed asked the taxi driver to wait while he asked his father for the fare. Steed was surprised and not a little humbled when the cabby said, 'Have this one on me mate, you deserve it and more,' and promptly drove off into the night.

Steed's father opened the door in his dressing gown. The old soldier immediately noted the bandaged head and dishevelled uniform. 'Harry! What's happened?'

'It's okay Dad. I had an argument with the Luftwaffe over Dunkirk and had to ditch in the sea. I came home in the Rochester Queen, you remember the paddle steamer that you and Mum used to take me on to Southend when I was a boy.'

'But you're hurt.'

'No Dad, it's just a scratch. I banged my head on the gun sight when I ditched in the sea. The medicos fixed me up.' Steed's mother appeared at the top of the stairs. 'Hello Mum, just dropped in for the night. I could murder a cuppa.'

Steed recounted the day's happenings to his parents. 'Don't say too much about all of this to anyone else, although I haven't said anything to you that the Germans don't know already. But please don't tell anyone that the Royal Navy shot me down, that wouldn't go down too well in certain quarters.'

'The perishers should polish up on aircraft recognition,' snorted his father.

'I don't really blame them Dad, the German dive bombers were giving them hell. The navy types were shooting at anything that they saw. I should have kept out of their way. Those boys are doing a fantastic job in getting our troops home.' Steed looked at his father. 'The army boys were all in, but virtually all of them still carried their rifles. It made you proud to see it.'

Steed's mother insisted that he should have a bath before bed. The old tin bath brought back memories of his childhood. In latter years, before joining the RAF, he had bathed at the local baths rather than in the traditional tin bath in front of the fire, but it was nice to wash away the smell of the Channel.

The next morning Steed was up bright and early, fully refreshed. His father had kept his Ariel Four in good running order, and she started easily. It was raining, so Steed put his wet weather clothing over warm civilian clothes, and stowed his damp uniform, flying jacket and boots in a suitcase strapped to the pannier. The motorcycle journey to Colne Martin was uneventful, though very wet, and he arrived shortly after ten in the morning.

Steed reported to Chamberlain, who was still acting squadron leader. After Steed had finished telling his story Chamberlain said, 'Well done Hawk, we are glad to have you back in one piece. It's diabolical that you should be shot down by the matelots. I'll report that up the chain, maybe they will think twice before assuming that every kite up there is German.'

So there it was. Steed had been saddled with his nickname, and the acting squadron leader was using it rather than the usual Sergeant Steed. Perhaps it signalled that he had been accepted into the fold. He was no longer the new boy.

Chamberlain continued, 'On the credit side, the squadron bagged two Stukas during your last trip, three with yours. Billy Bishop also bagged a 109. We were up again yesterday evening, and unfortunately we lost Billy. He was flying tail-end Charley over Dunkirk, alongside Sergeant Adams. One minute he was there, and the next he wasn't. Even Sergeant Adams didn't see what happened to him. Let's hope that he turns up on the next paddle steamer, just like you.'

Steed was becoming used to fellow pilots dying or going missing. It had been the same during training; flying was a dangerous business, even without the attentions of the Luftwaffe. Dougie Smith, Bunny Burroughs, Teddy Edwards, Stephen Cavendish, Jimmy Hunniford, all of these 126-Squadron pilots had gone down in recent days, but Billy Bishop was different. The others had been fellow pilots and colleagues, some of them even casual friends, but Steed had developed a special respect and liking for the amiable lad from East Anglia. Billy had a quiet, confident manner and was a good section leader as well as being a good pilot. Steed had felt completely at ease, both professionally and socially, with the fair-haired ex-Gladiator pilot; the difference between their ranks had made no difference to Billy.

It was strange how Billy Bishop had suddenly disappeared. The weavers were an asset to the squadron but, isolated at the back, these 'tail-end Charlies' as they were now known, had to keep their wits about them. Jimmy Hunniford and Stephen Cavendish had been dispatched by the bogeymen in much the same way when flying as a weavers only a couple of days ago; nobody had seen their assassins, but everybody had heard poor Stephen's screams over the radio as he burnt to death in the fireball that was once his Hurricane. And now Billy Bishop. Steed surmised that a pair of German fighters had been stalking the squadron and had crept up behind unseen and taken out poor Billy. He was absolutely right in his speculation!

Chamberlain continued speaking, shaking Steed out of his languor. 'The weather is foul here today, and much the same over Dunkirk we are told. We are on standby, but we are not going up in this,' he waved towards the rain outside the window. 'I am expecting three replacement pilots today, but until they turn up the squadron is down to seven pilots. I am not counting you Hawk, although we sure as hell need you, because I am ordering you to get a full check over from the Doc right away. You look dead beat.'

'I'm fine, really I am,' said Steed. 'I had a headache yesterday, but today it's just the cuts and bruising. I'll go to see the Doc straight away, but I'm sure he'll pass me fit. How's the aircraft situation? Do we have any spare Hurricanes?'

'We're not too badly off for kites. Have a word with the flight sergeant in charge of maintenance. I am sure that you will want to synchronise your guns at 250 yards.' Steed's jaw dropped. 'It's my job to know such things,' continued Chamberlain, now smiling. 'One or two pilots have moved away from the official Dowding spread. That's okay with me, as long as they are experienced and good shots, otherwise it's a bad move. In your case, you jumped the gun a bit, but I think that you have now proved that it suits your style.'

'Thank you sir,' stammered Steed. 'I didn't want to upset the apple cart by asking Squadron Leader Tomlinson officially if I could move away from the Dowding spread, but I thought that I would probably get better results if I synchronised at 250, so I decided to quietly give it a try.'

'Hmm,' contemplated Chamberlain. 'And what made you think that, get better results I mean?'

'Well sir, my air shooting results in training were good, and I saw what Mr Dix did to the target drogue when he took me up for some air to air firing shortly after I arrived here. I thought that if I ever got a German in my sights I should like to see the same effect on his kite.'

Chamberlain laughed, 'So you know that Hugh has his guns synchronised to 250 yards as well do you? I won't ask how you came by that information. But it only works if you are a good shot, which you obviously are. Have you shot before joining the RAF, hunted pheasants or grouse, something like that I mean?'

'I used to shoot clays in Civvy Street,' said Steed. He added thoughtfully, 'I think clay shooting is good practice for air to air deflection shooting.'

'I guessed as much. I take your point about deflection shooting. It's the same with grouse. It might be good fun to set up a competition clay shoot amongst the pilots if things ever quieten down. Off you go now and see the Doc.'

The Doctor gave Steed a thorough examination and passed him fit for flying, although he recommended to Chamberlain that Steed should be given a day off unless things were really desperate. Steed was surprised at the reception he received from the other pilots; they all seemed delighted to see him back. Steed still had in the back of his mind the roasting that he had received from Tomlinson and still thought, incorrectly, that some of the other pilots regarded him as a glory seeker, more interested in his personal score than in the success of the squadron. Steed now had six victories and he was a little embarrassed that he remained the squadron's top scorer.

The other pilots were also surprised at just how bad things were in Dunkirk, and most were hurt and a little affronted to hear that the soldiers thought the RAF was letting them down, leaving them with little protection from the onslaught of the Luftwaffe. Steed's ground crew, who both wanted to have chapter and verse on his recent exploits, greeted him warmly. Pip Courtauld had bagged one of the brand new Hurricanes, fresh from the factory, so Steed was allocated Courtauld's old aircraft. 'The privileges of rank,' said the flight sergeant. 'But she's all checked out. We'll get the guns set up on the range for you right now. Everything will be ready in an hour if you need her.'

Later that day, Dix interrupted Steed's game of darts in the crew room. 'The weather in Northern France is just as bad as it is here, so I don't think we will be needed over Dunkirk today. So, I'm standing you down Sergeant Steed. However, there is one thing that you could do for me. I went to see Squadron Leader Tomlinson in Colchester military hospital yesterday evening. They had to amputate his hand you know. He has asked to see you. You can take my car, and give him this book at the same time.' Steed's face registered surprise as Dix continued, 'The squadron leader is an honourable man. I think that he wants to clear up any misunderstandings following events of the other day. You should understand, Sergeant Steed, that squadron leaders do not justify their decisions to sergeant pilots. But you should also understand that he had been given the top priority task of breaking up those enemy bomber streams. We are all feeling the strain, but Mr Tomlinson has the additional responsibility of leadership. He may not show it, but the loss of so many of our pilots in battle has affected him badly.'

Steed surmised that Dix had chosen his words carefully. Deciphering the code seemed to indicate that Tomlinson now regretted the dressing down that he had inflicted on Steed in front of the other pilots. The Boss had wanted a maximum effort devoted to breaking up the bomber formation, and had been affronted by the sight of one of his junior pilots chasing a retiring bomber rather than returning to the fray and helping out his colleagues. Maybe he had a point.

Dix, like Tomlinson, was 'old school' RAF. Virtually all the other pilots now called Steed either by his Christian name or by his nickname. Even Chamberlain, the acting squadron leader, used Hawk during less formal moments. Dix, however, stuck rigidly to the correct 'Sergeant Steed' at all times. Still, that was reasonable. Dix was his flight commander, so perhaps needed to keep his distance. There was no doubt that Dix was an exceptional pilot, probably the best in the squadron. He was also a damn good air leader. Steed was certain that Dix would one day have his own squadron.

Tomlinson had a private room in the military hospital. Steed entered, came to attention and saluted, 'Good afternoon sir, I have a book for you from Mr Dix. How are you feeling?' Tomlinson was sitting up in the bed, the stump of his right arm heavily bandaged. His face was ashen, but he spoke in a clear and confident voice.

'Ah, Sergeant Steed. Pleased to see you. Good of you to come. Hugh Dix told me yesterday that you had been shot down over Dunkirk, but that you were on your way home in a pleasure boat. Were you wounded?' Tomlinson was looking at Steed's bandaged head.

'No sir. I banged my head on the gun sight when I ditched in the sea. It's just a cut. I will be flying again tomorrow.'

'Well come along Sergeant, tell me all about it.'

Steed narrated his story once again. He was getting quite used to it by now. Tomlinson tut-tutted when Steed described how the RN destroyer shot him down, and when Steed spoke of the general feeling of antipathy shown by the soldiers towards the RAF Tomlinson's face flushed with annoyance.

'Bad show that Sergeant Steed. Our people are dying over there, protecting the troops from the Hun bombers, our own squadron has lost a third of its strength in the past week. What more do they expect?'

Steed nodded his agreement. 'I know sir. I tried to explain that the RAF fighters were above the clouds, breaking up the bomber streams inland, trying to prevent the Jerries from reaching the beaches, but I think that the soldiers were just too tired to understand. They were taking a terrible pasting from the Luftwaffe, and from their perspective the RAF was nowhere to be seen. It seems that it was much the same story during their retreat though Belgium, lots of Jerry planes but none of ours.'

At the end of it all the squadron leader said quietly, 'Well done Sergeant Steed. With that Stuka you have, what, six victories?'

Steed gave an inward sigh. Was this a criticism? Was this a suggestion that he was more concerned with personal glory than with the breaking up of the enemy bomber force and the protection of the troops? Surely not.

'Yes sir, three fighters, two Stukas and a Heinkel.'

Tomlinson gave a thin smile, 'Ah yes, that Heinkel.' He continued after a short pause, looking Steed straight in the eyes. 'Sergeant Steed. I may have said things the other day that you could have misinterpreted. You have proved your courage on a number of occasions, and I certainly would never presume to call you a coward. No, don't interrupt. On your very first day in action, you shielded a shot-up Peter Chamberlain from two Me-109s, shooting down one of them in the process. On my last flight, when I too was pretty well defenceless and Hugh Dix was out of ammunition, you repeated the process, this time taking on four of the blighters, shooting one down and driving the others off.'

'I didn't actually shoot it down sir, the pilot made a mistake and crashed into the sea.' He paused. 'I am very sorry about the Heinkel.'

'Hmm, maybe Sergeant Steed. Our duty was, still is, to break up the bombers before they can hit the beaches or the shipping. You have now seen with your own eyes what it is like for our troops on the ground; we simply have to stop the sods from getting through. My intention was to keep the whole squadron together, attacking their main force, and I took umbrage when I saw you chasing off after one of the damaged buggers. But I accept that I should have chosen my words a little more carefully in front of the other pilots. It wasn't so much what you said in reply that irritated me, it was the way that you said it. Anyway, all water under the bridge now. I accept that you misunderstood my orders and that your intentions were honourable.'

Steed simply replied, 'Yes sir.'

Again that thin smile from the squadron leader, and he continued, 'But what you said in the crew room made sense as well. You were right. Your Heinkel will not be coming back for another go, and neither will the crew.'

'Yes sir, if the Heinkel had been the only target, I believe it would have been my duty to shoot it down. But there were other targets that day, Heinkels that still had bomb loads. I know now that I should have climbed up towards the main bomber force.'

'That's exactly as I see it Sergeant Steed. In the crew room, when you defended your actions, you seemed to me quite bloodthirsty in your desire to kill the crew of that Heinkel. Personally, I believe that our task is to shoot down their aeroplanes. I have no hatred of the crew; if they bale out, good luck to them.'

Steed sensed that this time Tomlinson would not rebuke him for taking a different viewpoint.

'May I speak freely sir?' Tomlinson nodded.

'In my view there isn't room for chivalry. War is brutal. The greatest air aces of the last war did not better the enemy, did not survive even, by being chivalrous. The best way of killing an enemy was, and still is, to creep up behind him and shoot him in the back. Or attack him unseen out of the sun, then escape before his mates find out what you are about. That's what the Germans are doing to us sir. That's why we are losing our tail-end Charlies, I mean our weavers sir.'

'An interesting observation Sergeant Steed. Is that how you have been so successful, by being an assassin?'

Steed answered honestly, 'I'm not sure sir, but given a choice that's how I would try to fight. Do to the Huns what the Huns are tying to do to us, but do it first, if you know what I mean. Kill them before they kill us!'

'But taken to its logical conclusion, your argument would have us shooting enemy pilots in their parachutes. The Germans haven't stooped that low as yet to my knowledge. I am interested to know what you think about that Sergeant Steed. You can speak freely.'

'I have thought about that one a lot sir. Firstly, I don't think that we should shoot enemy pilots in their parachutes over our own lines, because they would soon become prisoners of war. But if they are over their own lines, that's a different matter. I believe that we should shoot them. Pilots are no different to other soldiers. If we had the opportunity we would kill German soldiers on the ground by machine-gunning them, even if they were unarmed at the time. So why not kill pilots in their parachutes? We hear that German pilots are already machine-gunning French civilians. If we don't kill them, they will return to kill us, or worse they will kill our women and children with their bombs.'

Tomlinson was shocked, 'Shooting defenceless aircrew in their parachutes is a brutal thing to do. If there is no room for chivalry in air-to-air fighting then we pilots are reduced to the level of the trenches.'

Steed looked uncomfortable. He had been asked for his opinion and he had given it, but this man was from another age and another class. Perhaps he should have moderated his beliefs and language. He added, 'I have discussed this with Mr Dix sir. He has made it very clear that I should not shoot at parachutes, so of course I follow his orders.'

Tomlinson nodded and continued. 'Well, on the positive side Sergeant Steed, you are undoubtedly an efficient assassin. And I also suspect that the RAF, indeed our country, may have need of killers like you in the very near future. I am doomed to fly a desk from now on,' Tomlinson looked ruefully at his stump. 'Anyway, I wanted to thank you personally for what you did the other day, when I was shot up I mean. Now get the hell back to the squadron and buy the boys a drink to celebrate your return from Dunkirk.'

The next morning, the last day in May, Chamberlain addressed his pilots in the crew room. 'Gentlemen, for those of you that haven't yet met them, let me introduce three new additions to our merry band, Pilot Officers 'Nick' Nichols, Bernie Foulks and Ian Smith.' There was a chorus of catcalls. 'Now settle down. We are expecting more replacements any day now, but for the moment there are still only eleven of us. It is a big ask for the three new arrivals to join us in the air fighting without being given the time to settle in, but we will all fly today to put in a maximum effort over Dunkirk. We must break up the bombers and give our troops the cover that they deserve.' There followed murmurings of approval.

Chamberlain continued, 'Group have decreed a slight change of tactics, or I should say a refinement of tactics. As usual, the Hurricane and Spitfire squadrons will stay high to break up the bombers. But now Coastal Command has been tasked with dealing with any low-flying Huns over the beaches. The Coastal Command boys are now flying what is now being called the 'Sands Patrol', using Avro Ansons and Lockheed Hudsons. I know it sounds strange, but it seems to be working. We have heard from Sergeant Steed what our troops are going through over there, and the disillusionment of some of them with the RAF. These gripes are unfounded, as we all know. The troops on the ground cannot see what goes on above the clouds and away from the beaches.

Now, in addition to the usual patrol over Dunkirk, the squadron has also been asked to provide a section to cover a bombing raid by some Blenheims on a military target to the north of Dunkirk. Flight Lieutenant Dix will lead this section with Ian Smith and Sergeant Steed as his wingmen. The rest of us will form up into two vic sections with two weavers at the back. Bernie and Pip, you two will be my wingmen in Red Section. Roger will lead Yellow Section with Sergeant Walker and Nick. Tail-end Charlies in Green section will be Sergeant Adams and Ian Graham; the details are on the board. The observant amongst you will have noticed the fog outside; the forecast is for that to clear later in the morning, both here and over in France. Take off at 12.00 for the main squadron, 12.15 for Flight Lieutenant Dix's Blue Section.'

Dix briefed his section separately. 'Sergeant Steed, you are Blue-2 and Ian, you are Blue-3. We already have one Ian in the outfit, so do you mind if we call you Smithy? Good, that's settled. We rendezvous with the Blenheims over Southend at 12.30 and follow them at low-level towards Dunkirk. When we get near to Dunkirk, you cannot miss it Smithy, you can see the burning oil tanks for miles around, we climb to 3,000 feet or to the cloud base if that is lower and follow the Blenheims. The bomber boys will stay down on the deck. If enemy fighters try to intervene, we shoot them down or drive them off. Easy eh? The target is an enemy artillery position that is giving the troops within the Dunkirk perimeter a hard time. After the Blenheims complete their bombing run they will turn for the sea. Once they are clear and heading at full pelt and at low-level for Blighty, our orders are to return to strafe targets of opportunity to the north of Dunkirk. We will go down to low-level, line astern, and look for enemy troops along the road. When we have used up most of our ammunition we will head back home.'

The Blenheims and Dix's Blue Section arrived over Southend simultaneously. The bomber leader waggled his wings and headed out over the estuary, dropping down to sea level as he did so. His two charges followed suit, the Blenheims adopting a familiar vic formation. The Hurricanes settled in behind them, weaving gently in order to hold station with the slower, bomb-laden Blenheims. The fog had lifted to a degree, but there was still a translucent mist over the sea that made judging their height above the waves a tricky business. The pilots observed radio silence as the six aircraft set course for Dunkirk, but since the Hurricanes and the Blenheims were using different radio frequencies, radio communication between the fighters and the bombers was in any case impossible.

As they neared Dunkirk, Dix climbed above and behind the light bombers to 2,000 feet, as high as he dare go while still keeping the Blenheims in view. As the Blenheims crossed the coast just north of Dunkirk, they immediately drew the attention of some light flak. The bomber leader apparently knew where he was and where he was going because he suddenly made a sharp turn to the left and commenced his bombing run, followed by the other two aircraft now in line astern. The flak was suddenly much worse, all directed at the Blenheims, the Hurricanes for the moment being ignored.

Flashes on the ground indicated bomb strikes and the three Blenheims made another left turn and headed for the sea. But the centre Blenheim was in trouble, with smoke, then flame gushing from the port engine. Gamely the aircraft tried to make height, but then fell back into a shallow drive, crashing into a small wood and exploding in a ball of orange fire. The other two Blenheims crossed the coast and headed out to sea. Dix followed them for a while and then closed on the leader. Steed could clearly see the pilot wave his hand in thanks as the Hurricanes took their departure and headed back towards Dunkirk.

Blue Section crossed the coast again and flew inland for a couple of miles. Then Dix spotted a road running east towards Belgium. The Hurricanes dropped down in line astern and, well spaced out, followed the road, looking for targets of opportunity. Dix was in the lead, followed by Steed, with Smith at the back. At this low-level, while following his leader, Steed found it very difficult to keep a good lookout for enemy aircraft.

A group of army trucks appeared, coming towards them on the road. Dix opened fire at the targets, and Steed followed suit. Steed watched mesmerised as his tracers tore through the tarpaulin of the army supply trucks, watching soldiers dive for cover or being thrown into the air like rag dolls by his bullets. He had killed before, but this seemed very personal, very immediate, and very up-close. There was a burst of accurate flak from somewhere below and Steed's aircraft shuddered under the impact of the cannon shells. The road was abruptly empty again as the three Hurricanes hurtled along above it at treetop height.

Steed could not see Smith behind any more but he craned his neck searching the sky as best that he could for any German fighters on the prowl. Dix's voice came over the radio, 'Military traffic ahead.' Steed had a fleeting glimpse of soldiers and vehicles on the road as Dix opened fire in front. As Steed too opened fire, he was amazed to see that the transport was horse drawn, and he recoiled to see his bullets smash into the poor dumb creatures. And then they were gone.

Dix pulled away from the road and headed back towards the sea at low-level. As he followed his leader, Steed glanced down at the array of gauges in front of him. All seemed to be in order and his Hurricane also appeared to be responding to the controls normally, but there was a large hole on the starboard wing and he could smell cordite. Then they were crossing the coast, with a farewell burst of flak from somewhere behind. Once over the sea, Steed had more opportunity to look around. He could now see Smith behind and to his left. Steed eased up behind and to the right of Dix, and Smith drew alongside on his left into the classic vic formation. Dix spoke. 'Blue section from leader, everyone all right?'

Steed replied, 'Leader from Blue-2, I took some flak hits but everything still seems to be working.' Smith also transmitted, 'Leader from Blue-3, same for me. I felt some hits from the ground fire, but everything here seems normal.'

Dix replied, 'Well done boys. Home for tea.'

They landed before the rest of the squadron and, when Steed examined his Hurricane with his ground crew, he was astounded at the amount of damage it had sustained from the flak. In addition to the large hole on the starboard wing, the rear fuselage had also taken hits. 'What do you think about that Colin?' Steed asked his rigger as they surveyed the damage, 'Amazing thing is that she still seemed to fly pretty well. Is it a big job to repair, or will I need another aeroplane for tomorrow?'

Colin Stuart stroked his chin. 'I need to have a proper look under the fabric Sarge, but the moths have certainly been at it! There is not much in the fuselage behind you, wood and metal struts mostly, covered with fabric, so with a bit of luck we should be able to repair it overnight. You were lucky the Hun gunners did not hit you further forward. The hole in the wing is not too bad either; it's missed your control wires thank goodness. If it had hit further in, well you have the guns and wing tank to worry about of course.'

The three pilots walked across to the crew room for debriefing by the Spy. Steed still found time to run with the Spy's dog Dion, and he now regarded the amiable academic as a friend. The Spy was very approachable and a source of considerable knowledge about Luftwaffe aircraft and tactics, subject matter that was often aired in the officers' mess but that did not always permeate down to the sergeant pilots.

The Spy usually debriefed each pilot individually, but today he interviewed the three pilots together. They were talking about the attack by the Hurricanes on the second troop convoy. Steed commented, 'I thought that the German army was mechanised, you know tanks and armoured cars everywhere. But I was amazed to see those horses. I hated to shoot up the horses, they hadn't done anything wrong.'

'Yes, we think of the German Army as being super-modern,' said the Spy. 'But unlike our people, the Germans use horses a lot. The transport that you hit was probably bringing up ammunition and other supplies to their front line troops trying to break through at Dunkirk, so it was a very necessary job that you did today.'

'Do you think the poor nags walked all the way from Germany? They got through Belgium pretty quickly if they did.'

The Spy thought for a moment. 'Who can say? They may even have been French horses and carts requisitioned by the Germans.' The Spy moved to a related subject, 'Tell me about their flak. Were anti-aircraft guns travelling with their transport, and what calibre were they?'

Dix said, 'I didn't see any flak along the road, although I now know that Sergeant Steed and Smithy were hit there. The Germans certainly seem to have light flak guns all along that stretch of the coast, north of Dunkirk I mean. And the flak was very heavy over the bombers' target, all directed at the Blenheims, poor sods. As I said, one of them went down.'

Steed added, 'The flak that got me came up when we attacked the first group of vehicles. I didn't see where it came from, but there are three holes in the fuselage behind me, with one hole in the wing. Maybe someone with more experience could say what calibre the guns were from the damage to my plane, but my guess would be 20mm cannon; certainly cannon and not rifle-calibre machine-guns.'

Smith looked a little embarrassed, 'It all happened so very fast. Harry was in front of me and I saw tracer coming up as we attacked the first group of lorries, but I couldn't say exactly where it came from. I felt my aircraft hit so I took evasive action. I am sorry to say that my shooting at that point was less effective than it should have been.' He looked at Dix who simply nodded. Smith continued, 'I was a fair way behind Harry when we attacked the horse transport, but I didn't see any flak then. There seemed to be quite a bit of damage already, resulting from the strafing by the first two Hurricanes. I saw upturned wagons and bolting horses and I opened fire. I simply pressed the button and aimed at the road as I passed above the convoy.'

Smith omitted to say in his shame that he had forgotten to switch his guns to fire before the attack on the first convoy, and so had not fired a shot in anger at the German trucks! He took his secret to his grave. The rest of the squadron landed shortly afterwards. They had remained above the clouds and had not seen any action.

On the first day of June, before dawn, Chamberlain briefed the pilots. 'The happy tidings this morning gentlemen is that Billy Bishop is safe. I have just heard that he came back yesterday in a Royal Navy destroyer.' There was applause and cheering from all of the pilots. 'I don't yet know the full details, and I don't know if he is injured. We only know that he was landed at Dover sometime yesterday. The second piece of news is that the powers that be in Group have given me 126-Squadron. I am now officially your C/O.'

Again there were cheers and shouts of congratulation as Chamberlain smiled and raised his sleeve, where all could see the two thick and one thin stripes of a squadron leader. 'Now settle down please, because there are some other changes. Roger Daily is now acting flight lieutenant and will lead A-Flight.' There were more cheers. Chamberlain continued, 'The Navy is doing a fine job, but Group thinks that we have one or two more days at the most before the Germans break through and put those of our boys who have not managed to get out of Dunkirk into the bag. So, once again it is maximum effort over the beaches to protect our troops and the shipping from the attentions of the Luftwaffe. This morning we have eleven pilots available, so I intend us to operate in three vics with two weavers in Green Section, namely Sergeant Steed and Smithy.'

Chamberlain looked around the room, surveying his pilots. He continued, 'I know that I am asking some people to move between sections almost on a daily basis, and I realise that is far from ideal. But we have lost experienced pilots and while this flap is on I think the present arrangement gives us the best balance between the more experienced people and the new boys. When things settle down and we get replacements, then maybe we will get more stability.'

After the general briefing, Chamberlain spoke to the two weavers. 'Smithy, I spoke to you last night about the duties of a weaver. Basically you are there to keep a look out behind and to your right. Hawk will cover the other side, looking behind and to the left. Both of you need to weave in order to cover the blind spots behind and below. Hawk has been doing the job for some time now, and he is very good at it. He always spots the Huns, and I am counting on you Smithy to do the same. Hawk will be Green leader today, so if we go into action you must move across behind Hawk and follow him. Hawk, we have a spare ten minutes, I want you to have a quick word with Smithy about the tricks of the arse-end Charlie trade, especially that bit about not getting bumped off by the crafty, sneaky Huns!'

When Chamberlain walked away to talk to someone else, Smithy turned to Steed, 'What are these tricks of the trade Harry? Or was he joking?'

Steed grinned, 'No, I don't think that he was joking. We started to use weavers because the Hun fighters were bouncing the squadron too often. People were paying too much attention to maintaining a tight formation and not enough attention to looking around for the Jerry fighters. We found that stationing a couple of guys at the back, whose job it was to look behind and to the side, tended to give us better warning of any Hun fighters on the prowl. If you see a bogey, you tell the squadron leader. You must use the correct wireless procedure. If you spot fighters coming down on us, and there is no time to inform the squadron leader, then you have to call the break to the rest of the squadron. Are you clear on all of this or would you like me to go over it for you?'

'No, that's okay Harry. Chamberlain went through it all with me in the mess last night.'

'Good,' said Steed. 'Try to stay more or less level with me while we are acting as weavers. I will take station behind and above the rest of the squadron unless we are about to go into cloud, in which case I will close right up to the section in front. You must do the same. We don't want to lose the rest of them in cloud do we? If we go into action, listen to the instructions from the leader. He may for example order us to go into echelon starboard or something like that. When we attack I will try to close up to the section in front. I've discovered that it's not a good idea to attack a bomber formation after the rest of the lads have passed through; every Hun gunner turns on you as his only target! If all else fails, just follow me, but always keep a good lookout behind and in the sun.'

'They didn't say anything about weavers at the OTU,' said Smithy.

'No, it's a fairly new idea,' replied Steed. 'I think that it was first used by the squadrons in France, but different squadrons do things in different ways. In 126, we tend to use three weavers when we are at full squadron strength, but some other squadrons only use one; some don't bother at all with weavers. In any case the man, or men, at the back are called either tail-end Charlies or arse-end Charlies, depending upon your upbringing.' He smiled. 'The problem is that the Jerry fighter pilots know what we are up to, and they think that the tail-end Charlies make tempting targets at the back, all on their lonesome. If there are only a couple of Jerries, they like to sneak up on the Charlies, perhaps using the clouds or the sun as cover, or they come up from behind and below. Chamberlain is dead right, you have to keep looking around, or those crafty, sneaky Huns will bump you off.'

'Chamberlain called you Hawk, and I've also heard one or two other people call you that or Hawkeye. Do you prefer Harry or Hawk?'

'In the air you must always use the proper wireless procedure, so today I am Green-Leader. Sometimes you will hear people's names or nicknames being used over the radio, but you are much better off using call signs. In the RAF nicknames are very common. Already you are Smithy and not Ian. Chamberlain coined the nickname Hawkeye for me because he thinks that I have good eyesight. Other people have started using it as well, and it has now mostly been shortened to Hawk. The senior officers usually address sergeant pilots like me by their rank, you know, as Sergeant Steed. When we are in less formal situations, or off duty, I think that some of the seniors may find it easier calling me Hawk rather than Harry. To be honest, I don't mind what people call me, I answer to anything.'

'Well, I will call you Harry. Do you have exceptional eyesight? They tell me that you are the squadron's top scorer, an ace.'

'I think that I have good eyesight, but I wouldn't say exceptional,' reflected Steed. 'I think that it's more a question of technique, seeing the German fighters first I mean. You need to search the sky methodically, and you need to second guess where they might be hiding, in the sun for example.'

'So, why have you been so successful?'

Again Steed laughed, 'Luck probably!'

'No advice for a novice like me?'

Steed was serious this time, 'Well, it takes time to be aware of what is going on around you. When you are new, a novice if you like, things seem to happen very quickly. You have so many things to do all at once. You have to fly the aeroplane, follow the leader, look around for a target and try to keep from becoming one. As you get more experience, things get easier; you seem to have more time to think. You also become much more aware of what is going on around you, and most importantly you become a more accomplished pilot; you fly instinctively. My advice is to simply be extra careful for the first couple of missions. Rookies are always the easiest targets. Don't become one. If you get involved in a dogfight, remember that your Hurricane can out turn anything the Germans have, but their Me-109s can out climb and out dive you. Their Me-110s are much more sluggish and make juicier targets. Never fly straight and level in the dogfight area for more than a few seconds. Watch out for the Hun in the sun and behind you. Survive the first few operations and you are no longer a novice; statistically you are safer.'

'You make it seem like the Germans always have the upper hand. All the time we are worrying about them attacking us. Shouldn't they be worried about us rather than the other way around?'

'A very good point Smithy, you are spot on. Yes they should worry about us, especially if they are a bomber or Stuka crew. But remember, our job as weavers is to look out for the fighters trying to bounce our squadron. It's the squadron leader's job to look for a target, something that we can bounce if you like. I'm certainly not saying that you should be over cautious when we attack, on the contrary, it is our job to hit the bombers as hard as we can; we must break them up before they can hit our troops on the beaches or sink our ships. Get in close to the bastards before you open fire and try to ignore their return fire. But if you are dog fighting a 109 and he dives away, watch out. They come in pairs. If you follow him, you may find his wingman on your tail. Be aware of the dangers and you will live longer.'

As the pilots walked towards their aircraft, Steed reflected on his conversation with Smithy. Should he have mentioned the goggles? Steed used lightweight and lightly tinted pre-war glass goggles, expensive and purchased privately, and he kept them scrupulously clean. But nowadays, when the sky was not too bright and especially when acting as a weaver, he tended not to wear them at all, pushing them up onto his flying helmet in order to have a better chance of spotting the enemy. But there was a severe disadvantage to this practice, which was one reason that he had not mentioned it to Smithy. Fire in a Hurricane was an ever-present danger with a petrol tank a few feet in front of the pilot. The heavy duty goggles with celluloid lenses that Smithy carried would at least offer some protection in case of a sudden conflagration, possibly giving him a few more seconds to pull back the canopy and bail out with his eyesight intact. Without goggles one had a better chance of seeing the Huns, preferably before they saw you, and this could save your life and maybe earn you victories, but if there was a fire… Steed pushed the thought to the back of his mind.

The squadron took off in the twilight before dawn. As they passed over Margate at 5,000 feet, the sun had just broken above the eastern horizon, its rays dancing on the canopies of the eleven Hurricanes. As they headed out, past the North Foreland and into the Channel, Steed could just make out an assortment of small boats and ships, heading for the safety of English harbours. Ten minutes later, now at 10,000 feet as they approached the unmistakable begrimed column of smoke and dust above Dunkirk, it was light enough to clearly see the features of the coastline below. More ships were visible, hastily steering away from hostile territory and the savagery of the Luftwaffe.

Steed, conscious that Smith was a novice pilot, explored every inch of the sky, behind, right and left. Below, the sea was calm, with gentle surf at the shoreline. The sky was azure blue with a few white fluffy clouds scattered around. The first of June was going to be a glorious day, the sort of day that in peacetime would see bathers frolicking in the sea or sunbathing on the golden sands below. But this was not peacetime, and the destruction and carnage was evident in Dunkirk town, now ahead on the port side as Chamberlain led the squadron along the shoreline. At intervals along the beach Steed could see small makeshift jetties constructed from abandoned army trucks, but there was no sign of the lines of troops that he had witnessed from the deck of the Thames paddle steamer just a few days earlier. Presumably, most of the evacuation was being undertaken at night now.

Steed was methodically searching the sky when he spotted the enemy formation, for enemy formation it certainly was coming from that direction. He called Chamberlain, 'Tomcat leader from Green-1, about twenty bogeys at five o'clock, about the same height as us.' Although Steed felt certain that they could only be enemy bombers, he could not definitely identify the aircraft as such and so reported them as bogeys.

Steed looked above the enemy formation but saw nothing. If they were bombers, they would have a fighter escort somewhere up here.

Chamberlain replied, 'Thank you Green leader, I see them. Probably bombers or Stukas after the shipping.'

Chamberlain turned the squadron towards the enemy and started to climb. The German formation was now at one o'clock relative to the Tomcats, with both sets of protagonists heading towards the coast. It was now Chamberlain's responsibility to check ahead for any high cover escorting fighters.

A short while later Chamberlain's voice cut in again, 'Tomcat Squadron, vic echelon starboard GO.'

The vics spread out in echelon, with Chamberlain's Red Section in front on the left. They could all see the enemy formation clearly now.

'Tomcat Squadron from leader, around twenty-five Stukas ahead, I can't see any fighters but be aware everybody.'

The Hurricanes closed in on the Stukas. Both formations were now out over the Channel, with the Hurricanes behind and slightly above their enemy. The dive-bombers were obviously going for the shipping, now making a run for England with their cargo of soldiers. The Stukas were starting to circle above their prey, but they were also now the hunted as the Hurricanes advanced. Chamberlain had even managed to get the advantage of the low sun behind him.

Steed now saw the fighters, behind and much higher. But they were too far behind to prevent the squadron from intercepting the Stukas.' He called Chamberlain, 'Tomcat leader from Green-1, bogeys at six o'clock, about angels twenty. Too far back to hurt us yet.'

'Thank you Green-1.' Several Stukas were now peeling off into their dives, but the majority were still circling as the Hurricanes swooped. 'Be aware of fighters after the attack. Tallyho Tomcats.'

The Hurricane pilots each selected a target; there were plenty to go around. Steed throttled back and lined up on a Stuka as he followed Dix's section. He was aware of Smithy now coming across on his right.

The slow-moving Stuka grew swiftly in Steed's reflector sight as he approached from behind and above. The infamous dive-bomber seemed surprisingly large for a single engine aircraft. The rear gunner opened fire too early. A little correction for the relative movement between the two aircraft and Steed opened fire. Bright sparkles danced along the cowling and then along the canopy of the Stuka, silencing the gunner, and then continued their twinkling path along the rear fuselage. As Steed was passing the dive-bomber it exploded, violently throwing his aircraft into a spin. Steed recovered from the spin, somewhat shocked, two thousand feet lower. He looked around. Above, there were several smoke trails from stricken aircraft, but there was neither friend nor foe nearby. His Hurricane seemed to be none the worse from its recent ordeal, with all the gauges normal. Below, he could see two parachutes just opening.

The airwaves were full of shouts and oaths. For the umpteenth time Steed wished that pilots would stay off the air at times like these unless they had something vitally important to say. However, he became aware from these calls that Messerschmitt-109s had now entered the fray above his head. For a moment he was in two minds about what to do. He could drop down to 1,000 feet of so and hope to catch a Stuka heading for home after it had dropped its load, or he could claw his way upstairs to help his squadron colleagues deal with the Me-109s. He decided on the latter course of action and started to climb at full throttle.

The sky in the immediate vicinity was clear but, about 1000 feet higher, almost directly above his head, two fighters were circling. Steed's first thought was that a pair of Me-109s were considering coming down on his lonely Hurricane but, as he studied the two aircraft above, he could see that one was a Messerschmitt and the other a Hurricane. The Hurricane was almost behind the Me-109 in the turn when the German suddenly put his nose down and dived away; the Hurricane followed. Steed initially thought that the Me-109 might make a firing pass at his still climbing Hurricane on the way down, but the Messerschmitt pilot seemed not to have noticed him and curved away. The pursuing Hurricane was now so far behind that it wisely gave up the chase; it pulled out of its dive and headed in Steed's direction.

The newcomer was now closing head on with Steed at a combined speed of about five hundred miles per hour. Steed was concentrating on the Me-109, now seemingly uninterested in the two Hurricanes and heading away when, unaccountably, the Hurricane opened fire at Steed. Steed glimpsed its markings as it went past. It was Smithy! He turned sharply to follow Smith, who was also turning. 'Green-2 from Green leader, the last aeroplane that you fired on was me!'

A sheepish Smithy joined Steed, and together they climbed back towards the action. But the sky had suddenly become remarkably clear. The radio was also quiet, save for the usual static.

'Tomcat Squadron from Green-1, anybody there?' But there was no answer. Steed climbed to 12,000 feet and led Smithy back towards Dunkirk town, with its dirty black smoke marker. He called his wingman, 'Green-2, we have around five bogeys in front of us, about 2,000 feet lower.'

Chamberlain's came in, faint but distinct, 'Green section from Tomcat Leader, where are you?'

'Green Section approaching Dunkirk town from the east leader. I think that I see you in front of me.' The bogeys were now clearly identifiable as six Hurricanes, in a two vic formation, and so three aircraft were clearly missing. Steed and Smith took station behind as weavers. The rest of the patrol was uneventful.

When they landed, a very embarrassed Smithy met Steed by his Hurricane. 'Hey, look at this Smithy!' Steed and his ground crew were examining the damage to his aircraft, 'I shot up a Stuka, but as I went past the blighter it blew up, probably his bloody bomb!' Steed pointed to a piece of jagged metal jutting out of the underside of the Hurricane, 'That my dear boy is a bit of Stuka.' Steed turned to his rigger, 'Colin, will you save that bit for me please? I'd like it as a souvenir.'

As they walked towards to the crew room, Smithy said it a low voice, 'I say Harry, I am most terribly sorry about shooting at you back there. I suddenly saw what I thought was a 109 in front of me as I pulled out from a dive. It all happened so fast. I am very sorry.' His voice trailed away.

'No harm done,' said Steed cheerfully. 'It's lucky for me that you are such a rotten shot! I was below you and I saw you turning with the 109.'

'Yes,' said Smithy, 'I was just getting set up to open up on him when he suddenly put his nose down and just rocketed away in that dive.'

'And when you tried to follow him the poor old Merlin coughed and spluttered a bit before she would give you any power, so by the time you were able to follow him down he was out of range,' suggested Steed.

'That's right. Does that happen often?'

'The 109s have fuel injection and the Hurricane's Merlin has a carburettor. His engine can take negative G without getting fuel starvation, yours can't. The 109s often use that tactic. The only thing that you can do is to roll over as you dive to avoid the negative G, but that takes time so it doesn't really solve the problem. The 109s are faster in the dive and in the climb than us, faster in level flight as well come to think of it, so they can usually bottle out of a fight if they want to.'

'Anyway,' said Smithy, 'I really am very sorry about firing on you. It was a terrible thing to do, I could have killed you.'

'Put it down to experience, and maybe swot up on aircraft recognition a bit more. Don't mention it to anyone else, and neither will I.'

'That's most decent of you,' said Smithy sincerely; and they walked off for debriefing by the Spy.

Tomcat Squadron had realised a very productive morning's work. In addition to Steed's Stuka, four more Stukas were claimed as destroyed and several more as damaged. Dix also claimed a Me-109. Johnny Walker had escorted a shot up Nick Nichols back across the Channel. Nichols had made a crash landing at Marston, but escaped with only cuts and bruises. Bernie Foulks had not been so lucky. A Me-109 had latched onto him and sent the rookie down in flames.

Take-off for the next patrol over Dunkirk was scheduled for 13.00, so the pilots had time for rest and a light meal. The three sergeant pilots sat together for an early lunch in their mess. Johnny Walker turned to Steed, 'How's young Smithy shaping up Harry?'

'He's a bit green, like all of us were when we first arrived. Christ, here's me talking like a veteran and I've only been here six weeks or so myself. He'll be okay though.'

'I noticed that it was you who spotted the Stukas,' continued Walker, 'even though they were on Smithy's side of the sky. Come to think of it, it was you that spotted the 109s behind us as well.'

'You are being too hard on the lad Johnny. It was only his second op, and the first time as a Charlie. Remember that I've been doing the job for a while; you would expect me to be a darn sight better at it than Smithy. He will learn.'

'But that's my point Harry. All three of us sitting here had time to properly settle into the squadron before being sent on ops. We had a chance to get used to the aeroplanes, the tactics and the people. We had a sense of awareness. In other words we were properly trained before they let us loose on the Germans. But now look at the three sprogs that arrived here a couple of days ago. The day after they arrived they are sent on ops, and the day after that the 109s nail two of them. Bernie Foulks is shot down and Nick Nichols is lucky to get away with a crash landing. These boys are being sent into battle with too little training; that way they are simply cannon fodder.'

Toby Adams joined in the discussion 'I agree with you Johnny. Ideally the sprogs need to fly with the squadron for a bit and sharpen up on dog fighting and gunnery before they are thrown into the deep end. But what choice does Chamberlain have? If he lets them sit at home while the rest of us go looking for trouble over Dunkirk, the squadron ends up with only half a dozen Hurricanes to take on the Luftwaffe. He has to use the sprogs in order that we fly somewhere near squadron strength.'

After lunch, Steed met up with his ground crew. His rigger was apologetic. 'We're very sorry Sarge, but there was too much damage on your Hurricane to have her ready for you this afternoon. You will have to take a spare. We'll have your plane ready for you tomorrow though, that's a promise.'

'No worries Colin,' said Steed, 'It's my fault for allowing some stupid Stuka to blow himself up, all over my aeroplane.'

'Problem is,' said his fitter, 'the spare has its guns set in the Dowding spread. The engine's okay though. It's one of the older birds, but it's a good runner.'

'I'm sure that it is Denis. I'll try not to let the Jerries put any holes in her.'

There were only nine pilots available for the 13.00 sortie. Chamberlain moved Smithy from weaver to Red Section to replace Bernie Foulks, shot down that morning. Nick Nichols was still in transit from Marston, so Roger Daily and Johnny Walker flew as a Yellow Section pair rather than in a vic. That left Steed as a singleton tail-end Charlie.

Just before take off, Chamberlain took Steed to one side. 'Hawk, we both know that arse-end Charlie is a particularly dangerous position to fly. You make a tempting target for the Huns back there all alone. But you are our most experienced Charlie and I need your eyes. Don't get too far behind, and come up quickly at the first sign of trouble.'

The nine Hurricanes approached the Dunkirk beaches in the early afternoon. Down there somewhere, thought Steed, was the cremated remains of Pilot Officer Bernie Foulks. Hurricanes were tough aeroplanes, but they seemed to have developed a habit of catching fire all too quickly. Was it the main fuel tanks in the wings or the reserve tank just in front of where he was sitting that was the culprit? Mick Mannock, the Great War Royal Flying Corps ace, had a fear of being shot down in flames and burnt alive. As he weaved and scanned the sky behind his squadron, Steed thought of his forebears of twenty-odd years ago. British fighter pilots had no parachutes in those days, although rudimentary parachutes were available to German pilots later in the war, and also to British army observers in tethered balloons. The RFC leaders had deemed it inappropriate for pilots to have parachutes; these armchair warriors were concerned that the provision of parachutes would make their pilots less inclined to bring home a damaged aircraft.

But the flames had crept up on Mick Mannock in his SE5, just as they had on Bernie Foulks and Stephen Cavendish in their Hurricanes. In theory, Hurricane pilots could slide back the canopy and bail out if the worst happened, but that assumed that the canopy wasn't stuck or damaged by enemy fire and that there was sufficient altitude for the parachute to open. Steed remembered Cavendish's screams as he was burnt alive in his blazing Hurricane just a few days ago before.

Chamberlain was right. Tail-end Charlie was a lonely and dangerous position. The sky seemed empty, save for the nine Hurricanes, but those fluffy white clouds could hold dangers. The squadron leader's voice cut through Steed's thoughts. 'Tomcat Squadron, three bandits at one o'clock, 3,000 feet below. Tallyho!'

The Hurricanes streaked down towards the enemy aircraft, which Steed now identified as Dornier-17s. The Dorniers appeared to be lining up to bomb the suburbs of Dunkirk, but the bomber leader was alive to the danger posed by the Hurricanes and the Dorniers turned towards the safety of the nearby cloud as the Tomcats approached. Frustrated, Chamberlain circled around the clouds, but finding the German bombers was akin to finding the proverbial needle in the haystack. All the while Steed anxiously surveyed the sky behind. It was a lovely day, at least it would have been under different circumstances, but those appealing downy, cotton wool clouds could hide death within their vapours.

But it was German death that came first as the Tomcats meandered about, for above, silhouetted against a large cloud, were two Me-109s. The Tomcats were perfectly positioned, and the German pilots were uncharacteristically careless. The two Messerschmitts never knew what hit them; Chamberlain and Daily claimed the victories, and 126-Squadron turned for home in high spirits. Steed was relieved that the squadron was returning to Colne Martin. Although generally considered to be a dangerous position, Steed actually liked to fly tail-end Charlie; he also quite liked flying in that position alone. Steed enjoyed the freedom that it bestowed. But the weaver's job that afternoon was made much harder by the close proximity of so many fluffy clouds; so many hiding places to catch out the unwary, as the hapless Me-109 pilots had just discovered. Steed's neck muscles ached and he was tired. All that had happened over the last eight days, including his swim in the Channel, had taken its toll.

Maybe it was because of weariness, but more likely it was because he was up against two expert German fighter pilots, that Steed didn't at first see the two Me-109s that made a sudden exit from a nearby cloud. But see them he did at the last moment, and he put his Hurricane into a vicious climbing turn as tracer shot past his port wingtip. 'Tomcat Squadron break left!' he gasped. A garbled call maybe, but it was the best that he could manage under the circumstances. He straightened out briefly and looked around. Where was the enemy now? How many were there? His Hurricane shuddered under the impact of cannon shells and Steed again threw the Hurricane into a tight turn, this time to port. Jesus, he thought, the bastards are behind me!

Steed was partially correct. The leader was turning behind him, but the wingman was lining up for a deflection shot. Steed was caught in the trap. In desperation he pushed the Hurricane down, then immediately up into the loop, praying that he had sufficient speed to avoid the stall. Inverted, at the top of the loop, Steed caught a glimpse of the German wingman turning below. Steed completed the loop, dived to pick up speed, and then threw the Hurricane into yet another tight turn. Tracer sped past his canopy. Sod it! The Me-109 leader was still behind. Steed tensed his muscles, but he could feel the onset of blackout under the G-force. Surely the 109 couldn't live with this.

Steed was correct, the Me-109 leader was not able to follow the turn, but the wingman was coming up again. These boys are good, thought Steed, too bloody good, working as a pair. Where was the rest of his squadron, where was the cavalry? Where was the nearest cloud, that closeting veil in which he might hide?

Steed's mind raced. If he continued to circle in the hope of getting on the leader's tail, the wingman would get him for sure. Should he try the loop manoeuvre again? But then the wingman made his first mistake. He waited for the optimum moment to attack Steed, misjudging how much tighter Steed was turning than the Me-109 leader. The leader, however, was very aware of Steed's tighter turn and the likelihood that the Hurricane would soon be in a firing position on his tail; he adopted the standard Me-109 escape mechanism of diving away.

The wingman, slightly late, was coming in for the coup de grace. Steed threw the Hurricane into a diving turn in the opposite direction as the wingman opened fire. There was a loud bang somewhere close behind and a colossal thump into Steed's back, as the wingman whistled past. Steed now decided that discretion was the better part of valour. His aircraft had been hit, there was smoke in the cockpit and the numbness in his back suggested that he had been wounded. He corkscrew dived into the comforting safety of the woolly cloud below.

Once in the cloud, Steed assessed the situation. The radio was silent; there was not even the reassuring sound of static. Steed tried calling

Chamberlain but there was no response. His back ached, but otherwise he seemed to be okay and his limbs were moving freely. The instruments in front of him also seemed to be in order, and the Hurricane was answering to the controls. There was a load whistling noise from somewhere behind, and a draft. When Steed looked behind he saw that canopy was buckled just behind his head, where it met the back armour. He tried to pull back the canopy, just in case he needed to jump, but it wouldn't budge. It the back of his mind was the fear of fire, of being trapped in a burning Hurricane.

Steed, still in cloud, decided to head for home. He broke cloud over the Channel, about three miles out from Dunkirk. As far as he could see, he was alone in the sky. He reflected on the recent battle, although it was hardly that since he hadn't fired a shot, the tape was still in place over his gun ports. The two Me-109 pilots had been very good. He had faced tougher odds before, like the four Me-109s he had fought low over the Channel the day Tomlinson had lost his hand. But the two German boys today were in a different league. Steed knew that he had been lucky to come out of it alive.

After landing at Colne Martin, Steed was still unable to open the canopy and needed his ground crew to release him. On surveying the damage to his Hurricane, he was once again amazed at how much damage the aeroplane could take and still fly perfectly well. Machine-gun bullets had scythed a path across the rear fuselage, damaging the canopy. There was a gaping hole in the fabric, and a cannon shell had hit the radio behind his seat and exploded, hence the thump in his back. Steed was thankful for the seat armour plating.

The rest of the squadron had not yet returned, so Steed went off alone for debriefing with the Spy. Later, Chamberlain came to see him. 'What happened back there Hawk?'

'There were two Me-109s, at least I only saw two. They came up from behind. They must have been hiding in the clouds because I only saw them at the last moment. I shouted a break warning, did you hear it?'

'Yes.'

'They were very good, the German pilots I mean. They stayed to fight it out with me. Their attacks were fast and co-ordinated. If I tried to turn inside one of the blighters, the other one would line up on me to make a pass. Finally one of them hit me with cannon and machine-gun fire, smashing the radio and making a nasty mess of the fuselage just behind the seat. I made it to the clouds. I tried calling you of course, but my radio was smashed. When I broke cloud I was alone. My aircraft was damaged, so I came home.'

'I see,' said Chamberlain. 'Well, we heard your warning and broke left. We couldn't see you at first, and then we spotted you tussling with the two 109s, and we saw you dive for the cloud. We stormed in, but it all got a little disjointed. We missed the 109s, then chased around the clouds looking for them. I don't know how, but at some stage we lost Ian Graham. We heard him say that he had been hit, that's all. We simply lost contact with him. With luck he'll turn up. Billy Bishop is back by the way, and so is Nick Nichols.'

'Yes, with luck Ian will turn up,' said Steed. 'And it's good to see that Billy is back, Nick too. How are they, I mean are either of them injured?'

'I don't think so, but I haven't seen either of them yet. They are over in the mess.'

That evening, Billy Bishop came across to the sergeants' mess to see Steed and Toby Adams. Johnny Walker joined them as Billy recounted his experiences.

'Glad to see you made it back from Dunkirk Harry. I went down later the same day. I was flying arse-end Charlie with Toby and suddenly all hell broke loose behind me. My kite was knocked out of the sky and started to spin. Smoke filled the cockpit and I saw flames on the wing. It was a bit of an effort, but I eventually managed to bail out. Then came the greatest shock, a bloody great 109 circled around me when I was drifting down. I thought that the bastard was going to blow me away, but he just gave me a wave. Can you believe that? I guess he was the fellow that shot me down, I never saw him coming and I didn't even have time to radio that I was going down.'

Bishop took a swig of beer. 'That's better. Although the Jerry pilot didn't take a pot shot at me, one or two of the brown jobs below did! I could hear bullets whistling past me and a few holes appeared in the parachute canopy. I came down inside our lines fortunately, a couple of miles inland from the beach. Half a dozen Pongos appeared ready to brain me before they realised that I was British. Mind you, the RAF wasn't too popular amongst them, and I think one or two of them were still ready to have a go at me. They tell me that you had much the same experience Harry?'

'That's right,' said Steed. 'I became fed up trying to explain to people that the RAF was above the clouds, trying to break up the bomber formations before they hit the beach or the shipping. You couldn't really blame the brown jobs, every plane they saw was a German trying to bomb or strafe them.'

'They tell me that the Navy took such a dim view of seeing a RAF kite that they shot you down,' chuckled Bishop.

'Too right they did! Did you get a boat from the beach? My paddle steamer passed a whole flotilla of little ships on the way over to Dunkirk.'

'No,' said Bishop, 'I joined up with the brown jobs, who seemed to know where they were going thank goodness, and we eventually arrived at the dunes well after dark. There were a few boats coming in, but there were long queues and things were not moving very fast. It started to rain, and the fog came down. The weather was so miserable that even the Luftwaffe stayed away, although their artillery kept our heads down. By mid morning, I still could not find a boat and I was feeling pretty knackered, not having slept for over 24 hours. Some of the brown jobs had made makeshift jetties out of abandoned army trucks, and some of the others were up to their necks in the water waiting for a boat.

At about that time I spotted a Navy type by the shoreline, some sort of beach master I think, and I identified myself as an RAF officer. He told me the best chance of getting away was to head down to the Dunkirk mole around five miles away. The weather had cleared a bit by then and the Luftwaffe was coming over at intervals, so it was best to walk by the dunes where there was some cover. There were some of our kites flying low over the beach, mostly Coastal Command types like Hudsons and Ansons; I saw a couple of Lysanders as well. The only RAF fighter I saw was a Spitfire heading inland, trailing smoke, but I could sometimes hear Merlins above the cloud. I found some shelter amongst the Dunes and put my head down for a couple of hours. When I eventually reached the mole it was well after dark. There were long queues of soldiers leading to the mole. I didn't like to push in, and to be honest I kept a low profile, feelings towards the RAF being what they were. I queued with the army all night, but I wasn't able to get a boat. The next day it rained, but the dirty weather at least kept away the Luftwaffe. I eventually got onto a destroyer later that morning. We pulled into Dover a few hours later. The people there were marvellous, couldn't do enough for us. They were very keen to get everyone away from Dover on troop trains in case the Luftwaffe turned up. My train ended up at a holding camp in deepest Sussex. I was completely done in, so I got some shut-eye. It took me ages to get back to Colne Martin.'

The four pilots talked shop for a while, especially about the problems of being tail-end Charlies, and then turned in. Take off was set for 07.15 the next day.

Chamberlain gave his customary pilots' briefing in the crew room the next morning. 'Once again our job is to patrol the evacuation beaches. Group tell me that the evacuation is now mostly taking place at night, so when we get over there this morning we will probably see the stragglers starting to make their way back across the Channel. As usual, our job is to break up any bomber formations trying to attack the shipping or the beaches.'

The pilots already knew to which sections they were allocated, the list having been put up the previous evening but, as was his practice, Chamberlain confirmed the flight order at his briefing. 'We will use much the same formation as yesterday, but Nick Nichols will rejoin Flight Lieutenant Daily and Sergeant Walker in Yellow Section.' Nichols was missing two front teeth following his recent crash landing, but he had insisted that he was fit to fly. Chamberlain continued, 'Sergeant Steed will join Flight Lieutenant Dix and Sergeant Adams in Blue Section, which leaves Billy Bishop as our singleton tail-end Charlie.'

As 126-squadron approached Dunkirk, Bishop's voice cut in over the radio. 'Tomcat leader from Green-1, around twelve bogeys at four o'clock and about 3,000 feet above us.' Steed glanced over his right shoulder; they looked like Spitfires coming over from England.

Chamberlain responded, 'Thank you Green-1, they are probably friendly. Let me know when you have identified them.'

Down below, visible between the clouds, shipping of various descriptions was heading back across the Channel. A short while later Bishop's voice again came over the airwaves once more. 'Tomcat leader from Green-1, the aircraft at four o'clock are Spitfires.'

In front of the Tomcats, on the horizon over France, Steed could just make out a gaggle of dots. Coming from that direction they were certainly the enemy.

'Tomcat leader from Blue-3, a large number of bogies at eleven o'clock, about the same height as us.'

There was a short pause, and Steed was considering retransmitting when Chamberlain replied, 'Thank you Blue-3, I see them. Looks like fifty plus.'

Chamberlain started to climb as he headed for the enemy. Steed was gratified to see that the Spitfire squadron was heading in the same direction. There are more than fifty of the blighters thought Steed, more like a hundred. Away to the right and below, just appearing from behind a cloud was another squadron of Hurricanes. Steed gave it a moment to see if anyone else was on the ball. It was Dix who transmitted, 'Tomcat leader from Blue-1, twelve Hurricanes at three o'clock, 1,000 feet lower.'

Steed looked above the gaggle of German bombers for the inevitable fighter cover, but he couldn't see anything. The second Hurricane squadron was climbing to the same height as the Tomcats and sliding into position on their right. The Spitfire squadron had obviously increased to full throttle and was now positioned behind and above the two Hurricane squadrons. Everything was now set for the attack on the German bombers.

'Sections echelon starboard, GO,' ordered Chamberlain. Steed followed Dix as he moved to the right. Billy Bishop thankfully abandoned his tail-end Charlie position and moved up to the extreme right of the squadron, now in echelon. 'I don't see any fighter cover,' crackled Chamberlain, 'but it doesn't mean that it isn't there.' A few moments later he shouted enthusiastically, 'Break up those bombers, don't let them through to our ships. Tallyho Tomcats!'

The bombers were a mixture of Heinkel-111s and Dornier-17s in a stepped formation. The Tomcats closed the enemy in a shallow dive. Steed could see that Dix was aiming at the lower group of Heinkels at the front of the formation, so he selected his Heinkel within the same group. Steed throttled back and aligned his reflector gun sight on the glass canopy of his intended victim. He waited until the Heinkel filled the sight then opened fire. He had a fleeting vision of the Heinkel's canopy disappearing under the smoke and mayhem caused by the concentrated weight of bullets from his synchronised Brownings. And then he was diving past the nose of the Heinkel, following Dix and Adams ahead.

Dix led his section up again towards the underbellies of the aircraft near the centre of the formation. Steed followed, selecting the lead bomber of a group of three. Tracer from the German air gunners curved wickedly towards him, but he ignored it as best he could and concentrated on a difficult deflection shot. Once again, Steed's aiming point was the glass nose of his prey; German bomber crews liked to sit together, and under that glass they looked and felt vulnerable. Steed's shooting was accurate, and he watched the bullets strike the nose, and then creep down past the gondola, silencing the gunner; and then he was curving upwards past the bomber's tail.

Steed had expected Dix and Adams in front of him to dive away, but instead they continued up through the Heinkel formation to attack the upper layer. Steed was not carrying quite the same speed as the other two members of Blue Section, so he needed to go to emergency boost in order to keep up. His assault on the upper layer Heinkel followed almost exactly the same pattern as his attack on the Heinkel below, concentrated fire on the canopy, spreading along the underside of the fuselage past the gondola.

Dix did not continue upwards beyond the upper layer of the Heinkel formation, but once more led his section in a dive towards the bombers below. By now the Hurricanes had reached the tail end of the enemy formation. Steed's shooting was not quite so accurate in this last assault on the luckless Heinkels, his bullets missed the canopy aiming point, although he had the impression that some hit the wing between the fuselage and the starboard engine. And then he was clear of the enemy formation and closing up to Dix and Adams who were using the speed of their dive to once again climb behind the bombers. The three aircraft went up into a loop and then, when inverted at the top of the loop, rolled over into normal flight, completing the classical Immelmann turn.

The sight that met their eyes was truly amazing. The bombers in front and below were no longer in a tight, two-layer formation. Now they were spread all over the sky, harried by Spitfires and Hurricanes. Smoke trails and opening parachutes denoted that many aircraft, RAF fighters amongst them, would not be returning to their bases. Steed craned his neck, searching for any enemy fighters that could be approaching from the east, out of the sun, but the bombers seemed to be on their own this time.

Dix was now diving back towards the enemy formation. Following his leader, Steed could see that Dix was setting up a stern attack on a group of three Dornier 17s that were a little way behind the main formation and therefore denied their supporting fire. There was no need for Dix to give directions; the airwaves were in any case too busy. The three Hurricanes were in a vic formation, Dix in the centre, Adams on the right and Steed on the left. The Dorniers were also in a vic formation, so it was logical for Steed to select the Dornier on the left.

Dix led the section down in a dive behind the Dorniers, curving up to attack from behind and below. Presented with this synchronised attack, the Dorniers held formation with each bomber's air gunners firing at the particular Hurricane that was attacking them. As in most German bomber designs, the Dornier 17's crew sat near to each other in the nose of the aircraft. Dix's method of attack from behind and below, coupled with the bomber leader's brave decision to hold formation and to press on towards the target without taking any evasive action, meant that only the ventral machine-gun of each bomber could be brought to bear on each attacking Hurricane.

Steed steadied his Hurricane and throttled back, taking care not to overshoot his target. The ventral machine-gunner opened up early, but Steed held his fire as the Dornier started to fill his sights. Steed was confident that the single German machine gunner had no chance against the Hurricane's eight Brownings, each firing 1,000 rounds per minute. Not for the first time, he was surprised by the effectiveness of the return fire; German air gunners are brave lads he thought, and well trained. Yet again, the Great War maxim 'kill the gunner first' came into his head as he pressed the firing button. His deflection shooting was spot on as he watched mesmerised as his tracer danced around the bulging nose of the Dornier before creeping back to pepper the ventral gunner's position; the return fire ceased.

Steed dived and turned to avoid straying into the front gunners' arcs of fire, then climbed back towards his Dornier, which continued sedately on its course. The starboard bomber was twisting and turning away to the right as it attempted to avoid Adams' attention. The centre lead Dornier however was falling away, its port engine smoking. Steed caught a glimpse of Dix's Hurricane turning for a beam attack on the damaged bomber.

Once again Steed approached his Dornier from below and behind. This time there was no return fire from the ventral air gunner. He poured a long burst into the fat nose of the bomber. He saw hits all over the nose, but the bomber still continued towards the target. Once again he dived away and then returned for a third attack. Steed was always efficient with his ammunition, but he was becoming concerned that it must be getting close to empty by now. He commenced his third attack on the Dornier, again from behind and below where there would be no answering fire, and from where he would have a good chance of a long burst into the enemy aircraft.

The Dornier was continuing its run to the target, although now it had settled into a shallow dive. Why did it not take evasive action to bring its other guns into play, or at least to make it a more difficult target? Why was there no apparent damage? Steed was sure that he had poured many rounds at close range into the front of the Dornier. Was there armour plating under the nose that prevented his bullets from causing serious damage? Or perhaps the pilot was dead and the stable aircraft was flying itself? This time Steed decided to take out an engine. If the Dornier continued to fly in a straight line and without any return fire it should be easy to hit an engine.

As he settled into his attack run, for the umpteenth time Steed looked over his shoulders and checked his rear view mirror. Bloody hell! An enemy fighter was coming up behind him. Steed hauled his Hurricane into a tight climbing turn to starboard. The Hun fighters are too late to prevent their bomber force from being broken up, he thought, but not too late to catch out the unwary. And then he saw the 'enemy' fighter as it sped past; it was Dix!

Dix was heading for Steed's Dornier. Dix attacked from below and hit the port engine. Steed followed up and hit the starboard engine, but then ran out of ammunition. As Dix and Steed circled and climbed, the Dornier settled gracefully into a steeper dive with both engines smoking. As they watched, the dive became steeper and flames gushed from the starboard engine, spreading along the wing. The wing buckled and the aircraft began to spin, now in flames. There were no parachutes.

Dix and Steed were alone in the sky. For the first time since the attack on the bomber formation had started, Dix spoke. 'Half each for that one I think Blue-3. Well done!' Steed closed to formate on his leader as they headed for the coast and the retreating shipping. 'I have a sense of deja-vu Blue-3. I am out of ammunition.'

'So am I Blue leader,' replied Steed.

'Bloody good show that,' said Dix enthusiastically. 'There must have been nearly a hundred of the sods and we broke them up. Hun fighters kept out of it as well. Bloody good show!' A few Spitfires were circling the retreating shipping protectively, but the German bombers had turned for home without pressing home their attack. Dix tried calling Tomcat leader but without success, so the two Hurricanes headed for home.

The elation at their success was diminished by the news that three pilots had failed to return. Toby Adams had crash-landed in a field and was in hospital in Kent. Courtauld and Nichols were missing. Several Hurricanes were damaged and could not be made ready for the afternoon sortie. Steed claimed one half of the Dornier shared with Dix and three Heinkels damaged.

At midday, Chamberlain called his remaining pilots together. 'We have been pulled out of the fight boys. We have done enough. In a few days we will be heading up to Scotland to refit and receive replacement pilots and aircraft. Another squadron will take our place here. Group is proud of us; I am very proud of you all. The Dunkirk evacuation is all but over and 126-Squadron has more than done its bit. The Navy has achieved a miracle in bringing so many of our boys back from Dunkirk, and the RAF has kept the Luftwaffe at bay over the beaches. The army may not have realised it yet, but without the RAF many more German aircraft would have got through. This morning was the icing on the cake. Together with other RAF squadrons, we smashed a heavy raid on our shipping over Dunkirk. Our squadron alone destroyed seven bombers today, with many more damaged, all for the loss of two of our pilots who may yet return. But the last two weeks has taken a heavy toll on us all. We started out with fifteen pilots. During the battle we received three replacements, but we are now down to only seven pilots and a handful of serviceable aeroplanes. It is clear to me that we cannot throw inexperienced pilots in at the deep end without proper training and expect them to survive. Our job now is to rebuild the squadron, properly train the new pilots and get ready for what must now come.'

Chapter Seven – Battle of Britain

Steed sat back on his bed in the room that he shared with Johnny Walker and looked out through the open window. The cold, clammy Scottish mist still retained its tenuous grip on the border lowlands, exposing with a silver sheen the ensnaring spiders' webs that were strung across the foliage. The sky was a leaden grey, but at least it was not raining; the weather would not prevent the flying scheduled for that early July afternoon.

Steed had an hour in which to unwind. He was tired. Chamberlain had set a cracking pace and the squadron was now flying from dawn to dusk, weather permitting, in hard training. They had received an intake of new pilots to replace the casualties of Dunkirk, three RAFVR sergeant pilots, two Cranwell pilot officers, a Belgian pilot who had come to Britain via the Dunkirk evacuation, and a Pole who had arrived via a torturous and hazardous route through Hungary and Romania to France, then eventually to Britain.

The squadron had also received a complement of new Hurricane fighters and, for the first time, Steed was accorded his very own brand new aeroplane. He was touched to see that his ground crew had painted seven and one half swastikas on the fuselage below the canopy, representing his confirmed victories.

Much had happened in the four weeks that they had spent in this tranquil area of southwest Scotland. Italy had declared war on the Allies, anxious for a share in Hitler's spoils, and then France had effectively surrendered. Britain now stood alone. Well, not quite alone as the forthright Roger Daily had vehemently explained to all who would listen. 'At least you Poms have the Aussies standing with you, look who we've got!' That was true; there were now many foreign nationals joining the RAF, men from India and the Empire, New Zealand, Canada, Australia, South Africa and Rhodesia. Trained pilots had also escaped from Nazi occupied Europe, Poles and Czechs amongst them, welcome additions to the desperately under-strength RAF. But the mighty French army was no more. The French people were subjugated, as were those in half a dozen other European nations.

It was a sobering thought that half of 126-Squadron's pilots had been wiped out just two weeks of serious fighting. Mathematics suggested that the prospect of an RAF fighter pilot's survival in a shooting war was on a par with that of the Royal Flying Corps pilots of twenty odd years ago.

What would happen now? Invasion? The Royal Navy would certainly put up a strong fight to repel a seaborne invasion, but what about the air? Would the Luftwaffe be able to send the Navy's ships to the bottom of the Channel? The RN Destroyers had suffered badly at Dunkirk. Could German parachutists and glider troops gain a foothold in England? For these things to happen the Luftwaffe would need air supremacy; it would need to drive the RAF from the skies of Southern England.

Steed had a healthy degree of scepticism for the words of politicians, but Churchill's oratory had been truly inspiring, especially his 'Finest Hour' speech. He had said that the battle of France was over and the battle of Britain was about to begin. But things had been very quiet in Britain since Dunkirk. Perhaps this was the lull before the storm? The expected hordes of Luftwaffe bombers had not arrived, giving Britain, and especially her battered army and RAF, the chance to reorganise and to prepare for what must now come. The latest reports from the Spy suggested that business was now 'hotting up' over the Channel. The Luftwaffe was targeting the Channel convoys, and RAF fighters were being drawn into air battles over the shipping. Steed considered 126's respite in Scotland a real bonus; God knows that the squadron needed time to recover and refit.

Chamberlain had certainly seized the opportunity. The man was open to new ideas, and was not too proud to copy German tactics. Gone was the old tight formation flying and, with this constraint removed, pilots were now able to keep a far better lookout for the enemy. Gunnery was also on the menu. Sometimes they flew out over the Solway Firth, taking it in turn to shoot at their shadows on the water. They still flew vics when in full squadron formation, with the three aircraft of Green section nominated as weavers behind and above, although recently Chamberlain and some of his senior pilots had been experimenting with German type *schwarm* and *rotte* formations. This afternoon both Steed and Walker were scheduled to fly for the first time in an experimental '*schwarm*' with Dix and Billy Bishop.

Toby Adams had been discharged from hospital, but he was not yet fully fit to fly and was on leave back in South London. Toby's Hillman had been brought up to Scotland and had been commandeered by Steed and Johnny Walker. Steed's Ariel Square-4 motorcycle had also been brought up to Scotland on the back of an RAF lorry and seemed to thrive on the 100-octane petrol freely available from the aircraft browsers. Steed had the Ariel in perfect tune, and it reined supreme in the runway drag races organised by the pilots.

Chamberlain had organised a clay shoot, at which Steed had fancied his chances, but he had to be content with fourth place behind Dix, Chamberlain and one of the new pilots, 'Tommy' Tomlinson. These three were all expert shots, being a part of the country set and having taken part in many pheasant and grouse shoots. Steed was shaken from his reflections as Johnny Walker barged into the room.

'Wotcher Harry me old mate. I've just half-inched some juice for the jam-jar, but she's not running too well – a bit of hesitation when you put your foot down. Think it's the 100 octane?'

'Don't know Johnny. Could be dirt in the carb? Let's take a look after flying.'

'Well you can drive us over to dispersal now and see what you think. It's time to get cracking.'

That afternoon, while Chamberlain led the rest of the squadron on exercise, Dix briefed Steed and Walker on the forthcoming four aircraft section patrol.

'As Squadron Leader Chamberlain hinted the other day, it is probable that the squadron will be moving back to Colne Martin within the next couple of weeks. With so many new bods joining the squadron, the Boss thought it best for training purposes to stick with the tried and tested vics with weavers that we used during the shenanigans over Dunkirk. Much less confusion that way; we don't want to change too many things at once. Having said that, a few of the senior pilots have been flying together recently, experimenting with a four aircraft section much like the Germans use. We think that this type of formation has merit, so the idea is to introduce this technique to other members of the squadron, starting with those with the most combat experience. As sergeant pilots, you two would fly as wingmen in the number two or number four positions. This afternoon, I will lead the section and Sergeant Steed will fly as my wingman. Billy will fly Red-3 and Sergeant Walker Red-4. We will practice various observation, interception and break techniques.'

Dix started to chalk on the blackboard, illustrating the aircraft positions, the area of sky each of them should observe, how the aircraft should be positioned in turns and during an attack, and how they should break if they were attacked. Steed could see that much of this theory was based on how they had seen the German fighters operate over Dunkirk.

'Remember,' continued Dix, 'the leaders look ahead and it is the duty of the wingmen to guard the tail of their leader and to look behind. We position our aircraft so that each of us has an unobstructed view of the sun. We keep a fairly wide formation so that each of us is free to look around without fear of bumping into his neighbour, but we close up when going through cloud for obvious reasons.'

The training flight went well. Steed was impressed with the thought and expertise that the senior pilots, notably Chamberlain, Dix and Daily, had put into the new tactics. Other pilots were introduced into the new four-aircraft sections during the week, and by the end of the week the changeover was complete. Chamberlain was flying a full squadron comprising three sections of four aircraft. Steed invariably flew as number two to Dix in Blue section.

But their sojourn in the Scottish borders was coming to an end. Chamberlain called all his pilots together for a special briefing.

'Gentlemen,' he began, 'Group has now confirmed to me that 126-Squadron will moving south, returning to Colne Martin, at the end of next week. This means that we have just one more week to cement our new air fighting tactics. The lull since Dunkirk has given us time to re-build and retrain. It is obvious that the Hun will now try to do to us what he has already done to the rest of Europe. He will try to bully us into surrender by bombing our cities, just as he forced the Dutch to surrender by terror bombing Rotterdam. He may try to invade across the English Channel, but to do that he has to get past the Royal Navy, which will be far from easy.'

Chamberlain warmed to his point. 'Hitler must attain air superiority to have any chance of subjugating us. He must be able to bomb our cities at will in order to terrorise and demoralise our people. In any invasion attempt he must be able to unleash his bombers on the Royal Navy and support his troop landings. He must be able to get his parachutists through to their destinations without being shot down over the Channel. All of these things he must be able to do without fear of effective interference from the RAF.'

Chamberlain thumped the table with his fist as he continued, his voice now louder. 'That, then gentlemen, is our job now. We must not, indeed will not, allow German bombers to fly willy-nilly over our country, to drop their bombs on our towns and cities as they did in France, Holland, Belgium and all the other countries that the Nazis have overrun. If they dare to invade, we will destroy their bombers and Stukas. We will machine-gun and bomb their troops on our beaches, drop mustard gas on the bastards, whatever it takes.' Steed rather wondered if the squadron leader had been taking public speaking lessons from Churchill.

126-Squadron moved back to Colne Martin in mid July 1940. The grass airfield had seen some changes in the six weeks since Dunkirk. New concrete revetments had been built around the perimeter of the airfield to give some protection to the dispersed fighters against bomb blast damage. New anti-aircraft gun emplacements had appeared, better shelters had been provided and twenty soldiers had been deployed as a precaution against German parachutists. The officers still messed in the large country house a mile or so from the airfield, but Steed was pleased to see that the on-airfield sergeants' mess still retained its country pub charm.

The pilots were accorded a few days leave before the squadron became operational, so Steed went to see his parents in North London. He found a stoic attitude towards the war amongst his old friends and neighbours. There was a realisation and 'so be it' acceptance that Britain now stood alone against a powerful and ruthless enemy lurking just twenty miles the other side of the English Channel. There was faith in the capabilities of the Royal Navy, which had saved the men of the BEF, a proud and proven navy that was the nation's historical shield against invasion.

There was also a realisation that the RAF was very much in the front line, protecting British cities, Channel shipping and ports against the attentions of the Luftwaffe. Steed had been worried that the people may have heard stories from some of the soldiers returning from Dunkirk who blamed the RAF for not doing enough to protect the beaches and shipping from the German bombers. This was certainly not the attitude he found when he went with his parents to their local pub in the evening. His mother and father beamed with pride as friends and neighbours came up to shake their son's hand and admire the pilot's wings on his tunic. 'Just you give it to them Jerries son,' said the landlord, and that just about summed up the attitude of everybody that Steed met that night.

Steed left his parents house early in the morning of 20 July. As he started his motorcycle for the journey back to Colne Martin, his mother hugged him with tears in her eyes. 'Please be careful son,' she said quietly. 'You're all we have.'

'Don't worry Mum, I'm far too good to be shot down by any Jerry pilot, as one or two of them have found out already.' His father shook his hand. 'Good luck son, take care now.' And with that, Steed went back to the war.

There were now six sergeant pilots in the squadron, the three Dunkirk veterans Steed, Walker and Adams, for Toby Adams had returned to the squadron with the move to Colne Martin, and the three new RAFVR sergeants Derek Stillwell, Tony Parsons and Bernie Edwards. All six sat together in the mess that evening; the squadron was to become operational the following morning with a standing patrol over a Channel convoy.

Steed, as the squadron's top scorer with seven and a half kills, was by now used to the near hero worship bestowed upon him by the newer and younger NCO pilots. Derek Stillwell, universally known as 'Del', and Steed were the only two sergeant pilots to be chosen to fly on operations the next morning. Del was keen to talk shop.

'I was talking to one of the Spitfire types who have been minding the store here while we were up north. He said that these convoy patrols could either be very boring or very exciting. You either pootle up and down above two or three dirty colliers chugging along the Channel, with nothing much happening, or you're up to your neck in Junkers and Messerschmitts. Do you reckon that he was shooting a line Hawk?'

Steed still cringed a bit when he heard that moniker, but it was a name that had stuck. 'I'd say he was right Del. The Spy said much the same the other day. It looks like Jerry is testing our defences, hitting the convoys and the Channel ports. Sometimes the Hun doesn't even bother to bring up his bombers to hit the convoys, he just engages our fighters circling the ships. I gather the Spitfire boys have had a rough time of it recently. I bet they are looking forward to going up north for a rest.'

'It's a rest day for us tomorrow too,' chimed in Toby Adams. 'While you and Del are off paying your respects to the merchant navy, the rest of us jolly sergeant pilots are going for a practice spin around the local countryside. Seems that I need to brush up on the new four aircraft section tactics that you bods have been playing about with up in bonny Scotland.'

Tony Parsons changed the subject, 'What's the local nightlife like around here? Where do you find the dolls?'

Johnny Walker laughed at the Americanism. 'Not too many dollies in Colne Martin Tony. There is a pub in the village that isn't too bad, and we meet up with some of the local WAAFs there sometimes, but for the real nightlife we have to go into London.'

A call from the back of the mess interrupted their conversation. 'Hey Johnny, how about a tune?' Walker got up and headed for the piano, followed by the other sergeant pilots and their mugs of beer.

The next morning at dispersal, as was his custom, Chamberlain briefed his pilots.

'Well gentlemen, today the squadron returns to war. As you all know, the Luftwaffe is giving our Channel convoys, and our Channel ports such as Dover, some unwelcome attention. It is our job to put a stop to it. The English Channel is our bit of sea, not theirs! Today our job is to fly a standing patrol above one of the Channel convoys approaching the Thames estuary. We will join the convoy off The Naze and stay with them as they push on down the coast, until another squadron relieves us.'

Chamberlain paused to relight his pipe. 'Luftwaffe tactics vary. Sometimes they stay away altogether, in which case the job of our fighters is simply to circle above the ships for an hour or so until relieved. But increasingly now the Luftwaffe responds to the convoys by sending in bombers, or sometimes Stukas, to hit the ships while their fighters try to keep our fighters busy. Sometimes the Luftwaffe only sends fighters to engage our boys and so a dogfight develops. Sometimes both sides send in reinforcements, so a hell of a big dogfight breaks out. Terrific fun! Usually a flight of six aircraft is sent to patrol above the convoy, while the ground controllers have other aircraft on readiness in case things escalate. But today we are going to try something different. We will have the four aircraft of Blue section, led by Flight Lieutenant Dix, circling the convoy at fairly low level in the usual manner. Blue section will go for any bombers attacking the convoy. I will stay up in the sun with Red section. Our job will be to get the bounce on any enemy fighters attempting to interfere with Blue section. We have practiced this sort of thing up in Scotland many times. Now is our chance to try it out on the Luftwaffe. Remember, if a dogfight develops at low level it plays to the advantages of the Hurricane over the Me-109.'

Dix led the four Hurricanes of Blue Section in a series of sweeps, up and down, parallel to the coast and always to seaward of the small convoy. Steed, flying wingman to Dix at Blue-2, permitted himself a brief glimpse down at the three coasters and the escorting Royal Navy minesweeper. Not exactly an imposing demonstration of Britain's sea power perhaps, but a statement nevertheless that Britain sought to enforce command of both the sea and the skies around her coastline.

Steed continued with the search of his particular section of sky, always looking behind and also, as best that he could, into the sun. The formation was loose, easy and well practiced. The Hurricanes flew slowly, conserving fuel. On this leg, flying in the direction of the Thames estuary and with the sun at 10 o'clock, Steed's aircraft was on the extreme left and a little lower than the others in the formation, so that the other pilots had an unobstructed view of that area of the sky threatening the most danger.

Steed glanced across to Billy Bishop on the other side flying Blue-3, and behind him Del Stillwell. Beyond the four aircraft and the small convoy below, Steed could make out the small seaside town of Clacton, a holiday destination for the people of East London in happier times. The wireless had been quiet for some time now; there was no need for chatter because everybody knew what to do, and in any case radio silence was observed in order not to alert the Germans to the presence of the convoy.

Direction reversal at each end of a leg was executed by two successive 90-degree crossover turns without the need for any spoken orders, and the pilots automatically adjusted their relative heights to allow for the position of the sun. The many hours of practice in Scotland now paid handsome dividends. The Controller broke the silence.

'Tomcat Squadron, ten plus bogies reported to the east of you, angels ten.'

Steed immediately gave particular attention to that section of sky over his left shoulder, but he could see nothing of the enemy. Chamberlain's voice came across the RT next.

'Blue-1 from Tomcat leader, bogeys approaching from the east, angels fifteen. Looks like single engine fighters, about eight of the sods, no bombers visible as yet.'

Dix increased speed and climbed. Speed and height for manoeuvre were vital in a dogfight and Dix had no wish to be caught meandering along at a fuel-efficient cruising speed.

A reconnaissance Dornier had spotted the small convoy earlier that morning. The Germans had decided that the target wasn't worth a bomber strike, but that a fighter sweep against the RAF escort would probably reap dividends. The Luftwaffe's end objective was to destroy the RAF, through attrition if necessary. Messerschmitt-109s were now out looking for trouble.

Chamberlain, from his high vantage point, allowed the Me-109s to continue towards the coast unmolested. The German fighters were ten miles behind the convoy when they at last spotted it, and its attendant Blue-Section fighter escort. The Me-109s manoeuvred into position for an attack. The German leader first headed out to sea, then turned back so that he could come at Dix's Blue section from out of the sun. The German pilots failed to spot the high cover Hurricanes.

Chamberlain was already in position up-sun of the Messerschmitts. He gave a last look above to check that the Germans did not have any top cover, and then led his four Hurricanes down into the attack.

'Tallyho Red section!'

The bounce was almost perfect. The Germans saw the approaching Hurricanes at the last moment and broke, but it was too late for the Me-109 that now filled Chamberlain's gun sight. A short burst of well-directed fire and the German fighter stalled, belched black smoke and flame, and then fell away towards the cold, unwelcoming sea.

Dix was now leading his section up to join the dogfight. Steed watched the mêlée, while at the same time looking out for any approaching bombers; but there were none. The dogfight above broke up before their arrival, and the remaining Me-109s headed for home. The Tomcats continued an otherwise uneventful patrol until a section of six Spitfires relieved them.

Back at Colne Martin, Red section was cock-a-hoop. Chamberlain had a confirmed kill, and the Polish pilot 'King' Bazyli claimed a probable. Smithy Smith, flying wingman to Chamberlain, had collected a good number of bullet holes in his aeroplane, but crucially everybody was back in one piece and Chamberlain's new tactics had worked superbly. Privately, Chamberlain suspected that the Messerschmitt squadron was inexperienced. Things had been too easy. The Germans had made some elementary mistakes, much as 126-Squadron had done in the early days of Dunkirk. And he was right. This had been the first operation for the newly formed Me-109 squadron, but like the British they would learn; they would learn or they would die.

The following day Red and Yellow sections were on convoy patrol, while Blue section was stood down. Dix, though, had a job for Steed.

'Sergeant Steed, I want you to escort a Blenheim undertaking calibration testing for the Chain Home radio detection equipment. The Blenheim needs to beetle up and down off the coast on a specific course. You will need to keep him in sight, ideally sit a couple of thousand feet above him, and protect him from the bad guys. Take Sergeant Stillwell with you as Blue-2.' He handed Steed a sheet of paper containing the instructions for the task.

At midday, Steed and Del Stillwell rendezvoused with the Blenheim over Felixstowe. The pilot gave them a cheery wave, and then set course out to sea. The weather was fine and the visibility good, so Steed took station two thousand feet above the light bomber and weaved gently from side to side to match the bomber's speed. The flight was uneventful and in less than an hour the Blenheim waggled its wings and set course for home. As they crossed the coast and waved goodbye to the Blenheim the Controller called the Hurricane pair.

'Senate leader, we have a bogey off Harwich, probably a German reconnaissance plane. Are you able to take a look?'

Steed reported that the two Hurricanes had sufficient fuel and he was given a course towards the last reported position of the bogey three miles out to sea. Probably a wild goose chase thought Steed. The German pilot would be halfway across the North Sea by now with his photos, and standing orders forbade RAF forays too far out from the coastline. But then Steed caught sight of something moving fast, down at sea level, back towards the port of Harwich. It was a Junkers 88, no doubt after more pictures. But the German was out of luck.

The Ju-88 was a fast aeroplane, but the Hurricanes had the height advantage and were ideally positioned. 'Tallyho!' yelled Steed, and he put his Hurricane into a shallow dive, approaching the rear of the German aircraft. Steed was careful not to overshoot as he came up on the bomber. He concentrated on his target and relied on Stillwell to watch his tail. Four of his guns were loaded with standard .303 armour piercing ammunition, two with incendiary tracer and two with the new De Wilde ammunition. The incendiary ammunition burned from firing to the target, leaving a trail of smoke, but the De Wilde exhibited a flash on impact that confirmed to the pilot that his bullets were hitting the target. Steed very much liked the De Wilde ammunition.

The Ju-88 stayed low, nearly at sea level, and the pilot started to weave from side to side as Steed approached. The rear gunner opened up early with well-directed fire, but he only had the one rearward-facing gun against Steed's eight. Steed was a little higher than the German and his aiming point, as usual, was the glass-domed crew compartment. Bright lights from the De Wilde ammunition indicated hits on the fuselage. The German pilot threw his aircraft into a tight left-hand turn in an effort to evade the onslaught, but Steed corrected his aim and fired again. There were flashes on the glass dome, and this time there was no return fire from the gunner. Once more Steed took aim. The bomber was still travelling low and fast but the pilot was no longer taking evasive action; was he dead? They were approaching The Naze on the Essex coast. Soon they would be over land. Once again Steed fired, this time a long burst. Flashes sparkled on the glass dome once again, and then danced along the fuselage. Still the

Ju-88 sped on its way. What did it take to put this blighter into the sea? He was right behind the German in a perfect shooting position. The pilot was taking no evasive action and there was no return fire.

In fact the rear gunner was dead and, although the pilot's armour-protected seat had done its job, the pilot had been wounded in the right knee by a ricochet and was in considerable pain. The navigator was attempting to help the pilot while the ventral gunner, who had been unable to get a shot at either of the attacking Hurricanes, was getting very worried about the close proximity of the sea beneath his gondola. With The Naze approaching, Steed took aim once again at the shattered dome and fired. Several AP bullets slammed into the navigator who pitched forward into the stick, sending the aircraft into a dive. The inhospitable North Sea claimed yet another aircraft, and four more young lives.

Steed climbed away, heading inland over The Naze, and smelt glycol. The temperature gauge still indicated normal, but Steed knew that this would not last. Del Stillwell drew alongside.

'Senate leader, you are trailing white smoke.'

'Thank you Blue-2. I smell glycol in here too. The temperature gauge is still okay but I am going to climb so that I can glide down to Colne Martin if needs be.'

At 4,000 feet the temperature gauge moved into the red, so Steed shut down the engine and opened the canopy. But the welcoming airfield was now in sight. Cleared for an emergency approach, Steed made a perfect non-powered landing. That evening in the sergeants' mess they celebrated his eighth confirmed victory. Even as they did so his ground crew were adding another small swastika to the seven and one half that already garlanded his Hurricane.

In the days that followed, 126-Squadron settled into a routine. Invariably they were called upon to patrol above the Channel convoys off the Suffolk and Essex coastlines. Whenever possible, one section of four aircraft would patrol immediately above the convoy, ready to intercept any bombers or low-flying strafing fighters, and one section would fly high up-sun to provide top cover. Sometimes they were kept at readiness in reserve, to be scrambled as reinforcements if a big fight developed.

The Tomcats, for 126-Squadron retained the old call sign, patrolled predominantly that stretch of coastline immediately to the north of the Thames estuary. In this respect they avoided many of the larger dogfights, for the Luftwaffe tended to concentrate their attacks further south, closer to their airfields in the Calais region and where the Channel was narrower.

The Luftwaffe objective was clear, to wear down the RAF and to so prevent the RAF from effectively interfering in the planned German invasion along the Kent coast. To a degree, their strategy was succeeding. The squadrons based to the south of London were having a hard time of it; they were losing pilots and they were starting to suffer from fatigue. Air Chief Marshal Dowding rotated his squadrons where he could, sending battle-weary squadrons to the north out of harm's way and replenishing them with those rested.

But 126-Squadron stayed in the fight; they had been rested after Dunkirk and since their return they had not lost a pilot. It was true that there had been several crash landings and a couple of pilots had bailed out; Hurricanes had been lost, but nobody had been killed. As July closed, Sergeant Tony Parsons and Badger Armstrong were walking wounded, but otherwise the squadron was still at full complement. Steed now invariably flew as wingman to Hugh Dix. Steed's job was to guard his leader's tail, which he did so effectively that Dix was able to notch up his personal score to six destroyed, plus two probables.

It couldn't last; the Tomcats' luck ran out in early August. That morning the squadron were ordered south to refuel, and then on towards the Isle of Wight to cover a convoy of twenty merchant ships, plus naval escorts, bound for Dorset with a cargo of coal. The convoy had been the subject of numerous German attacks overnight and that morning.

126-Squadron was now part of a structured RAF defence of the convoy, so Chamberlain did not have the freedom to split his force in order to provide his preferred top cover. The Controller reported a strong force of German aircraft approaching the convoy, so the twelve Tomcats climbed at full boost over Hampshire, heading out over the Solent. The convoy appeared below, and then virtually everyone saw the mass of German aircraft coming from across the Channel. Chamberlain informed the controller that the enemy was in sight and positioned the Tomcats for a head-on attack. There looked to be about eighty enemy aircraft, a mix of Ju-87 Stukas and Me-110 fighters. The experienced Tomcat pilots licked their lips in anticipation. Stukas and Me-110s were easy meat, but was there a covering force of the formidable Me-109s?

Steed, scouring the sky to the rear, spotted a dozen single-engine aircraft emerging from cloud; they were Hurricanes. He was about to report the sighting to Chamberlain when an excited voice cut-in over the wireless, 'Tomcats break! 109s coming down from behind!' Everybody immediately took violent evasive action. Steed followed Dix into a sharp climbing turn.

Steed's voice was next over the radio. 'Tomcat leader from Blue-2, there is a squadron of Hurricanes above.' The friendly Hurricanes were now visible for all to see.

Chamberlain responded, 'Who called the break?'

A moment later an embarrassed Pilot Officer Armstrong called in. 'Tomcat leader from Yellow-4, I called the break, sorry, I thought they were Messerschmitts.'

'Better safe than sorry Yellow-4. Tomcat squadron reform on me.'

Reforming was easier said than done. 126-Squadron was spread out all over the sky. Looking back, Steed observed the other half of Dix's section, Bishop and Adams, climbing into position. With his section once again intact, Dix turned to join the orbiting Chamberlain. The other squadron of Hurricanes was by now approaching the gaggle of Me-110s and Stukas. Chamberlain was anxious to join in, not only to support the other squadron but also to strike the Stukas before they had a chance to drop their bombs on the convoy. But he wanted to hit the enemy hard as a single entity, to try to beak their formation. For this he needed his squadron together.

When ten of his aircraft had assembled around him, Chamberlain decided that he had waited for long enough and set course for the fight developing ahead. The other squadron of Hurricanes had ploughed into the enemy force, but the German formation was still intact and nearing the point where the Stukas would peel off into their dive.

Tomcat Squadron was at full boost and climbing to the attack when the Me-109s hit them. The Messerschmitts had been waiting in ambush, hidden by cloud, but now they came down in a decisive strike. Dix once again executed a tight climbing turn, closely followed by Steed. The airwaves were full of shouts and curses, but these were drowned by a terrible ear-piecing scream. Steed was aware of a Hurricane to his right plunging earthwards with flames enveloping the cockpit.

A Me-109 flashed in front of Steed, firing a wild burst in the general direction of the flight lieutenant; Steed shouted to Dix to break right and fired, but the Messerschmitt disappeared almost as quickly as it had arrived. Dix jinked and turned, but then headed on towards to Stukas, trusting Steed to clear his tail. There was no hope now of a solid punch from the combined squadron, it was up to every pilot to do what he could to turn the enemy away from the convoy.

As he followed his flight commander, Steed looked back, alert to the danger from the marauding Me-109s. He did not have to look far. As he weaved to cover the blind spot he saw two Me-109s coming up fast from behind and below, using the speed gained from their dive. Judging the moment, he instructed Dix to break left, just in time to watch the 109s climb away without firing a shot. Once again Dix set course for the dive-bomber formation in front. Looking behind, Steed saw several smoke trails from distressed aircraft and two parachutes.

As they came within range of the enemy formation, Dix and Steed realised that they were too late. The last of the Stukas was already commencing its dive towards the convoy, and some of the Me-110 fighters were starting to adopt their usual defensive tactic of flying in a wide circle, each aircraft defending the tail of its companion in front. But Dix was not interested in trading blows with the Me-110s, even though the Hurricane was more than a match for the less nimble twin engine German fighter. Dix put his Hurricane into a steep dive, following the Stukas.

Dix and Steed both knew that they would be unable to stay on the tail of a Stuka in a dive; the Stuka had air brakes, so the Hurricanes were bound to overshoot. But a Stuka at ground level, even without its bomb load, was much slower than a Hurricane and an easy target. It was too late to stop the dive-bombers; several ships below had already been hit, but Dix spiralled down to seaward in an effort to cut of the Stukas home run, trusting Steed to worry about any pursuing enemy fighters.

The ploy was successful, and Dix zeroed in on a luckless lone Stuka, just above the waves, heading back at its ridiculously slow maximum speed across the Channel after dropping its bombs. With Steed guarding his tail, Dix throttled back and took careful aim. The Stuka rear gunner tried his best to ward off his adversary, and his pilot tried his best to make his aircraft a difficult target, but to no avail; Dix's marksmanship was good. The rear gunner stopped firing, the Ju-87 trailed smoke and its engine stopped. Dix pulled up as the pilot ditched in the Channel, the German pilot making a pretty good landing. Steed thought that the heavy fixed undercarriage would have tipped the dive-bomber forward onto its nose as soon as it touched the water. But the pilot had pulled the nose up just before impact and the aircraft had stalled and flopped down into the water at low speed.

Dix, with Steed in attendance, circled looking for another target. Perhaps surprisingly, none of the German fighters had followed them down. The downed Stuka settled deeper into the water, nose first. The canopy was open and two figures could be seen inside. The pilot was standing and appeared to be helping the gunner to get out.

Another Hurricane appeared, low over the water. It turned towards the stricken Stuka and, at point blank range, it delivered a short and decisive burst of fire. The two figures jerked and fell back into the dive-bomber, which then settled deeper into the water. The tail rose high into the air and the dive-bomber and its two-man crew slipped beneath the waves. Dix and Steed looked on in astonishment as the Hurricane turned towards them and waggled its wings. They recognised it as belonging to the Polish Pilot Officer Piotr Bazyli, known to one and all as 'The King' because the English translation of his surname was King.

'Hello Blue Leader, Red-3 joining you,' said The King simply.

'What the hell do you think that you were doing?' retorted the shocked Dix.

There was a pause, and then The King replied quietly, 'Just pray that your country is never invaded by these swine Flight Lieutenant.' Dix left it at that. They searched for more targets, but everybody had gone home.

Shortly after they landed, the squadron was stood down for the day. A little later Steed was summoned to Chamberlain's office. The squadron leader was seated behind his desk; Dix was also there, sitting in a leather-winged chair in the corner of the small room.

'Ah Hawk, sit down will you,' said Chamberlain breezily, motioning Steed to a second battered leather armchair. 'There are a couple of things that we need to talk about. You've heard about today's squadron casualties?' The question was rhetorical and the squadron leader did not wait for an answer. 'It looks like we have lost two pilots killed, Sergeant Edwards and Pilot Officer Armstrong. I have just heard that Pilot Officer Eagles crash landed near Portsmouth and is in hospital with two broken legs, so he won't be back with us for a while. I will try for replacements, but they will be straight out of training with precious few hours on Hurricanes. I will be leaning on experienced chaps like you to show them the ropes. And that brings me onto happier news. We are promoting you to flight sergeant with immediate effect.'

Steed's face registered surprise. Both Toby Adams and Johnny Walker were senior, and Steed surmised that counted for a lot in the service. But he simply smiled and said, 'Thank you sir.'

'It's well deserved Hawk. You are one of our best pilots. I shall be looking to you to provide support and leadership to our young sergeant pilots. How are things in the sergeants' mess by the way? Most of us heard poor Sergeant Edwards' screams on the radio when the 109s came down. How did the other two new boys take that?'

Steed answered carefully. 'I suspect that things are much the same as in the officers' mess. We know that we have job to do and we will do it. We know the consequences of failure, so failure isn't an option. Nobody likes to hear a friend's cries as he is burnt alive – and I think that all of us have a secret dread of going down in a burning aeroplane with a jammed canopy.' Steed paused and then added, 'I don't think that you need to worry about lack of moral fibre in the sergeants' mess.'

'Of course not, of course not,' countered the squadron leader hastily. 'I wasn't suggesting that for one moment. But you have a couple of young impressionable chaps there, just as we have in the officers' mess. More young and inexperienced pilots will be arriving and the job, as you so eloquently put it, will get a lot tougher. Just keep your eye on them and offer paternal advice should you feel that they need it.'

'Yes sir, a father figure at twenty-two eh? Takes a bit of getting used to, but I know what you mean.'

'And now, changing the subject, I want to talk about what happened this afternoon. I have read your combat report. As usual, it is very comprehensive. About four times the length of those from most of the other pilots. And you always put in times and locations. How do you remember so much when you land?'

'I have a pad and pencil strapped to my knee in the cockpit. When I have a chance I scribble some notes. Not much, just enough to jog my memory for the report when I land.'

'Good show,' replied a somewhat bemused Chamberlain. 'As I say, your reports are always very comprehensive, and that is commendable. Now about the episode following the ditching of the Ju-87 in the sea today, you simply say that it sank and there were no survivors. Do you have any more to add to that?' Chamberlain looked at Steed quizzically. Steed glanced at Dix, who met his gaze impassively.

'My report is accurate as far as it goes. There is some more that I didn't think, eh, politic to put in writing. After Mr Dix had shot down the Stuka we circled. The Stuka had more or less come to a stop in the water and was starting to sink when I saw a figure emerging from the front of the cockpit; the canopy must have been open by then. I assume that it was the pilot. He appeared to be helping his gunner. The King appeared and opened fire on the Stuka. It was only a short burst but it was bang on target. The Stuka pilot fell back into the cockpit. Moments later the Stuka sank. Mr Dix asked The King what he thought that he was doing, or words to that effect, but The King simply replied that he hoped that our country would not be invaded. I thought his words were very poignant. The rest was as in my report.'

'Thank you Hawk. Have you mentioned this incident to anyone else as yet?'

'No sir.'

'Then I would be obliged if you would keep it under your hat, at least for the time being. I have some sympathy with The King, although I do not condone what he did. I know something of what he had been through after his country was invaded, and what has made him hate the Nazis so much. We will deal with this quietly and within the squadron.'

'Yes sir.'

The squadron leader smiled broadly and stood up; and so did Dix. Steed assumed that the interview was over and also got to his feet. Chamberlain beamed as he spoke. 'Flight Sergeant Steed, it gives me great pleasure to inform you that you have been awarded the Distinguished Flying Medal. The investiture will be by the King at Buckingham Palace next week.'

This time Steed's jaw really did drop.

'I, eh, I don't know what to say. It's a great honour.'

'And it is very well deserved my boy.' Chamberlain had produced a bottle of sherry and three glasses. The squadron leader glanced down towards a piece of paper on his desk. 'The DFM is given for an act, or acts, of valour, courage or devotion to duty whilst flying in active operations against the enemy. The citation mentions two of the incidents during the Dunkirk operations, the first when you defended me during your first trip over Dunkirk, and the second when you took on four of the Luftwaffe's finest single-handed, thereby protecting your wounded squadron leader.'

Chamberlain poured the sherry. 'Your very good health Flight Sergeant Steed.'

'Here, here,' added the beaming Dix. 'Very well deserved Hawk. You are invited to the officers' mess this evening for a celebration drink or two and, assuming that the officer pilots are all invited, the party will continue in the sergeants' mess.' So there it was. Flight Lieutenant Dix was now using the nickname 'Hawk' rather than the usual 'Sergeant Steed'. But it was now Flight Sergeant Steed of course, so perhaps, in Dix's eyes, the promotion made the moniker acceptable.

The party was a riotous affair. Steed was a popular pilot and it was a double celebration, his flight sergeant's crown and the DFM. Steed found the time to slip away to the workshops where he found, as he knew that he would, his fitter and rigger. His own Hurricane did not have a bullet hole in it, but many of the other squadron aircraft had been less fortunate that day, and the mechanics were busy.

The flight sergeant in charge of aircraft maintenance, Peter Hawkins, spotted Steed as he entered the hangar. 'Congratulations Harry, all the very best mate, well done and well deserved. Sorry I can't be at the celebrations, but as you can see we have our hands full tonight.' Hawkins held up a greasy palm as a signal that they should not shake hands.

'Thanks Peter, I wanted to say thank you to my ground crew. I have a bottle of whisky and a few glasses here, but it is entirely up to you of course. You may prefer that your men do not have a drink while on duty here.'

'I don't think that one dram each will do much harm Harry, and whisky is scarce these days,' and with that the flight sergeant called over Steed's fitter and rigger. The armourer was also working that night, and he joined them. After the drink and the small talk, the airmen returned to their work. Steed turned to the flight sergeant. 'We had another flamer today Peter, young Bernie Edwards.'

'Yes, I heard. A bad business.'

'The Hurricane seems prone to catching fire. Is there anything that we can do, at squadron level I mean, to protect the pilot? Give him a few more seconds to get the canopy open and bale out.'

Hawkins thought for a moment. 'Come over to this Hurricane Harry and I will show you the problem. The big danger of fire comes from petrol, so it follows that to reduce the fire risk we have to protect the fuel tanks in some way. Now armour plating is effective, but it adds weight. That makes the aeroplane slower and less manoeuvrable, which means that the Messerschmitts will get you! As you know, we have two main fuel tanks, one in each wing. Both of these are self-sealing to some extent because they are covered in Linatex. If the petrol tank is pierced and fuel escapes, the Linatex rubber expands to seal the gap.'

The two men climbed the ladder to peer into the Hurricane's engine compartment. The cowling covers had been removed, offering a better view. Hawkins continued. 'My personal view is that the main problem stems from this reserve petrol tank located right in front of the pilot. It contains twenty-eight gallons of fuel. It is sandwiched between these two bulkheads so it is a real bugger to get at. This reserve tank is not protected by Linatex.'

'Hmm,' said Steed. 'It begs the question why not? What are the chances of fitting a fire-resistant panel between the reserve tank and the pilot?'

'A very good question. We are talking to the Air Ministry about these things and others, and I believe that there are moves afoot to coat the reserve tank with Linatex. But there are also other vital areas on the aeroplane that could do with more protection. For example, when you chaps are attacking bombers, most of the German return fire is directed towards the front of the Hurricane. Therefore the glycol tank for the engine cooling, here in front of the reserve petrol tank, is vulnerable; likewise the oil tank down there at the leading edge of the port wing can also take hits. One could argue the case for a bit of extra armour in front of these components. That would help when you were taking return fire from dead ahead, but would be useless when the bullets came from another direction, ground fire for example, or the 109 on your tail. To provide armour all around for all these bits and pieces would make the aircraft far too heavy. We have to concentrate armour on where it is really needed, behind your seat for example. You see the problem?'

'Yes,' said Steed. 'It is all a bit of a compromise. The Hurricane struggles for speed and rate of climb against the Me-109 as it is. We can't afford to add extra weight, nice though a bit more armour would be. Thanks for the tour Peter. I had better get back to my party.'

In the days that followed, 126-Squadron was again employed on convoy duty north of the Thames estuary. There were no further losses, although several pilots had to nurse home damaged aeroplanes. Dix, Chamberlain and The King each claimed kills. The expected replacements did not arrive, so there was little chance of a rest day for any of the pilots.

Steed still found some time for cross-country running, usually around the airfield perimeter, and often accompanied by the Spy's black Labrador, Dion. Steed now regarded the jovial intelligence officer as a firm friend, and regularly solicited his opinions on German tactics and intentions. Chamberlain's briefings to his pilots at dispersal were very informative and welcome, but it was clear that some things were only for debate in the officers' mess.

One of the issues that Chamberlain had failed to mention in his briefings was the latest German ploy of sending 'hunting' Me-109 fighter sweeps over southern England. These, the Spy said, were aimed at drawing the RAF into fighter-on-fighter battles and a consequent wearing down of the British fighter force, so Dowding had instructed his controllers not to get sucked into such battles. To date, none of these Luftwaffe fighter sweeps had ventured out over Essex, but Steed was now especially alert for 'the Hun in the sun' right from take-off, and not just out over the Channel.

The investiture was a proud moment for Steed's parents, for they were invited to attend the ceremony at Buckingham Palace. Afterwards, his mother admired her son's medal. 'I can see that the face on the front of the medal is the King's, but who is this on the back Harry, is it Britannia?'

Steed replied, 'No Mum. That is Athena, Greek goddess of victory. She has a hawk on her arm, see?'

'Oh yes, I see. They call you Hawk, don't they son? The medal seems fitting somehow.'

'Well some of them call me that. They think that I can spot the Jerries coming well before anyone else sees them.'

'And can you son?'

'Absolutely Mum, I always see them before they see me. That's why I shoot 'em down so easily!'

'They shot you down once son,' said his mother uneasily, 'over Dunkirk.'

'Now then Mum, I've told you. It was the Royal Navy that did that, but we mustn't talk about it in case people think that the Navy go around shooting down Hurricanes. That's bad publicity for the Navy and good propaganda for Mr Hitler. Now let's go and find some tea.'

The following week the Luftwaffe changed tactics, providing a nasty shock to the Tomcats. Up until then the Germans had confined their offensive to the Channel convoys and coastal ports, with occasional fighter sweeps across Southern England. Then, one morning in mid August, Steed was lounging in a deckchair outside the dispersal hut reading a French textbook. He had resumed his schooldays study of the French language at the outbreak of the war when it seemed likely, to him at least, that he would be following in the footsteps of his father and his RFC heroes on the

Western Front. He was shaken from his study of French verb conjugation by the sound of the scramble bell.

Steed leaped from his deckchair and raced towards his parked Hurricane, some 200 metres away. He put on his Iving flying jacket as he ran, for it would be cold at fifteen thousand feet. In front of him he could see his rigger by the battery cart, which provided the power to turn the propeller, and his fitter leaning into the cockpit. The Hurricane's engine bellowed into life with a puff of black smoke. He seized his parachute from the wing of the Hurricane and clipped it on. Hampered by his equipment, Steed clumsily clambered up onto the wing root. His fitter helped him into the cramped cockpit and also helped to strap him into the fighter. Steed pulled on his flying helmet and connected the intercom lead and oxygen supply. The engine was now running sweetly so the rigger disconnected the battery plug and slammed shut the cover on the aircraft's nose. 'Good luck Flight,' shouted his ground crew in unison, and Steed was free to join the other aircraft taxiing for take-off. Only Blue and Yellow sections were at readiness that morning, and the eight-aircraft squadron was led by Dix.

Steed took position to the left and slightly behind Dix for take-off. Dix was unhappy that morning because his regular aircraft was being serviced and he was piloting a spare. As the two aircraft picked up speed, Steed became aware of multiple explosions away to his left. Christ, the airfield was being bombed! There were low-flying aircraft over there by the hangars and anti-aircraft fire was going up. As his Hurricane sped down the field, Steed glimpsed bombs falling behind him on the grass runway.

The Hurricane reached take-off speed and Steed immediately pulled back the stick and retracted the undercarriage. At that moment a Dornier skimmed past overhead, its dorsal gun winking wicked tracer towards Steed, who did not have the speed or height to take evasive action. Bullets ripped into the fabric of the Hurricane's wing. A huge explosion shook the ground, immediately ahead of Dix's aircraft. Steed watched in horror as the blast caught Dix's Hurricane and tossed it to one side like a child's toy. The same blast caught Steed's aircraft, although not with the same ferocity, since Steed was a little higher than Dix and to one side. Nevertheless, Steed's Hurricane was pitched violently to one side, losing height so that it only narrowly avoided digging a deep hole in the Essex countryside.

Having regained control, Steed twisted and turned his aircraft, as best as his low speed and height would allow, looking for friend or foe. Dix had gone. Steed caught sight of a burning aircraft on the runway behind; that could not be Dix, he thought, more likely to be one of the six Hurricanes that were behind during the squadron scramble, caught by the German attack.

Steed climbed higher. He tried the radio, but it was dead, not even static, probably hit by the German gunner or by the bomb blast he thought, because it would have been checked before take off. At least his aircraft appeared to be functioning predictably, in spite of its ill treatment by bombs and bullets, and all of the gauges were normal. Away to his left some of the airfield buildings were burning, but Steed could see no sign of the intruders. However, as he climbed higher he spotted two twin-engine aircraft heading back towards the station buildings. Presumably Germans coming in for a second bombing run. He turned his Hurricane, intending to cut them off, but the enemy, he could now see clearly that the two aircraft were Dornier-17s, had a head start and were once again approaching the devastation that was 126-Squadron's home. Steed felt deep resentment building up inside him against these arrogant Nazis who were dropping bombs on his airfield. It was time for some retribution.

The two Dorniers were machine-gunning targets of opportunity on the airfield. Were the anti-aircraft guns still returning fire? If they were, he could not see any tracer coming up. Steed was now behind the trailing bomber, travelling at about the same speed as the German but with a height advantage over it. The rest should be straightforward.

As Steed expected, the dorsal rear gunner opened fire early with short bursts, with the hope of putting off his attacker's aim. But Steed had been in this position before, and he knew exactly what he must do. The German pilot had few options. He was positioned well behind his leader, so he could expect little support from the second Dornier's guns. He could not quickly bring any of his other guns to bear, so he only had his dorsal gun to rely on for defensive fire. His only other option was to twist and turn in an attempt to deflect the Hurricane pilot's aim; this he did, but it was not enough. Ignoring the dorsal gunner's now quite accurate fire, Steed closed to his customary 250 yards range, allowing for the deflection and aiming, as usual, for the glazed nose section of the enemy aircraft.

His first burst was long and on target; the dorsal gunner was immediately silenced. Steed gave a rueful smile as he remembered, not for the first time, von Richthofen's maxim, 'kill the gunner first'. The Dornier was mortally hit. It lost height as Steed pulled up to avoid overshooting the bomber and thereby laying himself open to fire from its forward facing guns. The German hit the ground towards the perimeter of the airfield and appeared to make a passable attempt at a crash landing. But the crew was unlucky because the Dornier ploughed on through the perimeter fence into a small wood; the aircraft was brought to an abrupt halt amongst the shattered trees and burst into flames.

Steed set of in pursuit of the lead Dornier, but it had disappeared. He climbed, and circled the airfield. Once again he took stock of his aircraft. There were a number of holes in his starboard wing and his engine temperature was registering on the hot side of normal. His radio did not work; at least he could not receive. But apart from that he was not in bad shape. He tried transmitting a message to the effect that he was okay and circling the airfield with the aim of defending it against further attack, but he doubted that the apparatus was working. As he looked down, he could see two damaged Hurricanes on the grass runway; one was completely burnt out and was obviously a write off, an ambulance was alongside the second. A number of the squadron buildings had been damaged, including the main hangar. Altogether, a bit of a mess! The sky remained empty.

Steed remembered his leader. Had Dix survived the bomb blast or had he crashed beyond the airfield perimeter? Steed flew over the end of the runway and immediately spotted a burning Hurricane at the end of a deep furrow. It did not look good. From the furrow it appeared that Dix had at least been able to attempt a crash landing, but had he managed to escape from the aircraft before it burst into flames? The rescue vehicles had not yet arrived. Indeed they might not know that Dix was there, although they should have been alerted by the plume of black smoke now rising from the wreck. And then he saw a figure, some distance from the aircraft and lying on the ground. Mercifully, the flight commander waved as Steed flew overhead.

Steed was now convinced that his aircraft had been damaged. The temperature gauge had risen in spite of running at low engine revs for the past few minutes. He also thought that he could smell glycol, the radiator fluid. Steed made a few passes over the runway to check for bomb craters, of which there were several. He selected the best line of approach and came in to land; he looked for a warning flare from the control tower, but there was none. He gave a sigh of relief when he saw that his undercarriage was down and locked, but he still treated the Hurricane as if it were made of raw eggs during the landing, because he could not be sure that the bullets through his wing had not damaged a vital spar.

Steed taxied over to one of the crash crews, and waved one of the airmen over to the Hurricane. 'We have a crashed Hurricane just beyond the perimeter, over there, you can see the smoke. The pilot is out of the aircraft and is lying on the grass. He is conscious because he has just waved to me. Can you get someone over there quickly please?'

'We'll get an ambulance over there right away sir,' replied the airman.

'My radio is dead, so I haven't been able to tell anyone else. I believe the pilot is Flight Lieutenant Dix.'

'Okay sir, we will deal with it right away.'

Steed taxied carefully to dispersal, avoiding the bomb craters, and was relieved to see his waiting ground crew. 'Anybody hurt? Are you guys okay?' shouted Steed as his ground crew ran up to greet him.

'We're okay Flight, but the boys over there have taken a pasting.' His fitter gestured across the airfield towards the main hanger and squadron buildings. 'They got two Hurricanes of Yellow Section as they took off, Mr Daily and Sergeant Stillwell I think.'

His rigger broke into the conversation. 'Was that you who got that Jerry?' He jerked his thumb in the direction of the woods.

'I got the bastard Colin, but his leader got away.' Steed was by now out of his Hurricane and examining the damage. 'I took a number of hits in the starboard wing that I know about, and the aircraft was thrown about by bomb blast just as I left the ground on take-off, so there might be some damage from that. Also, the temperature gauge went high later in the flight and I think that I smelt glycol. Oh yes, my radio is duff as well, so I haven't heard from anybody. Have you any news on any of the others?'

'No Flight,' answered his fitter.

A car raced up to the three men, and the squadron leader jumped out. 'Good to see you are okay Hawk, was it you that took out the Hun over there?'

'Yes sir, a Dornier. Mr Dix and me were both hit by bomb blast as we took off. I think that he was rather more in the way of it than me. I lost contact with him but I have just seen a burning Hurricane just beyond the perimeter. The pilot, I think it must be Mr Dix, was some distance from the plane lying on his back, but he waved to me. I told the crash crews when I landed and they said that they would send an ambulance.'

'Good show. Jump in and you can tell me your story. It's a hell of a mess over there, but we have to get at least Red Section operational by noon.'

The airfield was indeed a shambles. The air raid warning had been sounded only as the first bombs began to fall, so many people had failed to reach the shelters in time and loss of life had been heavy. The main hangar had been damaged and several airfield buildings had been destroyed, including the small hospital come sickbay. This hampered the care of the many casualties. The sergeants' mess had survived!

An hour later, things were clearer. Del Stillwell had been killed on take-off. A bomb had exploded immediately in front of his aircraft, which had cart wheeled and bust into flames. Roger Daily's aircraft had similarly been blown over by a near miss, but his Hurricane had miraculously not caught fire, although brimmed full of fuel. Daily had been pulled from the wreckage, injured, with deep cuts to his legs and a loss of blood, but the tough Australian insisted that he would be flying again in a day or two. Dix was also injured, his face having smashed into the reflective gun sight during the crash landing. Both men had been taken to the local hospital.

Billy Bishop and Toby Adams, who had been flying Blue-3 and Blue-4 behind Dix and Steed, landed shortly after Steed with a story to tell. 'We were following you,' said Toby Adams to Steed, 'when out of nowhere there were bloody great bangs all around, grass and all sorts flying into the air. Then a sodding great Dornier flew past overhead with the cheeky rear gunner spraying bullets at us. Somehow, don't ask me how, Billy and me both managed to get off the ground in one piece. I saw you go off left, and you nearly hit the ground.'

'Tell me about it!' said Steed.

'Anyway, Billy said let's get that fucking Hun, so that's what we did. He was in front of us, pulling away and going hell for leather. I reckon the crew could see two Hurries chasing them and weren't waiting for us to join the party. There was a bit of cloud around, and I guess that they were hoping to get lost in the stuff. They made it to a cloudbank, but by this time Billy and me had picked up some speed. Unluckily for them the cloudbank was too small to hide in for long. Billy went above and I stayed below. When they popped out, we had them. It was obvious that they were trying for a larger clump of cloud, but Billy went in first and gave 'em a good dose of lead.'

'A good dose of lead! You sound like a Yank gangster' chuckled Steed.

'Yeah. Anyway, they kept on towards the next clump of cloud, wiggling this way and that, and Billy kept on firing. Then I had a go and one of their engines started smoking. Then it caught fire. The fire spread along the wing and that was it really. Billy and me pulled away and a couple of them managed to jump out before the thing went down into a steep dive, well on fire. Rotten thing was that it hit some houses below. Bloody great explosion, maybe they had a couple more bombs on board. I damn nearly gave the Huns a burst to send them to Nazi hell as they hung in their chutes; maybe I would have done if I had known then that they had killed poor Del. Anyway, we circled and saw the Huns land; they all landed in the same field. Some farm workers ran up and the Huns went quietly. Billy said that we should claim half a Hun each.'

That afternoon, all the pilots met in the dispersal hut. Chamberlain gave the score.

'The Jerries hit a number of our airfields today, all over Southern England. Here at Colne Martin we were scrambled of course, but totally unaware that our airfield was the target. I don't yet know how it happened but we received no warning of the raid until the blighters were on us. Maybe it was because they came in low. For sure, 126-Squadron has been on the receiving end today. We have lost Sergeant Stillwell, and our two flight lieutenants have been put into hospital. We have also lost a number of other people killed and injured, not to mention wrecked or damaged aircraft, equipment and buildings. We have, at this moment, only eight serviceable aircraft and nine pilots.'

Chamberlain paused and looked around the room. 'Things aren't all doom and gloom, though. Group has promised us some shiny new Hurricanes for later today, and we have three new pilots who arrived an hour ago, one pilot officer and two sergeants, all Volunteer Reserve. They are with the adjutant now. So, for this afternoon, Red and Blue sections are at readiness from 14.00. I will lead Red Section, which is unchanged. Billy Bishop will lead Blue Section with Sergeant Adams, Jean-Paul and Sergeant Walker.'

He looked across the room at Steed. 'Hawk, your aircraft is damaged but it will be ready tomorrow, or so I am told. I want you to go along to the adjutant's office, it is still there by the way, and brief the new chaps on the way we do things here. You know the score. Take them through the four aircraft section formation, duties of the wingman and so on. Tell them all about the nasty tricks the Jerries get up to. But don't scare the pants off them just yet.'

Later, in the adjutant's office, Steed was introduced to the new pilot intake.

'Gentlemen,' began the adjutant, 'allow me to introduce you to Flight Sergeant Harry Steed, known to one an all as Hawk because of his uncanny ability to spot the German aeroplanes coming before anyone else sees them. The flight sergeant is going to tell you all about squadron formations and tactics. Listen to him carefully; he knows what he is talking about. He is the squadron's top scorer with nine kills to his credit so far, including one of this morning's raiders, which he shot down over the airfield.'

The three young pilots looked suitably impressed. The adjutant introduced each pilot in turn as Steed shook their hands, 'Pilot Officer Chris Stevens, Sergeant Fred Farthing and Sergeant Gareth Evans. Hawk, the room next door is free. You will find a blackboard and chalk in there if you need it.'

Steed spent the next three hours trying to bring the young pilots up to date with the air war. He was shocked to find that each pilot had only four or five hours training on Hurricanes. That evening he asked for an appointment with the squadron leader. 'Come in Hawk, sit down.' The squadron leader looked tired. The squadron had been in combat again that afternoon, but fortunately had not suffered further losses. 'How did you get on with the new boys?'

'Sir, I am very worried about the training that they have received. They all have less than 100 hours total flying experience, and none of them has more than five hours on Hurricanes. They are all very keen and full of questions, very commendable, and I haven't seen them fly of course, but if we let them loose as they are, well, I have the feeling that they would simply be cannon fodder.'

'I know that Hawk,' said Chamberlain gravely, 'but we may have little choice. We are down to only nine pilots without the new chaps, so we need them to fly a twelve aircraft squadron. Otherwise we have to go into battle under strength, and Group won't like that.'

Chamberlain thought for a moment. 'Listen, our three new Hurricanes will be ready for ops. early tomorrow morning, plus those crates that our people can repair overnight, so it is not aircraft that are holding us back right now but pilots. I will tell Group that I am only able to put up eight aircraft tomorrow. That will buy some time to give the new guys a chance. It is your job to take the sprogs up tomorrow and try to teach them enough to survive. At least they will get in a few more hours on Hurricanes. I will want them and you back in the saddle the day after tomorrow. It is the best that I can do. The new boys will have to take their chances like the rest of us.'

Steed nodded, 'I'll try to give them the idiot's guide to air fighting. How are Mr Dix and Mr Daily?'

'I am just back from seeing them. Both of them are spending the night in the local hospital; looks like they will be there for a couple of days at least. They are in good spirits, but they are not allowed any visitors until tomorrow at least. The doctor only allowed me to see them because I am their C/O. Hugh has a number of nasty cuts around his face and he has lost a few teeth. One of his eyes is all but closed; he looks a bit of a mess. They think he has concussion. Roger isn't much better, he can hardly walk, but at least there are no bones broken. My guess is that neither of them will be flying again for at least a week, even though we are desperate to have them back.'

Steed nodded and said, 'Give them my regards sir,' and started to rise from his chair to leave.

Chamberlain motioned for him to be seated. 'No, sit down Hawk, since you are here, I have one or two things to say to you. I do not like to chop and change people around within sections if I can help it. Pilots get used to the people flying around them, leader and wingman and so on, teams within a team if you know what I mean.' Steed nodded and Chamberlain continued. 'We have been hit hard by the injuries to our two section leaders. As far as your Blue Section is concerned, Billy Bishop will lead until Hugh Dix returns, and Sergeant Adams will fly Billy's number two as usual. I want you to fly Blue-3 with Sergeant Evans as your Blue-4. Take Evans under your wing, will you?'

'Of course. I will try to look after him.'

That night in the sergeants' mess there was merriment and singing, with Johnny Walker on good form at the piano. Del Stillwell, or what was left of him after the fire, was in his coffin in a makeshift mortuary, the usual place of rest having been destroyed by the Luftwaffe's bombs. There was a toast to Del's memory; the sergeant pilots did not dwell on his death but moved on. Several of them had been across to the charred remains of Steed's Dornier and liberated a few souvenirs; a fabric swastika, cut from the tail plane, now hung above the bar.

True to his word, Chamberlain put only eight of his pilots on readiness the next day, leaving Steed to deliver essential survival training to the three new pilots. Steed addressed the pilots outside the dispersal hut.

'Today we will put into practice what we talked about yesterday. Tomorrow, it is likely that we will all be on operations mixing it with the Luftwaffe, so today is your last chance to iron out any deficiencies. One or two points to remember; we are at war and although I will try to keep us away from trouble, it is possible that we will run into the opposition. If we do, stick to me like glue and follow my orders. Remember, you must follow the orders of the designated air leader irrespective of rank. In the air today, I am the boss. If you find yourself all on your lonesome, do not fly in a straight line for more than a few seconds. Twist and turn, cover the blind spots and keep your eyes open for the Hun fighters, especially up in the sun.'

Steed paused and subconsciously studied the pilots. They were so young. Evans was only eighteen, the other three nineteen. They looked back attentively. Steed was acutely aware that their lives depended on what he would be able to teach them in a few short hours.

'We will fly the four-aircraft formation, just as we discussed yesterday. Our call-sign today as far as ground control is concerned is Pelican, but for transmissions between ourselves I am Blue Leader, Gareth is my wingman Blue-2, Chris is Blue-3 and Fred is Chris' wingman Blue-4. Everybody got that?' The young pilots nodded. 'Always use the correct wireless procedure; get used to it, and if we get into trouble don't block the airwaves with unnecessary chatter.'

'This morning I want to concentrate on loose formation flying and observation. It is obviously desirable to spot the Huns before they see us. The loose formation that we will fly today helps us to do that. Remember that we are the fighters. Enemy bombers over our territory need to worry about us, not the other way around. It is our job to shoot the bastards out of the sky. When you attack the bombers, ignore their return fire. Get in close, break up their formations and kill them! But the Huns have fighters too, and they like to live in the sun or come sneaking up behind you. Don't get shot down by their fighters before you have a chance to get to their bombers. So this morning I will show you how to spot and fend off a Hun fighter attack.

'We take off as two pairs and join up under the cloud. Nice tight formation going up through the cloud or we will lose each other. When we get topside spread out a little, not too much but just enough so you have time to look around without constantly having to worry about colliding with your companions. Remember, the secret is to keep looking around. Check the sun; and wingmen especially, keep a sharp lookout behind.'

Steed led his formation in a north-westerly direction, he hoped away from potential trouble. Steed was far from impressed by his pilots' station keeping as they climbed through the cloud; Fred Farthing lost contact altogether. He told them to close up again as they climbed into bright sunlight, but their formation flying was sloppy. He thought back to his fist flight with 126-Squadron before Dunkirk. Dix had certainly put him through his paces that day! What would the flight lieutenant think about the flying standard of the latest recruits?

'Pelicans from Leader. You have to be able to hold a tight formation as we climb through cloud, otherwise you will lose contact with your squadron just like Blue-4 did just then. Now that we are above the cloud, ease out a bit. Remember to switch on your oxygen; no one will remind you tomorrow. Now we will carry out some basic manoeuvres. Your job is to follow me and stay in a loose formation as we do so, and remember to keep a good lookout at all times.'

Steed led the formation in a series of, for him, gentle turns, climbs and dives. The pilots seemed to spread themselves all over the sky in their attempts to follow. Fred Farthing in particular was having a torrid time and spun away on several occasions. Steed made his manoeuvres less arduous and, gradually, the pilots managed to stay in a reasonable formation with each change in direction.

'Pelicans from Leader. Next exercise, Blue-3 and Blue-4, continue flying straight and level. Blue-2 follow me. We will make some practice attacks. Remember everybody, our guns are loaded so safety on please and do not get over-excited and press any buttons.'

Steed pulled away sharply, dived and turned, and then climbed steeply at full boost. He was pleased to see that Evans, although a little too far behind, stayed with him. He called to Stevens and Farthing. 'Blue-3 and 4 from Leader, can you see us?' There was a pause and the Stevens replied, 'I think so leader, are you up there in the sun?'

'That's right Blue-3. How about you Blue-4, can you see us? About 2,000 feet above you in the sun.'

'I think that I can see you Blue leader. But it's very difficult, looking into the sun I mean,' Farthing replied hesitantly.

Time was limited; Steed knew that he must push things along. 'We are now coming down to attack you from behind. Blue-3, you call the break. Please everyone, be careful, no collisions.'

Chris Stevens made a passable job of calling the break and the two Hurricanes turned to meet the attack. Steed reformed the section.

'Pelicans from Leader. Okay, we will try that once more. Keep a good lookout you two. Don't let us get within firing range.'

Again Steed climbed, turned sharply and climbed into the sun. He dived, turned and then climbed again, pleased to see that Evans was holding station behind him. Sensing that his quarry had lost sight of their 'enemy', he slid his Hurricane into the blind spot below and behind Farthing's aircraft. Farthing was making a feeble attempt at covering his tail by moving gently from side to side, but Steed and Evans were still able to creep up unseen to within 250 yards of Blue-4. After a minute, Steed transmitted, 'Blue-3 and 4 from Leader. Do you see us?'

'Leader from Blue-3. I don't think so. Are you in the sun?'

'No Blue-3. For the last couple of minutes we have been sitting a couple of hundred yards behind Blue-4. You must cover that blind spot behind and below Blue-4 or the Messerschmitts will have you for dinner. Weave. Have a good look, not a token glance, do it now.'

'Sorry Blue leader,' said Farthing, 'I see you now.'

'Okay boys, let's do it again,' Steed said cheerily, hoping to instil some confidence in his charges. 'When we have got it right Blue-3 and 4 can have a go at being the attackers.'

When they returned to Colne Martin to refuel, they found the squadron had been sent south to intercept Luftwaffe strikes on airfields. Steed did not allow his pilots to go to the mess for lunch; they had to make do with tea and a sandwich in the dispersal hut.

Steed sat back in an easy chair munching his bully beef sandwich. 'That was a good morning's work boys, you all did very well considering how few hours any of you has had on Hurricanes. A definite improvement as we went along. Any questions? Any thoughts?'

Steed looked around at his three companions. It was Chris Stevens who answered first. 'When we started, I found it almost impossible to see you chaps coming down out of the sun. And I also found it very difficult to know just when to call the break. But things did seem to get better as we went along. I know that they call you Hawk. Is it just that you have good eyesight, or is there some technique that you use?'

Steed smiled, 'I'm not sure that I use any special techniques. Obviously you cannot look directly into the sun, but with everybody moving about in the combat zone, the enemy is unlikely to be able to position himself directly in line with the sun as you see him anyway. So look to either side of the sun. I rely on frequent quick glances and I often hold my hand up to shield the sun so that I can see closer in if you know what I mean. How are your neck muscles?'

His pilots looked blank. Steed smiled again and continued, 'If you are doing your job properly, your neck muscles will be aching tonight. You should be looking around constantly. You may also have chafing on your neck where your shirt is rubbing. Try leaving your shirt collar open, and try wearing something soft around your neck.' Steed pointed to his silk scarf, 'This isn't my idea of fashion for the well dressed pilot; it stops my neck from getting sore.'

'Is there a chance that we can try some dogfighting this afternoon Hawk?' asked Gareth Evans in his Welsh singsong voice.

'Okay Gareth, we can play at air aces as well. But the main objective for this afternoon is to give you people the chance to fire your guns, since I understand that none of you has tried out any gunnery with the Hurricane.' The pilots murmured their agreement. 'Unfortunately, I haven't been able to fix up a drone for us to shoot at, but I have a few ideas on how we might practise deflection shooting. We are cleared to try out our gunnery over the sea, out over The Wash, so we can practice formation flying and observation on the way. On that note, I know I said that we fly a fairly loose formation, but some of you are moving about far too much. The Boss won't like it if you do it tomorrow. On the way up to The Wash, try to hold position a little bit better.' The pilots nodded. 'I know that it's difficult, but if you stray too far away you make yourself a target for the bad guys. Also, as Fred knows, if you don't fly a tight formation in cloud you get lost!' Fred Farthing smiled but coloured slightly.

Steed winked and then said, 'A little test question. Who can tell me roughly how many seconds continuous fire you can get from a Hurricane's guns?'

Stevens waited a moment for someone else to answer and then said, 'Fifteen seconds Flight.'

'Spot on. Remember that when we are firing our guns this afternoon. If I ask you to fire a two second burst, don't make it four seconds or you'll soon be out of ammo.'

Out over the Wash at sea level, Steed was gratified that a visible sun allowed four Hurricane shadows to skip along the tranquil sea. Steed spoke to Stevens.

'Blue-3 from leader. Hold your course and speed; the rest of you follow me.' Steed led the remaining two pilots into position above and behind Stevens's Hurricane, trailing its feathery shadow across the grey-green North Sea.

'Blue-2 and 4 from Leader, I am going to rake Blue-3's shadow with a two second burst. Watch carefully.' Steed dived down, allowed for the deflection, and then fired a two second burst. The water boiled around the shadow target. Steed returned to join Evans and Farthing.

'Pelicans from Leader. Please note the following instructions very carefully. Point one, do not shoot down Blue-3. Point two, do not crash into the sea. Point three, remember to allow for the deflection when you shoot. And point four, fire only a two second burst please. Okay Blue-2, in your own time. Give that shadow some stick!'

Evans dived down towards the shadow, his bullets scything a foaming path in the sea behind Stevens's aircraft. But he missed the target, his bullets always splattering the sea behind the swiftly moving shadow.

'Not bad Blue-2, but you hit behind the target. Remember the deflection. Best to fire too far in front of the target if anything, and then let the enemy run into your bullets as you correct. Your turn Blue-4.'

Farthing set off towards the trailed shadow. Of all his charges, Steed was most concerned about Farthing. The sergeant pilot's standard of flying was simply too poor; the boy found it difficult to maintain station and he had become separated from the others several times during their practice climbs through cloud. Steed watched as Farthing's aircraft hurtled down towards Stevens's shadow. Farthing fired. The splashes were right on target but Farthing was very low, his slipstream causing white spray to frolic in his wake. Farthing pulled up.

'Good shooting Blue-4, but you were very close to hitting the sea. Be careful about that next time.'

Steed continued with the gunnery exercises until his pilots were low on ammunition. On the way back he allowed his charges to dogfight with each other, but he found it ridiculously easy to get onto the tail of each of them, and to stay there as they attempted to shake him off.

When they landed at Colne Martin, they found that the squadron, all eight of them, were back. The ground crew immediately started work on refuelling and rearming their aircraft as Steed led the new pilots towards the dispersal hut. Chamberlain came out to greet them, 'How did you get on chaps?'

'Not bad sir,' replied Steed. 'We carried out formation and observation exercises this morning then, on the second flight, we had some firing practice at our shadows out over The Wash. We also played at dogfighting on the way back.'

'Capital,' replied the squadron leader. Looking towards the new pilots he added, 'You chaps are now operational. The squadron is at readiness. If we are scrambled, Chris, you will fly in Red Section as my wingman. Sergeant Evans, you will fly in Blue Section as Hawk's wingman. And Sergeant Farthing, you will fly in Yellow Section as Pilot Officer Colbert's wingman. The squadron formation is on the notice board, please take a look.'

As the new pilots entered the dispersal hut to do the squadron leader's bidding, Chamberlain motioned to Steed to walk with him outside. 'How do they shape up Hawk?'

Steed took a moment to consider as they walked, and then said, 'Pilot Officer Stevens is the best pilot. Sergeant Evans is not too far behind him, but Sergeant Farthing is simply not up to it yet. To be honest, none of them will come out on top in a dogfight against your typical 109 pilot, not unless their Jerry happens to be as green as they are. They should all be okay going at the bombers though. And all three of them are dead keen of course.'

'Much as I expected, but I don't have any choice Hawk, I must make them operational now. We just don't have the luxury of giving them any more training. I took eight aircraft up today against around fifty of the opposition. We were lucky to come away from it without any more losses. I need a full squadron up there. Everybody must pull their weight.' Steed surmised that the squadron leader was feeling the strain.

As Steed entered the dispersal hut the telephone rang. Anxious faces turned towards the duty corporal who answered. The corporal called through the open window to Chamberlain. 'Squadron stand down sir.'

'Right chaps,' shouted the squadron leader. 'We're finished for the day. Everybody off for tea!'

That evening the six sergeant pilots met up in the mess over beer. Johnny Walker was vociferous. 'What a day Harry. You boys did well to miss it. We were scrambled and headed out across the estuary, climbing hard all the time. We were well above twenty thousand feet when we first saw the bombers out in front. There must have been fifty of the buggers. We had plenty of height advantage on them, but the 109s were even higher than us, and there were loads of the sods. Not a friend in sight. There we were, eight little Hurricanes surrounded by half the Luftwaffe. The 109s came at us and it was every man for himself. You know what a lump the Hurri is compared with the 109 at that height. With Roger in hospital I was wingman to Smithy. I took pot shots of anything that came in front of me, but I doubt that I caused much damage. The 109s hit us, climbed away then came down on us again, time and again.'

'You're right there Johnny,' chimed in Toby Adams. 'The Hurri is a brick at that height. Billy and me got separated from everybody else right at the start. We had a whole gaggle of 109s on our tail and Billy decided to spiral down to lose the bastards; diving straight down would have been suicide. As it was, I got peppered by the sods, and a cannon shell blew out my radio. I think Billy was trying to make it to the bombers, then one of the 109s overshot and Billy got in a fair burst at him; didn't see the Hun go down though, so Billy claimed a damaged. The 109s chased us all the way down, the longest few minutes of my life! We didn't get a chance to have a go at the bombers. We were dead lucky to get home more or less in one piece.'

'We were in front,' said Tony Parsons. 'After the break, Chamberlain led us straight at the 109s. I was behind The King. I tell you, that Pole's got some guts. He bloody near rammed the lead 109, and just kept on going, blazing away at everything in sight. There were loads of the buggers, but I think that there were so many that they got in each other's way. They should have had us for breakfast. They had us outnumbered and at a height that gave their 109s a clear advantage over the Hurri. Like Johnny, I had snap shots at a number of the sods, but to be honest, mostly at maximum range and serious deflection shooting went out of the window!'

'I bet you boys are wondering what you have let yourselves into,' chuckled Johnny Walker, looking towards Evans and Farthing. 'Don't worry. We're all shooting a line. It wasn't as bad as we make out you know. After all we all came back didn't we? Tomorrow we will have some nice fat juicy bombers to shoot at. You will both come back aces. Right, that's enough shop for tonight, let's have a party.' Walker ambled over to the piano with his pint, and began to play 'roll out the barrel', a mess favourite. In no time he had a crowd around him singing along, and the party was in full swing.

Chamberlain gave his usual briefing the next morning at the dispersal hut.

'Settle down chaps and listen up. It is now clear that the enemy has changed his tactics. Up until a few days ago he was content to harass our Channel convoys and ports. Group believes that his intention was gain air superiority over the Channel as a precursor to invasion. His bombers did not penetrate too far inland, although he did mount fighter sweeps over Kent and Sussex, presumably with the aim of forcing fighter-on-fighter air battles and wearing us down. The RAF met and turned back these attacks, and we have denied the enemy air superiority over the English Channel and our homeland.'

There were shouts of agreement from the pilots. Chamberlain continued, 'We can all be very proud of the part that 126-Squadron has played so far. We have taken losses it's true, but we have given the Luftwaffe a bloody nose. We have proved that we are a force to be reckoned with if they are stupid enough to try an invasion.'

Again the pilots cheered. Steed's instinctive reaction was to shy away from jingoism; it had cost Britain dear in the Great War, but he admired the way in which Chamberlain could motivate his men. Chamberlain's words made sense, on balance the RAF had done well, very well in fact, although the Germans had also had their successes.

Chamberlain continued, 'Hitler is now trying something different. During the last few days he has been sending his bombers against our airfields, our RDF sites and our aircraft factories. His bombers have been coming over in numbers, very well supported by fighters. Hitler is trying to put the RAF out of action. There is only one reason for him to do this; he is setting himself up for an invasion. With us out of the picture his bombers will have a clear run at the Royal Navy warships trying to stop his landing craft, his paratrooper transports will not be shot out of the sky by our fighters, and his troops landing on our beaches will not have the shit knocked out of them by our bombers.'

Again Steed glanced around the dispersal hut to assess the pilots' reactions. He saw determination on their faces. Chamberlain certainly knew how to make a speech; he was almost as good as Churchill! But again, what Chamberlain was saying made perfect sense. If Hitler was going to mount a successful invasion he must first knock out the RAF. This was a fight that RAF Fighter Command simply had to win. It was implicit in Chamberlain's words that the pilots of 126-squadron must be prepared to make the ultimate sacrifice to make that happen.

'The Hurricane is a fine aeroplane,' continued Chamberlain. 'She is rugged and highly manoeuvrable, especially at low altitudes, and she is a stable gun platform. But as some of us discovered yesterday, up above twenty thousand feet her performance drops off badly when compared with the Me-109. Up there, the Spitfire has the edge. From now on, where possible, our controllers will direct the Spitfire squadrons to take on the escorting Hun top cover fighters upstairs, leaving the Hurricanes free to go for the bombers.'

There were nods and murmurings of approval from the pilots. 'Now this is not always going to work. Sod's law suggests that we will get involved with Hun fighters from time to time. The Luftwaffe is operating its fighters in three different ways. Firstly they use free roaming fighters, up high and in front of the bombers. These are looking for trouble, hoping the catch the RAF fighters on their way into battle, or to ambush the unwary. Secondly, they have top cover force of fighters high above the bombers. Thirdly, they have fighters providing close support to the bombers. The free roaming fighters will be left alone; the Spitfires will aim to keep the top cover busy, leaving us free to go for the bombers that are at a lower level where our Hurricanes exhibit their best performance.'

The squadron leader paused, looking around at his pilots. 'Now I must emphasise that our targets are the bombers. The Hun fighters by themselves are not damaging our aircraft factories and airfields. We must go in with maximum effort and break up their formations. The Hun bomber force relies on concentrated gunfire from the formation, but lone bombers away from their friends are easy meat. Break their formations and they are easier to deal with.'

Chamberlain looked directly at Steed and gave a wry smile, 'Show them no mercy. They are bombing our country, killing our people. If you see a bomber damaged, lagging behind his formation, put him down. That will be one less that returns next time. Chivalry belongs in the middle ages, not in twentieth century Britain.'

The King interrupted, 'Yes Squadron Leader, they are now bombing your country. I saw what they did in my country, to Warsaw. They slaughtered women and children. In Belgium too, eh John Paul?' Colbert nodded grimly. The King continued softly, 'I will kill your Germans for you Squadron Leader.' And all of the pilots knew that he meant exactly what he said.

'Yes, thank you King. Now, as I was saying,' continued Chamberlain, 'Where humanly possible 126-Squadron will go for the bombers. We will stay in squadron formation. In the early days we sometimes used a top cover flight when we were on our own, but that is no longer possible now that the Germans are sending over such large formations. We will have to rely on the Spitfire boys for our top cover.

The squadron scramble came at midday. The Tomcats were vectored across the Thames estuary towards Kent. They were at 12,000 feet when they saw the German formation ahead of them, in the vicinity of Margate. About fifty Heinkel bombers were in a stepped formation, escorted by twin-engine Messerschmitt-110 fighters. Instinctively, Steed looked above for the inevitable Me-109 top cover. He saw twisting vapour trails suggesting an aerial battle. Fantastic, the Spitfire boys were doing their job. As the Tomcats approached, the leading Me-110s rose to meet the challenge. Chamberlain's voice came over the wireless, calm and distinct.

'Tomcats from Leader, Sections Abreast. Fly through the fighters and go head-on into the bombers. Break up that formation! Tallyho!'

The Me-110 leader misjudged his interception and his formation was forced to swing around behind the Hurricanes. But the Hurricanes had the speed of their dive and easily outpaced the German fighters on their way towards their quarry. Steed lined up on one of the lead Heinkels. He was going very fast and was in fact now leading the Hurricane line. Below were the green fields of Kent, the garden of England, the fields where many of his friends from London had spent their summer holidays picking the hops. What right had these Hun warmongers to be here, dropping their filthy bombs on this peaceful countryside, killing innocent women and children?

The phalanx of bombers looked solid, impressive, unyielding; they had to be dispersed, broken up, turned back or shot down. There was no alternative. This was the time, and this was the place. He approached his target, head on, at a terrifying closing speed. Either he or the bomber pilot had to take avoiding action or there would be a mid-air collision. Steed was determined that he would not be the first to flinch. He pressed the firing button and saw his tracer hitting the bomber at point blank range. The German pilot held his nerve; they were going to collide. Steed, finger still on the firing button closed his eyes as the Heinkel filled his forward vision; he had a fleeting sensation of déjà vu, and then there was an almighty crash.

Steed was thrown forward in his harness. His aircraft smashed into the top of the Heinkel's glazed nose, the remains of his propeller decapitating the dorsal gunner as the wrecked Hurricane slid along the top of the bomber, tearing away the remains of the gunner's position and the radio aerial before finally demolishing the Heinlkel's large tail plane.

Steed's world was spinning wildly, the centrifugal force pinning him to his seat. Steed felt that he was in a dream. He fought through the confusion and dizziness with a sense of desperation. He was spinning; he knew that much. He must correct the spin and bring the aircraft under control. But the aircraft did not respond to the controls. The engine was screaming, the revs far in excess of tolerable running; he pulled the throttle lever back. He tried to assess the state of his Hurricane. The dials were spinning wildly; he could make no sense of them. Were the wings still in place? Yes but the engine that had been screaming had now stopped. Steed's orientation returned. The aircraft was spiralling down but the centrifugal force pinning him to his seat had lessened. The propeller had disappeared, the engine had probably seized. The aircraft was lost; he had been in a mid-air collision for Christ's sake! At least the Hurricane hadn't caught fire like so many others. The fields of Kent were fast approaching; time to get out if he could.

Steed took his hands from the stick and pulled on the canopy; it took an effort, but it slid back. Thank the Lord for that. He unbuckled his harness and disconnected his radio and oxygen leads. He heaved himself up out of the cockpit but was immediately caught by the slipstream, which pinned him to the back of the Hurricane, half in and half out of the cockpit. This was no time for finesse and clever attempts to miss the Hurricane's tail plane on exit, if indeed the tail plane was still there, he thought.

With a gargantuan effort he pushed himself out of the cockpit. The remains of his Hurricane sailed past without hitting him, and he pulled the ripcord. The thump of the harness against his shoulders and chest took his breath away, and the horizon at last reverted to its normal position. Looking down, he saw his aircraft crash into open country and explode. It was now time to think about his landing. The theory was that you turned the 'chute to land with the wind on your back. You hit the ground with bent knees, and then you fell down and rolled over onto your back.

Coming up fast was a field. Be grateful for small mercies, at least it wasn't a wood or a church steeple! But which way was the wind blowing? Steed hadn't a clue. He watched the ground rushing up towards him, relaxed, hoped that he didn't twist his ankle on landing and then hit the ground. His legs collapsed and he rolled forwards, his shoulder hitting the ground with a thump.

He lay on the ground for several seconds, trying to ascertain if he was still in one piece. He felt a tug as the light wind caught the open parachute and spun him around. He got unsteadily to his feet, pulled in the 'chute and at last freed himself from the harness. He sat down heavily on the grass, and for the first time noticed that he shared the field with a few dozen sheep. Away to his left he could see the smoke from his crashed Hurricane.

Everything ached, especially his shoulders, bruised by his harness when he had collided with the Heinkel he suspected. Gingerly he moved his limbs and visually inspected his body. Everything worked and he hadn't twisted his ankle. All in all, he considered himself very lucky. He had survived a mid-air collision with no more than bruising. He pocketed the ripcord; he must remember to tip the parachute packer when he returned to Colne Martin.

What to do now? He lay back on the grass. Up above the sky was empty of aeroplanes; he expected to see parachutes, but there were none. Where had everybody gone? It was quiet and the ground felt warm and comfortable. Somewhere nearby was the buzz of some insect, and a butterfly fluttered past. He had a headache; that was unusual, he never suffered from headaches. He closed his eyes; he felt that he deserved a little rest.

He was roused from his peaceful meditation by the sound of a motor. He sat up, and saw the reason for the noise; a small tractor was approaching carrying two people. As the machine came to a halt, Steed started to get to his feet, but immediately felt dizzy and remained for an instant on one knee as if in prayer. He got to his feet unsteadily and found himself looking at the barrel of a shotgun. The possessor of the weapon was an attractive woman of around forty. Steed held up his hands, 'I surrender,' he said wearily.

'Sprechen sie English' said her companion in a country accent.

'Oh ja,' said Steed now smiling, his hands still raised. 'Like a native. I'm an RAF pilot. Flight Sergeant Harry Steed at your service. That's the remains of my aeroplane over there.' He nodded towards the smoke rising in the distance. 'I am pleased to say it didn't hit anything – a house or something like that I mean,' he added. 'Can I put my hands down now?'

The woman lowered the shotgun. She looked at Steed with concern, 'Are you hurt young man? Yes of course you are. Can you make it up onto the tractor? We will take you to the farmhouse. It's just over there. Here, hold this against your head.' She offered Steed a clean handkerchief. Steed looked puzzled. 'Your head, it's bleeding she said, here.' She pressed the handkerchief to Steed's forehead.

'Ouch!' he exclaimed, 'Maybe that explains the headache.'

'How rude of me,' said the woman. 'I am Mrs Mary Blythe. We own this farm. This is Perkins, our shepherd.' She indicated the tractor driver.

'Where are you from sir, London?' asked Perkins as the tractor bounced along.

'That's right. I guess that you can tell by my accent. I was born and bred in North London, but since joining the RAF I've been all over the place. Are you from Kent?'

'I am a man of Kent,' the shepherd said proudly. 'That's a very important distinction in these parts. A man of Kent comes from the east of the River Medway. A Kentish man comes from west of the river, more towards London.'

'You learn something every day. I'll remember that in future Mr Perkins. A man of Kent.' The shepherd beamed.

Once at the farmhouse, Steed telephoned Colne Martin. 'The squadron isn't back yet m'boy,' said the adjutant, 'but I will get RAF Marston to collect you from your farmhouse. We will probably send somebody over this evening to fly you back here. Are you absolutely sure that you are not hurt?'

'Right as rain,' lied Steed.

'Well, the MO at Marston can have a look at you anyway.'

Steed sat in the offered armchair with a cup of tea. Mrs Blyth talked to him as she bandaged his head. 'Are you a Spitfire pilot, Flight Sergeant?'

'Not quite, I fly Hurricanes.'

'What happened to you up there? Are you allowed to say? I assume that you were shot down. Was it by a Messerschmitt?'

'I am afraid that we are not supposed to say too much, but it's a very straightforward story. I collided with a German bomber. My aircraft fell apart; I don't think that the bump did the bomber any good either. I bailed out and here I am.'

'I think that you are very brave.'

'No Mrs Blythe, I don't feel very brave or very clever. I am supposed to shoot down enemy bombers, not run into them and lose my aeroplane.'

'You make it sound like a road traffic accident. It isn't. But I'm sorry I'm embarrassing you. Why don't you get some rest? My husband will be back soon, and my son. They are both out with the flock. You can have something to eat with us if your people haven't arrived to collect you by then.'

Steed felt unusually tired; perhaps it was a reaction to recent events. He settled back into the comfortable armchair and was soon asleep.

He awoke two hours later, feeling much better, and with the smell of cooking in his nostrils. 'Ah, you are awake Flight Sergeant. Just in time for dinner. Your people from RAF Marston telephoned. They have been delayed, but they expect to pick you up by five o'clock. Steed enjoyed a bona fide farm dinner with the family. Shortly after five o'clock, the driver arrived from RAF Marston.

RAF Marston was not far from the seaside town of Ramsgate, very close to the coast and about twenty minutes drive from the farmhouse. The driver had been instructed to take Steed directly to the MO. Steed had visited RAF Marston on a number of occasions. It was a convenient refuelling stop before those long and boring Channel convoy patrols, and it was a very useful emergency field for damaged aeroplanes returning from a fight over the Channel.

But RAF Marston looked very different now after intimate attention from the Luftwaffe. There was rubble everywhere and the smell of burning. Hangars and buildings were in ruins. The driver spoke, 'We are too close to the Channel, Flight Sergeant. The bastards are on us before we know it. They caught a flight of Spitfires taking off today. A terrible mess!'

The MO diagnosed slight concussion, and also bruising around Steed's shoulders and ribcage. 'You are very lucky Flight. Not many pilots walk away from a mid-air collision. Your squadron leader wants you back tonight, so he is sending someone to fly you home. I will give your MO at Colne Martin a call. He will no doubt want to have a look at you tomorrow. In the meantime I am sorry that we cannot offer you more in the way of hospitality; blame the Luftwaffe. The sergeants' mess is a write off, but they have erected a tent where there is tea and hot soup. Early to bed when you get back home. Get some rest, Doctor's orders.'

Steed was tempted to say the same to the MO. The doctor looked all in. Steed could imagine what sort of a day the man had been through; the station must have taken many casualties. But he simply thanked the MO, saluted and went off to find the tea.

It was almost dusk when Johnny Walker arrived with the squadron Lysander. 'Good to see that you are still in the land of the living, you old sod,' said Walker. 'I didn't see your escapade with the Heinkel, but Gareth told me all about it. He called it a wizard prang, whatever that is!'

'I don't remember too much about it myself,' said Steed. 'I thought that if I went straight at the bastard with all guns blazing, he would have the sense to turn away, but the soppy sod came straight on. I didn't have a chance to get out of his way, and then there was a God Almighty bang. Next thing I know, I am hanging in the 'chute with the ground coming towards me at a fair rate of knots. The farmer's wife came trundling up on a tractor toting a bloody great shotgun. She thought that I was a Jerry, 'cause RAF fighter pilots don't get shot down do they? She gave me a fantastic dinner though. Just as well, because this place is in a mess.'

'Jammy bastard,' said Walker warmly. 'Gareth said that you went ahead of everybody else in the dive. You hit the Heinkel on his nose, and sort of skidded along the top of with bits of aeroplane flying off in all directions. You demolished his tail and then cart wheeled towards the next Hun in the formation. That feller must have been shit scared, because he pulled away to one side and darn nearly collided with his mate. We all went through their formation and then turned to have a second go. Those Me-110s are useless. Fine in a straight line, but hopeless with the twisty stuff. They couldn't protect the bombers. We came in again and this time poor old Fred flew straight into the side of one of the Heinkels. I saw that one. There was a bloody great explosion; I guess that his bombs must have gone off. With both Fred and you playing bumper cars with them, the Jerries must have thought that we had orders to ram them on purpose. Anyway from then on they lost all thoughts of holding formation. The Huns were twisting and turning in all directions. I got one of the sods, so did Toby. The Boss and The King got one each too, and more or less everybody said that they had scored hits. Oh, your Heinkel is confirmed as well. There will be a hell of a party tonight. We should get going.'

'We lost Fred?' said Steed, 'Anybody else hurt?'

'No, but there is no chance for Fred I'm afraid. I saw the whole thing. Whether he rammed the Hun on purpose following your example, or whether he misjudged it, we will never know. Quite a few of us had extra ventilation holes when we returned. Smithy's plane in particular looked pretty beaten up, but he put it down all right with a wheels-up. Anyway, let's get going. I never have been keen on night landings.'

'I'm not keen to try a night landing either with you as a pilot,' quipped Steed.

'I'd let you fly the bloody thing,' rejoined Walker, 'but if we meet a 109 you might try to ram it.'

'If we meet a 109 in this thing, I will have another go at bailing out, pretty dammed quick!'

As soon as they returned to Colne Martin, Steed went to see Chamberlain. 'Good to see you back Hawk,' said the squadron leader warmly. 'How are you, I hear that you have concussion?'

'I had a bit of a headache earlier sir, but it's gone now. I'm fine.' Steed knew what the squadron leader was really asking. 'Honestly, I am fit to fly tomorrow. No question about that.'

'Thank you Hawk. I would like to give you some time off. You deserve it of course. But you see how things are? We had a great day today, but I assume that Sergeant Walker has told you all about it. We bagged six of the blighters for the loss of only two of our own, and you are safe. On the debit side we lost Sergeant Farthing, I have just finished writing the letter.'

'Not the nicest of jobs,' said Steed.

'No,' said Chamberlain. 'And I don't want to have to write one to your parents either. It was very brave of you to go charging in like that, but it was also very foolhardy. We have to break up their formations it's true, and I have to admit that what you did was very effective. After you and Farthing put on a show, the Huns were convinced that we were all trying to ram them. Their formation went to pot and that made things easier for the rest of us. But Hawk, next time, leave yourself enough margin to get out of the way. That Heinkel did not have your manoeuvrability. When it was too late for him to get out of the way, you still had that chance. Don't push it as far as a collision.'

The parties in the officers' and sergeants' messes eventually combined in the local pub. There was jubilation at the squadron's most successful day so far. Everything had gone right. The Spitfires had kept away the Me-109's, the Me-110 close escorts had proved ineffective and the enemy bombing force had been given rough treatment. No one mentioned Fred Farthing.

The following day dawned cloudy, with a hint of drizzle. 126-Squadron was at readiness from dawn, but by noon they were still without trade. Strangely, the waiting made some of the pilots edgier than when they were flying into action. Steed had been given the use of Dix's Hurricane, which pleased him because it was in first class condition and the guns were synchronised to his liking.

Shortly after midday the air raid warning shattered the peace. The pilots and ground crews moved quickly towards the shelters and the gun crews dotted around the airfield closed up. Four Messerschmitt-110s appeared and promptly strafed the airfield with cannon fire. They were gone almost as quickly as they had arrived. Fortunately for 126-Squadron, the damage was not severe and none of the aircraft at dispersal were hit. However, two of Hurricanes under repair by the bomb-damaged main hangar were written off and two petrol tankers were caught by the Me-110s in the open and destroyed; several airmen were also killed.

On the credit side, four brand new Hurricanes materialized shortly after the raid, claimed as usual by the officers according to seniority. Steed retained Dix's aircraft because the flight commander would not need it for a while. Later in the day two fresh pilot officers arrived straight from training school. Towards evening Smithy, now promoted to flying officer, was detailed to take the new pilots up for a familiarisation flight around the local countryside. The Tomcats remained at readiness all day, but did not fly.

As August 1940 drew to a close, 126-Squadron was in action virtually every day. The Luftwaffe increased the pressure on the RAF by stepping up the bombing of airfields and aircraft factories. The air battle was finely balanced. If the RAF should lose it, then most people expected an invasion. Death came easily, most often to the new and inexperienced pilots, and most often from the Snappers, as the Messerschmitt-109s were now called over the wireless. The Tomcat pilots were feeling the strain.

A favourite and dangerous Snapper ploy was to come over at high altitude ahead of the bombers. The RAF controllers preferred not to engage such free hunting formations if they could possibly help it, but sometimes the snappers caught unwary RAF squadrons climbing to intercept the bombers. 126-Squadron's Hurricanes were at a particular disadvantage when attacked by free hunting Me-109s. The 109s easily outperformed the Hurricanes in terms of straight-line speed, climb and dive, and they were armed with a couple of very nasty 20mm cannons as well as machine-guns. The Snappers could therefore always beak off the fight at a time of their own choosing. The Snappers' favourite tactic was to dive on their prey from out of the sun, avoid a dogfight at lower altitudes with the more manoeuvrable Hurricanes and then climb away ready for another diving attack. It was very effective.

However, if the Tomcats could evade the free hunting patrols and close the bombers, then it was a different story. The bombers relied both on their stepped formation, to provide a concentration of defensive gunfire, and on a close escort of fighters. The close escort in the early days of Channel convoys was often the twin engine Me-110, but both sides had now learnt that the Me-110 was at a severe disadvantage in a dogfight, even with Hurricanes, so the close escort by the end of August was usually undertaken by Me-109s, increasing the workload on the pilots of the German single seat fighter.

The bombers came over at heights of between ten and fifteen thousand feet. At this altitude the Hurricane could easily turn inside the Me-109. The close escort fighters were duty bound to protect their bomber charges, so they could not use the dive and climb technique of the free hunters. They had to mix it with the Hurricanes in a close dogfight, and here they were at a disadvantage.

During one of his morning briefings Chamberlain spoke about the possibility of invasion.

'As many of you know, invasion barges have been spotted in French ports, so there is little doubt about what Hitler is considering. If they come, they will want Fighter Command out of the way. Hitler used his paratroops very successfully in Holland and Belgium,' here Jean-Paul Colbert gave a rueful nod. 'Group expects that German paratroops would be used to try to capture airfields here in the South of England. Hitler has several objectives in doing this. Firstly, he would be able to use the airfields to airlift in supplies and fresh troops. Remember, the Navy would be giving his shipping a tough time, so the more troops and munitions that he could ferry by air, the less that would have to go via sea. Secondly, he would deny the airfield to us, so that we would probably have to move further north, carrying what we could, that is providing that we could get away in time.

'If the German paratroops come, our army has the job of defending the airfield. Our job is to get into the air, if we can, so that we can shoot the buggers down. If we are caught on the ground, and there is no way of getting to our aircraft, then we will join the brown jobs in killing as many of the invaders as we can. Most of the officers already have revolvers, but I have a few more in the office for the sergeant pilots. Also, I have obtained three Lee Enfield rifles and some ammunition. I will leave these here at dispersal. We will have a shooting contest later. The best shots will have first call on the rifles if the paratroopers turn up.'

But the squadron was scrambled before they had a chance to try out the rifles. They were vectored to patrol over Southend-on-Sea. There was a covering of cloud, which obscured the seaside town, but above the climbing Tomcats was only a piercing azure sky of high summer. The wireless crackled and the Controller warned of a large formation of enemy aircraft in the vicinity of Whitstable. The squadron was heading out over the Thames estuary, when they saw the bomber formation ahead and to their right, and about one thousand feet below.

Chamberlain immediately turned the squadron into a beam attack. As usual, all eyes searched for escorting Snappers above the bomber formation. They were up there, but the twisting vapour trails suggested that the Spitfires were keeping them busy. The Tomcats were approaching at right angles to the bomber stream, which meant full deflection shooting. The close escort comprised Messerschmitt-110 Destroyers; even the Germans did not have an inexhaustible supply of single engine fighters, and the more nimble Me-109s could not be everywhere at once. The Me-110s were slow to respond, giving the Tomcats an unopposed first pass at the bombers. The Heinkels held a tight box formation, giving their air gunners the opportunity of catching the oncoming Tomcats in a vicious cone of fire.

Steed selected one of the leading Heinkels as his target. As usual, he ignored the German tracer coming towards him, and he held his fire until he was within effective range. He misjudged his aim though, and his long burst was, at first, well in front of the Heinkel; but he allowed the German to come on into his stream of bullets such that he was rewarded by seeing the twinkling flashes of the De Wilde ammunition running along the Heinkel's fuselage. As he passed the Heinkel he felt machine-gun bullets hammering into his Hurricane. He half rolled to put off the gunners' aim, but it was not enough. He levelled out below the German formation, the controls feeling very heavy. He attempted to climb back towards the bombers, but he had little power and the aircraft approached the stall, forcing him to level off again. Steed twisted his neck; where was the close escort of Me-110s? He was a sitting duck down here, flying straight and level with a sick aeroplane.

He heard Gareth Evans's excited voice. 'Blue-3, 110 on your tail Hawk…. I'm knocking bits off the bastard… I've got him. Take that Boyo!'

Steed side slipped as the Messerschmitt flashed past in a terminal dive, with Evans still firing at it from behind. Steed transmitted, 'Blue-4, don't follow it down, it's finished.'

The Messerschmitt was now trailing smoke. A parachute blossomed in its wake just before it entered the cloud below. Steed turned his sluggish machine as best he could and scoured the sky; he was concerned that other German fighters might single out his wounded

Hurricane for further attention, but the fight above had passed him by. Evans was now climbing up towards him, so he set course for home. The gauges appeared correct, but the Hurricane felt heavy on the controls and the engine would not rev, and he was slowly losing height.

Evans slipped in alongside, as Southend pier appeared though a gap in the cloud.

'Nice to have you riding shotgun Gareth. Take a look around the old bus will you? She feels a bit heavy and the motor won't rev.'

Evans could see nothing amiss, and so Steed decided that he could make Colne Martin. But as they descended down through the cloud, the engine suddenly stopped. Steed glided down and broke through the cloud over Chelmsford. He made a few rapid calculations in his head. He still had the chance to bale out, but very soon he would be too low for that option. He might just make Colne Martin if nothing else happened. Fire was the greatest danger, but there was no sign of smoke and the temperature gauge remained normal.

He radioed Evans, 'Blue-4, I think I can make Colne Martin. Tell them that I am gliding in with a dead engine.'

The airfield wasn't too far now. However, in a few more minutes it was clear that the Hurricane was not maintaining sufficient height in the glide; it was going to have to be a 'wheels up' landing in a farmer's field. Time to select a field now! Fortunately, the terrain in this part of Essex was flat.

'Blue-4, I'm going to pancake. Radio Colne to come and collect me please.'

'Will do Hawk. Good luck.'

The perfect field appeared over on the left, grass with a few sheep. They would run out of the way. A landing into the wind as well. Should be a piece of cake. He had pulled back the canopy some time ago. Now he tightened the straps, pulled out the plugs and switched everything off. He didn't want a face full of reflector gun sight like Dix.

It was only as he was about to touch down that he saw the poles. Damn it! Obstacles to prevent glider landings had sprung up everywhere. The bloody field looked like a hedgehog. Ah well, can't be helped. The Hurricane's belly made contact with the grass and she slid along smoothly, her feathered propeller bending on impact. Her wing root hit the first pole, but the pole was far less effective than the farmer had intended; it was simply uprooted without causing much impedance to the careering aeroplane.

The Hurricane ground to a halt after uprooting several more poles. Steed was slightly winded, but unhurt. He jumped out of the Hurricane smartly. As always, he was worried about fire. Evans was circling overhead. Steed waved and walked briskly away from the aeroplane. It didn't look too badly broken. Perhaps it could be repaired. He suddenly remembered that it wasn't his aeroplane; it belonged to Flight Lieutenant Dix. Oops!

Gareth Evans was waiting in the mess when Steed returned from his forced landing. Evans looked pleased with himself as Steed said, 'That was a good job today Gareth. You were the perfect wingman. When I was in trouble you were right behind me, just where you should have been. You were ideally placed to take out that Me-110. Damn good shooting.' Evans beamed, but Steed continued, 'But Gareth, what have I told you a thousand times? Never go down after a kill. You sacrifice height, and you never know who is behind you.' Evans looked a little downcast and nodded. Steed slapped him on the back, 'Come on Gareth, I'll buy you a beer, two in fact. One for your first victory and one for saving the skin of your flight sergeant!'

The next morning Steed arrived at dispersal early, courtesy of his Ariel motorcycle. He still rode the bike, but for some weeks now he had been scanning the local paper small ads. looking for a car. Cars were much cheaper now that petrol was getting scarce for the general public. Petrol wasn't a problem for Steed; authority turned a blind eye to petrol liberation by fighter pilots, as long as it wasn't too blatant. Steed was early at dispersal because he had heard that two more new Hurricanes had been delivered the previous afternoon. He knew that the airmen had been working late into the night repairing and preparing aircraft. Like the pilots, the ground crews too looked tired.

Steed wasn't disappointed; he had been allocated one of the new Hurricanes, and it was standing on the hardstand with his ground crew in attendance. But what did surprise Steed was the artistry that adorned the aircraft. A very good likeness of a sparrowhawk's head was painted on the cowling, and underneath was written 'The Hawk'. On the other side of the nose was a line of ten and a half swastikas, representing his victories. 'You're an ace twice over now Flight,' said his mechanic with a wink.

'This artwork is fantastic Denis,' said Steed. 'Who's the artist?'

'Jimmy Watson. Good isn't he? The armourer has set up your guns as you like 'em.'

As he chatted to his ground crew, the officers arrived. Two of them walked over. Steed turned to see Hugh Dix and Roger Daily. Neither was in flying kit and Roger walked with a limp. It was the first time that Steed had seen either of them since the airfield had been bombed several weeks ago. Daily greeted Steed in his own inimitable way. 'G'day Harry, how's it hanging?'

'Hello Roger, good to see you back. You too Mr Dix. Are you boys returning to flying?'

'I'm back on operations in a day or two, as soon as this dammed eye opens up a bit more,' said Dix. 'Likewise Roger, but we both intend to take a Hurricane up this afternoon for a stooge around, that is if you have left us any! They tell me that you not only wrote off my fine aeroplane yesterday, but that you have also been playing bumper cars with the Germans while we were on leave.'

'Ah, I'm very sorry about your Hurricane Mr Dix, she was a fine aeroplane. She didn't look too badly damaged, so maybe they can repair her. As for playing bumper cars, well, we drive on the left and they drive on the right. I'm surprised that we don't clout each other more often.'

As they spoke, Steed cast an eye over his flight commander's face. It still looked a mess, lacerated and bruised, with the right eye blackened and still not yet fully open. He had also lost some front teeth, such that he spoke with a slight lisp. Steed injected some humour, 'I must say your dodgy landing has given you that rugged fighter pilot look Mr Dix. A great improvement if I may be allowed to say so.'

'Well now,' said the flight lieutenant, 'we can't all be jammy blighters like you. Fly head on into a dirty great Heinkel loaded to the gunnels with bombs, and you walk away without a scratch. Then you write off my shiny Hurricane in a forced landing, and still you come out smelling of roses.'

'You haven't seen the bruises,' said Steed.

'And I don't want to either,' rejoined Dix.

Daily was examining Steed's Hurricane, 'Strewth, I want a picture like that on my kite too mate. How come you get pretty pictures of dicky birds on your Hurrie, when the rest of us have to make do with camouflage paint?'

'That's flight sergeant's privilege. Anyway, you've got a row of swastikas on yours, what more do you want? A kangaroo?'

'I might put a cricket bat on the front, just to remind you Poms of who always wins the ashes.'

Steed laughed, 'It's good to have you both back,' and he meant it. Adams's Hillman rattled to a halt alongside the dispersal hut and the four sergeant pilots emerged.

'Time for a cuppa,' said Daily.

After giving his customary daily briefing, Chamberlain turned to Steed. 'We are not at readiness for a bit, and things are in any case usually quiet first thing in the morning. I suggest you take your new aircraft up for a flight check. Be back within an hour please. By the way, do you want this?' The squadron leader held out a revolver, RAF web belt, holster, lanyard and an ammo pouch. 'Most of the officer pilots have the .45 Webley. This is a .38 Enfield number two; unfortunately it doesn't have the clout of the Webley, but it's all that I have left.'

'Thank you sir,' replied Steed, 'that'll do fine.'

On the ground, against paratroopers, he doubted that even a .45 revolver would be of much use; the effective range was only around 25 yards. No, it was in the air that Steed wanted the gun. As Steed took his leave of the squadron leader, he considered how he should wear the revolver in the cockpit. Some pilots over Dunkirk had stuffed their side arm in their boot. Steed decided to put the lanyard around his neck, with the revolver placed into his tunic breast pocket. Worn in this way, there was no danger of the gun flying around the cockpit during a dogfight, and it was easy to get to if required. He didn't need the ammo pouch in the air either; one bullet would be enough. Like so many of his fighter pilot heroes from the Great War, Steed did not want to be burnt alive. If the worst came to the worst and he couldn't jump, well, now he had the small .38 pistol.

Steed climbed into a cloudless cerulean dawn sky, with the sun glinting on his wings. Below, the early morning sun's rays had not yet reached the fields, which appeared dark and mottled. There was something magical about the English countryside viewed from the air, the patchwork fields, the small hamlets and villages. The early morning was the best time to appreciate their beauty, as the invading light of a new day brought them to life. Steed switched on his oxygen. He was quite alone in the Essex sky, overjoyed at being given time off by the Boss to play. The new Hurricane was performing beautifully. The instruments were in tune and she handled like a dream. He executed two rapid barrel rolls followed by a half loop, rolling out at the top into an Immelmann. Steed felt refreshed. What a magnificent morning.

The headphones crackled. The controller knew that Steed was on a test flight, and so warned him that an intruder had crossed the coast near the river Blackwater. Steed settled the Hurricane into level flight and carefully looked around; he was quite alone. The morning sun had climbed a little higher and now illuminated the countryside beneath. The sun glinted on something below, then again. Not a static reflection from a building window, but something moving, and moving too fast to be a road vehicle. Yes, there it was, a twin-engine aircraft. Steed increased speed in a dive. A cloudless sky, height advantage and a juicy Hun target, possibly a reconnaissance Ju-88 by the look of it. But as Steed descended and saw the aircraft more clearly. He recognised the shape of an RAF Blenheim flying almost at treetop height.

He was about to resume his playtime when something else caught his eye, astern of the RAF bomber. Christ, a Me-109! Steed was in the perfect bounce position, behind the Me-109 with height advantage and with the sun behind him. But likewise the Me-109 was in a perfect position behind the Blenheim. It was even money on whether the Me-109 would reach a firing position before Steed.

Steed increased speed in the dive. Where was the Hun's wingman? These bastards always flew in pairs. Steed weaved, rapidly searching for the missing wingman, but the German fighter seemed to be alone for a change. He lined up his sights on the Me-109, which had already opened fire on the Blenheim. Why did the bomber not take evasive action? Was the rear gunner asleep?

But the German too was caught napping as Steed put a long and accurate burst into the Messerschmitt at close range. Steed pulled up to avoid overshooting the Me-109 and for the first time noticed the approaching airfield. Of course, Sapling airfield, a light bomber base. These boys were busy most nights bombing the invasion barges along the French coast.

As he prepared to resume his attack on the Me-109, Steed saw that the German's engine had stopped and that its wheels were down. The pilot was heading for a landing at the approaching aerodrome, assuming that he had sufficient height. The Blenheim too was damaged; Steed could see the trail of smoke from the port engine. The Me-109 had by now pulled to one side of the Blenheim and was therefore in neither a shooting position nor a threat to the British bomber. Steed was content to allow the German pilot to land unhindered. Once again Steed checked unsuccessfully behind for the missing wingman.

The Blenheim made a passable wheels-up landing, slithering along the grass, and then coming to a halt; thankfully there was no fire. Steed circled the field as the Messerschmitt too came to a stop. The German pilot had made an excellent three-point landing without power. Fire tenders, ambulances and various other vehicles came racing towards the two stationary aircraft. The German pilot climbed out of his aircraft and stood on the wing; he waved at Steed, who could not resist a victory roll. He regretted the roll almost as soon as he finished it; the bomber boys would think it a line shoot.

Steed felt pleased with himself as he climbed away. A Me-109 shot down, the pilot and an almost intact enemy fighter captured, and all without a scratch on his brand new Hurricane. Steed hoped that the Blenheim's crew were uninjured; the forced landing had been passable but maybe the gunner had been hurt because Steed had not seen him return fire. Steed reported what had happened to his controller. The hour's playtime was up. It was time to head back to Colne Martin.

The rest of the day was an anticlimax. The squadron was scrambled at midday to meet a threat from German bombers, but the bombers turned south to hit other 11-Group airfields almost as soon as 126-Squadron were off the ground. The Tomcats patrolled just south of Chelmsford for an hour, and then returned to readiness at Colne Martin.

That evening, Smithy called Steed away from the party in the sergeants' mess celebrating his eleventh victory.

'Harry, we have the Jerry pilot that you shot down today over in the officers' mess. He wants to meet you.'

Steed thought for a moment. 'I'm not sure that I want to meet him. The Huns are killing our people. Why treat the bugger like a long lost comrade over in your mess? Send him off to the prisoner of war camp.'

'Don't be like that Harry. The Boss asked me to come over to fetch you. It's a tradition that we entertain downed enemy officers, and you shot him down. He's not a bad sort, bit of a lineshooter, that's all. He speaks very good English.'

'How did you get hold of him?' asked Steed as Smithy drove towards the officers' mess.

'The C/O at Sapling gave us a call,' said Smithy. 'The Hun wanted to meet the Spitfire pilot that shot him down. He was a bit miffed when he found out that you drive a Hurricane! Sapling sent him over with an escort this afternoon.'

'Did anyone ask how the Blenheim crew faired?' asked Steed.

'Don't know old boy,' was the reply.

Steed was ushered into the officers' mess. A group of pilots were standing around the German. The atmosphere seemed very convivial; everybody was laughing and joking and holding beer glasses. Chamberlain saw Steed as he entered and steered the German pilot away from the crowd and towards Steed. 'Oberleutnant Brauer, allow me to introduce Flight Sergeant Steed.'

Brauer beamed, 'Ah Flight Sergeant, you caught me sleeping today. I have been telling your comrades that my Katschmarek, you say wingman I believe, my Katschmarek lost me in cloud over the Channel and so I was alone over England. The fool will be in trouble when I return. You were able to surprise me because my Katschmarek was not guarding my tail. But it was your victory and I salute you.' Brauer offered his hand.

Steed accepted the handshake and assessed his former adversary. Herr Brauer seemed well lubricated and surprisingly happy, in spite of being a prisoner of war. Steed noticed that the Spy had moved with Chamberlain and now stood nonchalantly with his back towards the German but still within earshot. Steed was certain that the wily old fox was taking note of all that was going on, hoping to pick up some useful tit bit. Steed also noticed that The King and Jean-Paul Colbert were not a part of the group previously assembled around Brauer. Perhaps hospitality to the enemy was easier if they hadn't occupied your country.

Steed was polite and purposely over generous with his praise. 'I was very lucky today, Herr Oberleutnant. We have a great deal of respect for the Messerschmitt-109, and for the expertise of your pilots.'

Brauer beamed, 'Yes, the Messerschmitt-109 is much superior to your Hurricane. We call Hurricanes old puffers you know; we think that they are very old fashioned. We are much faster in a straight line, and in the dive and climb. I do not know how I can tell my comrades that I was shot down by a Hurricane when I get back. A Spitfire yes, it's a good aeroplane, not as fast as a Me-109 but still a good aeroplane, but a Hurricane, a puffer, how will I live down the shame?' Brauer laughed at his own humour.

Steed knew that he needed to be careful. Brauer was talkative and he seemed a little inebriated, but he must not realise that Steed was seeking intelligence. Maybe more flattery might work, might tease out an indiscretion. Steed continued, 'I wish that we had Spitfires too Herr Oberleutnant, but our high command does not have the foresight of your Reichsmarschall Goring. You are very lucky to have such a man who was a fighter pilot in the Great War and who understands a fighter pilot's needs. He is a great tactician. He gets everything right.'

Chamberlain's jaw dropped and he seemed about to chastise his NCO pilot; he frowned, he looked bemused, but he held his tongue. Brauer positively beamed. 'Our Reichsmarschall was indeed a great fighter pilot Flight Sergeant. He commanded Baron von Richthofen's squadron you know, after the Baron was killed.' Brauer paused, and then lowered his voice in a conspiratorial manner. 'We are all fighter pilots, us Germans and you English. We share the freedom of the sky, away from the ugliness of war on the ground and in the trenches. We are like the knights of old. We fight each other but we respect each other. There is chivalry between us. The fighter pilot is a hunter. He must hunt for his prey, unfettered by interference from the high command.'

Steed nodded his agreement, 'Yes Herr Oberleutnant, all fighter pilots, German and British, share the same thoughts. But this is where Reichsmarschall Goring's tactics are so much better than those of our own high command. You place your fighters in the best positions.'

'That's right Flight Sergeant, and we also have fighters sweeping the skies before our bombers arrive. This is good, and it is what fighters are supposed to do.' Brauer's eyes glinted. 'We are at war Flight Sergeant, and unfortunately that means that we must come over here to bomb your airfields and weapons-making factories. The fighter pilot's job is to protect our bombers of course, but we should not be tied to their skirts.'

'But forgive me Herr Oberleutnant, what is the problem? Your fighters are doing what fighters are supposed to do, and they are doing it very successfully.'

'The problem, Flight Sergeant, is that we have now been instructed to stay close to the bombers to protect them,' Brauer said bitterly. 'The bomber pilots complained to the Reichsmarschall that we have not been giving them sufficient protection. The high command has now told our fighter leaders to devote more resources to close escort. And close escort means just that. We must not go chasing Spitfires and Hurricanes, we must stay with the bombers.'

Steed was amazed at Brauer's indiscretion. Was this the truth, or was Brauer playing a game of double bluff? The Spy had moved in even closer, and Chamberlain no longer looked so shocked at Steed's conversation, in fact a hint of a smile had now appeared on the squadron leader's face. Steed continued, 'Even so Herr Oberleutnant, your strategy and your formations are clearly better than ours.'

'Yes, I agree with you. Your formation flying looks very pretty. Little vics look very good at air displays, but do you know what we call your squadron formations? I will tell you, rows of idiots! It is easy for us to come down from behind, shoot down the fighters at the back, and then climb away if we need to.'

Brauer was definitely slurring now. He put his arm around Steed's shoulder. 'Listen Flight Sergeant, I have already told your comrades. We should not be fighting each other. We are the same people. The English are Anglo Saxons, which means your ancestors are Germanic. Get rid of Churchill and unite with Germany. The RAF cannot win this battle, and England cannot win this war. We know how many aeroplanes you had at the beginning, we know how many you have lost, and we know that you do not have many left now. You have fought bravely but you are near the end. Your army is tiny compared with ours, and most of their equipment was lost at Dunkirk. Once our army is ashore you will be finished. I am sorry for being blunt, especially when you are showing me such fine hospitality, but it is the truth.'

Steed made a show of looking concerned, 'You make a very good case for a German victory Herr Oberleutnant, but what about the Royal Navy?'

'Ah yes, the Royal Navy, Britain's traditional saviour. Yes Fight Sergeant, you have a powerful navy but warfare has changed. Aeroplanes now drop bombs on ships and drop parachutists on land. With the Luftwaffe master of the sky, the invasion will succeed, have no doubt.'

Their conversation was interrupted by whoops and shrieks of laughter from the officer pilots, who now converged on their guest in a conga line. Chamberlain addressed Brauer, 'My officers would like to invite you to play some of our mess games.' The squadron leader turned to Steed, 'Drive yourself back Hawk, here are the keys to my car. Take it over to dispersal tomorrow morning please.'

When Steed got back to the sergeants' mess Johnny Walker greeted him, 'There's a pint here for you Harry. How was your Hun?'

'Cheers Johnny. He was remarkably happy, considering he's off to a POW camp. He was well tanked up, the boys are treating him well over there, but the sods didn't even offer me a drink.'

'When are they carting him off to the POW camp?'

'Christ only knows. When I left they were about to start their party games.'

'Overgrown schoolboys,' muttered Walker. 'What was it this time, trying to get around the room without touching the floor?' He didn't wait for an answer but headed for the piano. 'Come on Harry. Let's get our own party going.'

The following day 126-Squadron was at readiness until the afternoon. Although the pilots lounged in deck chairs and read magazines, it was not possible for many of them to relax; most were keyed up, Steed included, waiting for the dispersal telephone to ring signalling a scramble. Some, like Smithy, were over-restless and talked too much. Others like, Tony Parsons, withdrew into their shell and were morose. The pressure was starting to tell.

The scramble came at 2.15 in the afternoon. The Tomcats climbed hard, but when they saw the bombers they were still two thousand feet too low. Chamberlain had a difficult choice to make. He could climb straight into the bomber formation but that risked getting caught at climbing speed by the escorts, which would be disastrous. The alternative was to alter course while he gained more height, but that risked an engagement with the escorts before he could close the bombers. Chamberlain adopted the second course of action.

Steed looked for the inevitable gaggle of Me-109s high above the bomber force, but there were none. Maybe the Spitfire boys had engaged them earlier; maybe they had missed their rendezvous with the bombers. Whatever the reason, Steed was thankful for small mercies.

Chamberlain climbed and positioned his force in front of and slightly above the bombers and their close escort of Me-109s. The close escort had stayed with the bombers instead of coming over to engage the Hurricanes. Maybe Brauer had been telling the truth about the new orders for the close escort. Whatever the reason, it had given Chamberlain the advantage, and now he led his pilots in a head-on attack against the bombers. As they approached, the Me-109s came out to do battle.

In the melee that followed one of the new pilot officers was shot down and killed. Steed didn't see him go. The Tomcats were outnumbered, but in a way this was an advantage because the more numerous Germans seemed to get in each other's way. Steed twisted and turned, trying to get a telling strike on a bomber while at the same time avoiding the threats from the escorting Me-109s. He could only manage fleeting bursts as the

German fighters fought effectively to defend their charges. He was gratified that Gareth Evans was able to stay on his tail throughout the fight; the young sergeant pilot was doing well.

And then Evans was in trouble with a Me-109 on his tail, and he was shouting for help. Evans did the right thing. He put his Hurricane into a corkscrew dive. A Me-109 could go straight down faster than the Hurricane, but it could not easily follow a Hurricane in a twisting dive. Evans had listened to Steed's advice on air fighting, and now it saved his life. Steed came down behind the Messerschmitt. It was a difficult shot, because the Me-109 was twisting violently as the pilot attempted to target Evans. Steed fired. He was convinced that he hit the enemy fighter, but the German wasn't waiting around to be shot at again. He put on the power and went straight down, leaving the two Hurricanes in his wake. With the sky now empty of aeroplanes, Steed and Evans returned to Colne Martin, only to find that the Luftwaffe had knocked down a few more Nissen huts and had put a few more holes on the grass field.

That evening Steed was strolling around the airfield perimeter with the Spy and Dion, when Roger Daily pulled up in his car. 'Evening Harry, you have a visitor over in the officers' mess.' Steed looked quizzically at the flight lieutenant. 'It's the Blenheim pilot, the one that old Brauer shot down yesterday. Wants to say thanks and to buy you a drink.'

'That's jolly decent of him,' said Steed. 'Was everybody inside the Blenheim okay?'

'Fine,' said the Australian with a huge grin. 'Hop in mate, I'll give you a lift.'

When they walked into the officers' mess, a cheer went up from the pilots who turned towards Steed. They were standing in a circle, in the centre of which was an eye-catching brunette.

'Hello Harry,' she said softly. 'I thought that it might be you.'

'You know this guy?' said Daily incredulously.

Steed gazed at the woman in surprise. She was a little older now, slimmer if anything, and dressed impeccably in a tailored suit. She was still beautiful. How could he ever forget her?

'Good evening Mrs Richards,' he said, somewhat at a loss for anything else to say. She came towards him smiling and kissed him on the cheek.

'After all of this time, I really think that you can call me Sophie.' She stood back and regarded him attentively. 'Well, look at you now Flight Sergeant Steed. A fighter pilot with a DFM ribbon on you chest. Your C/O tells me that you have shot down eleven German aeroplanes, including the little sod that got me.'

Steed blushed as the penny dropped, 'So you were the Blenheim pilot! You are ferrying aircraft for the RAF now?' She nodded, now laughing. He looked around at Roger Daily who was also laughing. 'This wild colonial allowed me to believe that I was coming over here to meet a bomber squadron pilot.'

'Are you disappointed Harry?' she murmured in a mock seductive tone.

Steed had now recovered some semblance of composure, but all he could think of saying was, 'Oh no Sophie, you are much prettier than those bomber types.'

The officer pilots were still gathered around as Chamberlain cut into their conversation. 'The C/O at Sapling gave Mrs Richards an introduction, and she asked me if she could come over to say thank you to the pilot that shot down the 109. I had no idea that you two knew each other.'

Sophie Richards replied, 'I know Harry from our days with Epping Flying Club, it was there that we both learnt to fly.' Although Chamberlain and one or two of the other officer pilots knew that Steed had been a mechanic at the flying club before the war, from the way that she phrased her answer most of the rest of the young pilots gathered around assumed that Sophie Richards and Steed had been members. It would not have bothered Steed if she had referred to him as one of the mechanics, but she didn't; she had thoughtfully given the impression that they had been friends of equal standing.

'Were you hurt in the landing Sophie?' asked Steed with some concern. 'Were you carrying any crew?'

'No I wasn't hurt, no thanks to that bloody German!' She didn't bother to apologise for her colourful language. She was clearly at home amongst the young officers; she shared their background, and she shared their social class. She glanced around at her audience, 'Do you know that he wanted to meet the crew of the Blenheim that he had just shot down? The C/O at Sapling was having none of it. He sent him straight off to the cooler under armed guard.'

She looked back at Steed, 'We always fly alone Harry, and the aircraft that we fly are never armed. Pity, because a rear gunner would have been very useful the other day. I never saw the German and I never saw you. I was just approaching the airfield when there was a commotion behind. It sounds stupid, I know, but I didn't even realise that I was being shot at. I thought at first that there was something wrong with the aircraft. Then one of the engines stopped working and I could see that it was on fire. The hydraulics were u/s and wheels wouldn't come down. I was very lucky because by now the airfield was right in front of me. I just managed to tighten the straps before making a belly landing. It wasn't until I got out that the firemen told me what had happened and pointed out the Messerschmitt. By then you had gone. What can you tell me about it Harry?'

All eyes turned to Steed. 'There's not really much to tell Sophie. At first I thought that your aeroplane might be a hedgehopping German, but when I got lower I could see clearly that it was a Blenheim. It was only then that I saw the Messerschmitt-109 behind you. I am afraid that by the time I got into a shooting position he had already taken a pot shot at you. Anyway, he was so busy trying to put you away that he didn't see me. I hit him and then pulled up to avoid overshooting. By the time I had lined him up in my sights again I could see that he was in serious trouble and that his engine had stopped. I saw the airfield in front and, because he was no longer a threat to you, I allowed him to land. That's about it really.'

'Well I'm glad you showed up, because if you hadn't I'm darn sure that he would have finished me off; he wouldn't have been as chivalrous as you.'

'Oh, I'm far from being chivalrous Sophie. It was only because he was certain to be captured that I allowed him to land. If I had been behind a German aeroplane over France I would have done my best to shoot it down and kill the crew, even with an airfield in front.'

At this, several of the officer pilots looked a little embarrassed. The King, however, clapped Steed on the shoulder and exclaimed, 'You and me, Mister Hawk, we are of the same mind. But if it had been me behind Herr Brauer instead of you, he would now be in Valhalla, if that that where these Teutonic swine go, or maybe it is hell.'

'Steady on King,' said Chamberlain. 'There is a lady present.'

The King bowed solemnly towards Sophie Richards. 'Please accept my apologies dear madam. I sometimes forget myself when I talk about the Nazis.'

Sophie Richards chatted amiably with the pilots. She was the quintessential attractive older woman that all youths, especially virgin youths, find so exciting; sophisticated, slim, gay and easy to talk to, and above all with understated sexual experience.

Finally, it was time to leave and Steed walked her to her car. He half expected to see the Humber-12 in which he had lost his virginity, but her current car was a gorgeous SS Jaguar; the Richards family were obviously well heeled.

'Harry, I know how busy you are right now, remember that I deliver aircraft to RAF stations, but I would dearly like to take you out to dinner one night in London. I owe you my life; no, don't look so embarrassed, you know that it's true. It's my way of saying thank you. Please say that you will come, let's say tomorrow night.'

'That's very kind of you Sophie, but I would need to check with my C/O.'

Steed had half expected an invitation to another meeting. Would it just be a nice meal, or would their previous very brief affair be rekindled? He didn't want to start a relationship with a married woman, but seeing her again, smelling her perfume and feeling the softness of her cheek as she kissed him had reawakened his desire. Maybe it would just be dinner, but maybe, just maybe, it might go a little further. Life was short, and recently Steed had been getting the idea that it might be very much shorter than he would like.

'Please don't be cross darling, but I have already mentioned it to your C/O. He says that it will be fine, and that you people often go to London for the night.'

'In that case I would love to come. I could do with a decent meal. To be honest, the officers tend to go to London restaurants, clubs and parties and so on, but when I go to town it is usually to see my mum and dad.'

She had called him darling, but that was just a figure of speech, wasn't it? She probably used it all of the time in her circle of friends. He opened the door of her car and she slipped in behind the wheel, her tailored skirt rising just above her knee.

'I will pick you up here at seven o'clock tomorrow evening Harry. Your C/O said that would be a good time. I'll book a restaurant in London, but you must agree that the evening is my treat.

'Okay, that sounds marvellous Sophie, but let me drive you. I don't own a car, but I can borrow one.' He thought of Toby's beaten-up jalopy and added, 'Although I must admit it's not a patch on this.'

'It's probably easier if I pick you up Harry, it will save time. You can drive us to London in the Jaguar if you want to.' And so the evening was arranged. He bent down to shake her hand, but instead she kissed him goodbye very lightly on the lips. It was by no means a passionate kiss; an onlooker might have mistaken it for a kiss between relatives, but that innocuous touching of their lips made Steed's heart pound.

The following day Chamberlain lost another of his pilots; again it was one of the later arrivals, a young pilot officer, not yet nineteen. The Tomcats had been drawn into a fight with Me-109s. The Me-109 formation was not large, and for a change 126-Squadron was not outnumbered, but the Messerschmitts employed the perfect strategy against the Hurricanes. They came down out of the sun and forced the Tomcats to break. After making a single pass they climbed away and then repeated the process. The Me-109s were not interested in dog fighting Hurricanes at fifteen thousand feet. After ten minutes the Germans abandoned their game and flew away, presumably low on fuel. There was nothing that the Tomcats could do to prevent them. The 109s left behind a burning Hurricane plummeting towards the Essex soil, with its young pilot already dead it the cockpit.

Chamberlain recognised the strain that his young pilots had to endure. He tried hard to spread the load such that pilots had at least one day a week free from operations. It was not easy, and often an experienced pilot on a rest day would have to give hands-on instruction to one or two of the fledglings. When the Tomcats were stood down at the end of the day, Chamberlain called Steed over.

'Hawk, I know that Sophie Richards has invited you supper in London this evening by way of a thank you. I'm standing you down tomorrow, so a rest day with no flying. You don't have to hurry back tonight, so stay with your parents in London overnight if you like. Enjoy yourself Hawk, you deserve it.'

As Steed waited for Sophie Richards by the main gate he pondered Chamberlain's words. The squadron leader was a shrewd judge of character. Did he suspect that there was more to their relationship than a thank you meal? Surely not. Even Steed was uncertain of what the evening might have in store for him. Maybe it would just be a meal in a nice restaurant and he would be able to stay with his parents overnight. Nobody had mentioned Sophie's husband the previous day, although it was clear from her title that she was married, or at least that she had been married.

The Jaguar pulled up and Steed got in. Sophie Richards looked absolutely stunning. 'Hello Harry.' She kissed him on the cheek. 'Would you like to drive?'

'I'm happy as a passenger Sophie, but I will drive if you would like me to.'

'In which case, I will drive. I love this car, but I don't drive it so much as I used to. It drinks petrol, and the stuff isn't as easy to get these days. Do you still have your motorbike?'

The conversation flowed easily. Sophie Richards was an accomplished and fast driver. The miles flew by, and in no time they were approaching the outskirts of London. Steed felt that he had to ask the obvious question, 'Is your husband in the forces Sophie?'

She turned her head towards him. 'Yes, he's in the army, logistics, but he has been sent overseas, to Singapore.' The subject was not mentioned again.

The restaurant was popular and full, but a fresh table was prepared for them in an excellent position, near to the dance floor and with a good view of the small orchestra. As they sat down, Steed said, 'You obviously have influence here Sophie.'

She smiled, 'Not me darling, it's you. Haven't you noticed the way that people are looking at you? They can see your uniform, your wings, and they can see your DFM ribbon. You are one of Churchill's few, a national hero.'

Steed was acutely embarrassed. 'No, it's you they are looking at. And I don't blame them. You look absolutely fabulous this evening.'

Their drinks arrived, and then Sophie said, 'Shall we dance?'

Steed had not been to many dances, mostly those arranged at the various RAF camps. He was thankful that his elder cousin had taught him the steps to the more popular dances, so he was reasonably confident that he wouldn't make a fool of himself. The dance floor was crowded; that always helped the inexperienced.

'That would be wonderful,' he said, leading her onto the dance floor and into a slow foxtrot.

'You're not a bad dancer,' she said, 'quite light on your feet.'

'Don't sound so surprised,' Steed replied light-heartedly. 'I can manage a slow foxtrot, but if we get to a tango I'll crash and burn. I'll be quite heavy on your feet then!'

Over dinner the conversation again flowed easily. He had been on dates with girls of his own age, not many it was true, and he was quite friendly with a number of WAAFs at Colne Martin. He had even had a mild fling with a Norwegian girl in Dumfries, whom he suspected of being involved with the cloak and dagger brigade. But with Sophie it was so different. Steed felt as if a load had been lifted from his shoulders. Chamberlain was right. A night out, away from the mess, a chic nightspot with a beautiful and elegant woman; it was a real tonic. For a short while he could forget the day job. She was so easy to talk to, such fun to be with. She asked him about his friends in the squadron.

'My two closest friends are sergeant pilots,' he replied. 'The boys that you met yesterday are the officer pilots. We all do much the same job, but there is a difference. When we are flying, or rather sitting around waiting to fly, all the pilots, officers and NCOs, have a good repartee. But we do not mess together, and socially we tend to go our own separate ways. That's the way of the forces I guess; it would be bad for discipline if there was too much camaraderie.'

She nodded her understanding and Steed continued, 'You will remember Squadron Leader Chamberlain of course, our boss. He is a very good pilot and a fine leader, but I would never call him by his Christian name. The chap with the badly scarred face, that's Flight Lieutenant Dix, my flight commander. He is probably the best technical pilot in the squadron, but because he is my flight commander, I wouldn't call him by his Christian name either.'

'And they call you Hawk. I asked them about it and they told me the reason, Hawkeye eh? You have quite a reputation, and they also told me that you are the squadron's top scorer. I was lucky that it was you who came along the other day.'

'Don't believe all that they tell you Sophie, they are a bunch of jokers and leg-pullers. Anyway, I was telling you about my friends. In spite of the barriers that the RAF imposes, there are several officers that I am proud to call friends. The chap that led me into the mess when I met you is Roger Daily. He's Australian, as if you couldn't guess, and he's a really down to earth bloke.'

Sophie Richards interrupted, 'I would say that he is a ladies' man. Am I right?'

'You bet. His surname is Daily, but Roger isn't his real Christian name. It took me a while to realise what they meant by calling him 'Roger' Daily.' Sophie Richards looked confused, and then giggled as she finally understood.

'He walks with a bit of a limp, was he injured flying?'

'That's right, he had a bumpy landing. Billy Bishop is a good friend of mine too. You may not remember him, he is a bit quieter than some of the others, and older too, about my age.'

'My, my Harry, your grey hairs are showing,' she teased. 'How old are you, twenty-two, twenty-three?'

'Twenty-two, but you can see how young some of the pilots are, only nineteen some of them.' He paused, remembering that the one eighteen-year-old pilot in the squadron had died that day. Another difficult letter for the boss to write.

'In case you are wondering, I am thirty-five,' she said easily.

'I wouldn't have put you a day over twenty-five,' he said with mock sincerity. 'And then we have two foreign pilots, aside from Roger that is, who are good friends of mine. The King is Polish. Nobody can pronounce his Christian name, and his surname means King in English, so that's what we call him. He had a rough time getting to England and hates Germans for what they have done to his country. He is totally fearless and a crack pilot. The powers that be wanted to transfer him to a Polish squadron in training, but he was having none of it. He wants to stay with us so that he can kill Germans. The other foreign pilot is Belgian. He wasn't in the mess yesterday, but he is teaching me French.'

'Tu parle Français?' she asked.

Steed pinched his nose in order to sound like a Frenchman. *'Je parle un peu Français. Je apprends le Français. Mon proffeseur s'appelle Jean-Paul Colbert.'*

'Tres Bien,' she laughed. 'Are you planning to go to France in the near future?'

'Well, before the Germans ruined everything, I thought that we might be posted to the Western Front, just like in the last war. I did a bit of French at school so I started revising from old textbooks a year or so ago. We sit around quite a lot, at readiness or waiting to scramble, so it passes the time. Jean-Paul, our Belgian, saw what I was doing. He has been helping me with my French pronunciation which, by the way, he says is terrible.'

'I think that you are all fine boys. We are all proud of what you are doing. You are all very brave,' she said with sincerity.

'I find it all a bit embarrassing,' said Steed. 'I hadn't fully realised until tonight just how much Churchill's speech, you know the one *'never in the field of human conflict has so much been owed by so many to so few'*, has had on ordinary people. RAF pilots are fighting the Germans it's true, but so are a good many other people. I wouldn't want to trade places with the Merchant Navy sailors who sail the Atlantic day after day, week after week, waiting for a torpedo from a German submarine. What chance do they have in the middle of the night, swimming in an icy cold sea with burning oil all around? Anyway, there is one other good friend that I have, and he wasn't in the mess either yesterday. Our intelligence officer is known to one and all as the Spy. He is a lovely man; he used to teach classics at a university. I often walk, or rather run, his dog Dion.

The conversation moved on. They spoke about music and American swing, about Glen Miller, Tommy Dorsey, Bing Crosby and the Andrews Sisters. They spoke about films and she was surprised to hear him talking about the directors as well as the actors.

'I like the films of Howard Hawks,' he said. 'I saw *Dawn Patrol* with my mum and dad years ago. I was mad keen an anything to do with aeroplanes even then. His most recent film is *Only Angels Have Wings.*'

'But *Dawn Patrol* is a modern film isn't it?'

'Yes, but that's a remake with Errol Flynn and David Niven; that's a good picture too. There are some very good flying sequences in the modern *Dawn Patrol*, but the original version starred Douglas Fairbanks and was directed by Howard Hawks. I saw that when I was a boy, well a teenager anyway. Have you seen the Errol Flynn version?'

'No,' she said, 'I don't see too many films, but I liked *The Wizard of Oz* and *Gone With The Wind.*'

Steed was glad to move away from the subject of *Dawn Patrol* in case Sophie asked too many questions about parallels to the present conflict. The plot centred around the relationship between the commander of a British fighter squadron on the Western Front in the Great War and his two most senior pilots. Novice pilots were being sent to the front with too little flying experience and were consequently being massacred by the Germans. Nothing much has changed there then, he thought to himself.

By the last dance, they were both a little light-headed. It had been a while since Steed had allowed himself to drink so much. A sore head did not mix well with dog fighting Me-109s at fifteen thousand feet, although many pilots insisted that the best cure for a hangover was a good dose of oxygen.

When they reached the car, Sophie Richards asked Steed to drive. He was about to start the engine when she touched his hand. 'Harry, what time do you need to be back at Colne Martin?'

'I am not flying tomorrow, so anytime. Would you like to go on somewhere else?'

She was now holding his hand. 'Harry, a long time ago something happened between us. Neither of us has mentioned it this evening, and from that I can see you have grown into the perfect gentleman. You were very young then, and maybe I shouldn't have taken advantage, but I did.'

Steed started to speak, but she held a finger to his lips. She spoke quickly and, unusually for her, a little nervously. 'My husband and I have led separate lives for some time now, and in any case he is in Singapore. You are very welcome to spend the night at my house; we would be alone. It is very important for both of us to understand that it would simply be a very nice ending to a very nice evening. There should be no obligation or commitment towards the future from either of us. There is a war on and we would be living for the moment. I realise that I am thirteen years...'

She didn't finish the sentence because Steed drew her to him and kissed her hungrily. She responded, her mouth opening slightly and her hands moving to caress his neck and hair. He grasped her breast, feeling his excitement grow, kissing her mouth ardently and hard. His hand moved down her silk dress towards her thigh. He kissed her neck, revelling in the smell of her perfume. She said gently, 'That is nice darling, but not here. Drive me home. We have all night.'

And so it was that Steed slept with a woman for the first time in his life. She had taken his virginity five years earlier and taught him the primary steps of lovemaking. That night he moved on to the more advanced lessons.

On the 7th September, Flight Lieutenant Dix returned to operational flying. Steed, who had been flying Blue-3 with Evans as his wingman, now reverted to Blue-2 behind Dix. He had enjoyed the responsibility and greater freedom that leading a pair of fighters endowed, and he had seen young Gareth Evans grow rapidly in competence as his wingman. The boy listened to what he was told, and with his increasing experience had come his victory over the Me-110.

But the Luftwaffe was wearing down Fighter Command. Slowly, but surely, airfields and their support services were being wrecked by constant air raids. Colne Martin was less affected than the airfields south of London, but even small grass airfields on the periphery of the main battle area, like Colne, bore the scars of the conflict. The pilots too were tired, very tired some of them, but so they reasoned were the pilots on the other side. They knew that they were taking a toll of the German bombers. The Stukas no longer came, they were too vulnerable unless they enjoyed virtual air superiority. The RAF had denied them that, at least for the time being.

Still the RAF rose to accept battle in the skies of southern England. Still the Commander in Chief, Air Chief Marshal Sir Hugh Dowding, refused to withdraw his forces to airfields in the north, out of range of the deadly Messerschmitt-109s. But the strain was showing and the RAF's losses were growing. The C-in-C knew that he had to preserve his forces in order to meet the expected invasion. The outcome of the battle rested on a knife-edge.

The morning was quiet. Bishop and Adams were scrambled around mid morning to intercept a German reconnaissance aircraft, but without success. Otherwise the pilots lounged around in the autumn sunshine, reading or playing cards. Steed, who had become bored with French verbs, was reading a book about the English civil war. One of the newer pilots, Pilot Officer Vivian Fenton-Williams, saw the cover of the book and expressed his opinion.

'Cromwell was a traitor to England; he murdered a King and he deserved his comeuppance.'

Steed looked up from his book. He didn't much care for this spotty-faced youth with the squeaky voice, but he simply smiled and went back to his reading. Fenton-Williams persisted.

'Cromwell was just like Hitler, a dictator. He wanted to be King himself. The country soon went back to having a proper King, Charles II you know, once Cromwell died.'

Again Steed looked up from his book. Perhaps it was because he was tired, or maybe he was simply irritated with the young officer who seemed to think himself superior to the sergeant pilots. Looking back Steed could remember several innuendoes concerning education and breeding emanating from the immature Fenton-William's lips. Steed decided to wind up the young brat.

'Cromwell didn't get his comeuppance, as you put it old man, until two years after his death, which incidentally was by natural causes. Charles II had his body dug up and mutilated, but by then Oliver was past caring. As for being a dictator, well. Charles I was the dictator. He thought that God had given him the absolute right to rule the country exactly as he liked. Cromwell thought that parliament should have a say in the matter and chopped the tyrant's head off. Good riddance too, a bit of regicide never harmed anyone. The French had the right idea. Get rid of the aristocrats; send them all to the guillotine.'

Fenton-Williams rose to the bait, He didn't realise that Steed was teasing him. 'Well their republic hasn't done the French much good has it? I suppose that you would like to cut off…..' he paused, about to say that Steed would like to cut the head off the present monarch, but he thought better of it. He continued '….would like to depose George VI and put a president in his place?'

This time Steed responded with a serious expression, 'William the Conqueror gave English land and power to his foreign mates nine hundred years ago. But why should their descendants sit in the House of Lords and rule over the rest of us based solely on their Norman birthright? You are right, I would like to see the House of Lords abolished and all the titles, Dukes, Lords, Earls and so on, abolished along with it.'

'We need a House of Lords,' countered Fenton-Williams. 'It has given our country stability for hundreds of years. And we need it to moderate the House of Commons. If you abolished their titles, where would that leave the King?'

Steed answered carefully, 'Personally, I would like to see the country governed solely by elected representatives, not those who are there simply through an accident of birth. That hardly seems democratic.'

'That's treason!' squeaked Fenton-Williams. 'We are at war and you are suggesting getting rid of our King. You are a communist Flight Sergeant.'

'No, no dear boy,' said Steed in a condescending manner. 'A communist believes in state control of all enterprises. A republican believes in government of the people by the people. Please don't call the Americans communists, or they will be mightily offended.'

Dix was sitting nearby. He did not like the way the conversation was going and he intervened. 'That's enough gentlemen, this subject is now closed.' Fenton-Williams opened his mouth to say more, but he saw the expression on the flight lieutenant's face and thought better of it. Steed went back to his history book.

Later, when the opportunity arose, Dix had a private word with Steed. 'Hawk, this is an unofficial chat, otherwise I would address you as Flight Sergeant. I realise that you were putting young Fenton-Williams in his place this morning, but he does have a valid point. We are at war, you are a member of His Majesty's armed forces, and you owe the King your allegiance. He is our supreme commander. Is that clear?'

'Yes sir,' Steed thought it better to leave it at that.

'Normally, we have a right to freedom of speech here in Britain; it is what sets us apart from Nazi Germany. In Civy Street, you have the right to speak for a republic. Precious few people would agree with you of course, but we live in a democracy, so you have freedom of speech. But not here in the RAF, and not now in wartime. We are soldiers of the King. Do I make myself clear?'

'Yes sir.'

'You are a good pilot, an exceptional pilot even. You have proved that many times, but are you a leader? The next step for you on the promotional ladder is a commission. As an officer you must lead men. You must inspire them with a sense of duty, of responsibility, of order. You must display the values expected of an officer. You must be careful not to appear too cynical. Do you understand what I am saying?'

'Yes sir. Thank you for the advice.'

'That's what it is Hawk, simply advice. But keep any views you may have about a republic to yourself in future, even if said in jest. Are we clear on that?'

'Yes Sir.' And that was that. Steed hadn't really thought about promotion to pilot officer and beyond. He was beginning to have serious doubts about his chances of surviving as a flight sergeant for much longer, so thoughts of a future career in the RAF seemed a bit academic. But Dix had seemed to say what Steed had already surmised, that he was simply not officer material, he wouldn't fit in. He came from a different background, of working class London rather than public schools and debutant balls. So be it. If the invasion came, the officers and the NCO pilots were all destined for the same dark future anyway. It was better to live for today and not to worry about tomorrow.

The scramble came at four o'clock in the afternoon. The squadron was ordered to patrol over Southend-on-Sea at fifteen thousand feet. They were then sent northwest past Chelmsford, then finally south to London. The pilots were shocked to see the smoke drifting over the London docks, but by then the Luftwaffe had departed.

Chamberlain's briefing the next morning was very worrying for Steed, and indeed for all of those pilots with friends or family in London. 'Yesterday afternoon,' began the squadron leader, 'the Luftwaffe raided London in considerable force. Our controllers deployed most of the available squadrons, including 126, to meet the usual attacks on our airfields. But the huge mass of German aircraft didn't split up to strike at individual airfields as we expected, instead they pressed on to London. They were protected by hundreds of fighters, so those of our fighters that did manage to intercept were not able get through to the bombers. The Luftwaffe returned last night to stoke up the fires left over from the daylight raid. I am sorry to say gentlemen, that London has suffered badly.'

'What part of London was hit sir?' asked one of the pilots. 'Smoke was coming up from the docks when we flew over them yesterday.'

'Yes, that's right,' said Chamberlain. 'Their main target seems to have been the dockland area in East London, warehouses and so on. They had perfect visibility for the daylight raid, so one assumes that they hit the targets that they were after. The fires were still burning after dark, so that made a marker for the night raiders. Group expects them to try for London again today. If so, we shall be ready for them.'

But the day was quiet and the Tomcats were not scrambled. Unfortunately for the Londoners, the bombers came again that night, virtually unopposed, and guided to their target by the fires that still burned. That night, and for the next sixty-five nights bar one, the German bombers wrought their devastation upon the capital. The great Blitz of London had begun.

The morning after the second night raid on London, Chamberlain called Steed aside. 'Hawk, I see that you came top of your class in the night flying exercise during your training. You apparently earned a rebuke for flying upside down at one stage, what happened?'

'It was a while ago sir. As I remember, there was an incident on the ground while I was doing night circuits, and I had to stay up while it was cleared. I thought that, since I had the opportunity, I would try something new.' He gave the squadron leader a look that suggested butter wouldn't melt in his mouth. 'Someone on the ground noticed that my navigation lights were the wrong way around, so they discovered what I was doing. It was very wrong of me of course and I was quite rightly hauled over the coals for it.'

The squadron leader tried hard to suppress a grin. 'Well the point is that the Luftwaffe is bombing London at night and there is precious little that Fighter Command seems able to do about it. We have a few Blenheim night fighters stooging around over London, but Group want to give the people more protection. The squadron has been asked to paint one of our Hurricanes black, fit it out for night fighting, and try our luck. I have decided that two or three of our more experienced pilots shall take it in turns to have a go. How do you feel about flying tonight?'

Steed answered immediately, 'I would be very pleased to try my luck at night fighting. My parents are down there. Thank you for the opportunity.'

'Good show. I want you to fly for the next five nights in a row, starting tonight. You are relieved of daytime flying until the 15th of September. You will be expected to fly one operation each night. You will be in radio contact with a controller who will direct you and tell the local anti-aircraft guns to cease-fire when you are in their area. See the adjutant for the briefing notes. My advice is to try to get some sleep this afternoon. Good luck.'

Excused flying, Steed took the opportunity to join the Spy in walking Dion. 'I am off flying a Hurricane over London tonight Spy,' said Steed. 'How effective are our AA guns? How many did they bring down last night?'

The Spy looked serious. 'This is not for broadcasting Harry, but the guns are pretty ineffective. The standard 3.7-inch guns use optical range finders, so first the crews have to see a bomber in the searchlights before they can find its range. Then their predictors tell them where to lay the gun, what fuse timing to set and when to pull the trigger so to speak. Some of the searchlights have a basic radio direction finder, but it is not very effective. The trouble is, on the odd occasion that a Jerry gets caught in a searchlight, he immediately ducks and dives, which makes the predictor useless; the predictor assumes that the Jerry is going to fly straight and level for the time the shell takes to reach him you see.'

'Yes, I see,' said Steed. 'The Boss has put me off day flying for a couple of days so that I can fly at night. The idea is to stay above the bomber stream and look down, hoping to pick out the bombers visually against the fires below. Apparently, the Controller can order the guns to stop firing when I'm in their area. I only hope that I can remember what little we did in night flying training. Night-time navigation's the tricky bit in a single-seater in a blackout!'

The Spy nodded his agreement, 'Tonight the gun crews have been told to keep firing, even if they do not have a recognisable target. Apparently it is good for public morale to hear our anti-aircraft guns hitting back.' The Spy thought for a few seconds, and then added, 'Harry, what I am now about to tell you is in the strictest confidence, you mustn't discuss this with anyone.'

'My lips are sealed Spy,' said Steed. 'You have my undivided attention. Spill the beans!'

'Before the war,' began the Spy, 'the consensus view was that the bomber would always get through. So far, at Dunkirk, and presently over Britain, that is not always the case. The German bombers need protection from their fighters. Without protection the bombers suffer unacceptable casualties from a well-organised fighter force such as ours. Worse for them, their only fighter worth having is the Me-109, and that has limited range. So, in daylight at least, and assuming that we retain a credible fighter force, they can only raid within the range of the Me-109.'

'Yes,' agreed Steed, 'That much is obvious. No big secret there.'

'But the problem we have is with German night bombing. Here the pre-war consensus is correct. The bomber will get through, and there is very little that we can do about it. Their only real problem is finding the target in the blackout. Our AA guns are ineffective and our night fighters are next to useless.'

'Thanks, just what a prospective ace night fighter pilot wants to hear.'

'Be patient young Mr Steed,' said the Spy with a gleam in his eye. 'Because this is the in strictest confidence part. As you know, we use Radio Direction Finding to locate enemy aircraft approaching our shores, and very effective it is too. It's the main reason that our controllers can vector you onto the bombers as they come over. Otherwise, you people would have to fly standing patrols like you did at Dunkirk and over the Channel convoys. I have never understood why the Germans didn't persist in bombing our RDF sites, but they didn't and that was our good fortune.

Anyway, I digress. We have large RDF sites along the coast to locate aircraft as they approach our shores, and we even have mobile RDF stations to help our searchlights and AA guns find their targets. Well, now the boffins have invented an RDF set that can fit into a Blenheim to guide the fighter to an air target.'

'Clever stuff,' exclaimed Steed. 'Can I have one of these hush-hush boxes of tricks for my Hurricane tonight please?'

'I'm afraid not,' replied The Spy. 'It's a full time job peering at the screen and interpreting the squiggles. You need an observer to do that and to tell the pilot which way to fly in order to locate the enemy. The observer has to direct the pilot to come up behind the bomber. When the pilot is close enough to see the enemy, he shoots him down. Simple eh?'

'So why isn't the ground littered with wrecked German bombers come morning?' muttered Steed, with more than a hint of irony.

'Because dear boy, the boffins' brainchild doesn't work too well, not yet anyway, and the poor old Blenheim night fighter is slower than some of the enemy bombers! But fear ye not, all is not lost. We have new aircraft coming on stream. The Defiants are being used as a stopgap, but here the observer in his turret also has to do the shooting. The new Beaufighter is a much better bet for the future. It is faster and much more heavily armed, and the pilot does the shooting.'

'Which is as it should be,' said Steed. 'So what you are telling me is don't give up the day job.'

At this, the Spy looked quizzically at Steed. 'Well, actually, I am wondering if you should give up the day job and transfer to a night fighter squadron.'

'Huh? Well it's nice to be wanted!' said Steed with feeling.

'No, seriously Harry. The squadron leader picked you as one of his pilots for night fighting because you are technically one of our best pilots. You have excellent eyesight, and you came top of your class in night flying training. He told me about your inverted flying as well. That shows real confidence.'

'That's not what they said when they bollocked me after I came down!'

'What I mean is, there is a real need for night fighter pilots. With a decent aircraft and an RDF operator that knows what he is doing, I think that you would do well.'

'Hmm. Well thanks for the advice, and the hush-hush stuff about the airborne RDF. Let's see how I get on tonight.'

It had been a long time since Steed had flown at night, and that was in a Miles Master trainer. He was pleased to see his own ground crew waiting for him alongside the black Hurricane. His fitter pointed to the exhaust pipes on the cowling.

'We have extended the pipes to cut down on the glare, otherwise your night vision would be upset and the Jerries would see you coming from miles away.' Steed had seen Hurricane engines run up at night; great blue flames streamed from the exhaust pipes. 'The armourer has also set up your guns.'

Steed cleared the end of the field and climbed into the night sky. Navigation at night was the tricky part of this exercise. A lot of it rested on compass bearings, airspeed, wind direction and timings. He made a few jottings on his pad, strapped to his thigh alongside his map and notes, and then switched off the torch-like map reading light and turned down the instrument illumination. Below, the ground was pitch-dark; the blackout was very effective.

Ahead, in the direction of London, there was a dull red glow in the night sky. As he neared the capital the sky appeared blood red and he could see the pencil beams of searchlights and the airbursts of the anti-aircraft shells. As he entered the inferno, Steed could see the fires and the occasional bomb bursts below. A mixture of anger and fear swelled up inside him; anger at the Huns dropping their bombs and fear for the safety of his parents, somewhere in the metropolis below.

Steed had been searching in vain for some recognisable landmark. He needed to give the controller his position otherwise there was a danger that he would be shot down by his own side. In spite of the light from the fires, it was more difficult to fix his position than he expected. And then he saw the River Thames below, and away to his left he thought that he glimpsed St Paul's Cathedral in the fire's glow. He reported to his controller that he was over Westminster. On a whim, Steed requested the controller to refrain from telling the guns to cease-fire. The sky was apparently full of Germans with only his lone Hurricane for company. On the grounds of probability, the guns were far more likely to hit a German than him.

Steed circled slowly, peering down, trying to make out the outline of a German bomber, but he could see only the fires and the occasional flashes from the high explosive bombs. If he could see a line of bomb flashes from a stick of HE bombs, then perhaps he could guess the position of the offending bomber. That was a good theory, but in practice the flashes from HE bombs looked fairly random to Steed. Sometimes there were two or three flashes in succession, but it was difficult to ascertain the direction of the bomber. The Spy had told him that the Germans had also been dropping a high number of incendiary bombs and occasional parachute mines, and these wouldn't show up as a line of flashes.

There were shell bursts from the anti-aircraft guns pretty well all over the sky, but the Hurricane circled smoothly without any semblance of buffeting from a near miss. After fifteen minutes of fruitless searching, Steed became aware of greater activity further downstream, towards the docks. Several searchlights were frantically waving across the sky, and the anti-aircraft gunfire over there was definitely heavier. Steed set course down river until he came to that unmistakable horseshoe bend enclosing the Isle of Dogs. Suddenly, below and to his right, he saw a twin-engine aeroplane caught in a searchlight beam like a silver moth. Other beams darted across the sky, like bony fingers, trying to converge on the German. But the bomber turned and dived into the darkness. The searchlights swept around, backwards and forwards like angry wasps, but the German had escaped.

Again Steed circled, peering down, hoping to catch a shadow of a German aircraft against the fires below, but without success. Several times he sighted a bomber trapped momentarily by one of the searchlight beams, but the enemy always slipped out of the beam almost as soon as he had been caught, and certainly before Steed had a chance to get anywhere near him.

After thirty minutes of fruitless searching, Steed decided to try his luck at a much lower altitude. He dropped down to five thousand feet, about as low as he dared go without risking snagging a barrage balloon cable. Here the anti-aircraft fire was more intense, and he had the feeling that he was becoming the target. The searchlights seemed to grope their way towards him, but without quite finding him. He resisted the temptation to call his controller and ask for the gunners to cease-fire, but he fared no better at this lower altitude, and his enemy still eluded him. After a while he climbed a little higher, but it was like searching for a needle in the proverbial haystack. Disappointed, he finally informed his controller that he was getting low on fuel and set a course for home.

Navigation in a single seat Hurricane at night, in a blackout, is never easy. Steed had first to get a fix over London before setting off for Colne Martin. Before setting out that night he had worked out a flight plan from the Isle of Dogs, that loop in the river Thames that he correctly guessed would be relatively easy to spot. From there he set a course and carefully maintained a steady speed. When, by his calculation, he was over Colne Martin, he requested a flare be sent up over the field. He was gratified to see a green light appear about two miles away to his right.

Steed was very disappointed with his stint as a night fighter pilot. The following four nights followed the same pattern as the first. The only saving grace was that Steed proved his ability to navigate to London to fulfil his mission, not too difficult bearing in mind the target illumination provided by the Luftwaffe, and most importantly to return to Colne Martin for an uneventful landing.

Several times he saw German aircraft caught momentarily in the searchlight beams, and on one occasion, when he deliberately flew into a patch of the sky where the AA fire was heaviest, he caught a glimpse of blue exhaust flames and the outline of a bomber, a Heinkel he thought. But the German was taking evasive action to avoid the attentions of the gunners below, and Steed lost the target. However, when he returned to Colne Martin, he found his aircraft peppered with 'friendly' shrapnel.

Having his days free of flying did have its advantages. With Chamberlain's permission, Steed was able to take his motorcycle into London to see his parents. Petrol was now difficult to obtain, at least it was if one didn't have access to a Hurricane's petrol tanker, so Steed carried a full can for the return trip. One advantage of petrol rationing was that the traffic was light, and he was able to make good time through the countryside along near deserted roads. He rode through East London and was saddened to see that the working class area of the East End had taken a battering from the German bombs but, so far at least, his parents' district of Islington further to the north seemed to have been spared the worst of the damage.

Steed took his father for a pint at the local pub while his mother prepared dinner. His father spoke about the night bombing in London. 'You mustn't worry about Mum and me in the bombing Harry. The chances of a bomb hitting us are a thousand to one.'

'But why don't you get an Anderson Shelter in the garden Dad? You could sleep there during the bombing. It would be much safer.'

'Your mum and me have talked about it son. We both feel the same way. We want to sleep in our own room, in our own bed. In the unlikely event that one of Jerry's bombs hits the house, the wardens know where to find us. We're much more worried about you.'

The old soldier lowered his voice. 'I have never spoken to you about these things before son. I had hoped that you would never see some of the things that I have seen. Because I have been where you are now Harry. I know what it is like to see mates die. Mates that you have shared everything with. For me it was the boys in the trenches, for you it is the pilots in your squadron. You try to kid yourself that it will never happen to you, but in your heart you know that you are playing a game of chance. I convinced myself that I was going to die in France. I gave up all hope of seeing Blighty again. But, you know, I didn't die. And neither will you.'

Steed looked into his father's moist eyes, saw the memories from long ago, the trenches, the machine-guns, the whiz-bangs and fallen comrades. 'Yes, I know Dad. But it's not quite the same for me. When you went over the top it was a game of chance; the machine-gun bullet hit either you or the next man. There wasn't much you could do to lengthen the odds. But for me it's different. When I'm dog fighting with a Messerschmitt, I am in control of my own destiny. I'm better at it than most of them Dad, honestly. It's Jerry that has to worry about not coming back, not me. So tell Mum not to worry.'

'I'll tell her son, but it won't do any good. You're still her little boy, and she'll worry about you until the day that she dies.'

'Yes, well that won't be sometime soon now will it?' Steed thought for a moment, and then looked his father in the eye. 'We both know that it is possible that I will get unlucky. If I do, well you know how to tie things up; everything that I own goes to you and Mum of course. You will get a letter from my C/O saying lots of nice things about me. I guess that your officers wrote much the same letters in the Great War; a sort of sanitised note of what happened. Don't let Mum spend every Sunday visiting my grave. You know my views on such things. You know that for me it is the inky blackness. I have no God. It was the inky blackness for me before I was born and it will be the same inky blackness for me after I die. When my brain stops working there will be no more me. A ghostly version of Harry Steed will not suddenly materialise complete with wings and harp, whatever the devil dodger might say! You know how I feel about you and Mum, I know how you feel about me, and there's nothing more that we need to say about it. I have no regrets. Now let's have another pint before dinner.' The subject was closed. The old soldier and his son had their pint, but the landlord would not take any money for it.

Steed went back to his day job on Sunday 15th September 1940, the date that was later to be celebrated as 'Battle of Britain' day. Smithy took over as the squadron's temporary night fighter pilot. During Steed's sojourn, the Tomcats had been involved in the air battles over London. Chamberlain, Daily and The King had claimed confirmed kills, and several other pilots had claimed probables. Two of the squadron's aircraft had been lost in these engagements, but both of the pilots were safe and unhurt. John Paul Colbert had made a forced landing on Southend beach, and new squadron member PO 'Pussy' Lions had been shot down on his first operational flight but had managed to bail out.

Steed was having a cup of tea in the dispersal hut with Toby Adams and Johnny Walker when the scramble came. The twelve Hurricanes climbed into the late morning sunshine and headed towards London. Steed was in his usual position, number two to Dix, with Bishop and Adams forming the remainder of Blue section. The Tomcats, now at sixteen thousand feet, arrived over London shortly after midday. There were aeroplanes everywhere.

'Snappers at three o'clock, angels twenty,' said an unidentified voice.

Steed peered at the supposed enemy; yes, he was certain, they were flying in vic formation, and maybe not quite that high. He transmitted, 'Tomcat leader from Blue-2. The bogies at three o'clock are in vic formation, so possibly friendly.'

Chamberlain's voice was next over the wireless, 'Tomcats, enemy bombers ahead at angels fifteen. Tally Ho.' This was the signal to the Controller that the enemy was in sight and no further directions were needed. Chamberlain led the Tomcats straight at the enemy, who Steed could now see were Dorniers starting their bombing run. Other RAF fighters were circling the Dorniers like hornets, darting in and out of the bombers' impeccable formation. But where were the escorts, the Snappers? As the Tomcats closed the enemy bombers, Steed was certain that he saw four Me-109s of the close escort make a sudden u-turn and head for home, leaving their charges to continue with their bombing run. The Me-109s were not under any immediate threat from the RAF fighters when they turned, so maybe they were low on fuel. London was at the limit of a 109s range, especially if they had been fighting off RAF fighters on the journey to the target.

As the Tomcats closed in on the bombers, Steed spotted fighter aircraft coming in behind and below the Tomcats; they were Spitfires. 'Tomcat Leader from Blue-2. Spitfire squadron behind and below us.' And then the Tomcats were into the bombers.

Chamberlain had brought his squadron down on the port rear quarter of the Dornier formation. Dix was heading for the lead bomber in a closely packed group of four. Steed's job was to protect his leader's tail from the escorts, but otherwise he was free to have a pop at the bombers. For the moment there was no threat to his leader from the escorts, so Steed aimed at the second Dornier in the line, immediately behind Dix's target. The Hurricanes were travelling fast, perhaps too fast, and there wasn't enough time to get in a good long burst as Steed would have liked. Nevertheless, he was gratified to see flashes from the De Wilde ammunition flitting along the rear fuselage of the Dornier. Damn! Should have allowed more deflection thought Steed as he half rolled away, following Dix. The Tomcats had made their first pass as a squadron, but now the pairs of Hurricanes were free to continue the action independently.

Dix pulled up, intending to cut through the bomber formation a second time. A Spitfire cut in from the right, and fastened onto his tail. For a second Steed hesitated. Was this a lost friend looking for support? No, this idiot had mistaken Dix's Hurricane for a Messerschmitt. 'Blue leader break right, break right! Spitfire on your tail.'

The Spitfire opened fire at about the same time that Dix threw his aircraft into a tight turn. Having more speed, the Spitfire overshot, but he turned to come back. Dix rotated his aircraft, presenting the Spitfire pilot with a clear silhouette of his Hurricane, displaying the RAF roundels. But the Spitfire was clearly coming in for another pass. For a second, Steed thought about giving this clot a two second burst, because he was perfectly positioned to do so, but common sense prevailed. Unexpectedly, the Spitfire broke away. Whether it was because he had realised his mistake, or because he had seen Steed's aircraft on his tail, Steed was not sure.

'Blue Leader, the Spitfire has broken off.'

The airwaves were full of shouts and warnings, much of it unnecessary as far as Steed was concerned, so Dix did not reply, or if he did his transmission was lost in the general hubbub. The bombers were on their own, without fighter cover. We should be able to slaughter them thought Steed; but the bombers were holding a tight formation and the mixture of RAF Spitfires and Hurricanes were getting in each other's way.

Dix climbed towards the phalanx of Dorniers in a stern attack, with Steed in close attendance behind. Just as he was closing his prey, Dix was caught in a wicked stream of crossfire from several of the German formation. The flight lieutenant's aircraft span away from the battle, losing height rapidly. Much as he hated to leave such tempting targets as unescorted Dornier bombers over London, Steed's duty was to follow and protect his leader. Eventually, he was gratified to see Dix correct the spin and level out at six thousand feet; but they had a lot to do if they were to rejoin the fight some ten thousand feet above them.

Dix's voice cut in loud and clear. 'Blue-2 from Leader, nice of you to stay with me. My crate handles like a carthorse, and I can see damage to the port aileron. Take a look around her would you? See if her hat's on straight.'

Steed flew a slow barrel roll around Dix's Hurricane, but could see no obvious signs of damage. 'She looks okay to me Blue leader, apart from your aileron of course.'

'All right you clever sod, stop showing off. Well she doesn't feel the least bit okay. I had the Devil's own job in getting out of that spin. We're going home.' And so the two aircraft returned to Colne Martin, followed shortly afterwards by the remainder of 126-Squadron.

The Tomcats had no sooner refuelled and rearmed when the order to scramble came for the second time that day. Dix by then had acquired a spare aircraft. They were ordered to patrol Chelmsford at eighteen thousand feet, but they were soon directed towards Dartford, on the outskirts of East London.

If the noon excursion over the capital had been an experience, it was nothing on this. As the Tomcats arrived over the river Thames, the sky was absolutely full of aeroplanes; Steed could see three large formations of German bombers in line abreast, well over one hundred of the buggers he thought. Unlike the morning raid, this time the enemy's fighters were out in force with both close escort and higher-level Me-109s. But the RAF was also out in force, and Steed could see a mixture of Spitfires and Hurricanes trying to break through to the bombers and being engaged by the enemy's close escort fighters, while high above he could see the vapour trails that indicated the Spitfire squadrons were keeping the 'Hun in the sun' busy.

Chamberlain altered course, and led the Tomcats towards the nearest large block of bombers, which Steed could now see actually comprised two separate formations, Dorniers in front followed by Heinkels. Chamberlain had the height advantage over the bombers and their close escort. He led the Tomcats down in a feinted attack on the trailing Heinkels, and then turned his squadron to strike at the rear of the Dornier formation. It was cleverly done and completely misled the defending enemy fighters.

This time Steed slipped in behind Dix as they closed the Dorniers. He was worried that he might lose his leader in the melee if he chose his own target and stayed in line abreast; there were too many Snappers around to risk that. Steed watched from behind as Dix homed in a Dornier towards the edge of the formation who seemed to be lagging behind his comrades, and was therefore not so well protected by their guns. Steed weaved to both check that his tail was clear and to drop back a little further from Dix; he wanted to have a clear shooting chance at the Dornier without endangering his leader out in front.

Dix came in fast from dead astern of the enemy bomber, firing at it from close range and then sweeping over it, so close that he almost took off its radio aerial, and then rolling to the left and diving away from the defensive gunfire. Steed chose a higher route in towards the Dornier so that he could aim his customary deflection shot at the bomber's glass nose. At the last moment Steed rolled and dived to the right, continuing his roll through 180 degrees beneath the bomber, so that he emerged on Dix's tail.

By now the flight commander was curving up and around for a second attack on the rear of the bomber pack. Steed was struggling to make up lost ground as he followed his leader, so he hit the emergency boost. Again Dix opened fire at close range into the luckless belly of one of the enemy formation, and Steed followed suit, but this time as they dived away Steed glimpsed the Me-109s coming down.

'Blue Leader, Snappers coming down behind us.'

Dix corkscrewed down, followed by Steed, but the Me-109s, conspicuous by their yellow propeller hubs, broke off the chase and returned to their charges. Once again it looks like good old Oberleutnant Brauer was telling the truth mused Steed. The close escort 109s are tied to the apron strings of the bombers.

'Blue-Leader, the Snappers have broken off.'

Dix and Steed made several more passes at the bomber stream, playing a cat and mouse game with the defending Me-109s. The German fighters would wait until the two Hurricanes approached the bombers, and then dive down in an effort to make the British pair turn away or engage fighter on fighter. The Me-109s never pursued their quarry, but always returned to their defensive duties with the bombers. The same game between the German and RAF fighters was being played out all over London.

Dix was a wily leader. He was not interested in fighter on fighter duels; he wanted the blood of the bombers. When at last only two Me-109s stood between him and the Dorniers he resolved to punch through. 'Blue-2, take the wingman,' was the only command he gave. The 109s were poorly placed, caught on the climb in their attempt to intercept the two Hurricanes. Dix turned sharply and turned again, dived, and then pulled up behind and below the leader. Steed mirrored his manoeuvre and similarly found himself in the blind spot of the wingman. It was a perfect shooting opportunity and Steed did not let it go to waste. He poured a long burst into the Me-109 and was rewarded with the sight of bits flying off. The Messerschmitt leader was a trifle more astute and immediately dived for safety, though not without suffering a parting shot from Dix.

Steed turned his attention from his Messerschmitt, which was obviously in serious trouble, to Dix, who was now climbing once more to the harass the Dornier formation, now much more depleted and spread out by the constant attention of the British fighters. One of the Dorniers was struggling. There was smoke belching from one of the engines and the aircraft was jettisoning her bombs on the unfortunate Londoners below. The German turned away from the formation and headed for a cloudbank. Dix cut off the Dornier before it could reach safety, and raked the German in a beam attack. Steed, behind Dix, followed suit. It is amazing how much punishment these German bombers could take thought Steed. The problem was that machine-gun bullets could pass straight through the fuselage without doing too much damage. Incendiaries were better, but what the Hurricane really needed was a couple of cannons with 20mm exploding shells.

Dix and Steed turned for a second pass before the Dornier could make the closeting comfort of the clouds. As they did so a Me-109 fastened onto Steed's tail.

'Blue Leader from Blue-2, 109 on my tail.'

Steed pulled the Hurricane into a vicious turn, but as he did so the Messerschmitt blew apart behind him. A Hurricane swept past; Steed recognised it as the King's. A shriek of joy blasted over the wireless, followed by a babble of Polish. Steed turned his aircraft to once again follow his leader, but by now Dix was way below, behind his Dornier. Steed watched as Dix opened fire at long range, but the Dornier had already reached the refuge of the clouds and disappeared into their welcoming shrouds; Dix, his blood now up, irrationally plunged into the clouds in the Dornier's wake.

Steed circled waiting for his leader to emerge from the cloud, and when he didn't Steed tried to reach him over the wireless, but without success. Up above the fight had moved on. The King had also disappeared. Well then, what about the waifs and strays? Steed looked around hopefully for lone and damaged German aircraft, trying to make it back home. He still had ammunition left and a reserve of petrol. There were a few parachutes floating down, and below there was broken cloud. That cloud will not make the bomb aimers' jobs easy he thought, but it is good cover in which the wounded might try to make their escape.

He dropped down, heading southeast, the way home for the Germans. The clouds were formed in two layers, about two thousand feet apart. But the clouds at the lower layer sometimes billowed up to reach the upper layer. Steed remembered such days pre-war, when he would frolic amongst the milky cotton wool in a Tiger Moth. Without a wingman to guard his tail he needed to constantly check those picturesque but dangerous cumuli for German fighters.

Eventually, as the Channel appeared below through a gap in the clouds, and with an eye on his fuel gauge, Steed turned for home. When he landed at Colne Martin, he found most of the pilots in an elated mood. Several pilots had claimed kills, and most people had claimed to hit something. Although many had collected battle damage, everyone had made it home. The Spy was doing a brisk trade, with excited pilots vying for his attention.

Dix came over and clapped Steed on the back. 'What did you think of that little show Hawk? Did you see what happened to our targets?'

Steed glanced down at his notepad. The first two Dorniers that we both fired at I would say we damaged, but I don't think that we could claim either as a probable. We then took on a 109 each. I got in a good burst on mine and I saw bits flying off, but again I can only claim it as damaged. The third Dornier was damaged already when we had a go at it. I don't know how the thing kept flying after the amount of fire that we poured into it, but I had to break off when one of those yellow-nosed 109s got onto my tail. The King came along and blew the sod to kingdom come, damn good shooting on his part. When I looked around for you, you were chasing the Dornier into cloud down below. I circled for a bit and called you on the wireless, but you didn't answer. Everybody else had disappeared too. I then went looking for more trade on my own, but I was out of luck.'

'Yes, sorry about that Hawk. I wanted to put the bugger away, but I lost him in the cloud. Changing the subject, what did you think of that stupid Spitfire pilot on this morning's outing? I bloody nearly shot the clot down. Did you get his number?'

'Afraid not. He bolted when he saw your roundels and realised his mistake. With so many aeroplanes of all types charging around up there, I'm surprised that pilots don't take pot shots at their own side more often.

Mind you, wasn't it nice to see so many friendly aircraft around today? Makes a nice change for us not to be outnumbered.'

Steed took his leave as the Spy called him over for debriefing. He passed The King on the way and put his hand around the Pole's shoulder.

'Mr King my noble friend, there I was, flying around minding my own business and enjoying the view, when I looked behind and saw a nasty yellow-nosed bastard on my tail with evil intent. The next moment he disappeared in a pretty red flash and you charged by. I am much obliged to you dear sir. Bloody good shooting.'

'Ah Mr Hawk. I thought that was you. All part of the service my fine fellow.'

The ground crews refuelled and rearmed the aircraft and the squadron returned to readiness, but there were no more sorties that day. That night, the BBC news broadcasts were full of the exploits of the RAF, and the pilots partied.

The next day the pilots lounged at readiness, but there was no trade. At midday Steed was sitting outside the dispersal hut in a deckchair reading the Daily Express. The newspaper claimed that 175 German aircraft had been shot down the previous day. Steed looked up from the paper as Chamberlain walked over.

'Can I have a word please Hawk?' The squadron leader looked serious as he motioned for Steed to follow him out of earshot of the others. 'I am very sorry Hawk, but there is no other way to say this. Last night your parents were both killed by a German bomb. I am afraid that there is no mistake. The adjutant has checked carefully this morning with the local ARP and their bodies have been positively identified. I am so very sorry.'

Steed's world collapsed. For a moment the trees and sky seemed to spin around above his head; he felt his arm gripped tightly by Chamberlain's hand. The feeling of momentary faintness passed and he opened his mouth to speak, but no words came out. The only two people that were really close to him, whom he loved so absolutely and who loved him in return, were gone. A feeling of utter emptiness seized him. Could there be some mistake? Chamberlain was speaking again.

'Listen Hawk, the adjutant will help you to sort things out. The RAF is very good in circumstances such as these. You will have our full support and whatever help that you need. You know how things are here. If there is an invasion we will need you to come back pretty dammed quick, but in the meantime you are on compassionate leave to get things tidied up.

You must go to see the adjutant right now. He will advise you what to do next.'

By now, like most of the pilots, Steed was hardened to death. He had seen friends and colleagues perish both during training and during the battles over Dunkirk and Britain. He half expected to die himself any day, and he was convinced that he would depart this life in defence of his country should the invasion ever materialise. But the death of both of his parents, so unexpectedly and so suddenly, was different.

It had been a parachute mine. Usually, these devices had a delayed action fuse to cause maximum disruption, but this one had exploded almost immediately upon landing. It had destroyed a row of terraced houses. His parents' house was near the centre of the explosion and it had been completely flattened. His mother and father had died together in their bed. There was absolutely nothing left to salvage. Friends and neighbours had also perished in the same blast, people that Steed had known for all his life. His grandparents had died before the war; there were uncles, aunts and cousins of course, but as far as close family ties were concerned he was now alone in the world.

Affairs were tidied up and his parents laid to rest within a few days. There was nothing more to keep Steed in London; he returned to his squadron at Colne Martin in the late afternoon of 18th September. So far in this war Steed had retained some understanding, and even sympathy, for the typical German serviceman. The German in the trench, or in the aeroplane or the submarine for that matter, was simply doing what he believed to be his duty for his country. It was the Nazi politicians who were the real culprits. It was true that Steed believed in killing Germans before they had a chance to kill him, but so far he had not shared the hatred for the Germans that The King so clearly displayed. Now things were different. The German machine had killed those dearest to him; his mind had been twisted and he now wanted revenge.

There had been a daylight raid on the capital that day, and the Tomcats had been in the thick of the action. By and large they had been successful. The Tomcats had been joined by other friendly squadrons and the raid and been broken up. Several pilots had claimed victories, but two Tomcat aircraft failed to return. Later that evening the news came through. Fenton-Williams had parachuted to safety and was unhurt. The other pilot had been found dead in his crashed Hurricane. The other pilot was Johnny Walker.

That evening in the sergeants' mess the atmosphere was far from subdued; death was by now an accepted fact of life. But there was no singing around the piano because the mess's chief piano player was lying in his coffin. Steed stood at the bar deep in thought. Alongside him, Toby Adams and Gareth Evans were chatting to each other about London and girls.

Enough, said Steed quietly to himself, and he ambled over to the piano. He remembered the old piano at home, now so much firewood, and he remembered his mother's tuition and practice sessions that he so hated in the cold parlour. But those lessons had borne fruit and Steed had become an accomplished pianist. He sat down at the piano, thinking of the many times that he had entertained his parents and their friends, playing the old songs. He thought of the times that he played light classics both for and with his mother. Only a week ago he had been playing with her, just as he had when a child. He shook himself from these melancholy thoughts, opened the piano lid and began to play. His choice was Fur Elise, something that he was confident of playing from memory without the sheet music in front of him.

He immediately drew a crowd around the piano. A surprised Toby Adams exclaimed, 'You're a dark horse Harry.' Somebody else yelled, 'What's this Hawk. Can't you play anything brighter?'

'This, my good man,' countered Steed, 'is one of Ludwig Van Beethoven's finest. It's called Fur Elise. That means 'For Elise' in Jerry language for all of you uneducated buffoons.'

'Can you play roll out the barrel?'

Steed went into a medley of popular hits. The party started; the sergeants' mess had a new pianist.

There was poor weather and little activity for the next few days. Apart from a few words of condolence when he returned to duty, nobody had mentioned Steed's parents, for which he was grateful. The day the weather cleared the Tomcats were scrambled to intercept a raid over Southeast England. They were ordered to climb to 25,000 feet, much higher than they had intercepted bomber raids in the past. At this altitude the Hurricane's performance was dreadful. Even experienced pilots like Steed did not relish meeting the yellow-nosed bastards, as RAF parlance now referred to the Me-109s, at this height. Fortunately for the Tomcats they failed to intercept the raid, which was in fact a Luftwaffe fighter sweep, and they went home with the fabric still covering their gun ports.

In the last days of September, the Luftwaffe tried for the final time to win the battle in the skies over London. The Tomcats were scrambled to deal with a large formation of JU-88s hell bent on attacking London. Steed was, as usual, Dix's wingman. Another Hurricane squadron joined the Tomcats shortly before the engagement, and the squadron pair made a head-on attack with the aim of breaking up the bomber force. The usual close escort of Me-109s was in attendance, while vapour trails above indicated that the Spitfires were skirmishing with the German top cover. One thing about German attacks on London, thought Steed, our controllers have the time to vector in a sufficient number of our aircraft to make sure that we are not too outnumbered.

The close escort yellow-nosed bastards came out from the bomber stream to meet the Hurricanes, first climbing and then swooping down in a beam attack. The British squadrons were forced to meet the thrust, diverting their attention from the bombers in front and below. Steed stuck to his leader like glue as Dix turned towards the 109s. One of the German fighters engaged Dix directly; Steed observed the brief exchange of fire between the two opponents, but in following Dix he did not have a target to aim at, and so did not fire. Dix turned back towards the bomber stream as the 109s swept past. It would be a close run thing for the pair of them to reach the bombers before the Me-109s could swing around behind the Hurricanes' tails. Steed hit the emergency boost button and followed Dix in the dive.

They were going fast. At this speed there would be time for only a brief burst from their Brownings as they flashed through the bomber formation. Steed was now very close behind his leader and was concerned that he might hit Dix if they aimed at the same bomber. Steed jinked his Hurricane to one side in order to select his own target. As soon as they were through the Ju-88s, he would need to worry about the Me-109 escort sure to be on their tails. He fired a short burst at his Ju-88, but he was going too fast to see the effect of his work. He looked for Dix. His leader was going straight down. That would be suicide for Steed if the 109s were behind. Steed started to corkscrew, struggling to see if the 109s were following him down. No, his tail was clear, but they were leaving the Ju-88s well behind. Dix was still going down in a steep dive below. Then it dawned on Steed. His leader was in trouble.

'Blue Leader pull out! Pull out Mr Dix!'

Below, at last, the Hurricane seemed to be responding. It must be doing over four hundred miles per hour, thought Steed, but it's definitely starting to level out. When Steed eventually caught up with his leader they were low over the suburbs of London, too close to the barrage balloons for comfort.

'Blue Leader from Blue-2,' transmitted Steed. 'What is your situation?'

Dix's voice came in, clearly, if a little unsteady. 'My situation is a lot better than it was a minute ago Hawk. I had a real problem pulling out of that dive. Take a look at my kite. Can you spot any damage.'

'Will do leader, but can we climb a bit first? We are awfully close to those balloons.' A little later Steed reported, 'Can't see any damage Blue Leader. Do you have a problem?'

'A cannon shell came into the cockpit as we went through those 109s. It exploded by my leg. Otherwise everything seems to be okay.'

Steed considered his options. 'Blue Leader, suggest that we climb in case you need to bail out. Are you losing blood?'

'It's not too bad Hawk. Let's go home.'

Dix made a passable landing back at Colne Martin, but he needed to be lifted from the cockpit into the waiting ambulance.

The next day the Luftwaffe made their last major daylight raid on the capital using conventional bombers. The Tomcats were scrambled but failed to intercept. As autumn moved on and September gave way to October, it was clear that the Germans had changed tactics. The slower Heinkel and Dornier bombers were now used solely for night bombing. Me-110s and even some Me-109 fighters were fitted with bomb racks and carried out nuisance tip and run raids during the day. Goring sent over daylight fighter sweeps at high altitude, to which the British now felt duty bound to respond. The Tomcats in their Hurricanes were at a severe disadvantage. They did not have the speed to effectively deal with the tip and run raids, and they were very uncomfortable taking on the yellow-nose bastards, who now flew at 30,000 feet.

Those old hands like Steed, those that were left anyway, who had been through the Dunkirk battles and through what was now termed the Battle of Britain, were desperately tired. The inevitable happened in early October. The squadron was moved north for a rest and to re-equip with Spitfires. But not all of the pilots were to move with the squadron. Dix, who had been injured twice during the Battle of Britain and who was still recovering from the removal of cannon splinters from his thigh, was sent to train as a controller. Toby Adams and Steed were sent to different OTUs as instructors.

Chapter Eight – Rhubarbs and Circus

By this stage of the air war, Fighter Command had determined that experienced pilots, who had been through the recent air battles, were the best people to instruct fighter tactics to the fledgling pilots now joining the Operational Training Units. Steed was sent to OTU-34 near Penzance in Cornwall.

Steed viewed the posting with mixed feelings. He was sorry to leave the squadron, but in truth he now realised that he was jaded and in need of a break from operations. The loss of his parents had hit him hard, and he now recognised that his anger towards the Germans in the weeks following their deaths had clouded his judgement. Experienced fighter pilots knew when discretion was the better part of valour, but Steed's grief and sense of outrage had distorted his tactical awareness. If he had not been duty bound to protect his leader's tail during his last few weeks with the squadron, he now knew that he would have accepted unnecessary and unequal combat with the Me-109 fighter sweeps, most likely with disastrous consequences.

He felt very pleased with what he had achieved with the Tomcats, eleven and a half confirmed kills, the DFM presented by the King and the deep satisfaction of knowing that they had weathered the storm. With winter fast approaching, and the RAF in control of the skies over Britain, a German invasion would not be attempted until at least next spring. By then he would be back in an operational squadron.

Steed had never been to Cornwall before his posting, and he fell in love with that marvellous county and its rugged coastline, interspersed with pretty coves and glorious beaches. His conversion to a Spitfire consisted of reading the manual, familiarising himself with the layout of the cockpit for half an hour, followed by a takeoff and an hour's joyride.

He had a sense of déjà vu and his first venture in a Hurricane; was that only six months ago? Steed had a great fondness for the Hurricane. It was a solid gun platform, tough and easy to repair. It could also out-turn any front-line fighter at low level. But, in the latter stages of the Battle of Britain, Hurricane pilots had despaired of its lack of speed and poor performance at altitude in comparison with the Me-109. Height and positioning up-sun were key factors in air fighting. Up against Hurricanes, at anything above 15,000 feet, the yellow-nosed bastards held all the aces.

The Spitfire was different. It had almost the same manoeuvrability as the Hurricane at low altitude, and in this respect was superior to the Me-

109, but it could also match the German fighter for speed and overall performance at higher altitudes. The Spit handled like a dream, about its only drawback was that its cockpit was even smaller than the Hurricane's; at least it had a side door to aid entry in a scramble.

Cornwall was a long way from Colne Martin; in fact it was a long way from anywhere! By the time that he left the Tomcats, Steed's Ariel motorcycle had reached a high mileage and was requiring more and more of his time to keep it in good order. With his flight sergeant's pay and no outside responsibilities, Steed reasoned that he could afford a car. He did not relish another winter of motorcycle riding, and second-hand private cars were now much cheaper than in peacetime, most by now off the road due to lack of petrol. Steed sold the Ariel at a knock down price to his fitter when he left the Tomcats.

The car he chose as a replacement, a few weeks after arriving in Cornwall, was a red MG-TA two-seater sports car. He spotted the car for sale in the local paper, and fell in love with it at first sight. It had rock-hard suspension and suspect all-weather protection, but these deficiencies were of little concern to a hardened motorcyclist. It offered open-top motoring, a stylish design and it was simple to maintain, yet it would reach nearly eighty miles per hour given a long straight road.

Steed's sojourn at OTU-34 lasted almost seven months. He was a good instructor, and he was given the time to properly train his students such that they would not be as ill-prepared for action as so many of the Tomcat fledgling's in the Battle of Britain. Tactical thinking had changed as a result of the lessons learnt during the recent battles, and this was reflected in the final polish given to students by OTU instructors like Steed. The Fighting Area Attacks had been abandoned, as had the vulnerable vic of three fighters. RAF practice now copied that of the Germans, with a basic fighter element of two aircraft, leader and wingman, and sections of four aircraft in a 'finger four' formation, very similar to that devised by Chamberlain and his flight lieutenants.

By mid-April 1941, Steed reasoned that he would soon be due for a return to operational flying. His first thought was to approach Chamberlain, with a view towards returning to 126-Squadron before somebody else determined his posting, but to his dismay he discovered that his former squadron leader had been killed in a flying accident a month earlier. In any case, the Tomcats would have changed from his day; it was probably better to make a fresh start. He considered other options. He could try for an overseas squadron, perhaps the Western Desert or Malta. Possibly he should try for night fighters, as suggested by the Spy. In the end he decided to stick to what he knew best. Dix, his stint as a controller finished, now commanded a Spitfire squadron in Southeast England. Steed decided to ask his old flight commander for a job.

Dix was very helpful and pulled strings. Consequently, in mid May 1941, Steed reported to 294-Squadron based at RAF Stourden in Kent. The airfield had been constructed on the edge of Romney Marsh during the winter with the aim of providing an additional fighter station close to the English Channel, thereby permitting Spitfire operations deeper into Northern France. The airfield had only been operational for a couple of months and 294-Squadron was its only resident.

Steed was shown into Dix's office. He came to attention and saluted; Dix was old-school RAF and it didn't pay to be over-familiar, despite their history.

'Flight Sergeant Steed reporting for duty sir.' The squadron leader rose from his chair to shake Steed's hand.

'Hawk, good to see you, and glad to have you aboard. Pull up a chair.'

They exchanged a few pleasantries about their days with the Tomcats, and both expressed their sadness at the loss of Squadron Leader Chamberlain. But the deaths of friends and colleagues were now commonplace and their conversation moved on.

'You remember Smithy from the old days of course,' said Dix. 'He left 126-Squadron about the same time that you did and went off as an instructor to a flying training school up north somewhere. Anyway, he joined us a few weeks ago, so you will see at least one familiar face, apart from mine.'

Dix briefed Steed on their current situation. '294 is a new squadron, but we have a nucleus of experienced pilots, and I count you among them of course. We had our shakedown in Yorkshire, and we moved in here at the beginning of March. We became operational a couple of weeks later. Since then we have undertaken a number of sorties, which mainly fall into three areas. Firstly, we intercept the occasional daylight raider; these are usually reconnaissance or tip and run fighter-bombers. Secondly, we sometimes nip across the Channel at low level, usually with just two Spitfires, and look for targets of opportunity. These can be military, for example a train, German transport and so on, or even electricity pylons. But our main business is the Circus. We rendezvous with five or six other Spitfire squadrons and escort a handful of Blenheims on a bombing mission over France. The idea is to persuade the Huns to come up and fight. Sometimes they do, and sometimes they don't. I'm going to put you in A-Flight. Your flight commander will be Al Meredith. Al's a rugby playing New Zealander and a bloody good pilot. He missed out on Dunkirk, but he was flying a Spitfire in the thick of the Battle of Britain action. I'd better not tread on any toes, so I'll let Al brief you on the set-up here.'

Dix smiled, 'This reminds me of the first time we met, in Squadron Leader Tomlinson's office. I seem to remember that afterwards I took you up for a spot of formation flying and a bit of a dogfight.'

'That was just about a year ago, it seems an awful lot more.'

'We've both aged a bit since then,' reflected Dix. 'Come along, I'll introduce you to your flight commander.'

Steed immediately liked the genial New Zealander. The Kiwi's laid back, no-nonsense attitude reminded Steed very much of the Australian Roger Daily. Meredith briefed Steed on the Circus operations.

'Basically a Circus consists of a large number of RAF fighters escorting a few light bombers to targets in Northern France. The bombers are there to provoke the Luftwaffe into a fight. There are several objectives to Circus operations. One is to show the French people under the German cosh that the RAF can fly at will over France, and that the Luftwaffe can do precious little about it. The French see that we are still in the fight against the Germans so there is still hope that France will be free someday. Another objective is to carry the daylight air war to the Germans, over their territory. It is a bit like the Battle of Britain in reverse. By going over with large numbers of fighters we hope to be able to shoot down more of them than they can shoot down of us. We establish our air superiority over their territory, however briefly.'

'Where's the deepest that you have been into France sir? I guess that the Spitfire's limited range presents a problem, especially of you get involved in a fight.'

'A very good question Hawk. We now have the same problem that the 109s had during the Battle of Britain; we spend a lot of time gawking at our petrol gauges. The deepest that we have been into France so far is Lille, but we have only been there once. Lille is about seventy miles inland from Le Touquet and it is just about the limit of our range with the Spit Mark II. But we should be getting the Spitfire Mark Vb any day now. This has a supercharger and a lot more power, which will be very welcome for fisticuffs with the 109s, but it also has the advantage that we can fit a 30-gallon drop-tank, so we should get much greater range. The Spitfire Vb also gives us more punch, two 20mm cannons and four Brownings, There are also sixty more rounds per machine-gun compared with the Mark II.'

The New Zealander stood up. 'First things first. I'll get you settled in, and give you loads of bumph to read. Later on, I will introduce you to the flight sergeant in charge of the ground crews; he has an aeroplane ready for you. When it is set up, probably tomorrow, take it for a spin and get to know the local surroundings. Watch out for the South Downs if it is cloudy! The day after tomorrow, assuming that the weather is suitable, you and I will go for a sightseeing trip across the Channel. We call these operations Rhubarbs, low level search and destroy stuff. Great fun!'

The set-up at Stourden was similar in many respects to that at Colne Martin, although here the officers' mess was on the airfield. Steed was pleased to see that the sergeants' mess was cosy and well-appointed. His experience of the RAF so far suggested that the sergeants always lived well and their mess committees were always on the ball. There were four sergeant pilots currently with the squadron; all were RAFVR and had joined the squadron during the winter directly from OTUs. Dix introduced Steed to the other pilots as 'Hawk', and that is what he was called by everybody except Smithy, who called him Harry. Thankfully, as far as Steed was concerned, Dix did not mention the nickname's connotation with Hawkeye and Steed's ability to spot the enemy before most of the other pilots in his old squadron.

Flight Lieutenant Meredith briefed Steed on the planned 'Rhubarb' sortie over France. 'You're an experienced pilot Hawk, and Hugh Dix has told me of the sterling job that you did over Dunkirk and during the Battle of Britain. He has also told me that you were the best number two that he has ever had, so I won't try to teach my grandmother to suck eggs. If you have any questions, I'm sure that you will ask, okay?'

'Okay sir.'

'Good, let's start off on the right foot. I'm a wild colonial and less stuck up than some of the RAF types that I've met. We both shoot down Germans for a living, and we both take the same risks. When we are at formal gatherings, or in front of the great and mighty, I am your flight commander and we are obliged to follow the rules and etiquette. You call me sir or whatever and I call you flight sergeant. But when we are off duty, or together like this, my name's Al; that okay with you?'

'Sure thing Al.'

'Good. You know the drill as a number two; keep an eye open behind and in the sun, and watch my tail. I will worry about finding the targets.' They looked at the map. 'We only go out on 'Rhubarbs' when it is cloudy, like today. That way we can always escape from a superior force of enemy fighters. My plan is to head out over the Channel at low-level. When we get near to the enemy coast we increase speed and go over the coastal defences low and fast. There are certain places on the enemy coast where the flak defences are particularly strong, you saw the notes that I gave you the other day?'

'Yes, the ports are heavily defended, Calais and Boulogne in particular.'

'That's right. We avoid those areas like the plague. I aim to cross here.' Meredith indicated a point on the map. 'The other choice we have is to climb above the cloud before we cross the enemy coast and let down after we are past the coastal belt AA defences. Personally I don't like that option. You can't trust the altimeter and you are never sure of the terrain below. If you get down to 500 feet on the altimeter, and if you are still in cloud, then you have to call the whole thing off. So we go in fast and low where we think that the flak is weakest.' Meredith again pointed to an area on the map. 'We will go inland, throttle back, and then beetle around this sector at low-level looking for targets of opportunity.'

'What sort of targets are we looking for?' Steed interjected.

'Anything interesting that crops up, ideally German troops and transport. Trains are fair game, so we will follow this railway line for a bit. We may also try this canal. Barges and even lock gates are targets, as are gasometers and electricity pylons if we can't find anything else.'

'How about airfields?'

'Hun airfields are very well defended with stacks of light flak. We do sometimes go for them, but such operations need to be carefully co-ordinated. It is too much for the two of us to take on today. There are several Hun fighter airfields here in the Abbeville area,' Meredith indicated the position on the map, 'a bit further down the coast from where I intend to cross, but we will steer clear of those.'

The two Spitfires flew out over the Channel, below the cloud. The Channel looked grey and cold, despite the approaching summer. Sea horses capped the waves, and dismal clouds hung overhead; the sun was noticeable by its absence. The Channel was devoid of shipping, and the Spitfires were alone. They crossed the French coast south of Boulogne at top speed and headed inland, staying low; their incursion into enemy territory went unchallenged.

Rural France flashed by below. It looked peaceful and settled; a village, a church, and the crops in the fields. Meredith throttled back. A farmer appeared with a horse drawn wagon. The horse reared as the two Spitfires roared overhead. Was he pleased to see the RAF fighters? Meredith followed a road, but there were no German troop convoys, no marching soldiers and no enemy tanks. A woman on a bicycle pulled to the side of the road and stopped as they approached. She looked up. Meredith banked to display the RAF roundels on his Spitfire's wings, and Steed followed suit. As the two fighters swung back to follow the road, Steed could see the woman waving.

A railway line appeared ahead, and Meredith left the road to follow the tracks. After a few miles, Meredith spotted some covered railway rolling stock parked in a siding amongst some trees. He banked his Spitfire and came around in a wide circle, now heading for the wagons.

'Red-2, target the railway trucks ahead.'

Steed dropped back in order to have a clear shot as they came in. As Meredith opened fire, accurate flak came up from the trees towards the flight lieutenant. Steed could not see the German gun firing at Meredith, but he could see the approximate position that the tracer was coming from. Steed just had time to change his aiming point, and he sent a stream of machine-gun bullets into the trees behind the wagons. He followed Meredith as his leader rejoined the main railway line.

'Bastards!' said Meredith with feeling. 'Are you okay Red-2?'

'Fine Leader. I gave the Hun a burst as we went by.'

Their persistence in following the railway line was rewarded when a small railway locomotive hauling three passenger coaches came into view, travelling in the same direction as the fighters.

'Give the train a chance to stop,' Meredith transmitted as he banked his Spitfire, clearly displaying the roundels to the locomotive crew. Steed followed his leader in a wide circle. The locomotive driver applied his brakes; he knew what was coming.

'Red-2 from Leader, the target is the engine.'

Steed throttled back to give himself an unobstructed clear shot at the locomotive. The carriages were probably full of French people; he didn't want to hit those. The train had now stopped and Steed could see the driver and fireman leaping out of the engine and making a run for it. Meredith opened fire at the engine, and then it was Steed's turn. He was by now travelling quite slowly and he put in an accurate three second burst;

thankfully the French crew was now clear. The effect was dramatic. Steam blew out of the locomotive's ruptured tank, and then the little engine exploded. Steed was surprised that machine-gun bullets, even amour piecing machine-gun bullets, could have that effect.

The two Spitfires circled. People poured out of the carriages. The carriage immediately behind the engine had been pushed off the rails by the blast. People were sitting on the ground, some looked hurt. Here and there Steed saw the field grey uniforms of German soldiers, but the British fighters were unable to shoot at the Germans through fear of hitting the much more numerous French civilians.

Meredith left the railway and followed another road. They still had plenty of ammunition left. All the time, Steed undertook the task of a number-two and searched the cloudy skies above for German aircraft, but there were none. There was little traffic on the road either, so eventually, and with their eyes on their petrol gauges, the two Spitfires used a line of electricity pylons for target practice. Steed enjoyed this game enormously. A short burst at the insulators at 250 yards range, and down came the electricity high tension cables in a shower of sparks.

Meredith climbed above the clouds before heading back over the coast towards home. The Germans sent up a few dirty black puffs of anti-aircraft fire as a leaving present, and then they were out over the Channel. Meredith was careful to cross the English coast at well over 2,000 feet and at a designated point; not to do so would risk unwelcome attention from the AA gunners.

Back home, Meredith's Spitfire sported a hole from a 20mm cannon shell. The intelligence officer at Stourden, also known as the Spy in common with RAF parlance, was especially interested in the railway wagons. He debriefed Meredith first, and then Steed. He asked Steed, 'Do you think that the flak gun was positioned to defend the rolling stock in the siding?'

'I would say so sir. I could clearly see tracer coming from a position in the trees beyond the railway wagons. That would be the best place to have a clear, zero-deflection shot at any aircraft coming along the railway track towards them.'

'And what about the effect of Flight Lieutenant Meredith's machine-gun fire on the rolling stock? Did you see any fires or explosions?' continued the Spy.

'No, but I didn't get the chance to have a good look. I changed my target as soon as I saw the German AA position.'

'Why did you do that, change target I mean?'

'The orders were targets of opportunity. I reasoned a German AA crew to be a juicier target than a couple of possibly empty railway wagons in a siding.'

'Quite right,' said the Spy. 'Do you think that you hit the gun?'

'I don't know, but I am pretty sure that I hit the position where the flak tracer was coming from, and the gun didn't fire at me, at least if it did I didn't see it.'

'Do you think that the rolling stock might have been put there as a decoy, to trap any of our planes on a 'Rhubarb' mission?'

Steed considered the question for a moment, 'I think that it is possible. As I said, the AA was perfectly positioned. The wagons were sited just off the main railway line, easily visible to anyone flying along the line looking for a target. They were covered, so they may have been empty. It's possible that they were decoys and the Germans may have been sitting there waiting for us.'

Two days later the weather had cleared and a Circus operation was ordered. 294-Squadron was to be a part of the close escort wing surrounding nine Blenheim light bombers. The target was Lille. Meredith, at Red-1, would lead the squadron because Dix would not be flying that day. Steed was down to fly Red-4 as Smithy's wingman.

The pilots sat in the briefing room in front of a large map of Northern France. Red tape streamers were pinned to the map illustrating the route to the target. The names and positions of those selected for the mission were chalked on the blackboard alongside; Steed noted his confirmation to fly Red-4 and the squadron's usual call sign 'Sampson'. Lille, the pilots were told, was a strategic communications centre with important factories supporting the German war effort. So, thought Steed, the French factories and the unlucky French workers were to be bombed because they were forced to make guns and steel helmets for the Germans. War was a dirty business when you had to bomb, and probably kill, your recent ally.

294-Squadron formed up over Beachy Head with the two other Spitfire squadrons that made up the close-escort wing. They were joined by their nine Blenheim charges. The only job of the close-escort wing was to defend the bombers. Another three squadrons of Spitfires, making up the escort-cover, took station around and a little higher than the close-escort wing. In the event of a fight with enemy fighters, 294-Squadron, as close-escort, would be tied to the apron strings of the bombers, while the escort-cover would have more freedom to engage and pursue the enemy. This closely packed group of over eighty aeroplanes was termed a beehive. Steed could see why! But that was not all. Up above, the high-cover and top-cover wings were stacked to protect the beehive from being bounced by the German fighters. Furthermore, yet more Spitfires would meet the Beehive as it turned for home and cover the withdrawal.

The Beehive set out over the Channel. Steed and his companions had to weave gently from side to side to keep station with the bombers and their full bomb load. As the formation passed over the costal defences, accurate flak came up from the formidable 88mm guns hidden in the dunes below. Steed was surprised to see all three squadron leaders in the close escort wing lead their squadrons in a gentle climb away from the dangerous black puffs, dropping back down to their stations as the shell bursts fell behind. During this time the bombers pressed resolutely on, holding their height, course and speed.

Steed looked for enemy fighters, but found this a much more difficult job than in the days of Dunkirk or the Battle of Britain. The sky was full of friendly aeroplanes, over eighty in the Beehive, plus another seventy odd Spitfires well above the Beehive in the high-cover and top-cover wings.

The Me-109s appeared in a co-ordinated attack. There were warnings shouted from the Spitfire squadrons above that yellow-nosed bastards were coming down at the Beehive. Steed looked up to see four Me-109s in a high-speed dive from six-o'clock high, followed by a disorganised gang of Spitfires. At the same time, the escort-cover Spitfire squadrons turned to deal with other German fighter attacks from the flanks.

Steed followed Smithy around in a tight banking turn as the Me-109s came hurtling down from above and behind. For a moment chaos reigned. The four Me-109s went diving through the Beehive with all guns blazing, followed by the pack of chasing Spitfires from the cover squadrons above. Steed did not have a chance to fire his guns, he was far too busy trying to avoid collisions with the Spitfires wheeling and diving around him. The escort-cover squadrons turned away the Me-109 attacks from the flanks and the Beehive settled down again. Steed followed Smithy as they once again took up their position in the squadron.

Steed looked around. The previous order of the Beehive had been disturbed, and several aircraft of the escort-cover squadrons in particular had yet to resume their station. The bombers, on the other hand, were still in perfect formation and droned serenely on. Below, several Spitfires were climbing to rejoin their squadrons after chasing the enemy away.

As far as he could tell, nobody had been damaged in the attack. The three close-escort squadrons had stayed together after the break and were all now back in position. Level with the Sampsons and over to the left, a group of four Spitfires, presumably from one of the escort-cover squadrons, was gently making its way through the close-escort wing. Something about the Spitfires made Steed take a closer look. Jesus H. Christ!

'Sampson leader from Red-4, four Me-109s at nine o'clock, inside the Beehive!'

After a moment's hesitation, Meredith responded, 'Sampson Squadron Tallyho.'

Meredith let his men into a banking turn and a direct beam attack on the intruders. But the four Me-109s were alert, and all immediately went into a steep dive. Steed followed Smithy in a roll to starboard and a dive as his leader tried to close the nearest Messerschmitt. Smithy let off a burst of machine-gun fire at long range, almost in frustration, but he had little chance of hitting the German. Smithy broke of the attack and, followed dutifully by Steed, climbed to once again to assume his place in the Beehive.

The Sampsons regrouped and continued on their way. Meredith's voice crackled over the airwaves. 'Red-4 from Sampson Leader; well spotted Hawk.'

Ahead, Lille appeared through patchy cloud. The German 88 anti-aircraft guns welcomed the Beehive, and once again the close-escort squadrons surreptitiously turned to one side and climbed a thousand feet above their charges as the Blenheims commenced their bombing run. It probably made sense for the flimsy fighters to climb away out of harm's way when the flak came up; the bombers had no choice other than to stay at their bombing height. Even so, Steed wondered what the bombers' crews thought about it.

Bombs dropped, the Beehive wheeled around and headed for home. But all was not well with one of the Blenheims; it was falling back behind its friends. When it was clear that the wounded bomber could not keep station, the wing commander ordered the Sampsons to escort the damaged bomber until relieved by the withdrawal cover, whose job it was to look after the waifs and strays.

The Blenheim fell behind the Beehive, and the twelve Spitfires took station above and behind it. The bomber started to lose height and then Steed spotted the telltale signs of smoke, then fire, on the port engine. The pilot stopped the motor and feathered the propeller, but the fire spread. The bomber was by now losing height fast and was clearly doomed. The crew bailed out, first one, then two parachutes. The pilot had held it together for his crew to bail out, but now the nose of the bomber dropped and it started to curve around in a shallow dive. The Spitfires circled overhead watching for the third parachute. Eventually they were rewarded; the pilot had made it. The stricken aircraft, now with the whole port wing alight, continued its twisting plunge earthwards. 294-squadron increased speed to rejoin the Beehive.

After they landed, Meredith trotted across to meet Smithy and Steed, 'Hi there Hawk, what did you think of your first Circus?'

'Very interesting; like the Battle of Britain in reverse. There were so many of us that I think that we got in each other's way. I don't know how we avoided a collision when those 109s came down. There were only four of them, as far as I could see, but they certainly caused enough confusion.'

'Yes, Jerry has some very skilful pilots,' admitted Meredith. 'And some cheeky bastards as well! I've never heard of that trick before, infiltrating the Beehive I mean. The Spy will be interested in that one. Well spotted Hawk.'

'One thing that I was wondering about,' commented Steed, 'last year the Luftwaffe easily outnumbered us, and that was over our own turf. This year we seem to outnumber them. We go over there with hundreds of fighters, and Jerry only puts up a couple of dozen against us. Why? He has all of the advantages of fighting over his own territory. Why doesn't he want a big shootout with us?'

'Good question,' said Meredith. 'I asked the Spy the same thing and he doesn't have a clue either.'

'Maybe Jerry has sent all his fighters over to Greece and the Desert,' suggested Smithy, 'and he doesn't have many left to put up against us.'

'You could be right,' agreed Meredith. 'Or perhaps Adolf spends his money on tanks rather than aeroplanes these days, but I'm certainly not complaining about it.'

Springtime turned into early summer, and Steed settled into his new squadron. He regularly played the piano in the sergeants' mess and, as in the past, kept fit with cross-country running whenever he wasn't flying. The barriers between officer and sergeant pilots, although still there, were now steadily being broken down as more 'hostilities only' pilots joined the squadrons. There was now much more social interaction between the two groups than during Steed's early days with the Tomcats, and the 294-Squadron pilots now made regular forays to the London nightspots.

The dour, lifeless, government-induced attitude to entertainment of the phoney war, with closed cinemas and theatres, and only organ music and news broadcasts on the BBC, had given way to a vibrant 'live now and the devil with tomorrow' attitude. Nowhere was this more prevalent than in the capital's cosmopolitan nightspots, in spite of, or perhaps because of, the London Blitz.

Steed also reprised his flexible relationship with Sophie Richards. It had been difficult to see her during his posing to far away Cornwall but now that he was back within an evening's drive of her home the liaison was rekindled. She had many other social contacts of course, including no doubt other men friends. But the flexible, no questions asked, no responsibilities owing, nature of their relationship suited them both admirably. She was usually available as his glamorous escort for a dinner-dance date at some fashionable West End nightclub, and for her part she yearned for the youthful sex that he inevitably provided at the end of the evening.

Steed also made good use of his MG-TA sports car for dates with local WAAF girlfriends. However, he felt no desire for a deeper relationship with any of them and therefore always played the gentleman in the carnal aspects of these encounters.

As for the day job, he flew on Circus operations usually as Smithy's wingman. He preferred to be outside the Beehive, the supporting squadrons had more freedom. He couldn't help thinking back to his meeting with Oberleutnant Brauer, the Messerschmitt pilot that he had shot down back in the dark days of the Battle of Britain. He now had some sympathy for Brauer's views on close-escort duties.

Unlike most pilots in the squadron, Steed preferred the freedom of 'Rhubarbs'. He thought these offered more scope for a pilot's initiative, although one had to be careful with German decoys and flak traps of course. The German anti-aircraft defences were very effective. Steed's favoured option was to cross the enemy coast at high altitude and let down below the clouds once past the coastal AA batteries, rather than Meredith's preferred fast and low approach. He sometimes flew 'Rhubarbs' as Smithy's wingman, but one of the sergeant pilots, Ben Clayton, also liked to fly 'Rhubarbs' with Steed, in which case Steed, as the senior rank and the more experienced pilot, was permitted the luxury of leading the pair.

During Dunkirk and the Battle of Britain, Steed's victories had come thick and fast. German bombers did not have the speed to escape and the German fighters were keen to stay and fight. But these days, especially as a wingman to Smithy, there were simply not the same opportunities to nail a German aeroplane. The best that he could manage up until the end of June with his new squadron was a single 'damaged' 109.

Towards the end of June came the news that Germany had invaded Russia. 'Hitler's gone too far now,' exclaimed a delighted Steed to Smithy as they sat outside a country pub near Hastings. 'Russia's a huge country with a large army and millions of men. There is no way that the Germans can fight on two fronts and expect to win.'

'I'm not so sure about that,' said Smithy circumspectly. 'The Russians did very badly against Finland. Stalin got his way in the end of course, but the Finns showed that the Russian army isn't up to much, despite its size.'

'You have a point there,' conceded Steed. 'But it's a classic military mistake to open a war on two fronts. Britain must be safe from invasion now.'

Smithy was again doubtful. 'Look at history Harry. The Germans waged a war on two fronts during the Great War and they defeated the Russians then didn't they? It's the Americans that we need in this war, not the Russians. I think that Stalin is as bad as Hitler. Look what he did to Poland. Remember what The King thought about Stalin?'

Steed did indeed remember what the Polish Hurricane pilot thought about Stalin. The King hated Stalin almost as much as he hated Hitler. But Steed continued with his side of the argument.

'The Yanks will stay out of the war. American mothers know that to come in will see many of their sons die. Europe is a long way away for them. Quite a few Yanks, like Lindbergh, have German sympathies anyway, and Irish Americans like Joe Kennedy have no particular love for England. But what you have to remember is that Hitler has to garrison his troops in every country that he overruns; Norway, Denmark, France, Holland, Belgium, Greece, the Balkans, now Russia. In none of these countries are the natives friendly towards Germany. Imagine the number of troops that Hitler will need in Russia alone to protect his supply lines. The

Russians can retreat well beyond Moscow if needs be, and the Germans will have to deal with the Russian winter. Look what happened to Napoleon.'

'But you have to remember Harry that with every country he overruns, Hitler gains industrial muscle. That's why we are forced to bomb French factories. I agree with you that it is a damn good show that we are no longer fighting that man alone, but I just don't see that the Russians are as good as you think that they are.'

'Anyway,' concluded Steed, 'we now know why we are not facing the entire might of the Luftwaffe when we fly across the Channel. The Huns are taking their holidays in Mother Russia this year. Now then young Mr Smith, your glass is empty and it is my round. Another pint?'

The Spitfire Vb fighters started to arrive at the beginning of July. They had better performance and better armament than the Spitfire IIs that the squadron was relinquishing. Steed especially liked the punch of the twin 20mm cannons. The old problem of petrol starvation under zero gravity manoeuvres had been resolved and the new aircraft could be fitted with a flush-fitting 30-gallon drop tank, called a slipper tank, to increase range. All the Sampson pilots considered the Spitfire Vb to be superior to its main opponent, the Me-109F.

Steed's twelfth victory was a long time coming, but when it did it was one of the easiest. For his first operational sortie with a Spitfire Vb, Steed led Sergeant Ben Clayton on a 'Rhubarb'. Once across the French coast, Steed let down through the cloud and began to look for worthwhile targets. He followed a road, but could only find French civilian traffic. His attention was drawn upwards. There, in front and above, just below the cloud, was a Messerschmitt-109. The enemy fighter was alone, cruising peacefully in the same general direction as the two Spitfires, seemingly without a care in the world. Not wishing to alert the German controller by calling Clayton on the radio, Steed waggled his wings to attract his wingman's attention. As Clayton drew alongside, Steed pointed upwards. Clayton nodded and fell back behind his leader as Steed stealthily stalked the unwary German, surely a novice, probably doing a spot of instrument testing.

Steed came up behind and slightly lower than the German fighter, in the blind spot. Steed was now convinced that the German pilot was a beginner. He was flying straight and level and not bothering to weave to cover his tail. Was this a trap? No there was nothing else around. The kill was easy. A small allowance for deflection, then a three second burst of cannon and machine-gun fire at point blank range. Bits flew from the

German fighter, then it exploded; Steed had to fly through the blast. The pilot had no chance. Pieces of Me-109 mixed with pieces of Hun pilot went spinning earthwards. Steed was mightily impressed with the results of 20mm cannon fire from his new Spitfire. 'That's for you Mum and Dad,' he whispered to himself.

The RAF was busy during that summer of 1941. The British Government and RAF high command were keen to tie down as many Luftwaffe aircraft as possible over Northern France, in the valid assumption that by doing so pressure might be relieved on other fronts. In particular the Luftwaffe was strongly supporting the German army's deep penetration into the Soviet Union using Blitzkrieg tactics; the Russians needed all the help that they could get. The RAF flew Circus operations whenever the weather permitted.

One evening, the pilots attended a briefing on escape and evasion techniques. The lecturer stated that it was an officer's duty to evade capture if shot down over enemy territory and, if captured, it was his duty to try to escape. This tied down German manpower in searching for the escapee and so helped the war effort. Steed rather wondered if the man was really suggesting that this dictum applied only to officers and that flight sergeants need not bother! That aside, Steed thought that the lecture was quite useful and raised some interesting points.

The next day, he asked Dix for some French currency. In due course he was invited to sign for two packs of French francs in sealed waterproof envelopes. 'There you are Hawk,' said Dix, 'but please don't go overboard on escape preparations like Tiny and Jimmy.' Steed knew what his squadron leader was talking about. The two officer pilots in question were fastidious about their escape preparations, and could be seen fussing over their small escape kits before every Circus operation. Dix continued, 'You know, once you get into a mind set about what to do if you get shot down, you start to think about being shot down. You become the hunted and not the hunter.'

'Don't worry,' Steed replied. 'I'm not about to become an old woman just yet! But what the man said made sense to me. I don't think any Hun, not in a one-on-one fight anyway, is going to shoot me down, but it only takes a bit of flak on a Rhubarb....' He left the sentence unfinished. 'If I do go down in France, I fully intend to come back home again and not rot in some PoW camp.'

Over the next few days, Steed made himself a small evasion kit, which he put into a bag that he carried tied surreptitiously inside his flying jacket. He also took to flying in his walking boots and socks, rather than his flying boots. His feet were colder at 20,000 feet, but if he did come down in France, at least he would be able to cover distance on foot without getting blisters.

The entire squadron was now equipped with Spitfire Mk Vbs, with the option of slipper drop tanks, and they could therefore penetrate much deeper into France than before. In mid August they were part of a Spitfire wing that was providing forward-support to a Beehive targeting an industrial area near Lens in Northern France. The forward-support wing was positioned between Lens and the German fighter airfields around Abbeville, with 294-Squadron at 20,000 feet and the other two squadrons of the wing providing top-cover at 30,000 feet.

Dix spotted the German fighters first, eight of them climbing out of the haze and broken cloud that hung over Amiens. The wing leader ordered 294-Squadron down to accept combat, leaving the other two Spitfire squadrons for the moment as top cover. The fighters were German; that much was certain from the black crosses on their wings and fuselages. But they were not Me-109s. These Huns had radial engines. They were the new Focke-Wulf-190s, and 294-Squadron was soon in trouble!

Steed followed Smithy down towards the German fighters, who broke to meet the attack. In the dogfight that followed, Smithy tried to get onto the tail of one of the FW-190s, but the German zoomed into a step climb, easily outpacing the two chasing Spitfires. Another Fw-190 slipped in behind Steed, who was forced to break away from covering Smithy's tail.

'Red-3 from Red-4, Steed gasped as the g-force caused him to grey out, 'Bandit on my tail.' With this manoeuvre Steed expected to turn inside his opponent, which would have been the result with a Me-109. But he was shocked to see the German radial engine fighter still behind, almost in a firing position. Steed was sweating. This bastard is bloody good. He can turn inside me and he can out climb me. Can he out dive me?

Steed pointed his Spitfire at the cloud layer below and corkscrewed down; it was all that he could think of. Tracer came floating past his canopy, he felt hits on the airframe and then he was in that comforting, all-enveloping clammy vapour. He pulled the Spitfire into a tight 360-degree turn and then continued the dive. He emerged from the underside of the cloud to find his aggressor fortuitously immediately in front. Steed didn't miss the opportunity and opened fire. His opponent flipped around and started to dive to safety, but he was too late. Steed's cannon fire had been decisive. The German fighter was smoking and, as the German rolled, Steed saw red flame from the underside of the fuselage.

The pilot realised that the game was up; the FW-190 rolled onto its back and a shape fell out of the cockpit. The parachute opened several thousand feet below.

Steed circled assessing the damage to his aircraft. Everything still worked, although he knew that the Spitfire had taken hits. He glanced down at the parachute drifting below. That pilot would land, probably uninjured, and tomorrow would be up in another aeroplane. Steed had been lucky to survive; this Hun was undoubtedly an expert. If Steed allowed him to live, the German would almost certainly kill RAF pilots.

Steed remembered one of Dix's lectures to his pilots, forbidding them to shoot any German that had taken to his parachute on pain of courts martial. Dix had said that the Huns had, by and large, played fair during the Battle of Britain and refrained from machine-gunning RAF pilots in their parachutes. But Steed didn't buy into the hogwash that it was the aeroplane that one was trying to shoot down, not the pilot. We bomb soldiers and we shell soldiers for only one reason. We do it to kill them, to stop them from waging war on us, and to stop them from killing our own people in the future. Why should it be different for that Hun down there in his parachute? There was nobody around; Dix would never get to hear about it. It would be very easy to drop down a few thousand feet and nail this character, thereby almost certainly saving the lives of other RAF pilots. The Huns had killed his parents for God's sake, why worry about killing one of them in a parachute?

Steed shrugged his shoulders. He should be getting back to the war. His squadron was fighting for their lives somewhere up there above the clouds. His duty was to get back up there to help them. It would take time to drop down to shoot that Hun, and still more time to climb up again to the fight above. That's what he told himself as he climbed through the cloud. But topside, everyone had disappeared. He tried transmitting, but the airwaves were dead, not even static. The Hun must have taken out the radio.

It was dangerous piloting a lone Spitfire so deep into enemy territory, with the Abbeville fighter airfields so close. But Steed wasn't unduly worried. He was confident in his own ability to spot danger coming, and there was plenty of cloud cover around to dive into if too many of the bad guys came along. He might even get a pot-shot at an unwary Hun on his way home.

But then it happened. White smoke entered the cockpit. That meant a glycol coolant leak. Yes, he could smell the glycol now! A coolant line must have been ruptured during the fight, and now it had given up, or maybe it was the radiator? The temperature gauge moved into the red. Fuck! It was terminal. He was forced to cut the engine before it had a chance to catch fire. He was gliding now at what, eighteen thousand feet. Steed had only minutes left. What should he do, take to his parachute or try a wheels-up landing in a French field? His duty was to make sure that his aircraft did not fall into enemy hands. Allowing it to crash with a half-full petrol tank was the best way to do that. So the parachute it was then!

West of Amiens there was unbroken cloud. That would hide a parachute from prying eyes on the ground. It was rural country over in that direction too. Steed gently turned the Spitfire, flying just above the stall, trying to extend the glide. Below, through a gap in the clouds, he saw the Somme. It was the first time he had been this deep into France. So that was where so many soldiers had lost their lives, and these were the skies that the Great War aces patrolled.

All the while, Steed looked around for enemy fighters, but surprisingly he remained alone. Steed reached the point where he thought it best to bail out. He undid the straps and pulled back the hood. He had everything that he needed to take with him; it was time to get out. He turned the Spitfire west into the low sun. She was nicely trimmed in the glide. With luck the aircraft would keep going for a good few miles yet before crashing. That might put the Germans off his track, assuming that they didn't spot his parachute. The best way out of the Spitfire would have been to turn it upside down and simply drop out, but that would defeat the object of getting the thing to crash as far away from his parachute landing as possible. He heaved himself out of the cockpit and was caught momentarily in the slipstream, and then he was falling mercifully clear of the tailplane.

Chapter Nine - On the Run

Steed pulled the ripcord. There was a jolt; the world resumed its natural orientation and he was floating peacefully into the cloud. Remember to relax, bend the knees and roll when you hit the ground. And don't sprain your ankle! These were the thoughts that flashed through his head. The cloud was thicker than he had imagined, so that when he emerged he was not too far above the ground. Below all seemed quiet, meadowland, crop fields, but no people and no livestock. Best of all, no Germans with rifles! In the distance he could see a few buildings, a farm or a small hamlet perhaps. Immediately below was a grass field, which was where he was going to land. Maybe 600 yards to his right, on the other side of a hedge, was a fairly large wood.

He hit the ground, bent his knees and rolled. The gentle breeze took the parachute, but it did not pull him along and it was easy for him to gather it together. Not a bad landing, much better than the first time in Kent. Steed knelt on the ground with his parachute in his arms and warily looked around. Good, no one in sight, got everything? Well then, off we go. He set off at a trot for the hedge.

The hedge, he discovered, concealed a ditch that gave good cover. He knelt, assessing the best route to the distant wood. All seemed clear, nobody about. He sprinted over the grassland and plunged into the trees. He crawled back to the edge of the wood and, hidden by the undergrowth, surveyed the landscape. Everything was quiet. There were no German soldiers in hot pursuit. Steed moved stealthily into the wood's depths. He made up his mind to stay there until dark, still some hours away. He carefully, and very thoroughly, hid his parachute and flying helmet. He then thought about his next move.

The best thing to do, he reasoned, was to move south, travelling only at night, hiding by day. Much depended upon where his Spitfire had crashed, but if he was unlucky the Germans could be looking for him in this area. There may also be other downed RAF pilots in the vicinity after today's air battle. He needed to move out of the search area. If he could stay out of trouble for say five nights, maybe covering five or six miles per night, he would be in a much better position. Then he could consider approaching a likely looking Frenchman for help, or at least for food.

So what did he have in his escape kit? The gun of course, carried as usual in a lanyard around his neck and stuffed into his tunic breast pocket. But that was primarily for suicide in a burning aerial coffin, although the Spitfire, thank God, didn't have the Hurricane's tendency for pyrotechnics. A .38 was useless anyway in a shootout with rifle-toting German soldiers. That would indeed be suicide! The small torch, compass and map of France were essential for night-time navigation, although the map scale was insufficient to show the local terrain and villages. He also had his pilot's map of this part of Northern France. There was a small pair of opera glasses and a pocket-knife with a multitude of attachments. He also still had the small pad strapped to his leg that he used for his notes while flying. He destroyed the page of scribbled notes, but retained the pad and pencil.

How about water and food? Water was much more important than food. He could quite easily go without food for a couple of days, although more than that and the energy deficit would affect his fitness. He had a full army canteen of water, which would need to be refilled at some stage. He would avoid suspect water sources like rivers and ditches, so the canteen would have to be clandestinely replenished at farm standpipes or water butts. As for food, he had three tins of bully beef, a dozen Horlicks tablets and some chocolate. That would have to do for a bit. He had a snare and was reasonably confident that he could catch rabbits, squirrels or local game. He might also be able to steal the odd chicken or eggs from a farm. He also had a tinderbox, but he dare not light a fire, not yet and not around here at any rate.

Longer term, well, he would head for Spain. He would need civilian clothes and transport of some kind of course. He could steal clothes and maybe a bicycle from a farm. His training as a mechanic even endowed him with the skills to steal a motorcycle or a car. But he would certainly come up against checkpoints and roadblocks where they would demand identity papers, and that would be that!

There was no doubt in his mind that at some point he would need help from the local populace. Forged papers and a train ticket looked to be the best route home. He had the French francs that Dix had given to him, and he also had a small French dictionary. He hoped that he would be able to make himself understood when the time came. There was also the small matter of getting across borders, either covertly or with forged papers. Ah well, one step at a time, and with that Steed settled back in his hiding place and waited for dark.

Steed moved to the southern edge of the wood at dusk, but he waited for full darkness before venturing out over the fields on the other side. He was thankful for the experience of his poaching days with Bill Wheeler. He had become used to illicit country walks on dark nights with Bill. He hoped that he was still adept at avoiding those out to catch him.

The big difference was that back home in Essex he knew the country intimately. Here, he was all but lost.

Moving across country at night following a compass direction was much more difficult than Steed had expected. There was a half moon dodging in and out of the clouds, which helped and made his navigation easier, but it was still slow going. He took a compass bearing, noted a landmark as best he could in the darkness, and then moved towards it, keeping low and avoiding open ground.

Several times he came to minor roads, but he did not risk travelling along them. He came across a few farmhouses, but he didn't see a soul. It was hot work on a summer's night, and he soon took off his flying jacket. Finally, with the sky in the east becoming lighter, he looked for somewhere to hide during the daylight hours. He considered a derelict stone farm building, but eventually decided on another wood. Farm buildings offered shelter, but there was more chance of being discovered. The wood was safer and, so long as it wasn't raining, Steed didn't need a roof over his head. He ate a half tin of bully beef, two of his Horlicks tablets and some chocolate. He was tired and soon asleep. He awoke at around ten in the morning, stiff and aching a little, but otherwise in good spirits.

His hiding place was not quite as secluded as he had imagined in the half-light of dawn, so he carefully reconnoitred his surroundings. A small farmhouse with outbuildings was located just behind the wood, on slightly lower ground. He would need to refill his water bottle that night, so he peered through the opera glasses looking for a standpipe. He was in luck. There was a tall hand pump, probably taking water from a borehole or well. Later he saw a woman draw some water into a bucket and take it into a shed. Possibly chickens inside thought Steed.

What he really needed was something to hide his RAF uniform; a set of overalls would be best. But finding a set of overalls just lying around that would fit his large frame was not going to be easy. Then he saw the dog, curled up outside the side door of the farmhouse. Fortunately not a large dog, but he would have to be careful that night. It would be best just to take the water and then move on; save the pilfering until he was clear of the area.

In the event, refilling his canteen that night was not a problem. Nobody was disturbed in the farmhouse and the dog neither barked nor came to investigate. Steed still wore the warm clothing that helped to insulate him from the cold at high altitude. He had his walking boots and thick socks, his RAF uniform of course, a thick pullover and his flying jacket. The nights were warm and dry at the moment, so the heavy jacket in particular was a bit of a burden. Steed was loath to get rid of it, in a couple of weeks it would be September and maybe not quite so warm. If he was still on the run then he might be glad of its warmth and the weather protection that it offered. But he was clearly not going to be able to wear it in public, even over overalls or civilian clothes. He decided to keep it with him for the moment.

The second night's travelling on the run was even more successful than the first. He came across a track, it would not be fair to call it a road, which ran more or less due south for two or three miles. He risked following it, and made good speed before the track came to an intersection with what appeared to be a French D-class road and a small village. He briefly considered following the road in the hope of picking up a signpost and discovering his location on the map. But he resolved to follow his original plan and, after keeping watch on the road for five minutes, he crossed to the field on the other side and continued his cross-country expedition southwards.

Dawn found Steed anxiously looking for a safe place to hide. The best he could manage was a deep ditch between two fields, shielded by a small copse of trees. He settled in, scratched by thorns and bracken but well hidden from view and dry. He was thankful for the flying jacket, which he had nearly discarded. At least it offered protection from the sharp barbs. He ate the remaining bully beef in the tin, a couple of Horlicks tablets and the rest of his chocolate; the chocolate had partially melted in yesterday's warm weather so he thought it best to eat it all before it was spoilt. He now had two tins of bully beef and eight Horlicks tablets left. He slept fitfully until mid-morning.

He awoke, stiff and still tired, to the sound of aircraft overhead. There was no way that he could be spotted in his hideout, even from above, but out of curiosity he shifted his position and peered out over the field in the direction of the receding noise. He was just in time to see two Me-109s at low-level, flying in their usual *rotte* formation, disappearing over the horizon; probably from one of the Abbeville airfields he thought. The field contained some type of crop, beans by the look of them. He would help himself to some of those come nightfall and eat them raw. He watched the field for a few minutes from his hiding place, but there was no sign of any farm workers.

He crawled to the other side of the ditch, avoiding the sludge at the bottom. He was surprised to see a road not more than a hundred yards away, running parallel to the ditch. He took up a position where he had a clear view of the road, but by the same token was well hidden from view.

Two cyclists were pedalling steadily along the road; Steed observed them through his opera glasses. Viewed as a larger image, Steed could see that they were both young women, chatting to each other as they pedalled along side by side. It was too soon to make contact with the locals; a few more days and a few more miles and he might think about it. The girls disappeared, and a vehicle came along in the opposite direction, a German open-top utility vehicle with a driver and two officers by the look of them.

Steed watched the traffic on the road for some time, not that there was much of it. A few cyclists, some French commercial and agricultural vehicles, a shiny black Citroen whose occupants he couldn't see even with his opera glasses, and an open German lorry with half a dozen soldiers in it. Along the road to the southwest, and in the distance, he could see some houses and what looked like a crossroads. After dark he would look for a signpost at the crossroads and try to locate his position on his map.

In the late afternoon, two men appeared in the field adjacent to Steed's ditch. The men started to walk around the perimeter of the field, stopping at intervals to examine the crop. More importantly, they also stopped to peer into a ditch that ran along the other side of the field. Steed burrowed into his hideout and waited. Presently he could hear voices as the two farm workers approached. They appeared to stop close to his hideout and continued talking. He could hear them clearly; they were speaking in French but he didn't understand a word that they said. They moved off and were gone.

Steed emerged at dusk from the bracken and gathered some of the beans from the field, for they were indeed beans, not quite ready for picking but edible nonetheless. He moved along the edge of the field, alongside the ditch, towards the crossroads, keeping low, wary of any traffic on the road. His earlier vigil suggested traffic could mean Germans. But all was quiet. There were houses by the crossroads, and in the fading light he could just make out a signpost, but he was unable to read it from his vantage point, even with the aid of his opera glasses. There was no sign of a German checkpoint at the crossroads, but if he wanted to read the signpost he would have to cross an open space in full view of the houses, then he would have to cross the road. The houses were quiet, and there was so little traffic on the road now that he thought it worth the risk.

He waited half an hour for true darkness and then set off. He still carried the notepad and pencil that was normally strapped to his leg when flying. He risked a few quick flashes of his torch to illuminate the signpost and wrote down the place names and distances. One of the roads appeared to run due south. He knew that he would cover distance much more quickly and easily along a road, and even during daylight it was clear that the area was not exactly crawling with the enemy. So for the first time he risked moving along a road, always wary of the possibility of a German checkpoint or a patrol.

Steed followed the road for a couple of miles before he came to a village. The sound of singing came from one of the houses. He listened, crouched by the side of the road. It was French singing, that much was clear. He looked through his opera glasses. There was light shining from a chink in the blind behind one of the ground floor windows. Did the Germans insist on blackout curtains here in France? From its illumination he could just make out an unoccupied table and two or three chairs outside. Perhaps a bar or café? In any event, the locals were enjoying a singsong with their wine. Steed wished that he could join them, but instead he took to the fields again, giving the village a wide berth.

He followed the road for several hours, leaving it whenever he came to signs of civilisation. It was quiet in the early hours of the morning, but his poacher's senses were tuned into his environment. He could hear an owl in the distance and the unmistakable sound of a cricket. He was aware of rabbits in the field by the road, and then something else, a vehicle engine. He immediately left the road and sprinted across the field, tripped, fell heavily, and then lay still.

The vehicle, a truck by the sound of the diesel engine, was now coming around a bend in the road. All he could make out at this distance were the headlamps, illuminating the road ahead. Steed felt reasonably secure, lying flat on his belly in the long grass and hidden by the darkness. He was twenty yards from the road and well clear of the headlight beam. He slowly lifted his head to have a better view. He guessed that at this time in the morning there would be a curfew; the Germans administered this part of Northern France. The truck was either German military or it contained Frenchmen up to no good. But, as it trundled by, Steed could not be sure which.

Steed retraced his steps to the road and continued on his journey. Fortunately, although the old tree stump that he had tripped over had bruised his shin, he was still able to walk without discomfort. After a short distance, a farm track left the road and headed across the same field where he had taken his unplanned rest. He guessed that it led to a farmhouse. His army canteen was getting low on water; it was likely that he could refill it at the farm. It would be light in a couple of hours, a bit early to stop his trek southwards, but the rabbits in the field had stimulated his appetite. He fixed on a plan. Fill the canteen at the farmhouse, assuming that there was one at the end of this track, scout around for a good hiding place, then set a snare for a rabbit.

The first part of the plan went almost like clockwork. There was indeed a farmhouse at the end of the lane, and he had no problem in locating a water butt and filling his canteen. Sounds emanating from a shed suggested chickens, and Steed was on the point of investigating further when he heard the sound of geese. He knew from his poaching days that farmyard geese were better than guard dogs when it came to deterring pilferers, so he beat a hasty retreat.

It took time to find a decent hiding place, but with the first hint of dawn he located a wood on some rising ground. He knelt at the edge of the wood and, as the light improved, he selected the place for his snare. Steed had been adept at catching rabbits in the old days, and he hoped that his skills had not deserted him. He located a well-used rabbit run and then placed his snare, carefully concealing it from the rabbit. He hoped that it was off the beaten track, and would not be stumbled upon by the locals. He then moved deeper into the wood, found a suitable spot and settled down to eat his bully beef and Horlicks tablets. Rabbit for lunch, with any luck! He curled up on the soft dank woodland earth, snug in his flying jacket, and was soon asleep.

Steed awoke around midday, and immediately thought about his snare. But it was prudent to first reconnoitre the environs. It was a reasonably sized wood, located on a small hillside. The farmhouse, where he had filled his canteen the previous night, was visible from the tree line. He could see the farm track that led to the road through his opera glasses, but the road itself was out of sight. Steed smiled to himself as he watched a small flock of farmyard geese foraging near the suspected chicken shed.

He moved through the wood to the other side, which looked out over open farmland. This little wood is good place to hole up, he thought. A secluded spot where a small fire would not be noticed. If he didn't manage to catch a rabbit today he would give the snare another chance overnight. He could do with a night's rest from travelling, especially with roast rabbit over a wood fire on the menu. He searched his maps for the names of the villages that he had scribbled on his notepad, but in vain. No matter, he would simply keep travelling south.

He checked his snare later that afternoon and was overjoyed to discover a rabbit, still alive and kicking. He broke its neck swiftly and cleanly, and then moved into the heart of the wood where he skinned and gutted the animal with his pocket-knife. He lit a small fire, starting it using his tinderbox, some sheets from his notebook and some dry twigs. He skewered the rabbit with a stout twig, appropriately cut and sharpened, and supported it above the fire by two branches to make a crude but effective spit. He turned the rabbit at intervals, and delighted in the exquisite smell.

When the rabbit was suitably roasted he kicked out the fire, it wouldn't do to take too many chances, and then settled back for his feast. He was just finishing licking the final bones, and feeling particularly pleased with himself, when the dog bounded up. Steed looked around, taking care not to startle the animal because he wasn't sure how friendly it might be. The dog was a type of collie and appeared affable, wagging its tail and looking hopefully towards the remains of the rabbit. It appeared to be alone, no doubt attracted by the smell of his supper.

'Hello boy,' said Steed. 'I'm afraid that it's all gone. Where have you come from?' A young woman appeared from the trees and stared at Steed. Had she heard him speaking English to the dog? Probably.

'Hi doll,' said Steed brightly in French. It has to be said that the French lessons given to Steed by the Belgian pilot Jean-Paul Colbert left much to be desired. The young woman, she looked to be about twenty, gazed at him as if he had come from Mars. He tried again, this time more formally. *'Bonjour Mademoiselle.'*

She replied with a stream of French delivered at super high speed. Steed didn't understand a word. He spoke, slowly and deliberately, the French phrases that he had rehearsed. He almost held his nose to improve his accent, but he thought that might be going a bit too far.

'I speak a little French. Speak slowly please and maybe I am understanding you. I am English. A fighter pilot. RAF.'

Not quite the perfect French grammar that he was aiming at perhaps, but at least the girl nodded her head in understanding.

He was sitting in his RAF uniform shirt and trousers, with his tunic top, pullover and flying jacket lying by his side. He picked up his tunic top to show the girl the wings and slowly got to his feet. The girl spoke again, more slowly this time, but still Steed did not understand her. He considered speaking in English, but he persevered with French.

'I don't understand,' he said. 'Please speak very, very slowly. Help me please. I need clothes. I need food.'

He was aware of the risks that any Frenchman, or Frenchwoman for that matter, would be taking by helping him. If he were captured, the chances were that he would be taken to a prisoner of war camp and treated more or less in accordance with the Geneva Convention. Any French people helping him would end up in a concentration camp if they were lucky, but would more likely be shot. They would also, no doubt, be subjected to some very nasty interviews with the Gestapo. He wanted to say to this young girl that he knew the risk she would be taking if she helped him, so it would be okay if she simply walked away. Just don't tell anyone. But his French was not up to this level of complexity.

The girl was still looking at him; the collie had lost interest, since there was no rabbit, and went sniffing elsewhere. Steed made up his mind. In halting French he said, 'I am very sorry Mademoiselle, for you it is dangerous. The Germans.... I am going this evening. Please...' He hesitated, searching his brain hopelessly for the correct French words. In the end he simply put his finger to his lips in the universal request for silence. 'Goodbye Mademoiselle, and good luck.' Once again he put his finger to his lips. 'The Germans. Silence, yes?'

But she did not go. Instead she said very slowly and clearly in French, so that even Steed understood her, 'Come with me.' And she smiled.

Steed put on his pullover, tunic top and flying jacket, and checked that he had his escape kit bag of goodies. The gun was in its usual place, hidden away in his tunic pocket. He took care that the fire had been properly extinguished, and then scattered the ashes. He hid the remains of the rabbit and generally tidied the ground to eliminate all signs of his presence there.

The girl watched all this with interest, and then she pointed to Steed's multi-layers of clothing. 'Are you cold?' She was now speaking very slowly and deliberately.

Steed smiled at her. 'It is cold in my Spitfire.' He pointed at the sky, but he couldn't remember the French for high. 'It is cold very altitude,' was all that he could manage.

He followed the girl to the edge of the wood. From here he could see the farmhouse where he had helped himself to water the previous night. The girl pointed to the farmhouse. 'My farm,' she said. 'My house.' She continued speaking, but about all that Steed could understand was 'My father' and 'Wait here.'

He wanted to be sure that he had understood her, but once again his grasp on French grammar and tenses deserted him, and he said, 'I am waiting here. You are coming back. Your father is coming back.'

'Yes,' said the girl. 'Wait here.' She held up five fingers. 'I will return in five minutes with my father.' Steed made a mental note concerning the French future tense.

He watched her through his opera glasses as she went into the house. She re-emerged a few minutes later with a short stocky man that Steed guessed to be her father. The two of them hurried up the incline towards the wood. As they entered the wood, Steed stepped out from behind a tree and politely introduced himself. *'Bonjour Monsieur, Je m'appelle Flight Sergeant Harry Steed, RAF.'* The man looked at Steed for a moment, and then stepped forward to embrace him. The man introduced himself as Henri-Paul and said that he was the father of the girl, whom he called Nicole.

Steed was ushered down to the farmhouse, where Henri-Paul's wife gave him bread and cheese and some red wine. A youth appeared, whom the farmer introduced as his son Mathew. While the farmer's wife went off to the kitchen to prepare an evening meal, Steed sat at a large wooden table with Henri-Paul and his two children. There followed a taxing couple of hours for the four of them as they struggled to make themselves understood with copious use of Steed's dictionary. None of the family spoke any English, so that their discussion was entirely in French.

Steed explained that he had been on the run for four days since parachuting from his stricken Spitfire. His aim was to get back to England and rejoin his squadron. He thought that the best way back would be to head for Spain. If necessary he would continue travelling on foot, and at night, because that was safer and he had a better chance of avoiding the Germans. Steed said that he had been told that French people who helped pilots to escape ran a serious risk of being shot by the Gestapo. He did not want to put the family in danger. He would like food and clothes, perhaps overalls to wear over his RAF tunic – he remembered the polite form of the French verb to want. He would also like help with directions and information on the Germans. Were there many Germans in the area? Where were they located, in the towns, in barracks? Was there a night-time curfew? Were there German roadblocks and checkpoints operating at night? Did the Germans search farm outbuildings at night, perhaps looking for escaped British airman?

At one stage, Steed produced his map and asked his hosts to indicate on the map where he was. Henri-Paul studied the map for a moment, and then indicated a point about fifteen miles southwest of Amiens. Steed was left in no doubt that he should not mark the map, and he should never tell the Germans that people from this area had helped him.

Henri-Paul said that there was indeed a curfew at night, which was enforced by both the Germans and the French police. Sometimes checkpoints were set up, but they were more likely to be on the major roads or by important installations like power stations and railway lines. Road bridges over railway lines were also often guarded.

German activity in this area had been stepped up since Russia had entered the war. Communists, especially in the major cities, sometimes disrupted communications or killed Germans. When this happened the Germans took reprisals on the local population, shooting many innocent people for every German killed. So far, there had been very little of this kind of activity locally. Things were generally quiet, and the German soldiers had behaved very correctly.

Germans sometimes carried out random searches of farms, but there were fewer of them around since the war with Russia had started. German activity had not been stepped up in the last four days, so Henri-Paul doubted that the Germans suspected that a British airman was at large in the area. Most British planes were shot down further to the east, especially the night bombers targeting Germany, so it was unlikely that the Germans would devote too many resources to looking for fugitive pilots locally.

Travelling cross-country at night on foot would be the safest option, but it would take forever to reach Spain, and the Flight Sergeant would need to buy several new pairs of boots on the way. Nicole giggled at her father's little joke. Henri-Paul said that he had a few ideas of how to help Steed, but he would not elaborate.

At that point Henri-Paul's wife appeared and took Steed's arm. Without saying a word, she led Steed into a washroom where a tin bath had been filled with hot water. She handed Steed soap, a razor and a towel. She also handed him civilian clothes, underwear, trousers and a shirt. 'My son's clothes.'

The youth that he had left in the other room was much smaller than Steed, but these clothes looked to be a good fit. 'You have two sons Madam?'

'My other son is a prisoner of the Boche monsieur, a prisoner of war. Do you understand?'

'Yes Madam,' said Steed reverently. The woman left the room to allow Steed to continue his ablutions. The effect on his appearance of four days on the run had taken its toll. His clothes were dirty, and so was he. He had the beginnings of a beard and he did not exactly smell fresh. No wonder the good woman thought that he was in need of a bath. He had left his tunic top, with the handgun in the breast pocket, in the other room with Henri-Paul and Nicole. Ah well, if the Germans came in mob handed with their rifles at the ready, his little popgun would be useless anyway. He settled back in his bath. He reappeared, clean and shaved, just in time for dinner, a delicious stew served with more red wine and bread.

Steed thanked his hosts for their hospitality and the clothes, and prepared to take his leave. He said, in bad and halting French, and with generous use of his dictionary, that the family would be shot if the Germans were to find him on the farm. He would continue to head south, travelling at night. If the Germans caught him he would say that he stole the clothes from a washing line, but that he couldn't remember where.

Steed was touched when the whole family objected strongly to his departure and made it very clear that he should stay. Henri-Paul said solemnly that he had fought the Boche in the Great War, at Verdun, and he hated them for what they had done to France. Steed responded proudly that his father had also fought the Germans, in Flanders. Nicole suggested that his parents would be worried about their son, but Steed confided that German bombs had killed both of his parents. At this both Nicole and Madam sadly hugged and kissed him. Henri-Paul gravely put his hands on Steed's shoulders and kissed him on both cheeks. 'Monsieur,' said the old soldier, 'We will try to help you to reach unoccupied France. From there it will be easier for you to reach Spain. It is possible that we can help. I must talk with friends. Please stay here and give me time.'

That night, Steed slept as the family's guest in their prisoner-of-war son's room. He felt exhausted, not so much with the physical effort of covering twenty miles cross country over the last four days, nor even with the mental strain of being on the run and hiding from the Germans. It was the strain of understanding, and trying to make himself understood, in a foreign language that he had found most wearisome.

Over the next few days Nicole and Henri-Paul told Steed more about life in post-war, armistice France. Henri-Paul and his wife were peasant farmers. They owned a small mixed farm of arable and livestock, namely cereals, chickens, geese and a few goats and pigs. Before the war Nicole and her elder brother Alain helped their parents to run the farm. When Alain had joined the army, the younger brother Mathew, who was now sixteen, left school to work on the farm. Henri-Paul explained resentfully to Steed that the Boche, he never called them Germans, had imposed severe taxes on the French population as a part of the armistice terms. For example, France had to pay for the German troops garrisoned in France, and she had to pay at a ridiculous and punitive rate of exchange between the Franc and the Mark. Worse, although the war was over for France, the Boche retained their son and many others as prisoners of war in Germany. 'They want them as slave labourers,' said the farmer bitterly.

Steed learnt from his hosts that the area north of the Somme was administered by the German military, however their farm was south of the Somme and so administered by the French. It did not make a great deal of difference because they were still in the German occupied zone. However, the Germans, as Steed was well aware, did not occupy the southern part of France, although the French Vichy government was pro-German.

The Vichy regime was obviously a sore subject for Henri-Paul. The old soldier explained that he had been serving with the French Second Army in 1916 at the fortress of Verdun when the Boche launched a devastating attack, supported by a terrible artillery bombardment. Things looked very bad for Henri-Paul and his comrades until General Philippe Pétain took command. Pétain was not only a capable General, but he also showed compassion and caring for the troops under his command. Gradually the French soldiers stopped the Boche advance, which was threatening Paris, and then they retook all the ground lost earlier. Pétain became a hero not just to the soldiers but also to all of France, the saviour of Verdun.

Pétain, now in his eighties, became Prime Minister of France after the British withdrawal at Dunkirk, when defeat by the Boche seemed certain. Pétain was appointed Chief of the French State after the armistice, and now governed the country from the town of Vichy in the unoccupied zone of France. But Pétain now collaborated with the Boche and had adopted Nazi ethics for France. Work, family and fatherland had replaced the republican motto liberty, equality and fraternity. Pétain wanted to take France back to an authoritarian age, where working men were content with their lot and accepted paternal government from their betters.

Henri-Paul and his two children worked outside on the farm for most of the daylight hours, since it was now approaching harvest time. Even Madam, for it still did not seem appropriate for Steed to address Henri-Paul's wife by her Christian name, busied herself with the chickens and geese when she was not busy with her cooking and housework. Steed remained inside the farmhouse out of sight for most of the time, and he began to feel guilty doing nothing; time was going by. He wanted to get back on the road before the weather turned wetter and colder. He was confident that he could survive on his own for several weeks while the weather held, travelling by night, living off the land and perhaps pilfering from the farms. But Henri-Paul was adamant that Steed should stay, saying that he might have a plan.

One evening, Henri-Paul came back to the farmhouse with a stranger, a middle-aged man who immediately shook Steed's hand vigorously, and started to speak to him in fluent English.

'Good evening young man, Henri-Paul has asked me to speak with you. You can call me Pierre, it is not my real name of course, but it is safer that way.' Nicole and Mathew followed their father into the farmhouse and Henri-Paul invited everybody to sit at the table. Madam, brought in bread and wine, and she too sat down. They all looked at Pierre.

The stranger leaned forward and again addressed Steed in almost perfect English. 'They tell me that you speak some French, but not very well. In fact,' he indicated the family, 'they can hardly understand you at times. We need to make sure that there is no misunderstanding, because there are important things to say. Please tell me your story, how you came to be here.'

Steed repeated in English what he had laboriously explained to the family on the afternoon of his arrival. Pierre nodded, and then spoke with the family. Steed could not follow their conversation, but he was aware that Pierre was recounting the story and that the family were agreeing with it.

Pierre again turned to Steed. 'Well, that is exactly what they thought you had said, so your French can't be too bad. You can make yourself understood, but they say that you could never fool a French speaking German that you are French.'

Steed agreed. 'I read French much better than I can speak it, but I find it very hard to understand, especially when you all speak quickly, as you did just then, and I can get it all very wrong. For example, I thought Nicole said just then that I am a German!'

'Not quite,' laughed Pierre. 'She said that you look like a German. You do look much more like a German than a Frenchman by the way. You are tall and you have blond hair and blue eyes, very Arian. But of course you English are Anglo-Saxons, so that probably accounts for it. But Nicole doesn't think that you are German. She heard you speaking to her dog in English just before you saw her, and you speak French with a very strong

English accent. From your accent I would say that you are from London, yes?'

'That's right,' said Steed.

'We have to be careful,' continued Pierre. 'There are very strict penalties for those caught helping English airman to escape. In France today, the Germans shoot women and children.'

'I know,' continued Steed. 'I have told Henri-Paul that I am very grateful for his help, but it is now time for me to leave. Please assure him that I would never tell the Germans anything about this place, even if they stand me in front of a firing squad.'

'Yes, Henri-Paul has told me of your desire to leave. He is very complimentary about your, err, country ways and your ability to survive in the open; you are a poacher as well as an airman I understand.'

Steed held up his hands. 'That was a long time ago. I don't think that the local farmers in England were too worried if we took the occasional rabbit, and we only poached pheasants on large country estates owned by gentlemen farmers, not working people like here.' He smiled, 'I am reformed now. I only stalk Germans these days.'

Again Pierre translated for the family. Henri-Paul laughed and said something that Steed could not follow. Pierre continued, 'He thought that you still were a poacher, but he says that you often speak French in the present tense when you mean to speak in the past. He doesn't mind if you catch his rabbits, they eat his crops and he cannot control the rabbit population by shooting them because the Germans do not allow the French to keep guns, not even shotguns. Anyway, I digress. Henri-Paul has asked me to speak with you because he has a plan to help you to move on and he doesn't want you to misunderstand. You may be able to survive for weeks in the open, but even you cannot hope to walk to Spain. Do you have your map?'

Steed fetched his map of France and opened it on the table. Pierre continued, 'France is divided into the Occupied Zone, which of course is occupied and controlled by the Germans, and the Free Zone, unoccupied and controlled by the French. This area,' Pierre indicated a swathe of France with his finger, 'is the Free Zone. The town of Vichy, here, is the seat of the French government. There are no Germans in the Free Zone. If you want to get to Spain, you could trek down the western part of France, past Bordeaux, past Biarritz and cross into Spain here, near San Sebastian. The problem is that all of this land is part of the Occupied Zone. The

Germans occupy the whole of this western strip of France, all the way down to the Spanish border.' Again Pierre indicated the area on the map.'

'Instead, we recommend crossing into the Free Zone first, and then heading for the Spanish border. That will be a lot less dangerous than travelling the whole way through the German occupied part of France.'

Steed nodded. 'That is more or less my plan, but I agree with you, it's a long walk to Spain!'

'Well,' said Pierre slowly, 'that is where Henri-Paul may be able to help you. Henri-Paul has a brother who owns a farm near the town of Poitiers.' Pierre indicated the town of Poitiers, in Central-Western France, on Steed's map. 'The farm is close to the demarcation line between the Occupied and Free Zones. If we can get you to the farm, Henri-Paul's brother may know the best way of crossing over. To do it legally, you need a pass, but there may be other ways. To be honest we don't know, and it is dangerous to speak of such things in a letter. Our plan is to take you to Poitiers and then speak to Henri-Paul's brother. If the worst comes to the worst and he cannot help you, well, you will be a lot closer to Spain than you are here.'

'How do I get to Poitiers?' asked Steed.

'This will be the most dangerous part of your journey. You will need to take a train to Amiens, another train from Amiens to Paris, then cross Paris and take yet another train to Poitiers. You will almost certainly be asked for your papers several times, especially at the stations and on the trains. So, we need to get forged papers for you, and we also need to coach you in French phrases that you will need if challenged. Henri-Paul will go with you to Poitiers, but he will not walk with you nor sit with you. If you are arrested Henri-Paul must not be implicated, he will simply walk away. Is that clear?'

'Of course,' replied Steed.

'Henri-Paul has arranged for someone to come here to take your photograph. Henri-Paul will then take the photograph to the forger. There are people involved in the black market who make up false identity cards, ration books, German permits and all sorts of things, and for all sorts of reasons, all with no questions asked. Henri-Paul knows people who know people who do such things, if you know what I mean. But I am afraid that we will need some of your French money.'

'No problem,' said Steed. 'When will all of this happen?'

'The photograph will be taken tomorrow; the identity papers should be ready in about two or three weeks. If everything is on schedule, you will leave for Poitiers by the end of September. In the meantime, you have some homework to do. You need to memorise your new identities. We will have two identities for you, one to use in occupied France, and another to use in the Free Zone. You must be word perfect in a number of important phrases, but without your English accent. Henri-Paul and Nicole will be your tutors. One more thing, and this is very important. Be very careful whom you trust. Many people in France want to try to forget the war and move on to something new. They regard Pétain as a fatherly figure who has taken the shame of France's defeat onto his shoulders and is working with the Germans to create a new order in Europe, going back to the old conservative values of work, family and fatherland. Such people, maybe even a majority of the French nation, just want to get on with their lives and hope that, in time, things will return to normal and that the Germans will go home. The English are not popular with many people here. They would say that you ran away at Dunkirk and left France to its fate.'

Pierre held up his hand as Steed tried to interrupt, 'No, we do not think that my friend, but there are many that do. You have heard of Mérs El Kebir yes?' Steed looked puzzled. 'The French harbour near Oran in North Africa?' Steed nodded. He knew what the Frenchman was about to say. 'Two weeks after the armistice, the English fired on the French warships and killed over one thousand French sailors. Yes, I know the reason that Churchill gave. He was frightened that our fleet would fall into the hands of the Germans.'

'That was a terrible thing,' said Steed. 'But the French admiral was invited to either scuttle his fleet or sail it away from possible German control. He refused. Britain stood alone against a German nation that controlled all of mainland Europe. If Britain's sea lifeline to Canada were to be broken, her people would starve. The French ships, in German hands, might have been able to break that lifeline.'

'Yes, I know,' said Pierre. 'But this action at Mérs El Kebir caused shock and resentment amongst many French people. But some of us still have hope that the Germans can be beaten. You English are still fighting when most Frenchmen thought that you would have collapsed and sued for peace long ago. Now the Russians are also fighting the Germans, and De Gaulle promises that one day the French people will be free. A little further east from this farm are the old battlefields of the Somme. Henri-Paul's father farmed this land in those days. The Germans came very close; the front line was just the other side of Amiens at one time. Around here, the people have long memories and there is still resentment against the Germans for what they did then. But you should know that the French people are divided in their support for the English, and you must be very careful whom you approach, especially in Vichy France, that is the Free Zone. There are people who would betray you. Now, both of your identity cards will say that you are Georges Gallant, but they will have different addresses, one in the Occupied Zone and one in the Free Zone. So be very careful not to mix them up. When were you born?'

'24th January 1918.' Pierre wrote down the answer.

'Good, we will use your correct date of birth on both, it will be easier for you to remember if challenged. The first card will give your address as a village near Amiens. Your reason for going to Poitiers is to visit your sick mother. The second identity card will give your address as a small town between Poitiers and Limoges, inside the Free Zone. You may be on your own once in the Free Zone, if so my advice is to make for the Spanish border at either end of the Pyrenees, but not in the middle, it is far too mountainous for you to cross on foot.' Pierre again pointed to the map. 'See, here in the west, towards the Atlantic, between Pau and Pamplona, or here in the east towards the Mediterranean, near Perpignan.'

The photographer came the following morning as promised. Steed was dressed in shirt jacket and tie for the head and shoulders photograph. The photographer didn't speak to Steed, and Steed didn't speak to the photographer. It was all over in a matter of minutes. Henri-Paul said simply, 'A good friend.'

Steed worked mostly with Nicole on a set of responses that tried to anticipate questions about his identity, where he was going and why. It was clear that Steed would be in trouble if the questioning became detailed, but Henri-Paul said that detailed questioning was unusual unless the French policeman, or the Gestapo officer, was suspicious. In some respects, a check by the Boche was preferable, because they would be less able to detect his English accent.

He now had to decide what to take on his trip. Obviously he would wear Alain's civilian clothes, kindly offered by Madam; Henri-Paul said that he would burn the uniform and flying jacket. His walking boots were essential if he was going to make it over the Pyrenees, so he chose warm comfortable clothing from Alain's wardrobe in keeping with the boots. He also accepted a warm woolly hat from Henri-Paul, again with a trek over the mountains in mind.

Madam offered him the choice of a small suitcase or a rucksack with which to carry some additional clothing; extra layers would be useful crossing the Pyrenees in autumn. He chose the rucksack because it was more convenient to carry, and probably more in keeping with the clothes that he had chosen.

He was bound to meet routine checkpoints where he would be asked for his papers. They might want to look into his rucksack, and maybe even his pockets. If searching and questioning went beyond that, and they suspected that he was English, the game would be up anyway; his command of the French language was simply not good enough to fool them. He therefore decided to retain his identity tag worn around his neck.

He thought long and hard about his escape kit. Should he hide it away in his rucksack and take a chance on being searched? He decided to hide the important items as best he could around his person. Henri-Paul purchased a French version of his map of France that he could carry inside his rucksack without raising too much suspicion. His cover story was that his sick mother was staying with her sister and the map was to help him to find the village; he burnt his own maps. The English-French dictionary was essential, but a real giveaway. He replaced the dust jacket with that of a detective novel from Alain's collection and slipped it into his pocket. That would have to do.

But what if he were to be caught by the Germans? With the clothes, rucksack, false identity papers and other goodies, it would be obvious that French civilians had helped him. He could invent a cock-and-bull story about stealing the clothes and meeting a crook in a bar who took his photograph and provided him with false papers, but the Germans would never swallow that and would want to know the truth. They might become quite persuasive, especially if he was caught by, or handed over to, the Gestapo. Teeth and fingernails might be pulled out, nasty things might be done with red-hot pokers, and private parts might be subjected to amputations. These bully-boys were quite capable of such things.

So, if caught, should he go quietly or should he make a heroic last stand with his Enfield Mk II revolver and five bullets? Or should he leave the gun behind, bury it in the woods perhaps? It was, after all, heavy and difficult to conceal. Clearly, if he went around shooting Germans in order to get away from them he would be condemning innocent Frenchmen to death, because he now knew that the Germans shot many hostages for every German soldier murdered. He decided to bury the gun. When he told Henri-Paul of his intention, the farmer smiled. 'I will bury it for you alongside my own shotgun. You can collect it after the war when France is free.'

The identity papers arrived, printed on the necessary special type of paper and looking quite convincing. Madam sewed the papers for the Free Zone inside his jacket lining; he could retrieve them when, and if, he made it over the border. Henri-Paul and Steed were ready to go.

Two days before their departure, Pierre made another visit. It was a pleasure to hear English after so much cramming in French. 'Nicole tells me that your accent is improving Monsieur Gallant, but keep it very simple. If you stray from the phrases that you have been practising, a Frenchman will know immediately that you are a foreigner. Speak only if you really have to.'

'Yes, I know,' said Steed. 'If someone tries to engage me in social chit-chat, I apologise, point to my throat and say that it is sore. If someone questions my accent, I am supposed to say that I have had a speech impediment since childhood, a medical condition, smile politely and shrug my shoulders.' He demonstrated the learnt French phrase.

Pierre laughed, 'Not bad, that will have to do. Now there are a few things to say about your trip. I know that Henri-Paul has already spoken with you of some of these things, but we must be sure that you understand; that is why I am here. What you do not know yet is that Henri-Paul's sister lives in Paris, and that you are going to stay overnight in Paris at her apartment. Neither Henri-Paul's sister in Paris, nor his brother near Poitiers, know that Henri-Paul is bringing, shall we say, a friend to stay. So when you reach either of these places, Henri-Paul will leave you to your own devices while he tells his siblings who you are and checks that the coast is clear.'

Steed said that he understood, and Pierre continued, 'You know that you must not walk with Henri-Paul, but follow him at a discrete distance. Should you lose him, he has told you where to go to meet up with him again. Are you clear on these locations? Where would you go to in Paris for instance?'

'If I lose him in Paris, I must make my way to Notre Dame Cathedral, on the Seine. I must take a seat on the ninth row from the front on the left and pretend to pray. You know, I am tempted to lose Henri-Paul just so that I can see Notre Dame.' Steed saw the look of alarm on Pierre's face. 'Only joking Pierre, honest.'

It was just after dawn on a dull and grey morning in late September, with more than a hint of autumn about it, when Henri-Paul and

Steed set off on the four-mile cycle ride to Poix de Picardie station. Nicole and Mathew had already left; their job was to return with Henri-Paul's and Steed's bicycles, for Henri-Paul's children were by now quite adept at riding one bicycle while steering another alongside. Steed had already expressed his heartfelt thanks and said his goodbyes at the farmhouse, promising to return after the war, and now they were on their way.

Steed followed 100 metres behind Henri-Paul as they both pedalled steadily along the minor country roads. Steed was glad to be out in the fresh air. He had been cooped up in the farmhouse for too long. His brain felt about to explode with all of the French language that had been crammed into it during the last month and a half. It was still early, so traffic on the road was light. Occasionally they met another cyclist, or a motor vehicle of some description, but there were no checkpoints and no Germans.

There was more traffic as they entered the little town of Poix de Picardie, so Steed closed the gap to his guide to avoid losing him as they made their way towards the railway station. Nicole and Mathew were waiting outside the station when the two men arrived and, without fuss, they took the two bicycles in tow and pedalled away.

Having seen his children safety away, Henri-Paul entered the station to buy the tickets. Steed crossed the road and pretended to look in a shop window. Henri-Paul emerged from the station, crossed the road, and bought two newspapers. He joined Steed by the shop window, discretely handed him one of the newspapers and walked on. Steed slipped his hand inside the folded newspaper and found, as he knew he would, his rail ticket. All very cloak and dagger thought Steed. He crossed the road again and walked nonchalantly into the station. He pretended to look at the timetables while getting his bearings, but his heart missed a beat as he observed two German soldiers at the gate, rifles slung over their shoulders, with a French policeman who seemed to be checking the identity cards of travellers both leaving and entering the platform. A railway employee was also checking the tickets.

Henri-Paul walked to the gate, showed his identity card and ticket and moved on to the platform. Steed followed suit. He approached the gate, ticket and identity card at the ready. The policeman looked at the identity card, and then looked Steed in the eye. Steed politely looked back. The two German soldiers looked bored. The policeman handed the card back and Steed moved on to have his ticket checked, and then he was through to the platform. Not a word had been exchanged.

Henri-Paul walked a little way down the platform, and then sat down on a bench. Steed followed, walked past the bench and then leant against the wall and pretended to read his newspaper. There was half an hour to wait for the train. The Rouen-Amiens express whistled by without stopping, but after that all was quiet. The appointed time for their train came and went. The people waiting on the platform had that weary look of resignation that suggested that it wasn't unusual for trains to be delayed in this part of the world. When their train did eventually arrive it was nearly one hour late. Steed followed Henri-Paul up the steps and into the carriage. All of the seats were occupied; the train was full. Now there was a surprise! Steed found a spot to stand near the door. There were four intermediate stops between Poix de Picardie and Amiens, few people seemed to get off but many more got on. By the time the train pulled into Amiens station, the passengers were jammed into every conceivable space.

It was at this point that Steed thought of his Rhubarb trips. Trains were prime targets. What would have happened if a couple of Spitfires had strafed this train, had caused the engine to explode and the train to be derailed? This packed humanity would not have stood a chance. There were no Germans on this local train that he could see, just hundreds of ordinary Frenchmen and women. Steed had heard it said that fighter pilots fought a clean war; it was you against the other guy and you killed at a distance. However, blowing up French trains brimmed full of innocent civilians suggested that it was far from clean. War was a dirty business.

Amiens station was very different from Poix de Picardie. There were plenty of Germans here. Henri-Paul had said that Amiens was a major railhead in the Great War, troops and supplies passed through here on their way to the front. Now, in the present war, it was still a busy place. Having missed their connection, they had three hours to wait for the next Paris train. At least the day had brightened and they spent their time wandering around Amiens city centre in the autumn sunshine before returning to the station to await the Paris train. The pavement cafés around the station were full of well-heeled French people and German soldiers. But this was in contrast to the majority of people scurrying around the city, who looked gloomy and drab. There were few private cars, but many bicycles. Some bicycles towed little trailers, either for goods or up to two passengers. There were also some peculiar vehicles that appeared to have wood burners added to them as an afterthought. He later discovered that these *gazogènes* burnt wood chippings or charcoal to produce methane, which then powered the normal vehicle engine via a modified carburetta.

They boarded the train and both got seats, although they did not sit together. There were many German soldiers on the train, and Luftwaffe people too. A group of Luftwaffe officers was sitting nearby; at least one of them was wearing a pilot's insignia. Probably some of the Abbeville boys off to Paris on a spot of leave guessed Steed. He was taken aback when a German soldier sat next to him. The soldier looked at him, nodded, and muttered the one word greeting *'Monsieur.'* Steed responded by also nodding and repeating clearly that same standard greeting *'Monsieur'*, a word that he had practised over and over again with Nicole. He then went back to studiously reading his newspaper. Was this guy going to sit next to him the whole way to Paris? Would the German try to strike up a conversation?

What was in the newspaper? Was he holding it upside down? Was he reading the women's page? It was about the soldiers of the glorious Third Reich and the pasting that they were giving to the Russians. The train trundled on through the French countryside. Out of the corner of his eye, Steed was aware of the German soldier looking past him and out of the window. Why hadn't this Jerry brought along a book to read on the way? The German tourist's guide to France perhaps, or maybe a composite guide to Europe, because the sods seemed to have conquered most of it!

One way of avoiding conversation was to pretend to be asleep. Not such a bad idea, it had been a tiring day so far. Steed put down his newspaper, settled back in his seat and closed his eyes. The rhythm of the train cluttering along the rails was pleasant and relaxing. His thoughts began to wander. Before joining the RAF he hadn't been much further than Southend on annual holiday with his parents. Until abandoning his Spitfire a month or so ago he had never set foot in a foreign country, not counting Scotland of course! He had been to Dunkirk, but only for a swim in the sea. He hadn't set foot on French soil. Now he was on his way to Paris. His French textbooks had been full of Paris; the Eiffel Tower, the Seine, Notre Dame, Sacre-Cour, the Moulin Rouge, the artists' quarter…..

Steed was shaken out of his daydreaming by a tap on the shoulder and the sound of a French voice. He opened his eyes. Jesus Christ, the Jerry was speaking to him in what sounded like pretty good French. What was he saying? He was saying, something about the *le jour*, the day. Was the bugger talking about the weather? Now the Jerry was repeating whatever it was that he had said. No it wasn't *le jour*, it was *le journal*, the newspaper. That's it! He wants to borrow my newspaper.

Steed reached down for his newspaper, smiled, and handed it to the German soldier. *'Merci Monsieur,'* said the fine example of the master race. Steed closed his eyes again. The Jerry did look every inch a member of Hitler's finest. He was about nineteen years old, tall, with blond hair and blue eyes. He looked pretty fit and, although Steed hated to admit it, pretty smart in his field grey uniform. I bet his boots are shiny too thought Steed, and then with a start he realised that he was not unlike the Jerry soldier himself in appearance. Maybe Nicole was right, he thought, I do look like a blasted Hun.

The train pulled into a station. More people got on, but it was now standing room only. As the train pulled away from the station Steed felt another tap on his shoulder. '*Merci Monsieur,*' said the soldier, standing up and handing back the newspaper. Steed was surprised to see that the conquering hero was offering his seat to a middle-aged Frenchwoman.

Not wishing to be engaged in conversation by his new travelling companion, Steed again closed his eyes. The rest of the journey was uneventful; halfway to Paris a ticket inspector moved through the carriage, but he simply looked at Steed's ticket and moved on.

The train pulled into the *Gare de Nord* only twenty minutes late. Steed followed Henri-Paul along the platform towards the ticket barrier. They joined a queue of French civilians waiting to get through. This was going to be tricky. There were German soldiers, a uniformed French policemen and what looked to be two plain-clothes policemen at the barrier, and everybody had to show their tickets and identity cards. Some people were pulled from the line and sent for interview by the plain-clothes heavies, who Steed was now convinced were Gestapo.

Up front, Henri-Paul showed his papers and after a few words with the French Policeman was allowed through. Immediately in front of Steed was a family of four, it looked like a mother, father and two young children. The policeman looked at the father and examined his identity card, but something must have been wrong. The policeman was asking questions, and now he was looking at the rest of the family's papers. Steed could hear the exchange clearly, but was dismayed that he couldn't understand a word. He knew then that he was lost. There was no escape. Henri-Paul was already on his way, melting into the crowd. The policeman signalled to the German soldiers to take the family to see the heavies. The father's protest was rewarded by a blow in the back by a rifle that knocked him to the ground. Steed moved up to the French policeman who looked at him for a moment, then at his identity card, and then waved him on. The ticket inspector stamped his ticket, and then he was through, heart thumping, walking forward into the busy station concourse. A little way in front of him was Henri-Paul; he followed his guide out of the station and into the street.

The two men walked for forty minutes towards the Parisian suburb of Saint-Denis. They then turned into a quiet side street, where Henri-Paul stopped. As Steed drew level, the Frenchman said simply, 'Here in thirty minutes.' This was the pre-arranged signal that they were near the safe house, and that Henri-Paul would now ask his sister and brother-in-law if they would accommodate a British pilot for the night, at great risk to themselves should they be caught. Steed walked on, past Henri-Paul, and then checked the time by his watch. Thirty minutes later he returned. Henri-Paul appeared, but this time the Frenchman walked alongside Steed until they came to an apartment block. As they entered the building, Henri-Paul started to speak to Steed. The concierge was inside her apartment, but looking out through the open door, as the pair made their way towards the stairs. The concierge knew Henri-Paul, and it was for her benefit that Henri-Paul gave Steed credibility as a bone fide guest. Like French concierges everywhere, she took her residents' security seriously and liked to keep an eye on visitors.

Henri-Paul knocked on the door of one of the apartments on the third floor. A small plump woman with auburn hair opened the door and ushered them inside. Steed was introduced to Henri-Paul's sister, Madam Pelloche. Although Henri-Paul had been unable to tell his sister in his letter that he was bringing an English guest to stay, Steed was made very welcome. Monsieur Pelloche arrived home from work later, and they all sat down to a chicken supper, supplied by Henri-Paul. Over supper, Steed told his hosts what had happened at the station, how the family in front of him had been roughly handled and sent for questioning, but that the French policeman had waved him through after only a glance at his identity card. 'It is because you do not look Jewish,' Henri-Paul's sister said simply.

Steed was then told something of present day life in occupied Paris. Although his hosts could not speak English, Steed could now understand enough of what was said to make sense of it, provided that they spoke slowly. Madam Pelloche said that there were severe shortages in Paris. Coffee was now fabricated using toasted barley and chicory. Petrol was in such short supply that many cars and trucks had been converted to generate gas by burning charcoal.

Most people simply tried to make the best of things. They kept their heads down, put up with the shortages and rationing and didn't concern themselves with politics; they simply tried to get on with their lives. Those that expressed anti-German or anti-government sentiments risked arrest. Since the war had started against Russia, the Gestapo had arrested many communists and trade union leaders. Jews were having a bad time as well. There had been a big influx of Jews into Paris from

Eastern Europe over the last few years, and the Germans now wanted to deport them. It had to be agreed, said Madam Pelloche darkly, that many Parisians supported this idea of deportation. Many Jews had been arrested in August and were being held in Drancy concentration camp just outside Paris. Even native French Jews were now being taken.

The ordinary German soldiers, by and large, behaved correctly. However, the German police were another matter. One would hear a commotion, look out of the window, and the Gestapo would be dragging some luckless individual off. The communists were starting to make trouble for the Germans, one or two soldiers had been murdered, and the Gestapo were responding harshly. There were many informers; one could trust nobody.

Although their train for Poitiers was not due to depart until midday, Steed asked Henri-Paul if they could leave the apartment early. 'I would like to see the Eiffel Tower please. Maybe also the Arc de Triumph and Notre Dame?' Henri-Paul looked at Steed incredulously. Steed tried to explain. 'This is my first visit to Paris. I have read so much.' He ended lamely, 'I may never see Paris again.'

Henri-Paul half smiled, understanding at last. 'Ah, the English tourist wants to see Paris. Very well. We will leave the apartment early. It is also safer for my sister if we go.' And so, on that sunny late September morning, Steed had his first ride on the Paris metro and saw just a little of the city about which he had read so much.

The Metro was about the only way Parisians could travel any distance around their city because there were no buses. The system was crowded, but efficient. There were no police checkpoints during their journey and the two men arrived in the centre of Paris, alongside the River Seine, without incident. The city centre cafes were crowded, mostly with German soldiers and seemingly prosperous civilians. Madame Pelloche had said that the black market was flourishing and its best customers were the affluent Germans. Traffic was heavier in the city centre too. There were German vehicles of all types and the charcoal-burning French trucks with their *gazogènes*. Steed then had a glorious two hours of sightseeing before they set off for the station, and the train for Poitiers. He even managed to see inside Notre Dame!

The journey to Poitiers was long and tiring. The train was crowded and made frequent stops, sometimes scheduled at stations and sometimes in the middle of nowhere and for no apparent reason. Steed was lucky; he had a window seat. Looking out of the window helped to pass the time and in doing so he was less likely to be engaged in conversation by any of his fellow passengers. French policemen checked Henri-Paul's and Steed's identity cards when they boarded the train, but they were not bothered again until the train pulled out of Orleans two hours later. Then the trouble started.

Steed was peering out of the window, trying to get a glimpse of the Loire River. Something made him turn his head. Behind, two suited gentlemen were moving through the carriage checking the passengers' papers; they had the air of the Gestapo about them. In his mind, Steed started to rehearse his key phrases. At least the Germans would be less likely to detect his English accent, but if the conversation with the hoods was prolonged.... Steed didn't like to think of the consequences. They were closer now; Steed could feel their presence. It affected his fellow passengers too, like a dark mist gradually enveloping the carriage, carrying with it the stench of fear, the dread of the unknown.

There was trouble just behind. The thugs were questioning a young man, and they obviously didn't like his answers. He could hear snatches of the conversation. 'You are lying,' one of the Germans was saying. 'This identity card is false. What is your real name? Tell me now.' Steed was thankful for small mercies. The German spoke bad French, slowly like Steed. At least he was understandable, not like the French who spoke so rapidly that much of what they said was beyond his comprehension. Steed wanted to look back, but he followed the example of his travelling companions. Eyes were averted, look anywhere but at the men from the Gestapo. Try to blend into the background and try to avoid being conspicuous. Henri-Paul was on the other side of the carriage, in front of Steed. His eyes too were looking away from the raised voices behind. There was a yelp of pain. This time Steed did turn around. The youth was still sitting in his seat, but blood was gushing from his nose. Two German soldiers had arrived and, at a signal from one of the hoods, the soldiers pulled the youth to his feet and marched him away.

The Gestapo men moved forwards, looking for new victims. 'Papers,' was all they said, addressing Steed and the man sitting next to him. They both handed over their papers. Steed wished that he still had his gun. If the worst came to the worst, he would have been able to take out both of these bastards before turning the weapon on himself. 'Where are you going?' said the first brute curtly, addressing Steed.

'To Poitiers Monsieur,' Steed replied politely, looking the hood in the face so that the German could more easily confirm the photograph on the identity card.

'Where in Poitiers?' The accent was guttural, but the French was spoken slowly and clearly.

'To Montamisé Monsieur, just outside Poitiers, to my aunt's house.' Montamisé was indeed just outside Poitiers, but it was not where Henri-Paul's brother lived. Steed hadn't been given that information as yet, for reasons of security. It now looked like a wise precaution.

'Address?'

'6, Rue des Jonquilles.' Fictitious, of course.

'Why?'

'My mother is very ill Monsieur. She is with my aunt.' Steed thoughts turned to his own mother, killed in the London Blitz, and a tear came into his eye. The hood handed back Steed's identity card and moved on.

Steed felt very pleased with himself. His French homework with Nicole had paid handsome dividends. He had been able to answer the goons' questions using only the stock-reply phrases that he had practiced, and he had been taken for a Frenchman. He turned his attention back to the Loire River, then closed his eyes and feigned sleep.

The train pulled into Tours railway station. Many people were preparing to leave the train here, including the gentleman that had been sitting next to him since Paris. They hadn't spoken to each other during the whole journey, which had suited Steed admirably. As the man stood to retrieve his suitcase, he leant over Steed. 'Good luck Monsieur,' he said quietly in perfect English, so that only Steed could hear. 'Speak only when you really have to, your accent is unmistakably English.' And then he was gone without giving Steed a chance to respond.

From Tours, all the way down to Poitiers, the railway line ran parallel to the demarcation line separating Occupied France from the Free Zone. The journey was uneventful, but because of the earlier delays it was evening when the train pulled into the station.

Henri-Paul's brother owned a small farm, five miles to the east of Poitiers. Henri-Paul and Steed had already discussed the options of how to get there from the station. There were no busses, and Henri-Paul did not want Steed to be drawn into any conversations with taxi drivers. His brother had told him that the drivers could not be trusted because some were police informers. Their chosen option was to walk.

There were a few battered 'gazogènes' equipped taxis waiting outside the station and several pedal taxis also plying for hire, but Steed followed Henri-Paul past them, on towards the town-centre. Steed liked what he saw of central Poitiers. It was picturesque and there were far fewer Germans around than he had seen in Paris. It was evening now, and Henri-Paul was keen to reach his brother's farm before nightfall; he set a fair pace towards the outskirts of the town so that Steed had to be careful not to lose him in the crowded narrow streets.

Once clear of the town, the roads became much quieter. Steed was certain that his guide was taking the scenic route and avoiding the major roads because some of the roads that they travelled along were little more than farm tracks. Eventually, as darkness set in, Henri-Paul motioned to Steed to wait under the cover of a small clump of trees. Again, it had been agreed that Henri-Paul would first check with his brother that an English guest would be welcome. 'I will be back in thirty minutes,' was all that he said, and then he was gone.

Henri-Paul was as good as his word. He returned and led Steed to his brother's farm. Steed entered into a large well-lit kitchen filled with people. Henri-Paul made the introductions. 'This is my brother Guy, his wife Marie and their children Pierre, Monique, Georges and Claude.' Henri-Paul introduced the children in descending age order, with Pierre about Steed's age and Claude a boy of around ten. 'Guy says that he is proud to have you stay in his house, and he will try to help you to cross into the Free Zone. Like me, my brother does not speak English, but Monique attends university in Poitiers and she speaks English fluently.' Monique, a stunningly attractive girl of about twenty, smiled demurely and added in English, 'I am pleased to meet you Mr RAF Flight Sergeant.'

Steed blushed slightly and said in halting French to the family in general, 'It is kind of you to help me. I know that you are taking a great risk.'

The family did indeed make him welcome. Henri-Paul told his brother's family in slow and easy French, so that Steed could more or less understand, that it was Steed's plan to cross the demarcation line into the Free Zone, take a train to the Pyrenees, and then cross into Spain. There followed some rapid French conversation amongst the family that he could not hope to follow.

Eventually Monique turned to Steed. 'We would like you to stay with us for a few days. We can show you where to cross into the Free Zone. It is a little dangerous, and you must cross the fields at night, avoiding the French police and the Germans. But it is also possible that we can help you further. My mother's family come from the Free Zone and my grandmother lives less than twenty kilometres from the demarcation line. One of us might be able to get an *Ausweis*, which is a pass from the Boche, to visit my grandmother. We can say that she is ill. If you could cross into the Free Zone over the fields, one of us could meet you on the other side of the demarcation line and help you on your way.'

Steed replied in English. 'That's very kind of you, but I don't want to put your family in danger while I am here. We are close to the border with the Free Zone and I guess that the police, or the Germans, make unannounced visits to farms like this. I would like to stay outside, in the woods or in one of the outbuildings. If I am discovered by the Germans, they must not suspect that you have hidden me.'

Monique translated for the family. There was the usual high-speed chatter amongst them, accompanied by much shaking of heads. At length Monique said, 'They do not agree with you Mr RAF Flight Sergeant. My father and uncle are old soldiers. They hate the Boche. It is you that take the risks; it is you that is in danger every time that you fly against the Boche in your Spitfire. And you want to get back to England so that you can fight them again. No Mr RAF Flight Sergeant, while you are with us you will stay in our house, you will eat with us and you will sleep in a comfortable bed. That is final and there can be no arguments.'

'But if the Germans raid the house...' began Steed.

Monique cut him short, 'The Germans and the French police sometimes come here, looking for, how can I say, fugitives, Jews mostly, who think that life will be better for them in the Free Zone. But the Germans never search the house, only the outbuildings, so you see you are safer in here. We have a good place for you to hide if they come.'

Guy's farm at Poitiers seemed to Steed to be a much larger and more prosperous outfit than Henri-Paul's smallholding. Certainly the farmhouse was much larger; it was immense. There seemed to be no problems with food rationing here either, if the supper prepared by Guy's wife Marie was anything to go by.

The whole family sat down to supper together around a large wooden table, festooned with cheeses, bread and wine. Steed learned that Guy and Marie had yet another son who was a prisoner of war in Germany, just like his cousin Alain. Pierre had been luckier because he was still serving with the French army in the south when the armistice was declared, and so he was demobbed. During supper Henri-Paul announced that he would be leaving for home the next morning, and that Steed would then be in his brother's capable hands.

After the meal Steed offered to help with the dishes, but was ushered away by Marie. Steed had started off by addressing Guy's wife politely as Madame, but the ebullient woman had insisted that he should use her Christian name, so Marie it was. Henri-Paul and Guy sat down in easy chairs with their wine and became engrossed in a serious conversation. Other members of the family went their own ways, leaving Steed and Monique alone together. She spoke to him in English.

'I have told my father that I must be the one to go the Free Zone. It is difficult to get an *Ausweis*, and the Boche are more likely to give one to a girl who wants to visit her sick grandmother than to a man. Anyway, I speak English so I will be able to communicate more easily with you.'

'So what is wrong with my French?' said Steed with feigned offence. 'I'll have you know that just today my accent was good enough to convince two gentlemen from the Gestapo that I was a native of these parts.' Monique giggled. Steed had told the story over supper of his pleasure at fooling the Germans, only to be deflated by his fellow passenger wishing him good luck and telling him not to speak, if he could help it, because he had an unmistakable English accent.

'Well Mr RAF Flight Sergeant, I have heard your accent, and you do not sound very French to me. In fact you sound very English. You would certainly not fool a Frenchman, so you will need me with you in the Free Zone or you will end up in prison.'

'Do I sound Belgian?' Monique gave him a quizzical look. 'When we were sitting by our aeroplanes during the Battle of Britain, waiting for the Luftwaffe to turn up, a Belgian pilot friend of mine saw that I was studying a French textbook. From then on he helped me with my French conversation. I am not sure that he taught me correctly. He told me how I should address a pretty French girl, should I be fortunate enough to meet one. He said that I should not say *Bonjour Mademoiselle* because it was too old fashioned, so when I first saw Nicole, your cousin, in the wood by their farm, I said *Ca va Poupée*.'

Monique burst out laughing, 'I should like to meet your Belgian friend, but he was leading you astray. *Ca va* is an informal greeting, but *Bonjour* is far better with a stranger. *Poupée* isn't rude, but it is very, very colloquial. You should certainly never use it to someone that you don't know very well. What did Nicole say?'

'She didn't say anything. She just gave me a peculiar look. I don't blame her. When she popped out of the trees I was sitting there, eating a rabbit and speaking in English to her dog. I had been sleeping in the open for four nights so my clothes were filthy and I had stubble on my face. I quickly changed to *Bonjour Mademoiselle*, at least I think I did; I was pretty flustered at the time. I managed to communicate to her that I was an RAF fighter pilot and needed help. She went to get her father and, to cut a long story short, here I am. But that's enough about me. Henri-Paul told me that you are studying at the university in Poitiers. What are you studying?'

'I am studying World History and English, a little strange for a farmer's daughter I know, but I wanted to travel before settling down, and I wanted to know something of the countries that I planned to visit. I studied English because the English language is widely spoken throughout the world today. The war has ended that idea, of travelling I mean. The English part of my course has been cut back so now I have a break until after Christmas. English isn't exactly popular with the government of *Maréchal Pétain* right now. Has my uncle told you anything about the current state of politics in France?'

'Yes. Many people just want to forget the war, get on with their lives and make the best of things. They hope that, in time, the Germans will go away and France will return to normal. Pétain offers them a solution, work with the Germans and maybe France can become number two in a German led Europe. I think that these people are wrong. Mr Hitler believes that the Germans are the master race and that everyone else, including the French, must be subservient. The countries that he has overrun are not his partners. The Germans will steal their industry and resources and they will take their land. Hitler wants more living space for his people, so he will steal it from the countries that he has taken.'

Monique nodded her agreement. 'You are so very right Mr RAF Flight Sergeant. Do you know the history of Alsace?'

'No Monique, but I am sure that you are about to tell me. And my friends, of whom I dearly hope that you are one, call me Harry.'

'Well then dear Harry, I am sure you know that Alsace is a region of France next to Germany. There was a war with Germany in 1870. As a result, France had to cede Alsace-Lorraine to the Boche. The loss was temporary, and the territory came back to France in 1918 after our victory in the Great War. But now Hitler has declared that Alsace is a part of Germany again. French people living there are now declared German citizens. They must speak German and the men must join the German army. The Boche are also going to settle in other parts of north-eastern France, not just Alsace; they are stealing our land for their people, just like in Poland. But you know Harry, so many people in France just accept it, even welcome it. Politically, some of the Catholic Right are openly hostile to democracy. They are frightened of communism, and even of socialism. They want a fascist regime here in France, just like across our borders in Spain, Italy and Germany.'

Marie called for the family to join her in an adjoining room. The exuberant woman was seated at a piano. Monique enlightened Steed, 'My father and uncle served in the Great War. They do not see each other in these hard times as much as they would like, but when they do and the wine flows, they like to sing the songs of the trenches. My mother is going to accompany them on the piano.'

The two old soldiers sang heartily to Marie's accompaniment. Henri-Paul, now merry on the rough red wine, called to Steed, 'I want to hear an English song.'

Steed moved across to the piano.

'With your permission Marie.'

Marie moved aside and Steed sat down. He had entertained his parents and their friends many times. He knew the soldiers songs of the Great War, and for those songs he didn't need sheet music. He said in halting French, 'My father was an old soldier too, a sergeant in the army. These are some of his songs.' He moved through his repertoire, accompanying his own singing on the piano. He was pleasantly surprised to find Henri-Paul and Guy joining in on many of the songs, on one occasion even singing in English. It seemed that the French and British soldiers knew one or two of each other's refrains.

That night Steed slept in a huge feather bed. It had been a long day and the party had lasted into the early hours. He had been earlier, he imagined, the only English tourist in German occupied Paris, and now he was within twenty miles of the border into unoccupied France. He slept well.

He awoke early, then washed and shaved in cold water. Although it was autumn, the climate this far south was mild. He went down into that huge farmhouse kitchen-diner where Henri-Paul was already at breakfast. They spoke together in Steed's tortured French until it was time for the old soldier to go. Guy owned a *gazogène*-equipped truck, so Henri-Paul had a lift to the station. Henri-Paul embraced Steed and kissed him on both cheeks before climbing into the foul smelling contraption. Once again Steed thanked his benefactor and promised to visit when the war was over.

After breakfast, when the family has dispersed to their duties around the farm and Claude had gone to school, Monique said to Steed, 'I will show you a place to hide in the unlikely event that the Germans pay us a visit.' She led Steed through a door at the back of the kitchen and down a flight of steps into a huge ill-lit cellar. 'You will need someone to help you hide, but we all know this place,' she said with a wink. 'On the other side of the cellar is another fight of steps,' she pointed into the shadows. 'They lead up to the back of the house, so there is another way out if you are in trouble.' She stopped beside a large wardrobe. 'Help me to push this back Harry.'

A door was revealed behind the heavy wardrobe, which led to an extension of the cellar. She threw a light switch to reveal a treasure trove of foodstuffs, wine and oils and even some bicycles. 'This is our little secret,' she said. 'People in the country buy direct from the farmers. Sometimes they barter goods in exchange for food. It is illegal of course, and there are strict penalties and fines if you are caught. My father supplies the black-market restaurants as well. Once the wardrobe is back in place, no one will find you, but do not switch on the light. You will have to sit in the dark until the coast is clear.'

So this was why Guy's farm was doing so well. The man probably had some useful contacts, maybe even amongst the French police. They left the hidden storage cave and went back up to the kitchen.

'It's best if you stay in the house, out of sight,' she said. 'There are people that come here, my father's business contacts you understand, who should not see you. When these people come, we must go upstairs.' She thought for a moment, and then added brightly, 'I have a gramophone in my room and a collection of French and American records. Would you like to hear some?' It was an invitation that Steed was hardly going to refuse. This girl was so beautiful, so vibrant and so easy to talk to. He hardly knew her, but every time that she walked into the room he could feel his heart beating faster.

Her upstairs corner room in the stone farmhouse was large. A double bed, bedside tables, wardrobes and a dressing table were located at one end of the room opposite a large picture window that offered spectacular views over the countryside. The other end of her room was furnished as a sitting room, with a second large bay window that also looked out over open farmland. Her room was immaculately furnished and spotlessly clean and tidy.

'Wow!' said Steed in obvious admiration. 'This certainly puts my small bedroom in my mum and dad's old house to shame. I am very envious.'

'Is that where you go when you have leave from the RAF?'

'I used to,' Steed said sadly, 'but the German's dropped a bomb on the house last year. Mum and Dad were both killed outright and the house collapsed. There is nothing left of it now.'

'I am so sorry Harry. Do you have any brothers and sisters?'

Steed shook his head. 'I don't have any brothers or sisters, and my grandparents died before the war. I have aunts and uncles and some cousins, but no close family to worry too much about my being reported missing.'

'That is so sad Harry, you are an orphan. Your parents should have given you brothers and sisters. I have four brothers, although it is a pity that my parents could not have arranged to give me just one sister. You must hate the Boche.'

'There was a time, just after my parents were killed, when I really hated them, but maybe now hate is too strong a word. I have only spoken to one German socially, a fighter pilot who had been shot down over England. He was rather the worse for drink at the time; he was friendly enough, but a bit arrogant. The Gestapo thugs that I met on the train I would have happily brained, given the chance. Maybe that sums it up. I hate the Nazis and their bully-boys, like the Gestapo and the SS, but not the twenty year-old German soldier who was sitting next to me on the train to Paris and politely gave up his seat to a middle-aged Frenchwoman. Don't misunderstand me, if that soldier was walking down the road and I was overhead in my Spitfire, I would machine-gun him down because he is my enemy and his kind are trying to kill my kinsmen and invade my country.' Steed looked a little sheepish, 'That's the end of my speech.'

'I think Harry,' she said seriously, 'that you would hate all the Boche if your country was occupied like ours.'

Steed's mind went back to August 1940, to The King's cold-blooded machine-gunning of the luckless crew of a Stuka dive bomber as they attempted to exit their sinking aircraft in the English Channel, and his subsequent radio transmission to the shocked Dix. *Just pray that your country is never invaded by these swine Flight Lieutenant.*

'Yes,' said Steed reflectively. 'We had a Polish pilot who said much the same thing. But enough of the war, what records do you have Monique?'

A gramophone and a radio were perched on a sideboard. She opened the sideboard door to reveal a pile of records. She selected one, and put in on the turnstile. Two easy chairs were placed either side of the gramophone, but the girl sat instead on a sofa on the other side of the room. Steed joined her there.

The music was beautiful and melancholic, a very French sentimental slow foxtrot, sung by woman with a wonderful and somewhat deep voice. 'This is beautiful,' said Steed appreciatively. 'She has a wonderful voice. Who is she?'

'Her name is Léo Marjane. She is one of my favourite singers. Can you translate it Harry?'

Steed listened, 'I am alone tonight, with my… er….lost it! I am alone tonight, without your love….er…. sorry, don't know that bit.'

She went back to the gramophone and replayed the passage. Softly, she spoke the English translation.

'I am alone tonight,

With my dreams,

I am alone tonight,

Without your love,

Night falls, my joy is over,

Everything breaks in my heart.'

She sat down beside him again as they listened to the music. 'This song is about solitude, and is very popular now in France. I think many women in France today feel alone. Husbands or fiancés are prisoners of war, or worse dead.'

Steed's thoughts were in a whirl. This girl was absolutely wonderful, far too wonderful to be unattached. She must have a boyfriend at least, probably a fiancé. But so what? There was no future in a relationship with Monique. He was in occupied France, trying to escape back to his squadron. He would be leaving this girl in a few days. But he had to know the answer. 'Is your fiancé a prisoner Monique?'

She was sitting next to him, seemingly a little closer than before. 'No Harry. I do not have a fiancé. And you Harry, do you have a sweetheart waiting for you back in England?'

'No. There is nobody back there worrying about me.'

He changed the subject. 'The music is so beautiful. Would you like to dance Monique?'

'I would love to Harry. I'll start the record again.'

He put his arm around her waist, and gently took her hand. The music started and they moved around her room in a slow foxtrot. She was a good dancer. 'Do you have dances at the university?' For one stupid moment he thought about saying, 'Do you come here often?' but common sense prevailed.

'Yes we do. Poitiers is a university town. The nightlife used to be pretty good before the war, but I doubt that it matches London. Do you go to dances in London Harry? We hear that London is being heavily bombed. It must be very dangerous.'

'The bombing was quite bad during the winter, but Adolf has now taken many of his bomber crews off to visit Uncle Joe Stalin, so it isn't too bad these days. London is starting to look very cosmopolitan, many people in uniform, many different nationalities, including the French. Maybe it's the bombing, but people seem to want to live life to the full now, because tomorrow might be too late, so London nightlife is bustling. Sometimes I go up to London with people from my squadron. We go to restaurants where you can also dance to a band if you want to. But mostly in the evenings I go to the mess with friends from my squadron, or maybe to a local pub.'

He omitted to mention that he still occasionally met up with Sophie Richards in London, with whom he retained a very casual and flexible relationship. Although he was sure that Sophie had many other male friends, Steed very much enjoyed the occasional no-questions-asked evenings that they spent together in the London cafés, inevitably followed by love-making.

But his embryonic feelings for Monique were different. They played music, danced, chatted happily and discussed the British, French and American recording artists of the period. She had two other records by Léo Marjane that Steed liked, *La chapelle au clair de lune* and *En septembre sous la pluie*; 'I know that one, September in the rain,' he said.

Steed felt completely at ease in her company and the time passed very quickly.

Her mother called them down for lunch. Her father had returned and, together with his elder son Pierre, was studying two maps. Monique spoke with her father and brother in that high-speed French that Steed had no hope of following. There was a pause in the conversation, and they all turned to Steed as Monique said, 'We are discussing the best place for you to cross the demarcation line into the Free Zone, and the best route through France to the Pyrenees. As you know, my mother has family in the Free Zone, and they may be able to help us. Please let us talk this through between ourselves first, and then we can suggest to you some options. Is this all right with you?'

'Thank you,' said Steed in French. 'You are very kind. Thank you for your assistance.' He added in English to Monique, 'Please make it clear to your father that I do not want the family to take undue risks on my behalf. Please do not put yourselves in danger, especially with the Germans.'

'We have been through this before Harry. We hate the Boche and we want to do something to fight back. Getting you back to England so that you can climb into your Spitfire and shoot down Germans is something that we want to do. We accept the risks just as you do every time that you fly. In any case, once we are in the Free Zone there will be no Germans.' The rapid-fire French continued, with much pointing at the maps.

Eventually, Monique turned to Steed. 'There are two ways for you to cross the demarcation line. One way is to be smuggled past the Germans, hidden in the back of a truck, maybe in a barrel or in a false bottom. There are people that my father knows who would do this for a price. A number of Jews have made this trip already. But helping a British airman to escape almost certainly carries the death penalty for the smuggler. In your case, we know that you are fit and have woodcraft. We know that you have been a poacher. We think that the best way for you to cross into the Free Zone would be to creep across, alone and at night, at a lightly guarded point on the demarcation line. Now, this is very important. Can you swim, and if so how well?'

'I can swim quite well, not overly fast, but I can keep going for a couple of miles if necessary, say three or four kilometres, as long as the water isn't too cold and there isn't too much of a current.'

'Good, then here is a good spot to cross.' She indicated a point on a large-scale map of the border area. 'You first have to avoid the French observation posts. They are manned by French police or customs officers, and sometimes by French army units. None of the French like the idea of a divided France, and they are not enthusiastic about their job. They have been known to see people running across the fields in broad daylight and not to do anything about it.

'So, here you have a road that the French patrol. On the other side of the road is the field that you must cross; it is covered in long grass. There are French observation posts here and here. My Father has already checked them. There are signs warning of minefields, but there are no mines, we are sure of it. The field leads downhill to this stream, which marks the boundary between the Occupied and Free Zones. There is good cover here, but you have to be very careful. This is where the Germans patrol, along the occupied side of the stream. They have foot patrols, sometimes with dogs, and they have a boat patrol along the stream that has a searchlight and a machine-gun. You have to swim the stream, about twenty metres wide at this point, but with a two kilometre per hour current. Can you do that?'

Steed did a rapid conversion of yards to metres in his head. 'In swimming trunks I can swim about 30 metres in 30 seconds at full speed, but I will have boots and clothes. I will need to tie the boots around my neck I guess. How steep is the bank? Can I climb out easily enough on the other side, especially with a current running?'

'We have thought of that. You will be dressed in overalls with thick socks but no shoes. You will carry your clothes and boots in a waterproof bundle attached to four small floats, that is four empty and sealed oil cans. You will have a rope attached to the float tied to your wrist. The other side of the river is Free Zone territory, and the bank is not steep. You should be able to climb out, and again there is good cover. There are no guards along the other side of the stream; they are only at the designated crossing points. This route has been used before, and it works.'

'It sounds fantastic,' said Steed. 'When I get to the other side I dry off and change into my clothes. What do I do with the floats and overalls?'

'Take the lids off the oil cans so that they will sink and throw them into the stream. Take the overalls a good distance into the Free Zone and then hide them. Try not to give the opposition an idea of how we are getting people across. Remember, there may be others that follow you.

'You will make the crossing at night. You will then have a ten kilometre walk to this small town called Bourg-Souston.' She indicated the town on the map. 'You have to cross these fields, then you walk along this track to the road, turn left and keep walking. We will give you a large-scale map like this and you will have your compass and torch. In the centre of Bourg-Souston is a church; you cannot miss it, there is only one church in the town. I will be standing outside the church at precisely ten o'clock the next morning with two bicycles. We will go to my grandmother's house, where you can wash and get some sleep.'

She moved across to the second map, covering the South of France. 'We think that you should take a train for Perpignan. The Pyrenees are not so steep near the Mediterranean coast as they are further inland, so we think that is your best chance of crossing into Spain, somewhere around here.' Again she indicated the position on the map, her forefinger circling the border area just inland from the coast.

His eyes drifted from the map to instead contemplate her hand. What elegant hands she has. Her fingers are so long, absolutely beautiful with short but perfectly manicured nails. He shook himself out of his daydreaming. 'Is there a chance of obtaining a large scale map of this Spanish border area, a physical map showing contours and heights above sea level?'

She spoke with her father. 'Not here,' she said at length. 'But I will be coming with you to Perpignan. We can try in a bookshop there for a large scale local map.'

There was an issue that was bothering Steed, and now he raised it. 'My squadron leader gave me some French money to use if I was shot down and trying to escape. I have used a good deal of it on false papers and train tickets. I am not sure that I have enough left to cover my own train fare to Perpignan, let alone yours. Is there a chance that you father could lend me a few Francs, I will of course ensure that it is paid back after the war.'

'Dear Harry, don't be so silly,' she chided. 'My father will pay for everything. He can afford it. You have seen our secret cellar. I will always buy the train tickets, not that we don't trust your accent,' she said with a wink. 'But we will give you some money in case we get separated. We haven't finalised the route from my grandmother's house to Perpignan yet. It may be that we will take our bicycles on the train. It will take more than a day to get to Perpignan, and we are worried about booking into small hotels on the way because of your false papers and the police checks. My mother's sister and her husband, my aunt and uncle, live in a town called

Carcassonne, it's on the way to Perpignan. We might use it as a stopover, but we are not sure yet. So how does the plan sound to you Harry, shall we develop it a bit more?'

Steed enthusiastically agreed that it was a very good plan, much better than he had dared to hope. Over the next few days he worked with Pierre on constructing a waterproof sack that would hold his clothes, rucksack, escape kit and one or two other items donated by the family. They made a small frame to hold the sack and mounted four empty oil cans, sealed with tape so as to be watertight, to act as floats. They fitted two straps so that Steed could carry the contraption on his back, and a short length of rope so that he could swim with it and better drag it out of the water and up the opposite bank. If it became necessary the rope would also allow him to crawl along the ground and drag the sack behind him. Pierre tested it with a dummy load on a local pond, and it worked!

For the most part, Steed decided, Alain's clothes would suffice. He could build up undershirts, pullovers and a topcoat in layers that he hoped would protect him, to some degree at least, against the cold weather that he might expect during his journey through the mountains in October. Pierre contributed one garment that made very good sense, a military-style dark brown rain cape that could also be used as a ground sheet.

Steed spent a great deal of time with Monique. Sometimes she helped him to speak and understand French, but mostly they spoke in English. He found it so very easy to talk to her on a whole range of subjects; it was delightful just to be with her. She asked him to play the piano for her, and they danced to her records; and their dancing became ever closer.

Monique applied for, and received, her *Ausweis* permit enabling her to cross into the Free Zone. She said that she had been very lucky to get one because the Boche handed them out very sparingly. She had pretended that her grandmother was at death's door, and the German administrator had taken pity on her. Steed suspected the fact that she was also stunningly beautiful might have had something to do with it.

After a little over two weeks at the farm, it was time for Steed to move on. Monique set off for the nearest crossing point into the Free Zone, driven by her father in his truck. Steed accompanied them. If they were to be stopped, Guy would say that he was taking his daughter to the crossing point when they came across Steed walking along the road, and they offered him a lift. In the back of the truck were two bicycles that Monique would be taking with her. If questioned, Monique would say that one was hers and the other was a present for her uncle.

They stopped by a wood. 'Come with me Harry,' she said. 'This is where my father will leave you tomorrow.' They walked into the wood. Five minutes later they were on the other side of the wood, looking down a small incline to a road, and beyond that a field.

'The road marks the start of no man's land between the French and German border guards. The French police sometimes patrol it, and there are French observation posts over there, and over there,' she pointed to both sides. 'But you cannot see them from here. Beyond the road you can see the field that you must cross. Take no notice of the signs that say *Attention! Champ de mines.*' She saw the look in Steed's eyes. 'Trust me, there are no mines. Can you see the line of small trees and bushes at the far side of the field?' Steed was now looking through his opera glasses.

'Yes I see them.'

'The stream that marks the demarcation line is just behind them. It will be much more difficult to find your way at night so, tomorrow, when you are waiting for darkness, be sure to get your bearings.'

They walked back through the woods. Guy was waiting by the truck. The bonnet was raised and he was feigning a breakdown just in case inquisitive policemen came to ask why he was parked there. He saw Monique and Steed, and waved to them that the coast was clear. 'You stay here Harry. My father will take me to the crossing point and make sure that I get into the Free Zone without any problems. Then he will come back for you. I will see you the day after tomorrow at the Church.'

'Please take care Monique,' said Steed quietly.

'You too Harry, good luck.' She kissed him softly on the lips and hurried off towards her father. Steed withdrew into the woods and waited.

The following afternoon Steed returned with Guy, this time hidden in the back of the truck, covered by a tarpaulin. It was raining steadily. He was wearing overalls, woollen socks, boots and the rain cape, but precious little else. The original plan had been to change from his clothes into the overalls shortly before dark, but the rain had put paid to that strategy; he wanted to keep his change of clothing dry.

Guy embraced him and kissed him on both cheeks. Steed hoisted the waterproof sack, securely fastened to the wooden frame and floats, onto his back and disappeared into the woods. He retraced his steps of the previous day with Monique, and found himself looking out over a deserted and rain-swept road and fields. He selected a spot where there was good concealment by the vegetation and where he still had a good view of the road, but most importantly where the foliage of a tree gave at least some protection from the steady rain. Making sure that his field glasses were to hand at the top of the sack, he settled down to watch the road, and more especially the line of bushes and trees that hid the stream.

As darkness fell, he was pretty sure that he had observed the French and German border guards' routines. He timed their movements using the French wristwatch that Monique had given to him in exchange for his own. A French police car cruised along the track, right to left, once an hour, returning left to right ten minutes later, giving a fifty-minute window of opportunity to get clear of the road, for he doubted that the policemen would see him in the fields once it was dark, whereas the police car would betray its presence by the noise of its engine and the brightness of its lights.

Down by the stream, at the far side of the field, two German soldiers with one dog crossed from right to left once every hour, and returned twenty minutes later. He would have a forty-minute window free of German interference at the stream. That was the important window, but at least the rain would deaden the dog's sense of smell. He waited until it was almost dark and then slipped of his rain cape and put it into his sack. It gave excellent protection against the rain, and it provided some warmth, but it restricted his freedom of movement.

He set off at a jog, the sack and its associated frame and floats strapped to his back. He crossed the road, climbed the fence and dropped down to the other side; the field was very muddy. The rain was coming down heavier now and he could only just make out the tree line at the other end of the field. If he had left it much later he would have risked going around in circles in the darkness. He knelt and listened, but heard nothing. A light wind was blowing across the field. If the German patrol was keeping to the same schedule, the dog would be upwind of him on its approach, so it would probably be past him before it would pick up his scent, if indeed the brute could do so in this rain.

He bent low and started to jog towards the tree line and border. The policemen would find it extremely difficult to spot him from their observation posts in the darkness, and in any case he doubted that they would be too vigilant in this filthy weather. The noise from his pounding feet in the mud was louder than he would have liked, but on the other hand the sound of the rain probably masked most of the noise. He must be careful not to slip. He slowed down and bent lower as he approached the tree line, and then he stopped, crouched down and listened. The wind was in his face; that was the direction from which the German troops would be coming, if indeed they still adhered to their schedule on this wet and windy night. He couldn't hear a thing over the wind and rain. He moved forwards cautiously, the trees were getting ever closer, and then he was amongst their comforting, all-enveloping foliage. In front, he could hear the water. It was much darker amongst the trees, and he was almost on top of the stream before he saw it. He could just make out the other side, but the water was running at a darn sight more than two kilometres an hour, the rain had seen to that. This was no little stream; it was a bloody great river!

He moved to the edge of the water and slipped off his heavy backpack. The waterproof bag with its frame and floats held his every possession; he would be in a terrible mess if he lost it. He pulled off his boots and added them to the collection inside the sack, taking special care in the darkness to properly fasten and seal it.

Well, he could put it off no longer. He selected his launching spot and slid into the water. God it was cold! He could feel the current tugging at him. He gently pulled the bag with its frame and floats in after him. Let's hope that this contraption is a little more seaworthy than the Titanic was after its argument with the iceberg. The current took the rig and he felt a sharp tug on his wrist as it came to the end of the line. Fortunately, Steed was braced on an overhanging tree at the river's edge, and he was able to reel the sack in. At least it had remained upright. He gripped it with both hands and held it in front of his body. He pushed away from the Occupied Zone riverbank, kicking hard with breaststroke legs. The water raged about him, splashing over his head, the sack bobbing wildly in front of him. But his handiwork held together and the oil can floats worked.

After what seemed an age, he had a fleeting vision of the far bank in front of him, and then he crashed headlong into an overhanging tree bough. He struggled to find his footing, and somehow scrambled and slid to firmer ground in the shallows. The direction of the current confirmed that he had indeed reached the far bank and had not made an inadvertent u-turn in the water! He tugged at the rope, but his sack was held fast. He tied the rope securely to the tree, and then waded in to free his possessions. Ten minutes later, he had extracted his sack from the water, and lay exhausted, wet, freezing cold but happy on Free Zone territory. He had evaded the French policemen, the German troops and their dogs, and the machine-gun toting patrol boat, if it ever existed. Mind you, they would be brave sailors who navigated the river in those conditions. It had all been a bit of a doddle really!

Shivering, he removed his sack from the frame and floats, smashed the wood and threw the pieces into the river. The strong current would carry them far downstream, just so much more flotsam and jetsam. He removed the tape and screw tops from the oil cans so that they would sink, then hurled them too out into the main current. His first priority was to get clear of the border. His second priority was to find somewhere to shelter from the rain so that he could change into dry clothes. He slipped on his boots, and then left the riverbank to trek deeper into unoccupied France.

Steed found navigation on a dark, wet and windy night considerably more difficult than he had on those brighter first nights after he had been shot down, but eventually he found the track that he had been expecting. Better still, after a short distance he found a stone-built hut, the size of a garden shed, alongside the track. The heavy door wasn't locked, so Steed crept inside, closed the door and shone his torch around his shelter. From the smell, Steed guessed that the hut had been used as a storehouse; it had once contained animal feed, but now it was empty.

Steed stripped off and dried himself as best that he could, using one of his pullovers as a makeshift towel. He put on dry clothing and socks, paying a great deal of attention to drying out the insides of his boots. He rummaged through his sack, transferring his goodies to his rucksack or to his pockets. He then felt much better. He would rest here until first light, rather than blunder around in almost total blackness outside. He knew that he could easily cover ten kilometres in three hours once he had daylight, and so he was confident of reaching the church in Bourg-Souston by ten o'clock.

He set off again as the sky lightened. A light drizzle had replaced the earlier steady rain, but the rain cape offered good protection. He could see the path clearly enough in the half-light to drop into a jog. He felt refreshed; the light rain was cooling and he revelled in the sounds and smells of the countryside at dawn. It reminded him of his cross-county running days before the war, indeed of many early morning runs around airfield perimeters since joining the RAF. He came to the end of the path where, as expected, it met a minor road. He turned left and continued to jog along the road. Putting distance between himself and the Germans in occupied France felt good, and he ran at full speed for a couple of hundred yards out of sheer exhilaration. He came to a halt, panting. 'Jesus, young Harry, you are out of condition mate,' he said aloud. 'Too much soft living on Froggie farms, and too little exercise. Get back into training my son or you will never make it over the mountains.'

He continued on his way, walking now rather than jogging because he did not want to arrive at his destination too early. After a while he saw a group of houses on the road ahead. He had no need to look at his map; he knew that the road should shortly pass through a small hamlet called St Victor, only four kilometres from his Bourg-Souston rendezvous with Monique. It was light now, and he didn't want to be seen by anyone in those houses who might be suspicious of a stranger walking along the road so close to the border. He crouched at the side of the road and surveyed the scene through his field glasses. It was possible to skirt around the hamlet, but it was quite a diversion and the fields looked very muddy. The hamlet seemed quiet, not a soul was about. He continued along the road and reached the hamlet. The houses remained silent and nobody that he could see was peering out any of the windows.

A black car was parked by the side of the road, a smart Citroen town car without the wood burner, that looked just a little out of place in this small farming community. As Steed approached he saw that there was somebody sitting inside. His heart missed a beat but it was too late now. He had no option but to simply keep on going. Steed walked on, past the car, but he heard the door open and footsteps behind him. A man's voice babbling in French, the only word of which Steed understood being *Monsieur*. Why oh why did these people have to speak so quickly?

Steed stopped walking and turned around. A middle-aged man in a raincoat was holding up some form of identity card, but he put it down as Steed approached. To gain time, Steed said in his best French accent, '*Monsieur s'il vous plait,*' and pointed to the identity card, clearly asking for a better look. The man seemed surprised, but once again proffered his identification. Bugger! It was a plain-clothes *agent de police*. What the hell was he doing here, in the middle of nowhere, at this time in the morning?

Again there came a stream of high speed French. Steed tried one of his stock phrases. 'Please speak slowly Monsieur.' He pointed to his ear. 'It was the war,' he said with a shrug.

'So, do you have papers Monsieur?' said the policeman. It took Steed a moment to compute that the man was now speaking to him in very good English. Steed was trying to formulate a plan. Trying to persuade the cop that he was French was clearly now out of the question. He would hit this character, lay him out if he could, and steal his car. He would have to forget Monique at the Church but, depending upon how much petrol was in the tank, he might get fifty or even a hundred miles down the road towards Spain before he would have to ditch the thing. He needed to get his hands free of his rain cape though, in order to get in a good punch or two. He shrugged his shoulders in what he hoped was a Gallic gesture, '*Quoi?*'

Steed now had his rain cape raised slightly, and was sizing up the distance to the cop's jaw. He felt almost sorry for the older man. The policeman took his right hand from his pocket, where Steed now realised it had been all of the time. The hand held a pistol. He said in perfect English, 'So, you are what, an English soldier or airman, or perhaps a spy?'

The policeman stood just outside Steed's reach. No real chance of knocking the gun to one side, then belting him on the jaw, not yet anyway. And the rain cape was still too much of an impediment to such action to offer a good chance of success.

'I am an RAF pilot.'

Steed pulled back the rain cape and slowly raised the identity disc up through the neck of his shirt and showed it to the policeman. He now had better freedom of movement for a punch. He would make his move if the cop came forward for a better look at the disc.

'I am on my way back to England to carry on the fight against the Boche.' Steed used the idiomatic term in the hope of stirring some patriotism in the policeman's heart; the man certainly looked old enough to have served in the Great War.

The policeman spoke again in remarkably good English. 'We get visitors of all kinds here, smugglers, refugees, Jews, German spies, English spies. But this is the French Free Zone and these people are forbidden entry. So are English pilots.'

'I'll be leaving as soon as I can. I want to get back home to fight the Boche. One day we will beat them and all of France will be free. All of Europe will be free. There are many Frenchmen in England fighting with us, commanded by General de Gaulle. Belgians and Dutch too, and Poles, and Czechs.' Steed spread his hands and took a step closer to the policeman.

The cop raised his gun. 'Don't be stupid, one pace back please.' Steed did as he was told.

The policeman spoke again, it seemed more slowly and thoughtfully. 'When France fell, most of us thought that England would soon follow. But I will agree with you, more than a year later the Germans still haven't defeated you. You can thank your English Channel for that I think. But you will not be coming back to Dunkirk to drive out the Germans very soon, will you?' The policeman looked quizzically at Steed.

'One day we will. I admit that the Boche army is very strong right now, but their aeroplanes dare not fly over England in daylight, and their warships dare not challenge the Royal Navy on the high seas. We are fighting them in North Africa, and it is not just the British that are fighting.

There are many people from our Empire with us, and people who have escaped from all over Europe. That includes Free French soldiers and airmen. Now Hitler has invaded Russia. That is a huge country with millions of men. He cannot possibly hope to control all of the oppressed peoples that he has overrun. France will be free some day.'

The policeman nodded, 'But if you ask me whether I prefer German or Russian troops in my country, I will take the Germans every time. No Mr RAF pilot, it is not the Russians that you need in your war, it is the Americans.' He paused for thought, and then spoke again. 'From your accent you are obviously English. I do not think that you are a spy, because not even the English would be so stupid as to send a spy into France who cannot speak the language. No, I believe that you are what you say you are, an RAF pilot. How you came to be walking down the road in the Free Zone, alone and wearing civilian clothes, I will not bother to ask. Listen carefully to me. I am going to let you go, but only if you forget that you ever saw me. Do not tell anyone about me, not even your French contacts if you have any. It will be much safer for all of us that way. Go now please.'

A very relieved Steed stammered, '*Merci Monsieur, Vive la France,*' turned, and hurried on his way. Was the policeman really a patriot, or was this a clever trick aimed at rounding up Steed's French contacts? Would other people be watching him in Bourg-Souston, and would he be putting Monique in danger if he went through with the rendezvous at the church? Steed thought all of this unlikely, and that the policeman had no ulterior motive in letting him go, but his concern for Monique persuaded him to be ultra cautious.

By the time Bourg-Souston came into view, Steed had made up his mind. He would not go directly to the church. He consulted his map, left the road and skirted the small town, coming back to the road on the other side. Certain that he had not been followed, he selected a concealed spot with a good view of the road and settled down to wait. Fortunately, the rain had stopped, so he was able to stow away his rain cape. There was only one road through Bourg-Souston, and so it was fairly certain that Monique would approach the small town from this side. If he was wrong, and she hadn't arrived by ten o'clock, well the church was only a few minutes walk. The traffic was very light along the road, a few people on bicycles and absolutely no sign of a shiny black Citroen car.

At nine forty-five he was rewarded by the sight of Monique pedalling towards him, pushing the companion bicycle along beside her.

There was nobody else in sight. As she approached, he came out of his hiding place and waved to her. She stopped and dismounted.

'Harry, you are here! I am so glad.'

Steed put his forefinger to his lips and waved her into the trees. 'Bring your bicycles in here Monique, under cover. I need to talk to you.' He told her about the policeman. 'I think that the chap was genuine Monique, probably on the lookout for smugglers or refugees. Nobody has followed me, and he didn't even bother to search me or look at my identity papers; in fact he doesn't even have a clear idea of what clothes I am wearing, they were mostly hidden under the rain cape. But I don't want to put you or your family in danger. I have made it into the Free Zone, and you have given me the money for the rail ticket to Perpignan. I will be okay on my own from now.'

'No Harry,' she said softly. 'There are no Germans here to shoot French citizens if we dare to help evaders, although Pétain's government would consider it a crime. I will take you to Perpignan, and that is an end to it.' She giggled as she teased him, 'With your knowledge of French, you are more than likely to end up on a train back to Paris rather than to Perpignan. You need me Harry. I will hear no more about it.' She added more seriously, 'There are many like your policeman friend who will emerge to fight for France when they believe there is a realistic chance of throwing the Boche out of our country. But he is right; you need the Americans if you are going to beat the Nazis. You speak the same language, why do they not join you?'

'Maybe one day they will,' replied Steed wistfully. 'But America is a long way from Europe and Hitler is unlikely to demand living space from them. Many of their soldiers would die if they were to enter the war, so they would need a very good reason to come in. I guess that they simply haven't got one right now.'

'We should get going to my grandmother's house. You can tell me all about your adventures when we get there. Oh, it is so good to see you Harry, I was so worried about you crossing the demarcation line.' She was standing close to him now, each hand holding one of the bicycles. He slipped his arms around her waist and drew her towards him. Her mouth met his. He kissed her and she responded.

He released her and drew back, slightly flustered. She was the first to speak 'Both of my hands were full of bicycles Harry, and you took advantage. Here hold these.' She thrust both bicycles towards him so that he was forced to take them. Before he could utter a world of apology, she threw her arms around his neck, pulling him down to meet her lips. She kissed him enthusiastically.

'There, I hope that you have learnt your lesson. It is time that we started out. It is over an hour's journey to my grandmother's apartment. All of this kissing is making me feel hungry, and I left without breakfast this morning.'

The bicycle ride to her grandmother's apartment was uneventful. He stayed 100 metres behind her, but in spite of his arduous night and brush with the French constabulary, he felt overjoyed and elated. He was free, travelling in a France without Germans with an absolutely gorgeous girl with whom he was falling in love. It was stupid of course he told himself, it was the war, it was the surreal existence that he had been living over the past two months. He had known her for such a short time. But in spite of the logic from his head, his heart was soaring like a bird.

Her grandmother lived in a small town called St Justin. When they reached the town outskirts, Monique dismounted and waited for Steed to catch up. 'Harry, the concierge knows me. I told her yesterday that I would be bringing my fiancé to see my grandmother.' She winked, 'See what all of that kissing has brought you. You are engaged. The wedding is tomorrow. My father will be here later with his shotgun.'

Steed looked into those laughing eyes. 'I just wish that we had the time to get to know each other properly Monique. These last weeks with you have been absolutely marvellous. I have never met anybody quite like you before. It's just not fair. This war is a real pain.'

'I know Harry. I feel the same way. You know that. But we still have a few more days together.'

The concierge clucked like a mother hen as they walked past her window, and she exchanged a few words of greeting with Monique as they passed. Harry smiled and waved but, following Monique's instructions, did not say a word. They locked their bicycles in the storage area and then walked up the stairs. 'It is always best to have the concierge on your side,' whispered Monique.

Her grandmother welcomed Steed like a long lost son. It was clear that she hated the Boche for the shame that they had brought to her country. She did not speak a word of English, but Steed coped well with her French, once he had persuaded her to slow down a little. That evening the old lady retired early to bed, leaving Steed and Monique alone in the small living room.

'Are you clear about tomorrow Harry?'

'Yes. We leave early and cycle to Bellac. We take the bicycles on the train to Limoges. You buy the train tickets of course.' He made a face at her. 'We change trains at Limoges and travel on to Toulouse. Finally, we take another train to Carcassone where your aunt lives, and we hope that she is at home when we call.'

'That's right Harry, but if not we have to find a small farm in the country where we can rent a room for the night, somewhere discrete with no records. That should not be a problem for a young couple like us; this is France after all. The next day we will go on to Perpignan, and there I must leave you.'

They were sitting together on the sofa. He put his arm around her shoulders, and she turned towards him. 'Harry, I like you very much. You know that. And we have so little time left to us before you must go. You may be killed in the war and we may never see each other again. We both have feelings for each other, but there is something that I must tell you. I am a maiden, you understand? I want to be a maiden on my wedding night. This is very important to me. I want to kiss you; secretly I want to do more than that. But you must be the English gentleman that I know you are. I will sleep in the bedroom tonight, and you will sleep here on the couch. Do you understand Harry?'

'Yes Monique, of course I understand. I could never do anything to hurt you or to make you sad. I promise not to take advantage of your kindness. Am I allowed to kiss you?'

In answer she lent into him and kissed him softly on the lips.

'Do you remember when you kissed me for the first time?' he said.

'Of course I do Harry, when I left you to drive to the demarcation line with my father.' She giggled, 'He was surprised to see that I think. He reminded me that you are going back to England to fight a war and will probably get killed. He didn't want me to get hurt. But kissing you this morning was much more fun.'

'Your dad's right of course.' He kissed her on the cheek and moved on to nimble at her ear. 'I will come back to see you after the war, I owe your father money for one thing. But that may well be several years in the future. I lot can happen by then. You will probably be an old married lady with several children.' His tongue explored her ear briefly before his mouth returned to kiss her lips. She responded, kissing him firmly and with passion, holding his head in her hands.

She pulled away gently and moved her head forward to touch his forehead with hers. 'I know that we have only spent a few weeks together, and it is silly to get so attached in so short a time. You are right, and I should know better. But when it's all over, write to me Harry, promise me that. Write to me, if only to tell me that you are safe.'

He held her in his arms and they kissed for many minutes without saying anything. At length she said, 'It's time for me to go to bed, we have to be up early tomorrow and we have a long day in front of us.' She got up from the sofa, then bent down again to kiss him one final time. 'Don't get killed in that silly aeroplane of yours Harry, please.' And, as she stood up again, he saw the tear in her eye.

The next morning they were up early, cycling to the railway station in Bellac. The train was on time and, surprisingly, it was not full and they were able to sit together. The journey to Limoges took less than an hour. They recovered their bicycles from the goods wagon and walked arm in arm through the station. Monique spoke to Steed in French as they walked. 'What do you think of the railway station? It is quite famous. We are very proud of the *Gare des Bénédictins*. The architecture is amazing isn't it?'

She was speaking to him in French to make things look normal to the casual onlooker, to allay any suspicion. He didn't understand every word, but by now he was fluent enough to get the gist of her conversation. Steed looked up at the station roof. She was right, it certainly had London's grimy and shrapnel-splattered Liverpool Street Station beaten. Here at Limoges, there was a huge glass roof with stained glass widows and huge sculptures all around. There was also a large poster of a benevolent *Maréchal Pétain* with his slogan 'Work, Family and Fatherland'.

'Come outside,' she said. 'The outside is even better.' She was right. The station was built in an art deco style, with a lighthouse-type clock tower and a huge green-coppered dome. Their train for Toulouse did not leave for another hour and a half, so they ate their bread and cheese sitting in the park in the warm October sunshine.

The train journey from Limoges to Toulouse was equally uneventful. As before, the train was not crowded and they were able to sit together, Steed by the window. It was just as well because the train made many unscheduled stops and it was getting dark by the time that the train pulled into Toulouse. They collected their bicycles and consulted the train timetables.

'We have a problem,' whispered Monique. 'We have missed our connection. The next train to Carcassonne isn't until 07.55 tomorrow morning. I don't want to book into a hotel here, there are forms to fill in when you register and there are police checks. It's too risky with your false papers.'

'So we stay here in the station all night?' queried Steed.

'I don't like that idea either. The police could make checks on late night travellers waiting at railway stations.' She consulted the timetable. 'There is a local train that stops at every station. It goes as far as Casteinaudary, which is about half way to Carcassonne. It leaves in half an hour. We could take that and then pick up the train to Carcassonne when it stops at Casteinaudary in the morning.'

'Do you think that it is safer to wait in Casteinaudary station than here?'

'Well, I wouldn't stay at the station. Casteinaudary is a small town and we could cycle into the country in about five minutes and sleep in the open. It's not a bad night; you could give me a cuddle to keep me warm.'

'What are we waiting for?' enthused Steed.

It was nearly ten o'clock when the train pulled into its terminus at Casteinaudary. Their bicycles had no lights, but there was a moon and enough visibility to find their way along the country roads. It was not long before Steed saw what he had been looking for in the moonlight, a small wood close to the road. They wheeled their bicycles through the undergrowth. It was apparent, even by moonlight, that few people came this way.

They made camp in a small clearing. Steed found some dry moss and tinder, and soon had a fire going. They spread their rain capes on top of fallen leaves to make a passable mattress, and set out the bread, cheese and wine that they had brought with them. Steed left her tending the fire while he went off into the night with his torch and snare. He returned thirty minutes later with a rabbit. Monique was mightily impressed.

'I'm not quite as clever as you think,' he said sheepishly. 'I found a rabbit warren over on the other side of the field, on the slope, but other people had already set up snares. I liberated this fine specimen from one of them. We have been very lucky. There is not much game about here, even rabbits.'

'So, you stole a rabbit from someone else's trap?'

'I'm afraid that I did, but he will never know that. I reset his snare exactly as I found it, minus the rabbit of course.'

Steed skinned and gutted the rabbit, then cooked it over the open fire. She said that it was the most delicious rabbit that she had ever eaten. Warm and content after their feast, they settled back on their mattress in front of the fire, happy to be in each other's arms under the starlight.

'What did you like most about today Harry?' she murmured.

'Well, right now is easily the best bit.' He nuzzled his head into her hair, 'But I also found the journey down through France fascinating. The country around the Dordogne is really beautiful; I had never seen vineyards before. Come to think of it I had never set foot outside Britain before I was shot down. And I enjoyed our stop at Limoges too, and your railway station of course.'

'Yes, the Gare des *Bénédictins*, it was named after the monks you know. It was built over their old Abbey.'

'I would never have guessed that Benedictine Station was named after Benedictine monks… ouch!' He feigned mock pain as she nudged him in the ribs.

'Tell me about the railway stations in London Harry.'

'Some of them must have been built during the reign of Queen Victoria I think, in fact one of them is called Victoria Station. In their day they would have looked quite impressive, but now they are all looking rather worn out after all of the bombing. The glass roofs have been smashed and they all need a few coats of paint. In Paris, you have a station named after one of Napoleon's great battles, *Gare d'Austerlitz*. Well we have a station in London that is named after one of his great battles too, Waterloo Station… ouch!' She nudged him in the ribs again.

He changed the subject. 'The train that we will take to Carcassonne tomorrow, goes on to Narbonne doesn't it?'

'That's right Harry, I know what you are thinking. We no longer need to stop overnight at my aunt's house because we are now camping here. So, we should take the train to Narbonne tomorrow morning, and then take our final train to Perpignan from there. We should be in Perpignan by tomorrow afternoon, and you could be on your way over the mountains tomorrow night. Have you finalised your route?'

'I think so, but I really need a large-scale map of the border area. My idea is to cycle down to Banyuls sur Mer, then hole up somewhere between Banyuls and the border until dark.' He retrieved his map and torch from his rucksack to show her. 'Here, you see. There looks to be a route from Banyuls that goes southwest through a valley. There is a minor road shown on this map that goes past these villages and leads almost to the border. I am not sure that there is a recognised crossing into Spain because there does not seem to be a road on the Spanish side. I think that it is sure to be guarded close to the border, so I will have to leave the road a few kilometres before the border and track across country. The border is less than ten kilometres from Banyuls, so I might just make it over in one night. But in all depends on the terrain, and that's why I need a decent large-scale map with the height contours. I don't relish scrambling over steep and rough ground in the dark. If the terrain is bad, I will hide during the next day, and continue on overnight. I will need to take a little food with me, and I will need all of our water bottles.'

'We will find a bookshop in Perpignan. Walking in the Pyrenees was popular before the war, so we may be able to get a decent large-scale map for you.' She looked concerned and added, 'You must be very careful in the mountains at night Harry. You could easily fall and kill yourself in the darkness. It is rough country and there are some big drops. Maybe we should try to hire a guide?'

'We've been through this already Monique. Police informers would almost certainly get to know about it if we start asking around for a guide. My guess is that there are some pretty shady characters around, smugglers and the like, who would have no scruples in taking our money, then running off and leaving me in the lurch halfway up a mountain. No Monique, if I can get my hands on a decent scale map, I am sure that I will be able to navigate my way to Spain. It isn't that far once I get to Banyuls.'

'Okay Harry, but I will come to Banyuls with you. It is less suspicious for a boy and a girl to be cycling together by the seaside.'

'No Monique, you have done enough, no arguments. Buy the map for me, and then take the train back to your aunt's house. I may have to cycle quite fast to reach Banyuls before nightfall; it looks to be about thirty-five kilometres. Maybe you can buy some food for me too? It may be several days before I get to eat anything that I am not carrying.'

In spite of her protestations, the way forward was agreed. The train to Narbonne was on time, and they only had to wait thirty minutes at Narbonne station for the connecting train to Perpignan. The weather was warm but overcast; rain was in the air. They were directed to a bookstore and she was able to purchase a large-scale map of the region.

'This is much better than the other map Monique. You can see more clearly that there is a way through the mountains this way.' He pointed to the route. 'I will leave the road about here and then trek across country to the border. The contours show that it is not too steep. This map also shows a track on the Spanish side.'

'Will you give yourself up when you get to Spain?'

'No, not unless I really have to. The Spanish people have just been through a bitter civil war, and Franco's side won. But I am hoping that the Catalan people are sympathetic to those fighting Fascism. I will try hitch-hiking to Barcelona and then look for the British Consulate. If the Spanish police catch me, well it isn't the end of the world. They will put me in jail for a couple of weeks, then deport me through Gibraltar; that's what I was told back home anyway.'

It was time to say goodbye. There were tears in her eyes. 'When all of this is over, write to me Harry. I am not stupid. I know that things may change for both of us. But write to me, I need to know that you made it home, and made it through the war. Promise me, even if you are married with ten children, that you will write to me.'

'I promise Monique,' he said quietly. 'After all this is over I will write to you, I will return the money that your father has loaned to me, and we will take it from there.'

Steed pedalled at a steady pace, making good time and heading southeast towards the coast at St-Cyprien. He couldn't resist a small detour to see the beach of the small French seaside resort, and to see the Mediterranean for the first time. After a short break by the sea, he set off on the next leg of his journey to Argelès-sur-Mer. Steed estimated that he had only seven or eight miles more to go, as the crow flies, to reach Banyuls-sur-Mer, but he soon found that the going became very tough if one wasn't a crow because the road climbed and fell steeply.

He was amazed at the number of young men on racing cycles who sped past him, standing on their pedals. Of course, he reflected, cycling is a national sport in France. How he wished for a lightweight multi-geared machine like theirs. Better still, his old Ariel motorcycle would be very useful here. He was very tired and starting to ache by the time that he reached Banyuls. By careful map reading and consultation with his compass, he identified the road that he must take towards Spain and pushed on.

The Pyrenees now towered to either side. He forced himself to be realistic. The journey from Perpignan, especially the last part, had taken an awful lot out of him. Since leaving Banyuls the climbs seemed even steeper and he was pushing the bicycle far more often than riding it. It was probably only another five or six miles to the border, but he badly needed to rest. The temperature was dropping as the road climbed higher and as evening turned into night. He was wearing multiple layers of clothing, but he was still cold.

He made his decision; he would rest for a couple of hours, and then push on. He would try to get across the border by morning, but if his body would not allow that, he would seek shelter and then rest for the day out of sight. He would push on again tomorrow night. He moved away from the road to take shelter amongst rocks. He put his head on his knapsack, pulled down his hat and drew his rain cape over his head. He was tired and asleep within minutes.

When he awoke it was almost midnight. His bicycle was by now more hindrance than help, so he hid it amongst the rocks and set of on foot, following the road away from the coast and into the mountains. He knew from his earlier careful study of the map that he must not make a wrong turn now, or he would find the route into Spain blocked by a mountain. The overcast weather had cleared, and there was a half moon and stars in the sky; but it was cold at this altitude. The clear sky helped his navigation, because he could now see the Pyrenees towering to both sides. That was good, because it meant that he was moving through the valley. There was absolutely no traffic on the road. He had not seen a soul since leaving Banyuls. He expected next to come across a small hamlet where he would need to be careful. That would be a good place for customs men to watch the road.

He stopped, slowly dropped onto his belly, and then crawled to the verge. A house was immediately ahead. It was not showing any lights, but its outline was unmistakable. This was the hamlet that he had been expecting. The mountain towered to the right of the road, and the ground fell away to the left. Gingerly, Steed inched his way a few metres down the steep scrubland to the left of the road, and then moved forwards, remaining out of sight of the houses. It took him half an hour to bypass the hamlet because of the darkness and difficult terrain, but eventually he came back to the road several hundred metres past the last house. He now knew that he had only three miles to go before he reached Spain.

The valley was starting to widen now, although the road still hugged the mountain on the right. The map indicated that he should shortly see a track on his right, leading up the mountain. Steed began to think about leaving the road, for the crossing point into Spain was certain to be guarded. But away from the road, to the left, the terrain still dropped away steeply. He knew from his earlier experience of bypassing the hamlet that progress would be dreadfully slow. Also, it would be all too easy to slip and fall in the darkness, with potentially fatal results!

Ahead he saw the track that he had been looking for on the right. Good, the track confirmed that his navigation was spot on. No mean feat in the dark. He stopped, crouched and listened. All was quiet, but it was a good place for the police or customs men to watch the road leading to the border. He felt that he had no choice but to bypass the track. He crawled to the verge, left the road, slowly and carefully inched his way along its edge, then rejoined it twenty metres further on.

It was less than two miles to the border now. Steed was creeping along very carefully, stopping frequently, all senses tuned for the slightest sound or movement. He really needed a rest. Thirty minutes later he made his decision. The border must be about a mile or so to the southeast. It was time to leave the road and travel cross-country. The problem was, in this rough terrain and moving by moonlight, one could easily fall down a ravine and break one's bloody neck. He left the road and began to scramble over the rocky scrub. His body by now was screaming for respite. The safest option would be to find somewhere to hide and get some rest. When it was fully light he could scan his surroundings with his opera glasses to pick out a path for tomorrow night.

Once again he sought refuge amongst rocks and scrubland, covering himself with his brown rain cape. He was cut and bruised and felt dog-tired; he was cold and everything ached. He closed his eyes, but he did not sleep. An hour later it was starting to get a little lighter, not much, but just enough to travel. It was only a mile to the border, and he was still veiled from prying eyes by the dim, dawn light.

Feeling a little better, he left his shelter and moved on, travelling southwest at the best pace that he could manage over difficult uphill terrain, scrambling over the rocks and scrubland. It was bitterly cold. The adrenalin kicked in. Less than a mile to go and he would be free. Thirty minutes later it was becoming light. He could not see the road that he had left during the night, although the valley that it followed was below to his right, and the mountain beyond stood out clearly against the lightening sky. He was no longer sure if he was in France or Spain. There was no sign of the French police or customs people, so the obvious thing to do was to keep going.

An hour later it was fully light and Steed was convinced that he was in Spain. He stopped and looked out over the countryside through his opera glasses. The mountain to his right now seemed a little further away, and he was travelling parallel to a high peak on his left. He was also going downhill. Once again he consulted his map. He was sure of his position. He was in Spain. Still cautious, he found a suitable hiding spot, ate the remains of his bread and cheese, finished his penultimate bottle of water, and then sunk into a deep and undisturbed sleep.

He awoke around midday. According to his map, he should eventually come across a stream where he should hopefully be able to refill his water bottles, and there should be a forest immediately behind it. He stood up. Yes, he could see the forest in the distance. In spite of his aching limbs he set off again in good heart. The going was much easier now, downhill with fewer rocks baring the way. He should be able to find game in the forest ahead. Something hot to eat would be good.

Two hours later he saw the stream, but as he approached he realised the problem. He was going to have to ford the stream, and it looked to be deep and running fast. He consulted his map again. If he followed the stream to the right, he should sooner or later come to a track crossing his path. If he were to follow that track northeast, something that he was not going to do, he would come to the French border and the road that he had travelled the previous night. But the track also went to the southwest, and on through the forest. That suggested a bridge over the stream, or at least a crossing point.

Sure enough, when he came to the track, it did indeed cross the stream via a rickety bridge. Steed refilled his water bottles and set off over the bridge. According to his map he would now have about an eight-kilometre walk through the forest before he came to the first Spanish village. But the walk was cut short moments after he stepped off the bridge. He stopped and slowly raised his hands. Advancing towards him were half a dozen Spanish troops, rifles raised, led by an officer. The soldiers stopped a few paces in front of him and the officer let loose a flood of Spanish.

Steed, of course, didn't understand a word. When the torrent had ceased, Steed said slowly, 'I am English, *Inglés*. Please take me to the British embassy.'

The officer barked an order to one of his men, who thereupon shouldered his rifle and advanced towards Steed. The soldier pulled Steed's rucksack from his back and then proceeded to rifle through Steed's pockets. He found Steed's false French identity papers. Steed metaphorically kicked himself; he should have destroyed those once he entered Spain. Another barked order and the soldier picked up the rucksack and handed it to his officer, together with the false I.D.

Steed still had his hands raised. 'Identification,' he said, and slowly drew out his RAF dog tag from around his neck. 'I am an RAF pilot, *Inglés*.'

This time the officer spoke in English. 'This paper says that you are Georges Gallant, a Frenchman.'

'It is a forgery, made by a black marketer in France. I am Flight Sergeant Steed, RAF, and this is my identification.' Steed waved his dog tag. 'The British authorities will confirm my identity if you ask them.'

'You will come with us.' Steed did as he was told. He reflected on his capture. The Spaniards were well positioned. Anyone coming from or going to the border would have to either cross this bridge or ford the stream. Ah well, so be it. A spell of captivity in Spain would be followed by deportation via Gibraltar.

Chapter Ten – Epilogue.

Steed was taken first to Figueras prison, where he spent an uncomfortable week before being moved on to the infamous concentration camp of Miranda del Ebro. As he was marched through the gates, a familiar voice called out to him.

'*Bonjour Monsieur Hawk, comment ca va?*' A gaggle of people were waiting just inside the gates; one of them pushed forward towards Steed, a dark-haired swarthy individual wearing an overcoat that looked several sizes too large. It was Jean-Paul Colbert.

'Jean-Paul!' exclaimed Steed in amazement, 'Am I glad to see a familiar face!'

'We will meet later,' said the Belgian as a guard roughly pushed him away. 'After they have stuck their filthy needles into you.'

Jean-Paul was right. The welcome from the Spanish concentration camp authorities included a series of painful inoculations for God knows what. After the Spaniards had finished their formalities and released Steed into the compound, he found Jean-Paul waiting for him.

'This place is not a too bad Hawk. There are many nationalities here, including one or two RAF types. Bring your stuff over to our hut. We have a couple of spare bunks there. What brings you to Miranda del Ebro, the premier hotel in General Franco's beloved Spain? Tell me all.'

Steed told his story, but he was careful to say nothing that could identify Henri-Paul and his family; neither did he say anything about his close relationship with his guide through southern France.

'Much the same story for me,' said the Belgian. 'I had a spot of bother on an outing to Lille. I made it across into Belgium and met up with some people that I know.' He winked. 'They fixed me up with money and false papers and I took a train to Paris, then on to Tours, just like you. But I was foolish enough to swim the River Cher into the Free Zone one night. That was not funny, I damn near drowned! I travelled down into the Basque country where they speak a really peculiar language that is absolutely nothing like French or Spanish. I bribed a local to take me across into Spain, but he left me as soon as we crossed the border. The place was crawling with Franco's soldiers; I think that they are still having trouble from Republican freedom fighters left over from the civil war. I was captured, and here I am.'

Steed asked the question that had been worrying him. 'Do they know back home that you are here? I am not sure that they know about me, I have been away since August, so my squadron probably think by now that I have bought it.'

'Yes, they know. The Spanish are playing this by the book. I told the Spaniards that I was a British citizen by the way, not Belgian. A man from the British embassy turned up and sorted everything out. You should meet him shortly. The Spanish will keep us here for about a month, and then they will deport us through Gibraltar.'

Jean-Paul was right. A few days later Steed met a representative of His Majesty's Government, the Military Attaché from the Madrid embassy. It was a relief to know that the authorities back home at last knew where he was. The Attaché was very helpful, providing Steed with an allowance of money and food, and advising him that he would probably be deported after spending a few weeks in prison.

Life in Miranda del Ebro was not too bad. There were a number of petty regulations, and those that bucked the system were usually punished with beatings and solitary confinement. But the Spanish guards were on the whole humane, and the money provided by the Madrid embassy could be spent on better food and luxuries, even good quality wine. A Spanish concentration camp was clearly preferable to a German POW camp, especially since Steed knew that his confinement was only temporary. Most prisoners worked, and Steed managed to get a job logging in the adjacent forest. He was pleased to be away from the camp during the day, and out in the fresh air. The Miranda del Ebro camp was high in the mountains and consequently the November nights were very cold. Steed was very grateful for Alain's warm clothing, which he had been allowed to keep.

At last came the day when a party of seven British airmen, including Steed and Jean-Paul Colbert, were packed into an army truck and sent off to Madrid. Life was suddenly very much better. From Madrid they travelled down to Gibraltar, to where they were formally deported. Once on the colony, Steed re-entered RAF service life, donning a uniform with flight sergeant insignia and enjoying the hospitality of the sergeants' mess. He hoped to hitch a lift in an aircraft bound for the UK, but he was disappointed. Instead he took passage in a tramp steamer, a part of a convoy bound for Liverpool.

Steed reported to his squadron, still based at RAF Stourden in Kent. The weather that day in early December was foul, and flying was cancelled. He went immediately to his squadron leader's office. Dix welcomed him with open arms.

'Hawk, it's really good to see you. We heard in October that you were a guest of General Franco and we had one hell of a celebration. I knew that you would give the Huns the slip. Nobody saw what happened to you the day that you went down, but one or two people heard you say that you had a Hun on your tail.'

'That's right. I was covering Smithy when we got into a fight with some radial engine fighters. They were bloody good; they easily outpaced us in a climb. I saw one of them behind me, so I had to break. I tried a tight turn, but the sod could turn even tighter. The only thing that I could think of was to corkscrew down to the cloud. But he was still behind me and I felt hits on the Spit. I went into the cloud, levelled off, and then dived again. When I came out of the cloud he was right in front of me, and I managed to hit him. He went down and I saw him bail out. I was very lucky to come out of the cloud behind him like that. He was a very good pilot in a very good aeroplane.'

'Tell me about it!' said Dix. 'That was a Focke-Wulf 190, and those buggers have been giving us grief. The Fw-190 completely outclasses the Spitfire V. We lost other people the day that you went down, and we have lost more since then. What happened after that?'

'I started to climb back to the action upstairs. I called you guys on the wireless but I didn't get an answer. Then I smelt glycol, the engine overheated and I had to feather the prop. I pointed the aircraft west, hoping that it would crash well away from me, and took to my parachute. I must remember to tip the packers. I came down in open country, and went on the run. I travelled only at night, hiding by day. I then met some French people who helped me. I used the French currency that you gave to me to buy false identity papers, and the French helped me to get a train south. They introduced me to other people who showed me the best place to cross into Vichy France, which I did at night. They then helped me to get down to Perpignan by train. I promised the people who helped me that I would never identify them, even to my own people if I made it home. If the French are caught helping British airman, they are shot. I owe them money by the way, for train fares and so on. From there, with the aid of a map that they bought for me, I planned a route across the Pyrenees into Spain. I went across one night, but got captured by Spanish troops the next day. I spent time in Spanish prisons, met up with Jean-Paul Colbert at the last Spanish concentration camp, and was deported to Gibraltar, and here I am.'

'Fantastic. We heard about Jean-Paul. That must have been a surprise. By the way, you are now on leave for three weeks but you also have orders to see the spies.' Dix handed Steed an envelope. 'MI9 is an outfit that deals with escape and evasion. They want to debrief you. You have to go to Wilton Park in Buckinghamshire. But that's for later. Tonight we are having a party to celebrate your return.'

The escape and evasion people at Wilton Park were very interested in Steed's story. He was thoroughly debriefed, but he refused steadfastly to divulge the identity of his French contacts. He was also purposely vague on the precise location of his crossing point into the Free Zone. However, he was able to provide his inquisitors with significant detail on his journey over the Pyrenees, including the exact position of the waiting Spanish border guards. Finally, the lead MI9 agent asked, 'What do you think was the primary reason for your success in evading the Germans Flight Sergeant? And what particular advice would you have for others in your position?'

'I would never have made it without help from the local French people, so that was clearly the main reason that I got away. My advice to others would be to think about what to do after being shot down before the event. I think that my squadron leader might disagree with that though. He says that once you start to think about being shot down you develop the mindset of the hunted and not the hunter. That could be true for some people, but not I think for me. I had my escape kit, compass, torch and so on, and a decent pair of walking boots. That was a bit of a risk by the way, because I found out later that decent boots are now hard to come by in France. I am fairly certain that I could have kept going for quite a while, travelling at night and hiding by day. But to get to the Spanish border, or the Swiss border for that matter, you need to take trains. In that environment, sooner of later, you are going to have to show identity papers. My language skills are not up to the mark either. I needed help from my French friends to buy tickets and to find my way around the cities.'

'Anything that you didn't carry in your escape kit that you wished you had?'

'Identity papers and more money!'

Steed had back pay and three weeks leave, but sadly nowhere to go. His parents were dead and he had no close relatives. All of his friends were in the RAF. Britain in December 1941 was a dismal place to go sightseeing, and so Steed spent his leave at RAF Stourden. He thought about giving Sophie Richards a call, but in truth he was missing Monique.

The one girl in his life who he cared for, to whom he could relate, was incommunicado until the end of the war. And throwing the Germans out of France seemed a very long way off. At least the Russian soldiers, protected by their harsh winter weather, had stopped going backwards.

All that changed on Sunday 7th December when the Japanese carrier force attacked Pearl Harbour. Four days later Adolf Hitler declared war on the United States. What a stupid thing to do thought Steed. The Yanks were in the war now, and that was certain to make a big difference. Steed was reading a newspaper in the sergeants' mess when he received the summons from Dix.

Dix and Steed's flight commander were both in the squadron leader's office. 'Flight Sergeant Steed,' began Dix with a broad smile, 'it is my pleasant duty to inform you that you have been recommended for promotion to pilot officer. Do you accept?'

The last sentence was not quite as daft as it sounded. Life as a flight sergeant was in many ways preferable to that of the lowest officer grade in the RAF. Certainly the remuneration for a senior NCO was better, given the high cost of officers' uniforms and messing. They will take anyone now, thought Steed, not at all like pre-war.

'I would be delighted sir, thank you very much,' he replied.

THE END

Printed in Great Britain
by Amazon